Estes, Winston
  A simple act of kindness.

DATE DUE		
JUN 2 9 1973	.20	APR 2 3 '79
June 15	Oct. 29	NOV 6 '79
July 5	NOV 2 9 1973	FEB 9 '80
July 12	DEC 1 9 1973	MAR 5 '80
July 20	JAN 2 4	MAR 1 9 '80
July 30	JAN 3 0 1976	APR 1 1 '80
Aug. 15	FEB 7 1976	JAN 2 6 1987
Aug 22	APR 2 8 1976	FEB 2 3 1987
.6	MAY 1 2 1976	JAN 1 4 1991
Sept 19	MAY 1 9 1976	
Sept 26	MAR 5	
Oct. 17	AUG 22 '77	

JUN 12 '73

A Simple Act
of Kindness

Also by Winston M. Estes

WINSTON IN WONDERLAND
ANOTHER PART OF THE HOUSE
A STREETFUL OF PEOPLE

A Simple Act
of Kindness

A Novel

Winston M. Estes

J. B. LIPPINCOTT COMPANY
Philadelphia/New York

29.867

U.S. Library of Congress Cataloging in Publication Data

Estes, Winston M   birth date
    A simple act of kindness.

    I. Title.
PZ4.E794Si   [PS3555.S8]   813'.5'4   72–3877
ISBN–0–397–00943–7

For Janet Moore Estes

A Simple Act
of Kindness

☙ 1 ❧

I looked at Amy sitting patiently with Kenny cradled in her arms, and I had never seen her look prettier. I winked at her to reassure her that the waiting didn't bother me.

"They also serve who only stand and wait," I said. "That's me."

She dodged a chubby little hand that reached for her hat. The dangling red tassel had caught his eye. She was too late.

"I don't know why I don't cut off this doodad and just give it to him," she said, holding him away with one hand and pulling at her hat with the other.

I started to laugh, but Skeeter cut me short. He escaped from the pen I had made with my legs and darted across the waiting room.

I went after him and brought him back under one arm. He was almost two and squirmed with the strength of a bobcat. He set up a wail. I clamped a hand over his mouth and sat down again with him in my lap. I locked an arm around him and held him firmly. "Now sit still, or I'm going to throw you out the window," I said.

Amy laughed and then frowned. "I'm real sorry, darling, for you to use a perfectly good Saturday sitting around like this."

"Oh, well—it gives me a chance to see the doctor who gets all our money for telling us there's nothing wrong with our children." I tightened my grip on Skeeter.

She glanced at the door. "He's certainly taking his time. We've never waited this long before."

We lapsed into silence. I stared vacantly across the room, pretending an interest in a baby whose mother seemed to expect it. The man opposite us, about my own age and considerably more bored, was watching us. My eye caught his, and he looked away, embarrassed. Amy dangled a key chain in front of Kenny and fascinated Skeeter instead.

From the streets of downtown Fort Worth below came the honk of a horn, the screech of rubber on concrete and the angry blast of a policeman's whistle. In the distance, a siren shrieked, then faded. The gentle whir of the air conditioning was beginning to mesmerize me.

Suddenly, the sound of a buzzer shot through the stillness. The receptionist leaned forward and addressed the gray intercom on her desk. "Yes, Doctor?"

All heads turned toward her as if on a single pivot. Beyond her desk the door opened, and Carrie Holbrook came out.

I recognized her immediately; I recalled everything about her as though five minutes rather than five years had lapsed since I had seen her.

She looked marvelous, as beautiful as I remembered her. She wore a gray tailored suit, perfectly cut and fitted, and a saucy suggestion of a hat on her silky blond hair. Her tall statuesque figure, her lithe movements and regal poise erased five years as if by magic, and there stood Carrie Holbrook again with the sparkling green eyes, while everybody gaped at her in open admiration. She was holding a small boy by the hand.

Before the door clicked shut behind her, I was on my feet moving toward her with Skeeter under one arm. She smiled at the receptionist and then saw me. Ever so briefly, she hesitated, and a flicker of recognition appeared in her eyes. Her name was on my tongue, but before I could say it she looked away, tugged at the child and swept past me out into the corridor without saying a word. I was too startled to call after her.

I stared at the door. She had appeared and disappeared so swiftly that I doubted my own senses. The receptionist was talking into the intercom. A young woman with a baby was crossing the room. Amy's voice brought me to.

"Who was that?" she asked.

I continued to stare at the door and made no reply.

"Who was it?" she repeated with curiosity and amusement.

"Carrie Holbrook. . . ."

"You don't sound too sure."

"She didn't speak to me."

"Maybe she didn't recognize you."

"She did, though." I sat down again. "She did recognize me. I could tell."

Amy ran a hand under Kenny's pants to see if they were wet. "Carrie Holbrook . . . Holbrook . . . your friend in the war?"

"Ben Holbrook—you remember. From Erskine. He got lost over New Guinea. Carrie's his wife."

"I remember now—but you seldom mention them any more."

"We didn't stay in touch. But even after five years, I still miss Ben. We had lots of plans for after the war."

Skeeter was relaxed and drowsy in my lap. The room had thinned out, and the remaining people had settled down again to wait. Some were watching us as if listening. I lowered my voice.

"She remembers," I said stubbornly. "I was a third member of that household. We were a regular trio. Some people probably thought we were a triangle, but we weren't. We were good friends, that's all."

"It's peculiar that she didn't speak, then, isn't it?"

"Sure is," I said, shaking my head. "The last I heard of her, she was living in a place called Foley—a little ranch town the other side of San Angelo. It's not even on the main highway. I pass the turnoff every week. I used to think about taking an extra hour or two and driving over to see her, but it seems that I was always running late, and I just never got around to it. She was teaching school then, but she probably lives somewhere else by now. That was—let's see—late in 1945, as I remember. Almost four years ago."

"She doesn't look like the small-town type," Amy said.

"She's not. She's not the schoolteacher type, either. At least, I never had a teacher who looked like her."

"All mine were old maids with moustaches," Amy said.

"And baritone voices," I added.

Kenny tried to crawl out of Amy's lap. She pulled him back. Skeeter was asleep now.

"How did you know she lived in Foley?" Amy asked.

"After the war, she sent me some papers to sign. I had witnessed Ben's will and insurance—and I don't know what else. I sent the papers back and wrote her a letter, but she didn't answer. That was the last I knew about her."

"She's certainly attractive," she said. "And the little boy was a darling."

"Little boy?" The scene came sharply back into focus. "They didn't have any children. She must have got married again."

"Probably. People do it all the time."

"I guess they do. After all, it's been a long time. The last time Carrie saw Ben was in 1944—July fourteen, to be exact. We were leaving Indianapolis for San Francisco—the Port of Debarkation."

Amy was dabbing at the front of her dress. "I was listening," she said, glancing up, "but Kenny was drooling on me."

"I was just remembering," I said.

"Maybe her second husband is jealous," she suggested. "And wants to blot out his wife's first marriage and friends. Anyway, maybe the little boy isn't hers. He could be a neighbor's or a relative's."

"I doubt it. Carrie wasn't the baby-sitter type. I can't even imagine her tending her own. She was never the motherly type, either."

"Many women aren't until they have children of their own."

I grinned at her. We lapsed into silence and awaited our turn with the doctor. While we waited, I thought about the Holbrooks. Solemn, staid, straitlaced Ben and happy, carefree, gregarious Carrie came back at me larger than life. On the face of it, theirs had been an unlikely match, and I wondered briefly if she had married someone who reminded her of Ben. Then our turn with the doctor came.

ꕤ 2 ꕤ

The next week was a busy one for me, and I did not dwell on Carrie Holbrook and her peculiar behavior. From Monday through Friday each week, I stayed on the road for American Business Machines, and in that particular week one of my largest dealers, this one in Abilene, was threatening to change his account to a rival company. I was confident that I could prevent his defection, but Mr. Marsh, our vice president in charge of sales, apparently thought I couldn't do it without his personal assistance. He telephoned me three times during the week to tell me what to do and when to do it.

It would have been easy not to like Mr. Marsh, but the fact remained that I did. I also respected him immensely. He was a fine man. Rather small, he had a bald head fringed with white, a soft, cultivated voice and a benign way of looking through his rimless spectacles that made people think they were close to him personally—until they realized that his mind was on American Business Machines to the exclusion of everything else. I don't think I ever heard him mention his own family or even the weather. It was nothing new to have him make a nuisance of himself with his advice and guidance. Naturally I could not ignore him, but he did play havoc with my schedule. As I drove through the West Texas countryside, my mind worked busily from one town to the next, calculating and refiguring how to meet all my appointments and still get home by Friday night. I had blanketed West Texas with American Business Machines. After the war, dealers had been standing in line waiting for the manufacturers to retool, an eager and ready market for anything mechanical that came off the assembly line. My job had long since settled itself into a routine of keeping the dealers happy with new and improved models of typewriters, adding machines, calculators and whatever else the designers and engineers could devise and produce. My work had become so predictable that between Fort Worth and El Paso I stayed in the same hotels, ate my meals at the same restaurants and bought gas at the same service stations. I even had a standing reservation on the air flight from Midland to El Paso on Wednesdays and return on Thursdays. My work was pleasant, and it was satisfying. Perhaps I had made it too much my own personal possession and achievement, for on this trip, by the time I had reached San Angelo, I had begun to resent Mr. Marsh's guidance as outright interference.

And yet, as fully occupied as my mind was that week, I could not dismiss Carrie Holbrook's behavior altogether. She would not stay out of sight. She passed before me unbidden at odd and illogical moments; while waiting for a traffic light to change, over a cup of coffee with a customer, on a hotel elevator, crossing a street or tying my shoe, I saw her. With Ben no longer the link between us, perhaps I had become one of the memories that she had filed away to forget. Maybe she had designed a life for herself with no room in it for the past. At the same time, it seemed that she could have spoken to me for old time's sake if nothing else. Surely that would have posed no threat to her new way of living, whatever it was.

But for all that, I suppose that in time I would have put her out of my mind again, perhaps permanently, had it not been for the detour that actually led me through Foley.

Almost a month after that glimpse of her, I had spent the night in San Angelo, and my first appointment was in Fort

Stockton, 180 miles to the southwest. I had a second in Midland, another 90 miles north and back to the east. It was a frustrating itinerary, for my account in Fort Stockton was a small one, worth the trouble and expense of the drive only as a means to keep out the competition.

As you go west in Texas, the state gets bigger. Trim farms and fenced pastures yield to flattened, thirsty land that lies vast, hostile and shadowless in the hot Texas sun. Scrub oak gives way to mesquite, and grain fields to prickly pear and quivering sheets of prairie grass. Distances, sizes and shapes are deceptive, and what appears to be a hill rising out of the shin oak and sagebrush turns out to be merely an outcropping of limestone, and not a large one at that. A steep rise in the ground ahead proves to be so gentle that you don't realize you have reached its summit until you have gone beyond and trained your eyes on another. The gaunt skeleton of a windmill sits atop the earth like a colossus. A solitary house without features or detail blackens a scrap of sky miles away. This is sun country, where you can chase a heat mirage for mile after mile over land as flat as a tabletop to find, with no warning, the jagged gash of a ravine or a rocky canyon, and the earth taking up again on the other side as though the fracture had existed only in your mind. The sky is so big and so broad that, if you study it for a while, you might get a glimmer of what infinity is all about. The area is sparsely populated, and the countryside is relieved only by endless stretches of barbed wire that fences in nothing and wavering columns of telephone poles that go nowhere.

As San Angelo dropped over the horizon behind me and my rearview mirror reflected the same empty nothingness that lay ahead, I settled down for the dreary trip to Fort Stockton. An hour of steady, relentless driving brought me to a dilapidated filling station that stood guard over a side road from the left, and a pointed marker that read FOLEY—9 MILES. A barricade across the highway and a sign reading DETOUR, CLOSED FOR REPAIRS brought me to a halt. I studied the side road with misgivings. A narrow strip of asphalt winding out of sight, it was as uninviting as the terrain it bisected.

The October sun was high. I looked at my watch anxiously, shifted gears, turned left and set out on the asphalt road to Foley.

The road seemed to have been poured onto the flat earth without foundation or design. The edges were ragged as sawteeth, and the holes, eroded by weather and worn by age, had been left untended. As I bounced along, the vastness of the land before me, behind me and on all sides closed in and caught me up in a strange moodiness. A jackrabbit darted from behind a bush, the only sign of life I had seen since leaving the highway. If there were people at the end of the road, I could not visualize Carrie Holbrook ever having been among them.

I wondered whom she had married and if she had stayed in Foley after all. But surely not—not Carrie, with the beautiful dresses and outlandish hairdos; the first one on the dance floor when the orchestra struck up a lively tune.

"Come dance with me, Pete," she used to say. "This one's too fast for old slowpoke Ben."

Then she would wrinkle her nose affectionately at her husband, and we would go out onto the dance floor, leaving Ben at the table to look on with pride. Carrie was one of those people who had to dance. Something inside her would not be still. She danced as naturally as she breathed. She was weightless, in absolute harmony with the music. When I danced with her, I fancied I danced as well as she did. It was an illusion, but Carrie herself was something of an illusion. She had never been quite real to me, and I liked her that way.

Foley arose ahead of me, shimmering in the morning sun, fragile and tentative, ready to be swooped up by the wind and scattered with the dust. As I drew nearer, the buildings began to separate into the low, nondescript boxes I expected to see. They were dominated by a spidery water tower and a two-story structure that probably was a courthouse, maybe a church or a school.

The road curved into town past a scattering of squalid shacks, chicken coops and outbuildings flung at random across the dry earth. The town proper was scarcely more than a tick-tack-toe arrangement of a few wide, treeless streets and irregularly spaced frame houses.

Abruptly, I found myself between two clumps of low, red-brick buildings, separated by a street wide enough to have been a plaza. This was the business district: a grocery store, a bank, a post office, a drugstore, a café, a drygoods store, a barber shop, and one or two unidentifiable establishments. A pickup truck and several automobiles sat at haphazard angles in the middle of the street, but no people were visible. A silence hung over the place. It was a silence of too much time suspended in too large an area, of too little to do and too much space to do it in. The wind blew steadily and with determination.

I drove the short block past Foley's businesses, made a U-turn and drove back. Without plan or forethought, I parked in front of the drugstore and went inside. I was already through the screen door and surveying the dim cluttered interior before it came to me that I had no idea why I was there. A stooped, graying man of perhaps sixty was alone in the rear of the store. I climbed onto a stool at the soda fountain and waited for him to make his way to the front. He came up behind the soda fountain and faced me expectantly but with no apparent enthusiasm. He did not speak.

"Good morning!" I said. "What's the reason for the detour? The sign said repairs of some kind."

"You might say that," he said. "A big truck crashed through a bridge about four miles on down the road. The only way they could detour the traffic around it was to build another bridge. Instead of that, they detoured everybody through Foley. What'll you have?"

"Coffee, I guess—black."

"You'll have to go to the café if you want coffee. Two doors down."

"A Coke will be fine, then."

While he busied himself with the ice and a glass, I wheeled

around on the stool and took in the store. I remembered such a store from my childhood. The ceiling-high, glassed-fronted cases along the walls, the round white-enameled ice-cream tables and chairs with curved wire legs, the wrapping counter with its surface too cluttered to be of much use, the door at the rear through which I could see row upon row of prescription bottles lighted by an unshaded bulb, the sickly-sweet smell of drugs, cosmetics and ice cream filled me with a kind of nostalgia. I was surprised that such places still existed.

"How far is it back to the highway?" I asked.

"Which way you going?"

"To Fort Stockton."

"Not much further. Three miles is about all. Just follow the road you came in on."

He straightened up, placed the Coke in front of me and leaned forward, resting both hands on the back edge of the fountain.

"This your first time in Foley?"

"Yes, it is. I go from San Angelo to Fort Stockton and Midland every week, but this is the first time I ever took the Foley turnoff."

"I reckon you might say we're enjoying a boom," he said with a chuckle. "That detour has sent more traffic through here during the last week than we've had in twenty years put together. Nobody comes here much unless it's on business or unless they know somebody."

"I used to know somebody here," I said.

"That right? Then I reckon I know 'em, too." He warmed to my presence. "What's their name?"

"I don't know what it is now, but it used to be Holbrook. She taught—"

"You mean Carrie Holbrook?" The man's eyes brightened, and his face softened into a wide smile. "Is that who you mean?"

"Why, yes—I guess it is, but I didn't expect—"

"Carrie Holbrook," he repeated. "She's a widow lady. Her husband got killed in the war."

"That's her," I said quickly. "You seem to remember her well."

"Remember her?" He peered at me curiously. "Remembering doesn't have anything to do with it. She lives right here in Foley right now."

"But you called her *Holbrook.*"

"Well—so did you. That's her name. Wasn't that who you asked about?"

"Yes, but—why does—I mean what does she—"

He beamed. "She's a schoolteacher. All the kids think a lot of her. How did you know her?"

"I knew her husband during the war. We were overseas together."

"I bet she'd be glad to see you then," he said. "You can't catch her until noon, though." He glanced at the clock on the rear wall. "If you want to wait around until dinnertime, school lets out at twelve."

I'm not certain how much I was tempted, for now that I had stirred the memory of that brief encounter in Fort Worth, I discovered that it still smarted. I wanted to hear an explanation from Carrie's own lips, but in some perverse fashion, I was reluctant to give her the opportunity. Anyway, I had those appointments in Fort Stockton and Midland.

"Did Carrie—Mrs. Holbrook—didn't she get married again?"

"Not that I know of," the man said.

"Does she live alone?"

"Just her and the boy."

"The boy?"

"Ben—her son. He was born while his daddy was overseas— after he got killed, I think. His daddy never saw him. I know that much." Shaking his head sadly, he said, "He's a cute little fellow."

"How old is—Ben?"

He made some silent calculations. "Must be four years old, maybe five. I don't know for sure. He's not old enough to go to school, though. If you was with his daddy overseas, you could probably figure it up for yourself."

I said, "It's easy to lose track of the time."

"Sure is. Well, Carrie's a fine lady. Everybody in Foley thinks so. I guess you and her will have lots to talk about. Not many of her old-time friends come around that I know of. This place is out of the way, sort of."

I paid for my Coke and got up to leave.

The man turned to the cash register and rang up the sale. "If you want to go by the school and see if you can catch Carrie, it's just one block over."

"I don't believe I'll have time," I said.

"Then you can leave your name with me, if you want to, and I'll tell her you asked about her," he suggested. "She comes in here nearly every day."

With my hand on the door, I allowed myself time to consider this idea; then, without replying, I hurried outside and to my car.

I backed away from the curb and circled the block past a gaunt, two-story structure that stood on the baked earth like a lean, wizened old man. This was the school. Not one blade of grass, not the first suggestion of a tree broke up the brown waste that surrounded the building. The flag, high on its pole at the main entrance, stood out straight in the wind. A conglomeration of bicycles against the building, a few swings and seesaws, an isolated water fountain in the middle of the yard were the only indications that life might be somewhere close by.

Two days later, on my return trip, I drove through Foley without stopping.

❦ 3 ❧

Jones Hill, no doubt, resembled every other bedroom community in the United States, but not to Amy and me, for we lived there. Despite the countless look-alike houses lined up like dominoes along street after street and looped around one cul-de-sac after the other, Jones Hill held a unique charm for us. We were convinced that our two-bedroom, one-bath, white frame house with carport was exceptional. Even our neighbors, most of whom were as much like us as our houses—young parents, young professionals or businessmen, still economically unsure of themselves and all working in Fort Worth, less than thirty minutes away—struck us as the most distinctive and individual group of people in the State of Texas. All of us had bought our homes under the GI Bill of Rights, sodded our lawns, set out our shrubbery, added our chain fences and built our barbecue patios in our back yards as though playing follow-the-leader. None of which lessened the delight with which I turned onto our street on Fridays, sometimes before dark, if all had gone well since Monday.

Amy and the boys were glad to see me, but the week at home had not been easy. Kenny had run a fever for two days, and of course, the household had revolved around him until his temperature had dropped to normal.

"You should have called me," I said. "You knew how to get me."

"Worry wart!" she said, wrinkling her nose at me. "It wasn't exactly a crisis. My big problem was keeping Skeeter out of his face. Linda Smith took him over to her house one afternoon, and he wet her sofa! I'm still embarrassed." She laughed, and I kissed her again. "How did you make out with your Abilene problem —and Mr. Marsh?" she asked.

I gave her the details, then told her about my unplanned trip through Foley. "I just don't get it," I said when I had finished. "She and Ben didn't have a baby."

"Maybe she adopted one."

"But widows don't usually adopt children."

"There's no law against it, though."

"And Foley! You ought to see the place! It's not much more than a watering hole—and dried up at that."

"Well, I guess they needed a schoolteacher in Foley, and Carrie needed a job, so the two of them got together."

I watched her across the table. She was trying to feed Kenny his dinner and getting nowhere. She held a heap of mushy spinach to his mouth. He grabbed the spoon from her hand.

"Kenny! Stop it!"

Problems were developing on my side of the table, too. Skeeter was banging his spoon on his plate. I took it away from him. He let out a scream of complaint.

Amy pushed Kenny's high chair away from the table and removed his bowl. I got up and lifted Skeeter down. He toddled into the kitchen. I listened for a crash or a bang or some other commotion; nothing happened, and I returned to Foley.

"If you'll help me solve the mystery of Carrie Holbrook, I'll share the credit with you," I said. "How's that for an incentive?"

She shook her head. "I like to be excited by a mystery, but somehow I don't think Carrie's got it. Not for me, anyway." She laughed and started for the kitchen to investigate Skeeter's silence. She rumpled my hair as she passed me and said, "Just

(23)

don't get the idea I'm ready to share you with anybody, including Carrie Holbrook."

That seemed to dispose of the Case of Carrie Holbrook.

Late in October, two dealers canceled their appointments, leaving me with a half-day void, which I filled by shuffling my other appointments to give me Friday afternoon free and a rare opportunity to get home ahead of schedule. But I hadn't reckoned with Mr. Marsh. He telephoned me in Midland.

"Our dealer in Erskine is being plagued with maintenance and supply problems," he said. "He needs some assistance and guidance. So I was wondering if you could make a short detour and stop by there Friday on your way in?" He outlined the nature of the problem.

"What happened to the city salesmen?" I asked. Only nineteen miles from Fort Worth, Erskine was covered by our local representatives.

"We've run into trouble this week, Hamilton," he said. He detailed a series of unrelated reasons why none of our city sales force had the time for a trip to Erskine. "Do you think you can make it?" he asked.

"Well—naturally," I said. "I'll take the cutoff at Weatherford and stop by Erskine before I come into the office. Tell our man it will be three or four o'clock before I get there."

Nothing about Erskine will stick in your memory once you've driven through and beyond it, for in that part of Texas, all the small towns bear an undistinguished similarity to one another. Afloat on billows of prairie grass and farmlands, they speckle the state, small communities formed three quarters of a century earlier, seventy-five years in which to congeal their features and standardize their personalities. For the most part, they are thriving and active, although a stranger driving through on the highway might not detect that.

Their profiles seem to be shaped by identical assortments of courthouse domes, water towers and grain elevators, cotton gins and boxcars on railroad sidings. Their populations, advertised on

(24)

identical signs stuck into the ground by the Texas Highway Department at the city limits, have frozen somewhere around three thousand, and it makes little difference in their visual impact if their numbers expand to five thousand or shrink to two. To leave one is not much different from entering the other. You drive past a dusty clutter of filling stations, perhaps a motel, a drive-in restaurant, an auto body shop, a John Deere Implement agency, and suddenly you're on Main Street headed for the center of town and a traffic light and a war memorial on the courthouse lawn. Rotary Club meets on Thursday, Kiwanis on Wednesday, Speed Laws Are Strictly Enforced and the Chamber of Commerce welcomes you or invites you to hurry back, depending on whether you're coming or going.

In Erskine I spent no more than an hour with our dealer, a pleasant man named McCash. On impulse, as I was leaving, I asked him if he knew the Holbrook family.

"Everybody in Erskine knows the Holbrook family," he said. "Lots of money there."

"Did you know Ben, the son?"

"No. I came here after the war," he said.

"Ben was a good friend of mine," I explained. "We first met in cadet flight training and we were together from then on—until his plane went down over New Guinea. I ran into his wife a few weeks ago, and the Holbrooks have nagged at my conscience ever since."

"Did you ever meet his parents?"

"No, but I should have. I just never made it down here, though. That's what's been nagging at me." I looked at my watch. "I probably ought to run by and say hello. Is their house close by?"

Mr. McCash laughed. "In Erskine, everybody lives close by. The Holbrook house is on the edge of town, easy to find." He gave me directions, and as I was leaving, added, "Tell Mr. Marsh to get his people on the ball. You're the first one that's been down here in three weeks. And see if you can jar somebody loose on those parts orders I sent in."

"I'll do my best, Mr. McCash," I said.

"Holbrooks' is the last house in town," he called after me. "So don't think you've gone too far if the town seems to be running out."

I saw it from a distance, on a hill, but as I drew nearer, it lost itself in a blanket of trees, all colored with autumn. I turned in between two low concrete gateposts and followed a graveled road to the top where it broke out into a circular driveway fronting the house.

The Holbrook house had once been splendid, and even now, fifty or sixty years later, it still clung to its grandeur and elegance, like a painted, aging woman who had long ago been belle of the ball. It was a throwback to another age when display had triumphed over good taste, when grace had been sacrificed for bulk. The result was a heap of steep gables, faded red brick and twisted brown timbers, topped off by an absurd cupola. The house was wrapped around two sides by a deep veranda that came together at the corner and jutted out into a several-sided conservatory, as whimsical as the cupola on the roof. The windows and doors were tall and narrow and seemed to have been punched through the bricks at random. The lawn, as irregular as the angles of the house and with the same neglected air about it, had yielded to the season. Patchy with shoots of wild rye and scrubweed, it sloped down and away with the contours of the hill, terminating behind the house at an untended driveway and a sagging barn.

It was an unfriendly house in the weakening afternoon sun, pensive and moody amid its own shadows and silence. The contrast with the windswept openness of the town below was so startling that I turned for a reassuring look back down the hill and across the rolling land to remind myself of where I was.

I pulled over to the edge of the circular driveway and got out. The cavernous veranda caught me up in a dank, clammy coldness, and I shivered. I rang the bell. While I waited, I studied the dim assortment of stained-glass patches that surrounded the front door like an open fan.

A colored maid in white uniform, middle-aged, heavy, gray-haired and kindly of expression, opened the door. I told her my name.

"Is Mrs. Holbrook expectin' you?" she asked pleasantly.

"No. Please tell her that I was a friend of her son's."

She hesitated briefly; her thick lips parted in doubt. Then she opened the door wide. "Won't you come in, please?" she said.

The narrow, high-ceilinged hall was as gloomy as the outside of the house. Shadows bordered the walls like a black picture frame. A steep, ornate staircase mounted into the dimness. Broad doors through dark and forbidding woodwork opened into a parlor on one side and a small sitting room on the other. The maid asked me to wait in the sitting room.

A blocked-off fireplace on one wall, an empty bookshelf on another and a long bare library table along still another testified to the room's disuse. I sat uncomfortably on a faded brown sofa and looked out into the hall at the steep pitch of the stairs and the tasteless carvings of the balustrade.

I was wishing I hadn't come. This house was wrong. It was for old people—grim and crabby, probably. But the Holbrooks could not be so old. Ben would now be thirty—one year older than I. His parents therefore should be certainly not far into their sixties, unless—

"Mr. Hamilton?"

The slight, white-haired lady in the doorway was lovely. She stepped across the threshold and moved into the room with her hand outstretched. Her grip was warm, her smile friendly. As we shook hands, she studied my face, trying to remember, if remember she should. I think her eyes were the clearest blue I have ever seen. She wore a floor-length hostess robe of black velvet, tied around the waist with a silver cord. She wore no jewelry. The jet black of the garment and the snowy white of her hair made a startling contrast. Her complexion was flawless.

"I hope I'm not interrupting anything," I said.

"Nonsense! What is there to interrupt? Sit down, please." She moved to the sofa and indicated a chair opposite. "Alberta—my maid—tells me you were a friend of Ben's."

"Yes. In the war—from flight training on."

She stared at me intently. "You'll have to forgive me for not remembering. I'm sure Ben spoke of you many times, but so much has happened. Have we met before?"

"No. After the war, when I came back home, I meant to come, but things kept interfering."

"I understand perfectly," she said. "Nothing was the same again after the war, was it? I'm glad you could come now."

I found her as charming in manner as in appearance. She asked about my work and my family. She was a good listener and spoke with ease, but after a time, her blue eyes lost some of their luster, and she became still. Then she said, "Did you know that Mr. Holbrook passed away three years ago?"

"No. I didn't know. I'm sorry. Was he ill for a long time?"

"Yes, but not like you think. He wasted away." She had a faraway look, and I noticed a tightening of the muscles in her throat as if she were straining to make herself heard. "I think it was a broken heart. That's not listed in medical books, but perhaps it should be. He was a grand figure of a man—not the kind to have physical ailments at all. He was never sick a day in his life. He was huge—a giant. Six feet four in his stocking feet, with the broadest shoulders. . . . He filled the front seat of his car with his bulk." She smiled fondly. "He had a shock of bushy white hair that he couldn't control. It just wouldn't lie down, and he was always bareheaded. You could see his hair before you could see him."

She laughed softly. Somewhere in the house, a clock chimed. The wind had come up. The limb of a tree brushed a window.

"He worshiped Ben," she went on. "He adored the ground under his feet. He was never the same after Ben was killed. Were you with him when he was killed?"

"Not really," I said, relieved that she could speak of Ben in a matter-of-fact way. "Ben and I lived in the same tent, but we never flew the same missions. I wasn't on the schedule that day.

Before he left, he woke me to borrow some cigarettes. He left some letters on the table for me to mail."

I stopped. How could I make it sound credible to Mrs. Holbrook that one morning in that long-ago October her son simply flew away and disappeared from existence? The target that day was north of New Guinea, and the flight was over water. About an hour after takeoff Ben lost an engine, and the flight commander ordered him to turn back to the base. Members of the other crews watched the aircraft peel off the formation and turn around. No one ever saw Ben Holbrook and crew again. The casualty report, first listing him as "Missing in Action," was later changed to "Presumed Dead." Search after search turned up nothing. The sea had swallowed up the plane and the men aboard.

I explained all that to Mrs. Holbrook, trying to soften it where possible. She sat rigid, staring straight into my face.

"I wish I could tell you more," I said when I had finished. "But that's all any of us knows."

She sat quietly for a moment; then she sighed. "You have no idea what it means to hear it from someone who was there," she said quietly. "We had a letter from Ben's commanding officer, but it wasn't like hearing it from you. Mr. Holbrook never gave up hope of finding Ben. Oh, those 'Missing in Action' reports are ten times more cruel than an outright report of death. Mr. Holbrook studied maps of New Guinea and the entire area surrounding it. He went over them again and again until his eyes began to go bad. He knew as much about those islands as any person could possibly know without having been there. Had he lived, I think eventually he would have gone to New Guinea to see for himself. He talked about it often. Even a year and two years later, when I knew without admitting it that they would never find Ben, I didn't discourage Mr. Holbrook. It's a terrible thing to take away a person's hope."

"I wrote all the details to Carrie," I said. "As many as the censors would let me tell, you may remember."

A small, barely perceptible change came over her. "Did you know Carrie personally?" she asked stiffly.

"Yes. Carrie and I were good friends. She, Ben and I were together a long time."

"Have you kept up with her since the war?"

"Only to sign some legal papers she sent me. That was several years ago, of course."

"I hope they were what she wanted," she snapped.

I was startled by the sting in her words. "She chased off out into West Texas to some little place nobody ever heard of," she went on. "Somewhere around San Angelo. Foley, I think it was."

"I got a glimpse of her in Fort Worth several weeks ago," I said. "Lots of people were around, though, and I didn't get a chance to talk to her. I hope she's getting along all right."

"Oh, you don't need to worry about Carrie." Her voice was still waspish. "She'll get along all right. Carrie looks after Carrie. You can be sure of that!" She took a deep breath and let it out slowly. Then, as if the words came hard, she asked, "Did you know she had a baby?"

"She had a little boy with her that day in Fort Worth."

"Let me ask you something, Mr. Hamilton. And I want you to be truthful with me." She paused. "Did Ben ever mention a baby to you? I mean, did he ever say that Carrie was pregnant?"

I admitted that he had not.

"Did you know other boys whose wives back home were expecting babies?"

"Oh yes. A number of them."

"Did they ever talk about it?"

"Yes. Quite a bit."

"It was the natural thing to do, wasn't it?"

"Why yes, I guess it was."

"Then can you think of any reason why Ben should not have mentioned Carrie's pregnancy to you?"

"Not really. Unless—"

"Unless what?" she prompted me eagerly. "Unless he didn't know anything about it?"

(30)

"Well, I didn't mean to imply that—"

"Ben would have been so happy that he would have told everybody," she broke in. "So would Carrie, yet she told us nothing whatsoever about expecting a baby. She got herself a job in the office of a shipyard down at Port Arthur and hadn't been up to see us for several months. But she kept in touch. She was good about writing. Sometimes she sent Ben's letters or some snapshots. She telephoned often, too. After she got that awful telegram, she came up for a weekend. She offered to stop work and come stay with us, but we all agreed it would be better for her to keep busy. We didn't see her again for—I guess it was nearly a year, and then—"

Suddenly she stopped and sprang to her feet. I started to rise, but she motioned me back. With apprehension clouding her face, she pressed a forefinger against her lips and signaled me to silence while she tiptoed to the doorway and looked out into the hall.

"It's the maid," she whispered, turning to me. "Keep your voice low. I never know when she's listening."

I heard nothing.

"Poor Alberta," she said, resuming her seat. "She's been with me for years, but she's getting old, and I have to watch after her more than she watches after me. . . ." Her voice trailed off, and she sat lost in thought. Then she remembered me again.

"I'm sorry," she said. "As I was saying, it wasn't until the following October that Carrie showed up here with that baby. With no warning whatsoever, she walked in saying she'd like for us to meet our grandson. She said he was six months old. You can't imagine the shock! She said she'd been sick a lot—nearly had a miscarriage. She had a difficult labor and was a long time getting her strength back, and the baby was born sickly, and weeks went into months before she felt she could let us see either of them without worrying us—on top of our grief for Ben. She didn't want to worry us! Can you imagine a story as thin as all that? It was just too absurd. A baby to look forward to—even to worry about—might have been the one thing to bring us back to life."

She looked at me, waiting to see what I would say.

"If she was afraid she'd miscarry," I said tentatively, "that might explain why she didn't tell Ben."

"But nearly a whole year!" Mrs. Holbrook said. "And yet—we wanted to believe her so much, I think there was a period when we actually did. But it couldn't last; her story left too many unanswered questions. She said the baby was born in April, almost nine months to the day after the last time she saw Ben. I did some figuring. She would have been about four months along when she came to see us after Ben was lost. As well as I could remember, she had seemed quite normal. Why wouldn't we have sensed *something* if she was having difficulty? I hinted at this and she reminded me that we were all in a state of shock. That held me for a little while.

"Then Mr. Holbrook asked her, if she was so unwell all that time, how had she managed to keep on working, and writing so regularly and telephoning so often? She said, 'You may have noticed that I wrote you less and telephoned you more. Because phoning took less effort.' That was clever. It wasn't a thing you'd keep count of, but it could have been true. And she said, 'As for working, I didn't want you to know how many days I missed.' It seemed she had an answer for everything. All the same, we decided—"

She glanced nervously toward the hall. "Did you hear anything?"

I shook my head.

"It's so hard to tell in this big old house," she said. "You would think that after all these years I would recognize every creak and groan, but I don't. I came here as a bride. . . ."

Again her mind seemed to be far away; her eyes were on a spot above my head, and her fingers worked at the silver cord of her robe, twisting the ends together, then untwisting and holding them apart, over and over. Her lips were working too, and I strained to make something intelligible from her vague muttering that sounded as though she were coming out of a bad dream.

"It's too bad," she murmured. "It's too bad. . . ."

"I beg your pardon?"

"Oh, please forgive me, Mr. Hamilton," she said, collecting herself with an effort. "I don't know what's happening to me. My mind seems to wander. I was saying . . . saying . . . I was saying that we decided that baby wasn't Ben's." She caught her breath. "It was dreadful—you'll never know what it cost us to come to that conclusion."

She leaned forward and frowned. "You were a friend of Ben's," she said. "If he were alive, he'd tell you these things himself. You're the kind of person Ben would talk to. I can tell. But you must promise not to breathe a word of it to Alberta. She's a busybody, and I have no idea what she repeats when she gets among her own people."

I squirmed in my chair. "Really, Mrs. Holbrook, if you'd rather—"

"No. I want you to hear it all," she said. "The main thing was, I just knew that baby wasn't six months old. She said he'd been a very small baby since birth, and of course they do vary a lot. But then about the third week, Dr. Kriegel dropped in—he's an old, old family friend—and I got him aside and asked his opinion. He only muttered something about there being too many variables to say. I knew he didn't believe Carrie's story, though, and I knew he didn't want to break our hearts. So I spoke to Mr. Holbrook, and soon after that, we had a showdown with Carrie."

She picked up an end of silver cord, looked at it absently and dropped it in her lap.

"I accused her outright. 'Carrie, you've been lying about that baby, haven't you?' I said. She pretended to be shocked, and she cried—real tears, I'll say that much. Those tears were real. Of course, she denied everything. We had the most dreadful scene you can imagine. The upshot of it all was that Mr. Holbrook and I asked her to leave."

She paused again and shook her head sadly. "It nearly killed us. I still say that it hastened Mr. Holbrook's death. We loved Carrie like our own. Well—she *was* our own. That's what made it so hard. When she left, she said, 'I'm sorry you think what you do. This baby is Ben's, and nothing you can do will change that.' Those words have haunted me ever since. She was a good daughter-in-law until. . . ." Her voice trailed off again. Then she brought herself back. "You'll never know how often I've wondered if we were wrong. What if we were? Suppose Carrie was speaking the truth? Think of how we've wronged her!"

"But Mrs. Holbrook, wouldn't it have been simple to ask Carrie for Ben's birth certificate?" I asked.

"Mr. Holbrook did ask her for it," she replied. "She was offended and said if she had known she would be expected to document all her own words, she'd have picked up a copy from the Port Arthur courthouse and brought it along, although she doubted that we would have believed that either. It was horrible. She left immediately after that."

"Couldn't you have made your own check of the county records in Port Arthur?" I asked. Then I hastened to add, "I don't mean to be too inquisitive, but I'm just trying to get it straight."

"It's quite all right," she assured me. "Yes, we could have checked, but the entire business was so personal and private! We just didn't feel right about double-checking on a member of our own family as if we were spies. We thought of asking Mr. Tolliver, our attorney, to check for us, but Mr. Tolliver is—well, rather excitable. Anyway, Mr. Holbrook said he would rather go down and check it himself, but he wasn't feeling well—this was the illness that developed into his last—so he just never went."

She relaxed, her features softened, and a gentle wistfulness came into her eyes. "Do you know, Mr. Hamilton, losing Carrie was like losing Ben all over again. When she walked out that door, Mr. Holbrook and I cried like babies. We sat right here on this very sofa, just the two of us, and cried our eyes out. Some things are worse than death. Death is inevitable, and we manage to adjust to that. But this—this is so unnecessary. It's sordid and should never, never have happened. I'll never understand it. Maybe I was raised in the wrong generation. I'll never understand—never! You have no idea how it feels until it happens to one of your own."

She began to cry. After a time, she dabbed her eyes and composed herself. "Please try to overlook all this," she said. "I have no right to burden you with our family problems. I'm afraid I've taken advantage of you. Dr. Kriegel says we can endure whatever we're supposed to endure. He must be right."

She cleared her throat and leaned back on the sofa. It was more of a story than I had bargained for. Carrie and Ben had been so happy. . . .

"I hear from her every now and then," she said with a wave of her hand, "but I never answer her letters. She came back to Mr. Holbrook's funeral. She didn't stay, though. By then she was living in that Foley place, I guess. She brought the baby, and it was embarrassing. The house was full of people. The doctor—Dr. Kriegel—talked to her and made certain that I wasn't left alone with her. I don't know what either of us would have said."

"I don't mean to be nosy," I said, "but if you don't answer her letters, why does she continue to write?"

"Hmph! That's not hard to understand. We're not wealthy people—not by Texas standards, anyway—but Mr. Holbrook did well in cattle and investments. Besides, there's a great deal of land that's been in the family for years, and he added to it during his life. He was a good businessman. Anybody in this part of Texas will tell you that. Naturally, everything was to go to Ben and his family. That's what's so senseless about what Carrie did. She would have inherited every cent, every investment, every acre, every head of cattle. We would have settled it all on her. It was all hers—she was all we had after Ben died. But, of course, we hardly felt obligated to provide for an illegitimate child."

She drew herself up and set her lips firmly. "We're understanding people, Mr. Hamilton, but even understanding has its limits. We reasoned that Carrie wanted to establish the baby as the legal heir, so that if she remarried, the estate would still come into her hands. I don't know why she didn't marry the baby's real father. The idea of her remarrying would not have been distasteful to us. She's a beautiful child, and a young girl like her is not meant to live alone. She doesn't need to. Mr. Holbrook and I would have loved her the same."

In fascination, I listened, only partially absorbed by Mrs. Holbrook's words. The other part of me was thousands of miles away on one of those miserable little Pacific islands alongside first one and then another unsuspecting fellow whose marriage could not survive the cruel demands of the war. Some blamed the long separation, and who could say they were wrong? They received their "Dear Johns" with stoicism or with shame or with too much feeling to hide, all of them baffled by a war that asked for their lives and took their marriages instead. It was not in the bargain. Ben said that the shock was not altogether real.

"You can't kid me," he said. "These breakups don't come as total surprises to these guys. They're saving face. Their marriages were shaky all along, and they knew it. Don't you think I could tell—even from this distance—if all was not well between Carrie and me?"

Mrs. Holbrook saw me glance at my watch.

"Must you go?" she asked. "I've been a dreadful hostess. I haven't offered you a cup of tea or coffee. I might even find the ingredients of a highball if you can stay."

I apologized and explained my travel schedule. She walked to the door with me, asking for my address, telling me that she came into Fort Worth occasionally and perhaps she could call me. I gave her my card.

"I'll just get a wrap and walk out to the car with you," she said, fumbling among a pile of coats and sweaters on a hall tree by the front door. "I haven't been outside all day, and the weather looks lovely."

As she joined me on the veranda, I saw a changed person. All the warmth and gentleness had vanished. Her eyes had widened and were darting about wildly. She put a forefinger to her lips.

"Sssshhh."

She stood motionless for an instant, then turned her head slowly. Cautiously, she glanced about the veranda, across the driveway and then over her shoulder at the front door. She stepped out into the conservatory and back again on tiptoe, once more motioning for me to remain silent.

Suddenly, she leaped at me and grabbed my arm. "Mr. Hamilton!"

Her quick, catlike movements stunned me. Her body was tense, her voice a hoarse whisper. "You've got to help me." Her face was close to mine, her breath hot on my cheek. Her fingers dug into my arm like talons. "I want you to find Ben."

"What?"

She clapped her other hand over my mouth, pressing with surprising strength. "Not so loud!" she whispered. "Do you want Alberta to hear?" Glancing wildly at the front door again, she gripped my arm tighter. "You've got to find Ben," she insisted.

"But Mrs. Holbrook, it's been five years now. Don't you remember? The entire area was searched many times over."

"That doesn't matter. You can find him. You were his friend. You'll know where to look. They didn't know."

"But I'm afraid it would be—"

"I've got the money for the trip—all you want. And you can use Mr. Holbrook's maps. They're marked and ready to use."

Her poise and dignity were gone. She seemed smaller, somehow. Small, terrified and excited. "You've got to go soon!" she urged. "Soon! We can't wait any longer. He's been out there long enough. He misses us, and I know he's hungry. I'm the only person who knows what Ben likes to eat. He wants to come home. I know he does. He didn't even come home for his father's funeral. He misses us. . . ."

"But—"

"Don't mention it to anybody. Just bring him back here, and we'll have him all to ourselves. We won't tell Alberta or Carrie or the doctor or anybody else."

She looked again at the door. "I'll get the maps now. You can take them home and study them."

I opened my mouth to speak, but the words wouldn't come. Interpreting my silence as consent, she relaxed her grip on my arm and said, "Wait here. It'll only take a minute. I know exactly where they are—"

"Please, Mrs. Holbrook—"

She released me and turned toward the door. She stopped short and gasped.

Alberta stood framed by the doorway.

Mrs. Holbrook brought herself up to full height, then crumpled. Her shoulders drooped, her body sagged.

Alberta stepped out onto the veranda.

"It's time to rest before supper, Mrs. Holbrook," she said gently, putting an arm around her shoulders. Mrs. Holbrook was submissive.

"I'm sorry, Mr. Hamilton," Alberta said. "Maybe you can come back another time when she can talk longer."

"It's all right," I said. "I'm sorry. I didn't know. . . ."

"She'll be all right . . . she'll be fine . . . she'll be all right. . . ." Alberta's voice was soothing, half chant, half song.

Mrs. Holbrook preceded her into the house, a pitiful remnant of the splendid woman I had first met.

"Le's go upstairs and rest," Alberta was saying. "You can be makin' up your mind if you want to eat supper in your room or downstairs. Come on now . . . come on. . . ."

I turned to go. As I descended the steps onto the circular driveway, I listened to the click of the door as it closed gently behind me.

At the bottom of the hill, a blue station wagon turned in at the gate. A piece of gravel flew up and hit my windshield. I pulled over and let the car pass. The driver looked at me curiously. He was huge, almost a giant, filling the front seat with his massive bulk. And he was bareheaded. I did not get a good look at his face, for his most arresting feature was a shock of bushy, snowy-white hair that looked wild and uncontrollable.

(38)

❧ 4 ❧

Amy was intrigued by my description of the Holbrook house, its mistress and her strange behavior. Faced with a sinkful of dirty dishes, a clogged drain, a malfunctioning washing machine filled with half-washed laundry, a crying baby with wet pants, his brother who had that very day learned to climb out of his crib, Amy didn't miss a word.

"I'm not sure why I went," I said. "Seeing Carrie that day in the doctor's office and stopping in Foley probably prompted me, but—well, I don't know exactly—and I'm not sure it was the right thing to do."

"Maybe not," she said thoughtfully. "Your being there could have triggered her, but how could you have known? You simply stopped by to see the mother of a friend who got killed in the war. I think it was a grand thing for you to do. After all, you didn't create that situation."

"I'll bet I agitated it, though."

"Well, don't feel bad about it," she went on. "Your heart was in the right place. That ought to count for something."

She jiggled the switch on the washing machine, then cocked her ear to determine if she had accomplished anything. I moved across the kitchen to see for myself, and she stepped aside.

"It's all yours," she said. "And don't take too long, because when you finish, I'm saving two little boys to turn over to you, lock, stock and barrel—until you leave town again Monday."

Two weeks later, I got a letter from Mrs. Holbrook. It came on a Saturday morning while Amy was at the supermarket and I was minding Skeeter and Kenny. The handwriting on the envelope was delicately feminine. The sheet of fine white vellum contained a single paragraph:

My dear Mr. Hamilton:
Forgive me for bothering you, but I must see you about a matter that I cannot entrust to lawyers. I realize this is an imposition, but I don't know where else to turn. I will be grateful if you can spare me a few minutes of your time. Any time will do.

Very truly yours,
(Mrs.) Henrietta Holbrook

I tossed the letter onto the table with the other mail, then picked it up and read it again. I laid it aside the second time and took Skeeter and Kenny out into the back yard. When we went in again, Amy had returned and was reading the letter.

"What do you think?" I asked.

"I don't know," she said. "She must need you for something, or else she wouldn't have written."

"Do you think I ought to go?"

"Do you know how to refuse gracefully?"

"No, I guess I don't. Will you go with me?"

She laughed. "Yes. Yes, indeed—if you'll stay here with Skeeter and Kenny."

We discussed the matter off and on for the rest of the day and decided I should go. How to work the trip into my regular schedule was another matter.

"You know, if she wouldn't object to my coming early Monday, I think I could detour by Erskine for a few minutes without changing any appointments. I'd have to leave here a little earlier than usual, that's all."

Amy suggested that I telephone Mrs. Holbrook. She was charming and said she would be glad to see me around eight-thirty.

Monday was beautiful and clear, the wind crisp and cold. The old Holbrook house, awash with the richness of the November sun, looked fresher and less alone. The hard, brilliant sunlight flooded the veranda, dancing and winking on the colors of the stained glass around the door, like a kaleidoscope making patterns.

Alberta's greeting was effusive. "Why, Mr. Hamilton! Do come in. It's nice to see you again!"

I apologized for the unconventional hour of my call. "It's the only time I could arrange to come."

"That's all right. I already knowed about it. We is both early risers in this house, anyway. When Mrs. Holbrook seen you drive up the hill, she tole me to tell you she'd be right down."

She took my hat and coat and led me into the sitting room again. "I been hoping you'd come back so's I could explain about the las' time," she said.

"That was something of a shock," I said.

Deep furrows formed across her dark brow. She shook her head sadly. "She go off like that without no notice. Sometime jes' when I think she gettin' better, she have a whole string of bad spells. I could tell you was awful surprised the other day."

"I felt so sorry for her!"

"After you was here, she was in a bad way for two days."

"How is she today?"

Her face broadened into a smile. "She's fine. Jes' fine. She ain't had no bad spells for—let me see now—three days, I reckon it is."

"I suppose you know she wrote and asked me to come?"

"I didn't know it till you called the other day. I don't remember no letter, though, and she usually give me her letters to mail. Maybe she give it to the doctor."

"The doctor? She mentioned a doctor several times the other day. Is she under his care?"

"Oh, no, sir! He don't come like that! Dr. Kriegel, he been coming up here all his life, I reckon. He's jes' about the best friend Mr. and Mrs. Holbrook ever did have." She paused. "Did Mrs. Holbrook say in her letter what she want to see you about?"

I hesitated, and Alberta saw what was bothering me.

"You don't need to worry about me none, Mr. Hamilton," she said, laughing easily. "I done know more about Mrs. Holbrook's business than I wish I knowed. I jes' thought I might help you out if I knowed what she want to see you for. I'm always havin' to straighten things out for people who come up here."

Her manner was comforting and reassuring.

"She didn't say exactly. It was something she couldn't let her lawyers do for her."

"Oh, my!" She looked anxiously up the stairs. "They ain't no tellin' what it is, then. Sometimes she and that lawyer, they go roun' and roun'."

"I certainly don't want to cause another setback," I said anxiously. "If you think I shouldn't have come, just say so, and I'll make some kind of excuse and get out."

"Oh, no, sir! Please don't do that, Mr. Hamilton! It's all right. You jes' make yourself right at home, and I'll go get you some coffee. Mrs. Holbrook she'll be right down."

I strolled out into the hall and confirmed my first impression of the big house. The sunlight splashed through the front windows and flooded the dark corners of the parlor. The room was even mustier than I had first supposed. It was not well proportioned; the ceilings were too high and the windows too narrow, but the paneling on the walls was beautiful—rich and velvety, like cocoa. At the far end of the room was a wide, not too ornate marble mantel with edges gracefully turned. The fireplace itself looked as though it had been cold for years. Two rather ordinary vases sat at either end of the mantel. They were empty. A huge oil painting of the kind popular forty years earlier—a landscape and not a good one—hung over the mantel. The clutter of the high-backed chairs, the stiff settee covered with a dull maroon velour and the assortment of useless occasional tables crowded the room like furniture in a secondhand store. And the antimacassars! Everywhere I looked, I saw antimacassars—white, lacy, starched antimacassars. One glance would have sent Amy screaming down the hill.

Mrs. Holbrook appeared suddenly in the doorway.

"Mr. Hamilton, thank you for coming," she said.

She was wearing a dress of light blue open at the neck and belted around the middle to show off a trim, almost girlish figure. The heels of her black pumps were higher than one would expect on an elderly woman, but they complemented her marvelously shaped legs and well-turned ankles.

"I'm glad I could come," I said, "although I don't have much time. I have a long way to drive today."

She smiled. As she led me back into the sitting room, she said, "That makes me all the more grateful. Please sit down. Alberta will be along with coffee in a minute. You do have time for coffee with me, I hope."

I tried not to stare at her, but I was helpless. To reconcile her with the distressed, tortured creature I had seen last on the veranda was impossible. She seemed to have no recollection of the other Mrs. Holbrook. There was only one—a lovely lady, a gracious hostess, relaxed and poised, concerned only that her guest be at ease. I had dreamed the other.

While she inquired about Amy, Skeeter and Kenny, Alberta brought in the coffee tray and departed. Mrs. Holbrook busied herself with cups and saucers, smiling and chattering about the weather, the morning headlines, friends in Fort Worth whom I might know.

"I'm sure you're wondering why I asked you to come, Mr. Hamilton," she said after serving me coffee. "And you'll never know how I appreciate your response."

"Whatever I can do, Mrs. Holbrook."

She took a sip of coffee and put down her cup. Leaning back, she folded her hands in her lap and smiled.

"I want to beg a favor of you, and I hope I'm not presumptuous."

"Not at all. I believe you said it was a matter you couldn't turn over to your lawyer."

"Why, yes, I did," she said. "I want you to kill Carrie for me."

5

An eerie stillness hung over the room. If there was a sound anywhere, it was the echo of Mrs. Holbrook's words. The more I heard them, the less certain I was that she had spoken at all.

She sat serene and poised, watching me across the coffee table, a suggestion of a smile playing around her lips. A kind of satisfied merriment had come into her manner. She was relaxed. Nothing extraordinary had been said. Quite simply, she had made a request; now she was quietly awaiting my reply. Somewhere in the house, a door slammed.

Finally, I managed to speak. "What did you say?"

Her expression did not change. "I said I want you to kill Carrie for me."

"You're not serious," I said.

"I was never more serious in my life," she said. "She deserves to die. She made Ben unhappy, and has made us unhappy. She must pay for it."

"But she didn't make Ben unhappy," I said. "Ben was happy with Carrie. He loved her. Carrie loved him. They made each other happy. Surely you remember that."

"No! That's not true!" her voice rose. "He might have been happy at first, but not later. He couldn't have been happy after the things she did to him."

"But Mrs. Holbrook, that was after Ben—"

"Don't say it!" She touched her hand to her mouth. "Don't you *dare* say that! You think Ben is dead, too. I know you do!" She lifted her chin haughtily. "And I thought you were Ben's friend!"

"I was, but I was also Carrie's friend."

I glanced out into the hall hoping to see Alberta.

"You're like the rest of them—Alberta, the doctor and all the others! You're no different. You think I'm insane, don't you?" She paused and let her question hang for a moment. "Don't you?" she repeated. "*Don't you?* Why don't you say it? You think I'm a crazy woman who doesn't know what she's talking about." She bent forward. "Well—isn't that what you think?"

"Please, Mrs. Holbrook. Let me call Alberta."

She sprang to her feet and stood glaring down at me. Her flawless skin had turned splotchy and red. "Call Alberta! Call Alberta!" she mimicked. "That's all anybody thinks about. Well, go ahead and call Alberta. Go ahead."

Suddenly she was quiet again. She was short of breath. I watched her carefully, hoping her excitement had spent itself and exhausted her. But she narrowed her eyes and bent down, her face within inches of mine.

"What if Alberta is not here?" she asked slowly.

"But I saw her," I said, drawing back against the cushion of the chair.

She leaned into me further. "What if I sent her on an errand?" she asked. "How do you know that she is anywhere in this house?"

I had to get out of that chair or suffocate. Swiftly, I slid from under her and jumped to my feet. "I'll go find her myself," I exclaimed, starting for the door.

"Mr. Hamilton?"

The voice was soft and warm again. It drew me up short. I wheeled around unable to believe what I saw. She had resumed her seat and was reaching for her coffee cup. "Please sit down

(45)

and finish your coffee," she said, apparently unperturbed. "It's likely to get cold."

I gaped at her.

"If you don't feel that you can help me, just say so," she said kindly. "Naturally, I shall be disappointed, but at the same time, I realize you must have other things on your mind and your own affairs to look after."

Of the two of us, who was sane? Desperately, I cast about for a way to get out of that house, to get off that hill and away from Erskine forever.

"Mrs. Holbrook, you'll have to excuse me," I said. "I'll have to beg off." My remark was as crazy as the scene itself.

Her disappointment showed. "Oh? I'm sorry to hear that. But I should have realized that it was an imposition to ask."

"No—it's not that." This was the craziest remark of all. "I just have a busy schedule, that's all."

"I see. Well, it was an idea to save a lot of fuss and bother. I know your work takes you near Foley, and I thought perhaps you could save Carrie a trip here."

"But Carrie never comes here—you told me."

"She doesn't. But I wrote and invited her. I asked her to let bygones be bygones and to please forgive a lonely old lady. We could start all over, and I would make amends somehow."

"Do you think she'll come?"

"I have no doubt. It's what she's been waiting for."

"I'd better be on my way. . . ."

A change came over her. She looked out the window. "You'll have a nice day for driving," she said pleasantly. She was dismissing me. The visit had ended.

I got to my feet.

"I'm afraid I've taken up too much of your time," she apologized.

"It doesn't matter. I can make it up."

"I do appreciate your coming, and I'm sorry we couldn't get together on my little proposition. Maybe I can get the doctor to do it. If he won't, I'll have to do it myself."

She preceded me into the hall and called for Alberta, who appeared at the end of the hall and ducked into a closet under the stairs. When she reached us with my hat and coat, she was beaming at Mrs. Holbrook.

"It sure looks like you had a nice visit, Mrs. Holbrook," she said.

"Yes, it was lovely," Mrs. Holbrook answered, and said to me, "Please come any time you can."

Alberta helped me on with my coat. The door closed behind me. I was on the veranda alone. I turned and looked down the veranda into a parlor window.

Mrs. Holbrook was staring out at me.

6

This was not my affair. I knew that. Yet, I felt an obligation to discuss what I had witnessed with a responsible person, someone who had the resources for assessing it and acting accordingly. Although in all probability, Mrs. Holbrook's behavior was an old story to those who knew her best, her threat against Carrie—for that's what it was—might turn out to be a new chapter. It seemed to me that I could not in good conscience drive away from Erskine without telling it to someone who knew her better than I. I wanted to talk to Alberta, but I did not know how to arrange this outside Mrs. Holbrook's presence. And so I decided to seek out Mrs. Holbrook's friend Dr. Kriegel, who seemed to be closer to the family than anyone else.

His office was downtown, upstairs over a beauty shop. A plainly furnished and carelessly arranged office, it was spartan in its bareness. The waiting room was empty except for a receptionist in a white uniform who regarded me with indifference. Dr. Kriegel was busy with a patient, and inasmuch as I had no appointment and was not ill, she was reluctant to say that I could see him at all. Nevertheless, she agreed to ask him.

The wait seemed interminable. I had a long way to drive and many calls to make, and I should have been out on the road an hour earlier. Eventually the door opened, and I was startled but not really surprised that the man who appeared in the doorway was the bushy-haired driver of the blue station wagon, the white-haired giant Mrs. Holbrook had described as her late husband.

He ushered a faded, middle-aged lady past the receptionist's desk to the outer door. He was even larger than I had imagined, at least six feet five. His eyes were deep-set and buried under a pair of dense, overhanging brows. His hair was an unruly tangle. His hands were immense, and his feet, which he moved in a bumbling shuffle, appeared to be weights that were almost unmanageable. There was about him an aboriginal look, the air of a true primitive. I watched him in fascination as he talked to the lady for a moment, then patted her gently on the shoulder and sent her out into the corridor. As he shuffled back across the room, he looked at me curiously. He stopped in front of the receptionist and leaned on her desk, then turned to me.

"Mr. Hamilton? Won't you come in, please?" His voice was like distant thunder but with a body like his, it could have sounded no less.

I followed him into his office, awed by his massiveness. The tough texture of his skin, the roughhewn cast of his immense features would have harmonized with a cattle range or the dirty rig of an oil well. He closed the door and looked at me appraisingly.

"You're not from around here, are you?" he asked. It was more of a statement than a question. For all his booming thunder, he was not gruff. On the contrary, he gave a strange gentleness to the inflection of his words.

I explained who I was and why I was in Erskine.

"I don't believe I've heard Mrs. Holbrook mention you," he said agreeably.

"Probably not. This is only my second visit."

"I'm happy to meet a friend of Ben's," he said, motioning me to sit down. "He was a fine boy, and all of us still miss him." He dropped heavily into a chair at his cluttered desk and faced me. "Now, what can I do for you?"

"Well, I certainly don't want to snoop into things that are

none of my business, but I ran into a situation at Mrs. Holbrook's today that bothered me, and I thought maybe you ought to know about it."

He lifted his thick brows and smiled. "I thought I knew each and every situation at Mrs. Holbrook's, but perhaps not." He leaned forward and rested an elbow on the desk, regarding me with mild interest.

"In the first place, I came to Erskine today at Mrs. Holbrook's invitation—actually, it was a request. Something she wanted me to do, she said. But maybe it would be better if I backed up and told you first how *that* came about."

I began with Carrie's odd actions in Fort Worth and ended with Mrs. Holbrook's bizarre request that I kill her. It was a long story, but the doctor's attention never strayed.

". . . and so it seemed that you're the logical person to tell this to, and here I am," I said. "I'm sure you understand that the experience shook me up quite a bit."

"Yes, I certainly can understand that," he said. He drew a long breath. "And as strange as this may sound to you, there's no real cause for alarm. Mrs. Holbrook means a lot to me. I've taken care of her a long time. I've looked after the entire family for years. I delivered Ben and pulled him through all his childhood diseases and accidents. Ben's father was my best friend as well as my patient. I was with him when he died. I probably know more about the Holbrooks' private affairs than anyone else alive."

He paused, leaned back in his chair, took a crumpled package of cigarettes from his shirt pocket and held them toward me. I took one. He lighted mine, then his own, and watched the smoke for a moment.

"I tell you this so you can understand how close I am to the circumstances—to ease your mind, so to speak. From time to time I've considered hospitalizing her—and the day may come when I'll have to do it, but not just yet."

"Then you don't really consider her a menace or a danger, despite her threat to kill Carrie?"

"No, I don't." He smiled again. It was a professional smile, and well practiced. "The threat means nothing. By this time, she probably doesn't even remember saying it."

"Well—you certainly are reassuring," I said. I breathed somewhat more easily. "I just assumed that all such cases are for specialists, and I guess I'm a little surprised that she's not under a psychiatrist's care."

The smile disappeared. He leaned forward in his chair. His expression hardened slightly, and when he spoke, his voice was edged with impatience. "Mr. Hamilton, you're not in Fort Worth now. You're in Erskine, Texas, population three thousand. I don't know your experience with small towns, but let me explain something to you. In a town this small, the doctor plays many roles that have nothing to do with the profession of medicine. A doctor in a small town is required to do more than heal sick bodies."

He ground his half-smoked cigarette into an ashtray already filled with half-smoked cigarettes. "Henrietta Holbrook is one of my dearest friends," he went on. "I grieved over Ben as though he were my own, and I was as upset about Carrie and the way she behaved as Mr. and Mrs. Holbrook were. I have the run of the house. I'm at home when I'm on that hill."

He stopped for a moment, then began again. "You may be assured that I'll do what seems best for Mrs. Holbrook. At the moment, however, she's doing well without a psychiatrist. She has ample resources, and I have ample judgment, for bringing one in should it appear necessary."

"I'm sorry," I said sheepishly. "I wasn't being critical. It's just that I was unnerved about the whole business."

"It's all right. I appreciate your concern," he said affably. "And to ease your mind further, consider this: she's in familiar surroundings. She's comfortable, and she's with people she knows."

"I see," I said. "And I repeat—I'm sorry for butting in like this."

"Just keep one thing in mind," he said. "I'm caring for a woman in her sixties whose life is behind her. She stays at home bothering nobody; she rarely comes down from that hill. When she does, somebody comes along to look after her."

"Well, Doctor, since I've already put my foot in my mouth, let me put it there once more." I smiled. He smiled easily in return and nodded.

"Isn't it possible that some day—in a rash and unguarded moment—that she *could* harm somebody? Alberta, say."

"Oh, yes," he said. "There's always that possibility, but it's remote, I think. It's a calculated risk, and I think the care and devotion she receives help to minimize that risk." He grew thoughtful. "The cracks began to show soon after they got the 'Missing in Action' report. She could have adjusted to his death soon enough, but the not knowing seemed to be more than she could handle. Of course, all that business about Carrie and the baby, coming on top of the other, complicated matters. Then, Mr. Holbrook's death seemed to be a final blow of some kind. She sort of gave herself up to whatever fantasies happened to be running through her mind." He sighed. Then he shook his head and looked at me keenly. "To say that I've followed all these events is an understatement," he added. "I've been involved in them."

He spoke with finality, and I knew he was ready to terminate my visit.

"Do you think I should warn Carrie not to come?"

"As you wish, but I must remind you that you'll be warning her against nothing, actually," he said. "Henrietta won't harm *her*, but if the subject of Carrie upsets her now, then Carrie in person might be too much for her. Also, we'd have to assume that Carrie would bring the child—another risk, perhaps. But it really isn't your problem, though I do appreciate your concern. Don't worry—these things will work themselves out in their own time."

"Well, you've certainly made me feel a lot better," I said.

"That's because now you know the case better."

"Touché," I said. "Again I apologize—and thank you."

"Not at all!" he boomed, getting to his feet. He shuffled toward his office door. "Some of her friends drop in every now and then, so she doesn't get too lonesome. She has no relatives, and that makes it kind of hard on her." He put his hand on the doorknob. "Mr. Holbrook's two brothers died some years before he did, and neither left children. He was the last of a disappearing family. In fact, Mrs. Holbrook is the sole survivor of two families. It's rather unusual, isn't it? Of course, she doesn't count Carrie as a member of the family—not after she tried to palm that baby off as Ben's. An outrageous bit of business, if you ask me." He opened the door.

"I gather you agreed that the baby couldn't have been old enough to be Ben's," I said.

He frowned. "I didn't say that; babies vary enormously, and I never really examined Carrie's. It was those months and months of not telling them that I couldn't swallow. Her story was grossly inadequate. Well, good-bye."

❧ 7 ❧

The highway to Fort Stockton had been repaired, but on my return trip, I took the road to Foley anyway. The sun was low when I arrived, and the little community was having a gasp of activity before shutting down for the night. A few people moved about on the sidewalk; a woman carrying a parcel walked out into the wide street toward an automobile parked in the middle; a group of schoolboys lounged on the curb in front of the café; two men wearing cowboy hats and high-heeled boots stood propped against the post office, engrossed in conversation; a gray-haired man sat on the curb with his legs crossed and eyed me with curiosity as I drove past.

I pulled up to the curb and asked a young man in blue denim overalls for directions to Carrie's house. Two blocks down and one block over, he said, third house from the corner on the left, the one with the blue trimming.

A flat dreariness, whipped by the wind and baked to a turn by the sun, hung over the short street which petered out into a cow-path a few blocks in the distance. The frame houses that spotted the area were without style, without charm, without personality. Carrie's house could have been any one of them: white, rectangular and anonymous. Her yard, like the others, spilled over both ways into the next with no boundaries to define it, an empty expanse of dead grass and brown dust. Two small boys tossing a football in the yard beyond stopped their playing and watched me park on the street in front of Carrie's house.

I walked up onto the front porch, not at all confident that I would find Carrie Holbrook anywhere within miles of such a place. A blue plastic toy lay in the yard. A tricycle stood on the porch. A length of string tied to the porch railing fluttered in the wind. There was no doorbell. I rapped on the door. Inside, the jingle of a radio commercial was silenced abruptly. The *click-click* of heels moved through the house toward the front door. I put down an impulse to turn and run.

The door opened. Carrie Holbrook stood there, beautiful, cold and unsmiling. She wore a pair of blue slacks and a gray pullover jersey. They might have been ordinary clothes that Foley teachers wore at home after school was out for the day, but on Carrie Holbrook nothing looked ordinary. She would probably have looked chic in a Mother Hubbard.

"Hello, Pete," she said calmly.

She pushed open the screen door and stood aside.

I went in. "You don't seem very surprised," I said.

"I saw you through the window," she said. "Anyway, after I heard about the stranger in the drugstore, I knew. Why did you do that, Pete?" She was not unpleasant, but neither was she cordial.

"I could ask you a similar question," I countered.

"I suppose you could." She made a gesture toward the room at large. "But let's not stand here like posts. Sit down."

Carrie's living room was surprisingly ordinary. The gray overstuffed sofa and matching chair, the identical tables holding identical lamps, the plain coffee table with glass ashtrays stacked at one end, the gray figured wallpaper, the lace curtains at the windows, the cheap carpet with green swirls, all could have been purchased from Montgomery Ward on a single order blank. The only thing in the room that could have belonged to Carrie and no one else was a large photograph of Ben, solemn and unsmiling, on the wall by the dining-room door. He was wearing his flight suit with white silk scarf wrapped carefully around his neck and tucked into his open collar. I remembered when the photograph had been taken. Somewhere in my war paraphernalia I had a copy, and the chances were that Carrie had a similar pose of me stored away with Ben's things. She caught my appraising glance.

"What's the verdict?" she asked, still unsmiling.

"I don't know. It's just dawned on me that this is the first time I've been inside a place that's yours. During the war it was furnished apartments and hotel rooms. I never got around to wondering what your own place would be like."

"Don't start wondering yet," she said. "I rent this place from the local banker. I've been living here four years—temporary all the way." She motioned me into the overstuffed chair. I was looking hard for some trace of the old Carrie Holbrook. She wasn't there.

"Not even the furniture is mine," she was saying. "It came with the house. From the first I intended to get my own things, but San Angelo's the closest place I could find anything decent. Getting there's just been too big a hassle, what with working all day and raising a baby before and afterwards. So, here I am— still in a furnished place."

An awkward silence followed. We looked at one another uneasily. Suddenly, she broke into a laugh. It was happy, musical laughter. She came to life.

"Isn't this goofy?" she squealed. "This is the silliest thing I ever heard of!"

She leaped from her chair, laughing, and planted herself before me, her hands outstretched. "I'll tell you what," she said. "Let's go into the kitchen, and I'll see if I can find an old bottle of bourbon that must be at least three years old by now—if it hasn't evaporated. I've forgotten how a highball tastes."

I relaxed. A warm feeling gushed over me. The years fell away. "It's good to see you, Carrie," I said, smiling up into her face. I reached for her hands.

(56)

"It's good to see you too, Pete. Tell me about yourself and why I'm so honored after so many years."

"What about the bourbon?"

"Oh, yes." She tugged at me. I got to my feet and followed her into the kitchen. "Come on," she said. "You haven't seen Ben yet. He's around somewhere."

Ben came in from the back yard in answer to his mother's summons. A slight, brown-haired child with great, round eyes as dark as his hair, he examined me with no show of interest. Something wistful about him reminded me of the adult Ben Holbrook, but maybe it was my imagination. Alongside his mother's blond sparkle, his quiet manner and serious expression provided the same contrast that people had always been quick to notice in Carrie and her husband.

"He and Daddy flew airplanes together in the war," she told him. "We've got his picture in Daddy's scrapbook."

She turned to me. "We did have fun, didn't we? Do you remember that old hatchet-faced commander's wife who thought you were Ben and how disapproving she was to find out you weren't?"

I smiled. "She wouldn't have believed us if we'd told her Ben was going to meet us later."

"Oh, God, no! She was having too good a time making us into a scandal."

That set off a round of reminiscences. Little Ben stood and examined me further for a while, and if he was impressed, he concealed it well. He turned and wandered out of the room.

"He doesn't meet strangers very well," she apologized. "Maybe he'll get used to you after a while, but I don't guarantee it."

I watched him go through the doorway. "Carrie, I know I'm supposed to think he resembles somebody, but he doesn't."

She was scratching around in the pantry, moving boxes and rattling paper sacks. "I know," she said over her shoulder. "I wouldn't believe you if you said otherwise." She backed out of the pantry and glanced around for Ben. Her face grew serious.

(57)

"To be truthful, Pete, sometimes it's like having a little stranger in the house. There's a part of him that I don't think I'll ever reach. It's downright spooky when your own—"

"Where did you get him, Carrie?"

Her eyes leveled on me for an instant. Then she bent down again into the pantry. "Where do people usually get babies?" she asked.

She overdid it. She was too casual.

"Oh—here we are!" She backed out with a half-filled whiskey bottle. "You'll have to be bartender. I've forgotten how."

"You're a bum actress, Carrie," I said, taking the bottle. "You know exactly what I mean."

She studied my face, then spoke slowly and softly. "Yes, I guess I do."

She took a tray of ice from the refrigerator and handed it to me. While I mixed the drinks, she went to the back door and called to Ben. She got no response and went through the house looking for him. I took the drinks into the living room and sat down. In a minute she joined me. She turned on a couple of lamps.

"Honestly! He gets off to himself and gets so quiet that I forget he's in the house. Where's my drink? Oh—"

I handed her the glass. She sat on the sofa and took a deep breath.

"Now—"

"Well—is this a guessing game?" I asked.

She sipped her drink. "Mmmm, that's good. It's been so long since I've had a drink, I'll probably fall flat on my face."

She gazed into her glass. I waited.

"He's Ben's—not mine," she said quietly.

"Ben's?"

"That's why I was so snooty in Fort Worth that day. I didn't want to see you, because I was afraid I couldn't pull it off—not with you. You would spot something fishy along the way." She smiled wistfully.

"I don't understand."

"Does the name Marie Scott mean anything to you?"

"No. Should it?"

"Did you and Ben bump into a couple of girls from Texas University at the Top of the Mark your last night in San Francisco—just before you shipped out?"

"Obviously, you know we did or you wouldn't be asking. And if you say one of them was named Marie, I won't argue. I just don't remember. Anyway, what does that have to do with it?"

"Marie was Ben's old girl friend—back in college, before me. And little Ben is Marie's and Ben's."

"Now come on, Carrie! Do you expect me to believe that?"

"Probably not. I didn't believe it myself when I first heard it. But you did see them together that night."

"Yes. At the Top of the Mark. But if anything had happened between them, do you think Ben would have written you about seeing her at all?"

"Maybe—in case I heard it from somebody else—you or the other girl. Maggie somebody or other. I knew Marie before I knew Ben. In fact, she introduced me to him. She and I lived in the same dormitory, same floor. We weren't close friends, but we went to a lot of the same things, belonged to some of the same clubs. We always got along well. She and Ben went steady for—oh, I don't know how long—until he asked me for a date. Then, the first thing you know, Marie was out of the picture, and I was in it. I lost track of her after graduation."

She took a drink from her glass and set it on the coffee table. "Were you with them all evening in San Francisco?"

"No. I had a date. I left the three of them soon after that one drink."

"Oh. He didn't tell me that, so I assumed the four of you were together all evening. At any rate, I wasn't upset about Ben seeing Marie, because I knew that Ben wasn't interested in her any more. That is, until one night in September—that was 1945 —I was working in a shipyard in Port Arthur—Marie came to see me. She said she was living in San Antonio and working at Randolph Field. The real purpose of her visit, though, was to tell me that she had a baby and that Ben was the father. The baby was back in San Antonio. Of course, I didn't believe her."

She paused, as though trying to remember what should come next, then continued. "I can assure you that things were perfect between Ben and me—absolutely perfect. Well, I got my dander up in a hurry—naturally. How gullible did she think I was? God knows what all I must have said to the poor girl, but we went back and forth for the longest time. She said when she saw Ben, she didn't intend for anything to happen, and Ben didn't either. But it did. She said she still loved him, but that Ben loved me and she had no doubts about it."

Carrie smiled. "I still wasn't ready for all that. Maybe she did actually shack up with him, and maybe she did have an illegitimate child, but I didn't have to believe the baby was Ben's. There's a limit to how much you can swallow in one story, you know. She went on to say that when she found she was pregnant, she wrote and asked Ben what she should do."

She stopped suddenly and asked, "Did Ben ever mention such a thing to you?"

"No. And I think you *were* gullible."

"Did he ever seem upset about anything personal that he couldn't talk about? You know, Ben Holbrook wasn't the gabbiest person on earth."

"No. And I think Ben would have told me something like this."

"Give me a cigarette," she said. I gave her one and lighted it for her. She took a deep drag and coughed. "Whew! This is the first cigarette I've had in I don't know when. It's making me dizzy." She crushed it out and laughed. "Cigarettes and whiskey —what would the citizens of Foley think if they could see me now? Anyway, Marie said that Ben wrote her back—she had the letter—and, in effect, admitted the whole thing. He said he would think of something and not leave her stranded. You know—the kind of letter that Ben *would* have written."

"But Carrie, even Ben's admission to sleeping with Marie wouldn't necessarily prove that he was the father."

(60)

"Maybe not genetically, or however you prove such things," she said. "But if a man admits paternity, that's it, friend. It's all his. Don't you ever read the papers? Paternity suits are settled frequently when the man admits the act and accepts responsibility for the baby."

She picked up her glass and set it down again without drinking from it. "Anyway," she continued, "she had the baby in April. Of course, Ben was already missing by then. Soon afterwards, she went back to work, and her married sister took care of the baby. He was five months old when she came to see me. She had met this petroleum engineer who was being reassigned to Saudi Arabia. He wanted to marry her, but he didn't want the baby. And her sister couldn't keep him indefinitely, either. So she knew she'd have to go to an adoption agency, which she admitted she should have done as soon as the baby was born. Her only other choice, as she saw it, was go to the Holbrooks. Before she did either, she wanted my opinion on it. *Me*, of all people! What do you think of that?"

"I think you had been smoking opium, that's what I think."

"I know it must sound that way now. Marie said if she had gone to the Holbrooks, I would know it anyway, so she came to see me first. She went on to say that she didn't want to give the baby up, but if she had to, she thought his real grandparents should have some choice in the matter. But under the circumstances, she didn't know if it was right or wrong to tell them about the baby. 'You're the only one who can tell me the answer,' she said."

Carrie looked at me. "You'll have to agree, Pete—that was one hell of a question to wrestle with. Later on I seesawed back and forth about it, but at the time, my immediate reaction was to be violently opposed to heaping any more shock and grief on my in-laws, so I said, 'Don't tell them, Marie.' I—"

"Hold it, Carrie," I said. "You sound as though suddenly you believed her."

She pushed a stray strand of hair from her forehead. "Yes—suddenly, I did. All at once, she started to make sense. I already

(61)

knew her, you remember. I knew her as a fine person. I couldn't ignore that. I think she honestly loved Ben. As much as she cared what happened to the baby, she wasn't going to barge in on his parents if it was the wrong thing to do. So she came to see me, of all people. I don't know if I would have had the nerve to do that or not. So—well, hell, yes! I believed her!"

She looked out the window for a moment. It was dark outside now. She shook her head and turned back to me.

"Now, Pete, if I live to be a million years old, I'll never understand the next thing I did. As calmly as you please, I said, 'Let me take the baby, Marie.' Such a thought had not entered my head until that minute. It came out of my mouth as though someone else were speaking. But once I'd said it, the idea began to take hold. Ben and I had planned to have children, naturally, after the war when he came home to stay, but that dream had gone forever. . . ." Her voice softened to a whisper. She caught herself. "I—well, I just found myself wanting that baby, Pete! Desperately—even though I hadn't seen him. Maybe his being Ben's had a lot to do with it. I don't know. I can't explain it completely. Every woman wants a baby, but I wanted that particular one. I just did, that's all."

She paused again. "The upshot of it all is that Marie agreed, but it took a long time for me to convince her. Eventually, I won, though. Her only stipulation was that we never, never have any personal contact; no letters, no phone calls, no inquiries through mutual acquaintances and friends. That seemed reasonable, and I agreed. So she brought me the baby the next week, and I've had him ever since."

"That's a touching story, Carrie," I said. "It really is; I'm not being sarcastic or cute. But soap operas can be touching, too, if they don't strain your imagination too much. This one is putting a strain on mine."

"Oh, this is pure *Stella Dallas*—no question about it."

"It's pure sudsy soap opera, that's what it is."

"I'm not surprised that you don't believe it," she said. "This is

(62)

the first time I've ever told the story to anyone, and even while I was telling it, it began to sound unreal."

"Why didn't you tell Ben's parents the truth?"

"Wow! Don't think I didn't argue with myself over that one! After all, they were as involved as I was. I would convince myself that they were entitled to know, and by the time I'd get to the telephone, I'd chicken out. You wouldn't believe how many times I picked up that telephone and put it down again. I kept thinking of the tortures they were suffering over Ben's death . . . it had absolutely crushed them. They idolized him. I still marvel that I wormed my way into their affections at all, for the Holbrook family was a closed corporation, believe me. When they lost Ben, they lost their center of existence. For several days I wandered around trying to decide whether to call them or not. Ben was gone, and the Marie Scott business would only add to their misery. So I plain chickened out!

"The next morning after Marie's visit, I went into the office and quit. Just like that. It didn't cause any stir—they hired service wives who were always coming and going anyway. Then I went on the damnedest shopping spree you ever heard of. It takes a hell of a lot of equipment to raise a baby."

"I know," I said. "Did you adopt the baby legally?"

"No."

"Why not?"

"For one thing, it didn't seem necessary. If he was Ben's, he was mine, too, I reasoned. For another, adoption would have involved court proceedings, and the fact that little Ben wasn't mine would become a matter of official and public record. I didn't want that. Then, to be truthful, I simply didn't have the guts to go into court and explain where he came from. It would have been too messy."

"That sounds rather careless to me," I said. "Adoption would actually cover up his origins. The court issues new birth certificates in these cases, you know, so that children won't go through life with 'illegitimate' written on their birth certificates. It's been a Texas law for some time now."

"Yes, I know—now. I suppose I could still get it done somewhere. I've got his real birth certificate—the one Marie gave me. The Holbrooks asked me for his birth certificate, but I couldn't show it to them, could I? I trumped up a tale about it being recorded in Port Arthur and that I had not received it yet."

"What about the letter from Ben admitting paternity?" I said. "Why didn't you show that to the Holbrooks?"

"That was as crazy as the rest of this tale," Carrie said. "It didn't occur to me to look in the envelope that Marie gave me for several days. All the crying and newness and—*everything*—well, it just wasn't important at the time. Then when I *did* look, the birth certificate was there, but the letter wasn't. Marie had already disappeared, and I had no more idea than a spook where she was. I tried to find her, but I didn't get far. I didn't know her sister's name in San Antonio and—well, I just didn't know how to track her down. And let's face it, I wasn't anxious to make too much noise about all this, so the upshot of it all was that I had the birth certificate and no letter. With the letter, I think I might eventually have gone to the Holbrooks, but. . . ." She paused for a few moments. "I waited and waited, thinking maybe Marie would discover the oversight and mail me the letter, but she didn't. Then the time came when I couldn't wait any longer. I *had* to see the Holbrooks face to face sooner or later, so I stiffened my spine and took little Ben to see them and told them he was mine and Ben's. You know the rest."

Our glasses were empty; neither of us made a move to refill them.

"Isn't that the damnedest tale you ever heard?" she said.

"To put it mildly, yes," I said.

My instincts, my common sense, my better judgment all told me to take her story with a grain of salt. Yet, it somehow hung together, and she had told it with a lack of guile that made it sound plausible, no matter how improbable. Besides, if she had set out to fabricate a story, she was too intelligent to fabricate one as far-fetched as this. In other words, it was just bad enough to be true.

Ben had come into the living room and crawled into his mother's lap while she had been talking.

"Are you hungry, darling?" she asked, drawing him close and planting a kiss on the top of his head.

He did not reply. She made a move to get up.

"Come on, Pete, and let's feed Ben. You can make us another drink." She placed her hand under Ben's chin and tilted his face upwards. Her eyes glowed. "Why won't you talk to Mr. Hamilton?" she asked, wrinkling her nose at him. "He's an old, old friend, and he'd like to talk to you, I'll bet." Her voice was no more than a murmur.

We went into the kitchen where Ben lost some of his shyness and chattered nonsense, interrupting us at will. I perched myself on a kitchen stool while Carrie went about preparing his supper and talking to me over her shoulder, never failing to give Ben her full attention when he had something to say. At times, I could have tiptoed out of the house and neither of them would have noticed. I tried to fit the elder Ben Holbrook into the picture, and even he did not belong.

"We'll give Ben his supper, and you and I will eat later," she said.

"I think not, Carrie. I've got to get on to San Angelo."

"Over my dead body!" she exclaimed. "I'm not through talking to you. Besides, I'm so tired of cooking for just Ben and me that I could die. Even a recipe for two is too much. We've got one café in Foley, but I'm too fond of you to make you eat in it. You'll have to put up with my cooking. Tell me about your family."

"Carrie, you haven't changed a bit," I said. "You had me worried. I guess that's why I snooped on you in the drugstore."

"That was a dirty trick. When Mr. Andrews—the druggist—described you, I knew immediately. But it was a dirty trick."

"Okay—the score is tied. If you won't play any more dirty tricks on me, I won't play any on you."

"It's a deal," she said. "Now tell me about your family. Would I like Amy?"

"Amy? Everybody likes Amy. I'll guarantee her. She's honest and direct, no beating around the bush with her. She's a very practical lady."

"Pretty? Blond? Brunette? Tall? Short?"

"Brown hair, five feet five, very *very* pretty. Her college yearbook says she has an All-American wholesome charm—the girl next door kind of thing. She hates that, but it's a pretty good description."

I went on to tell her how Amy had grown up in St. Louis, about Skeeter and Kenny, about our GI house, our friends, my job. Meanwhile, she carried on a disjointed, running conversation with Ben whenever he chose to interrupt. We sat on either side of the kitchen table while he ate his supper. When he had finished and left the room, we stayed where we were and sat in silence for a while.

Then I said, "But Carrie, your taking the baby in the first place was crazy. Don't you realize that?"

"Certainly I realize it," she said pensively. "I realize lots of things now that I didn't realize then." She sighed deeply. "Down inside me, I knew they'd never find Ben. He was gone forever, and I knew it. You don't know what it is to look forward to nothing. No letters, no homecoming. Nothing. You know, Pete, I thought I'd lie down and die when the war ended and everyone was coming home to family reunions and celebrations. Little Ben helped me through all that more than you can know. Despite all the heartbreak that followed, I never think of where I got him. Not any more. He's mine. It's the same as if I had given birth to him, labor pains and all."

We lapsed into a silence again. Then Carrie spoke. "The Holbrooks had been good to me," she went on. "I was never close to my own family. I don't even remember my father, and my mother was always too busy making a living to pay much attention to me. The Holbrooks filled the gaps for me. Poor Daddy Holbrook died thinking the worst of me, and that hurts, God knows. He was a kind person, one of those cute, lovable little men—sort of like a Kewpie doll—one that you'd like to pet and

(66)

cuddle. If I live to be a thousand years old, I'll never forget how he looked at me when I left the house that day. His eyes filled with tears, and when he said, 'Good-bye, Carrie'—that's all—when he said that, it almost ruined me. On my way out to my car with the baby, I started bawling like a calf. When I got to the foot of the hill, I almost turned around and drove back, to tell them the whole story."

"You should have. They'd have got used to it eventually."

"And how many times do you suppose I've been through *that* exercise? I write to Mother Holbrook all along, but she never answers. The first year or so, I got so homesick for them I could hardly stand it."

"She thinks you're after her money," I said.

"Who?"

"Mrs. Holbrook."

"How do you know?" she asked absently.

"She told me."

She became rigid. "You've *seen* her?"

"That's the real reason I came here."

"You saw *Ben's* mother?" She half rose from the table.

"Twice."

She shook her head quickly. "I don't get it," she said.

"She's not well, Carrie. She's unbalanced mentally."

"I found that out when I went back to Daddy Holbrook's funeral." She sat down. "Tell me about seeing my mother-in-law twice." There was an edge in her voice. "You already knew they'd thrown me out when you came here, didn't you?"

"Yes, I knew," I said then went on to describe my first visit to Mrs. Holbrook. "The day I saw her, though," I added, "she seemed to be thinking perhaps they had wronged you. And then she suddenly started acting peculiar and asked me to go and find Ben. It was quite a shock."

"But you went back a second time."

"I had no intention of going back, but she wrote and asked me to come as a favor. And when I saw her that time, she was having one of her spells, as Alberta calls them. She was really in bad shape that day. She's got it in her mind to kill you, Carrie—that's really why I came to see you. To warn you. After I left her, I went to see Dr. Kriegel about it, and he assured me that there is no cause for alarm. Still, I thought you should know."

She didn't flinch.

"Doesn't that disturb you?" I asked.

"Certainly."

"You don't act like it."

"How am I supposed to act? Nobody's ever threatened to kill me before. I don't know what's required."

"She asked me to do it for her."

Her chin was resting on her hand. "She what?"

"Asked me to kill you."

She dropped her hand and leaned back in her chair. "That's awful!" she said. "She's in worse shape than I thought."

"That's why I came to warn you. Did you get a letter from her asking you to come back to Erskine?"

"No."

"She told me she wrote and asked you to bring Ben and come back to stay."

"I never received the letter."

"If you had received it, would you go?"

She studied my question. "Probably," she said at last.

I could hear her even breathing from across the table. After a time, she got up and went through the house turning on more lights and drawing shades. She did not say a word. I sat at the kitchen table and waited.

When she returned, she said, "It *is* a lot of money."

In the living room, Ben set up a wail. His mother gave no indication that she heard him.

8

"You don't need to look so shocked," she said, regaining some of her vigor. "What's wrong with wanting a lot of money? It's the Great American Dream, isn't it?"

I did not reply.

"And you don't need to look so disapproving, either," she added, her voice rising. "These past few years haven't been a picnic. Try raising a child on a schoolteacher's salary. Oh, I've got a widow's pension, but it's not much. And I got Ben's GI insurance, but my God! that didn't last forever. I've got little Ben to raise and send to college and—well, it takes more money than I've got. But aside from that, try burying yourself in a place like Foley, at the end of the world. Just try that. Do you have any idea what I do for entertainment? I go downtown and visit the clerks in the stores and the local citizens on the sidewalks. I go to PTA. I never miss a school play. I go to all the basketball games and cheer like hell when the Foley Wildcats make a basket. I went to an electioneering pie supper last year. Every once in a while I finagle myself a trip to Fort Worth or Dallas. Most of the time, though, I have to settle for San Angelo. And the worst part of it is that San Angelo looks like a metropolis to me."

She laughed bitterly.

"But hasn't there been anyone else?" I asked. "There must have been someone—some man—around to see you during the years."

"Oh, yes indeed. Even Foley turns up an occasional man who is eligible. There was a rancher from God knows where, wearing levis, cowboy boots, and the dirtiest, biggest hat north of the Mexican border. He took me to Fort Stockton to a movie. Then there was the high school principal. Yipes! By comparison, the cowboy was God's gift to womankind. The principal didn't take me anywhere. He came to see me. Get that, Pete Hamilton. We had a *parlor date* in this very room! At least, he knew the difference between *saw* and *seen* and *took* and *taken*—and he wore a coat and tie. I guess I've been here too long, because when he showed up in that coat and tie, I almost asked him if he'd been to a wedding or a funeral. Then let me see . . . oh yes . . . this is a peachy one. One summer the Baptist Church had a revival meeting, and somebody teamed me up with the visiting evangelist for a cake and coffee party after church and—oh, what the hell, Pete! There hasn't been anyone else, and there won't be—not here. I'm surprised that even that detour consented to come through Foley."

She calmed down. "If anyone in Foley heard me saying these things, they'd barbecue me on a spit."

"If you've got such a low opinion of the place, why haven't you moved away?"

"That's easy. I never could get enough ahead to pull it off. Among other things, Ben was sick a lot during that first year, and it seemed that I was spending all my money on doctors and an occasional day or two in the hospital in Fort Stockton. And, whatever I've said, the people here are good people, and they're good to me. I've got good friends here. I teach their children as they pass through the sixth grade, and they bring me presents and invite me to Sunday dinner. In the drugstore after school or on Saturdays, some gangling six-footer yells out 'Hi, Miz Holbrook,' and I take a second look to see that he's one of my ex-pupils who took a growing spell when I wasn't looking."

(70)

She paused, took a breath and said, "Only one thing will get me away from this and back to civilization, and that's money. M-O-N-E-Y. Now, tell me what's wrong with that." She leaned back, the lines on her face set, a half smile frozen on her lips.

"But it's like she said—you're after her money."

"No—not the way you're putting it," she snapped. "I've learned to be practical. I'm not so noble that I can turn up my nose at a fortune. What would that prove? What do you think will happen to all that money when Mother Holbrook dies? Have you thought of that?"

"I don't know how much it is."

"Plenty. She'll scatter it around and dissipate it where nobody will get much out of it. That is, unless there's a legal heir to claim it. *And I've got the legal heir.*" She lifted her chin defiantly.

"But you make it sound so—so—"

"Mercenary?"

"I wasn't going to—"

"You can say it. It won't hurt my feelings. Look. I could have stayed in Erskine and tried to battle it out, but I wouldn't have had a prayer—not against the town's leading citizens. So I left. I dusted off my degree and started shopping around for a teaching job. I picked San Angelo out of a hat. It was far away, but not too far. Then I heard about Foley. The money was better and the living cheaper. I never intended to stay. Just long enough to get on my feet financially and back into the good graces of the Holbrooks. Pipe dreams. Here, nobody asks about Ben. Why should they? I'm a war widow with a child. We're not an unusual spectacle—not even in Foley. The country's full of war widows with children."

"I don't know what to think," I said uneasily. "You're talking in a way that baffles me. Whatever I expected to hear you say, you haven't said it."

"Did you expect something like 'Blessed are the meek, for they shall inherit the earth'? Well, I don't want the earth. My wants are considerably more modest. I'm sorry if I disappoint you, Pete."

"Just what do you intend to do about it? The money, I mean."

"I'd always thought I'd just go on sweating it out, hoping that my letters would eventually turn the trick with Mother Holbrook. I didn't know there was any other way—until you showed up today."

"What have I got to do with it?"

"I'm going back to Erskine and dig in. I'm going to take Ben back where he belongs and get what's his—if you'll help me."

"Help you do what?"

"Help me set the record straight with Mother Holbrook. Wouldn't you stop by there for me, Pete?"

Her manner had softened. A new appeal in her voice and eyes touched me. Nevertheless, I hesitated.

"Well—I don't know, Carrie," I said. "I'm not sure that I haven't stuck my nose into the Holbrooks' business too far already. The only reason I came here today was to tell you about Mrs. Holbrook's threats, even though the doctor says she's harmless. I don't think I should get any more involved than that. It's a family matter."

"You're probably right," she said. "And I do appreciate what you've done, Pete. I agree with the doctor. Mother Holbrook won't harm me. She's the kindest, most gentle person on earth, but she's sick; and I'm not afraid of sick people. It's the others I'm afraid of."

"Who?"

"Oh, I don't know. But she's vulnerable. Somebody might take advantage of her—if they haven't already—and Ben and me in the process. Dr. Kriegel, for example."

"Why him?"

She shrugged. "He just came to mind, that's all. He's a widower, privy to all the family secrets. He's in a good position. Her lawyer—a swishy number named Tolliver—could do the same thing. Her banker, anybody she deals with. Rich old ladies are prime targets, you know." She paused. "What do you think of my chances?"

"How should I know? I hardly know Mrs. Holbrook. Each

time I've seen her she had one of her spells. I'm not even sure what the *real* Mrs. Holbrook is like."

"She's the lovely, charming lady she appears to be," said Carrie. "If she was willing to tell you so much about all of us, I think she would listen to you, Pete. I really do."

"Look, Carrie. It's not that I don't want to help you—you know that. But certain matters should be settled within a family, not by outsiders. We're not on such close terms that I can advise her how to run her life."

"Why were you so anxious to come out here and warn me about Mother Holbrook?" she asked abruptly. The hardness had returned.

"I explained that not more than one minute ago."

"Listen. For five years, I know nothing about you. Then all at once, here you are, brimming over with Holbrook family affairs. Now, pray tell, if you went far enough to learn about my in-laws' ill regard for me, why wouldn't you be willing to go one step further?"

"I stumbled onto all this," I said. "I wasn't snooping or trying to learn about your relationship with your mother-in-law. You make it sound like I did something underhanded or wrong."

"Oh, come off it, Pete! Stop it! Why this sudden interest in us?"

"It's not sudden. It goes back several years. We've just been out of touch, that's all."

"Now let's not play games. I simply asked you what's behind your sudden interest in the Holbrooks. Is that an unreasonable question?"

"With the implications you're putting on it—yes."

"Don't be so thin-skinned. I only asked you a question."

"Okay—here it is again, if you must have it. Seeing you in Fort Worth stirred up lots of memories for me. Ben meant a lot to me, and so did you. My interest in the Holbrooks got rekindled. That's it in a nutshell."

"My, my!" she said mockingly.

I pushed back from the kitchen table and got up. "This conversation took a wrong turn somewhere," I said. "You're reading something shady into my being here, and I don't understand it. Maybe we'd do well to knock it off here and now."

"You mean you're leaving?"

"I've got to go anyway. It's a long way to San Angelo, and I've got to get up early in the morning."

"But we haven't had supper yet! Can't you stay—please? I'd love to set the table in the dining room for a change. I'll even use my good china and crystal and silver. *Please?*"

I relented. "Okay, Carrie," I said. I laughed. "You win. But I really will have to go early. I've got some reports to write."

❧ 9 ❧

The ragged asphalt road back to the U. S. Highway was more treacherous by night than by day. I bounced in and out of holes, and once where the road curved unexpectedly, I ran off into a shallow ditch. Shifting gears and putting the car into motion again, I resolved to train my mind on where I was going and not so much on where I had been.

The trouble was that Carrie made too much sense. She was logical and practical whereas I was only squeamish. How could it be wrong if I influenced Mrs. Holbrook to take her daughter-in-law back into the family? What was wrong with it, indeed? I asked Amy, when I had told her Carrie's story.

She didn't know exactly, but she had doubts, nevertheless.

"Something doesn't hang together," she said. "Or maybe it hangs together too well," she added. "It's theatrical. Let's face it, Pete, Carrie's tale is too much of a tearjerker."

"What's wrong with tearjerkers?"

"Nothing—if you enjoy crying. A good tearjerker works on your emotions at the expense of your intelligence and reason. That's how *East Lynne* and *Way Down East* played to full houses for years. They asked for—and got—their audience's emotions, their tears, their righteous indignation, and most of all, their suspension of belief."

"Bravo!" I exclaimed. "That was a fine little lecture on the drama. Very literary and intellectual."

"It was rather highbrow, wasn't it?" she said, laughing at herself.

"Yes, but I rather enjoyed it." I poured another jigger of bourbon in her glass. "But seriously," I went on, "if Carrie wanted to lie, she wouldn't have invented such a long, elaborate lie as all that."

"I'll bet she can't repeat it with all the details intact."

"How can you say that? You don't even know her."

"You just told me her story," she said. "But whether it's true or false, you've done just about all you can do. Look, darling. Why not let them settle their own affairs? I'm afraid if you don't, you'll get involved over your head."

"Not necessarily," I said. "Listen, Amy. I didn't ask for this mess to be dumped in my lap, but there it is. I don't see anything wrong with helping a family patch itself up. Social workers and counselors get paid for doing it, you know. So what's wrong with my lending a hand?"

She shook her head thoughtfully. "I don't mean that helping someone is wrong," she said. "You've got a heart as big as all outdoors—everybody who knows you agrees on that. But I don't want you to get hurt. And I have an uneasy feeling about your delivering Carrie's message to her mother-in-law. Why doesn't she do her own talking?"

"She writes to Mrs. Holbrook, but she doesn't get any replies. Mrs. Holbrook wouldn't even see her alone when she went back to Mr. Holbrook's funeral. You've got to admit, Amy, there's always two sides to these things."

"But not three, darling," she said. "Let's face it—you just can't go around jumping into the middle of other people's lives and straightening out their family problems for them."

"But Carrie *asked* me to go, Amy! It's not as though I volunteered."

"But why *you*, Pete?"

"I don't know exactly. Because I happened to be passing the intersection when the accident occurred, I guess."

"Pete—you're kidding yourself. You said yourself you told Mrs. Holbrook you wouldn't go to Foley, and Dr. Kriegel assured you it was quite unnecessary. Maybe you honestly thought you ought to warn Carrie anyway, but my guess is that mainly you were curious as all getout—probably from the time she wouldn't speak to you in the doctor's office. Why not? Anybody would be." She came close and poked a finger in my chest, smiling up at me. "Now be honest—do you really believe you just happened to be passing?"

I gripped her finger and grinned. "I guess that wasn't quite accurate—but I do believe Carrie's story."

We dropped the subject and never got back to it during the weekend.

On Monday morning, I had already driven around the edge of Fort Worth and was approaching Highway 80 West when I decided to see Mrs. Holbrook, after all. The truth was, I did not know how to ignore Carrie's request. It made no difference that her breakup with the elder Holbrooks had been caused by her own mishandling of the situation. Did that rule out her right to a second chance? And how was she to get it? Apparently, there was no one she could turn to but me. I wouldn't try to straighten out their problems, as Amy had put it. I would just tell Mrs. Holbrook the story from a neutral position. No persuasion, no advocacy, no opinions, but simply the story as I knew it. She could accept it, or she could reject it. In either case, I would not try to influence her decision. My role would end with the bare telling.

I pulled up to the edge of Highway 80 West and stopped. When the traffic light turned green, I took the road to Erskine.

Mrs. Holbrook was charming and gracious, and as we chatted, the bizarre events of my previous visits seemed so remote as to be impossible. When our small talk played out, I gathered my courage and blurted out the essentials of the story as Carrie had told it to me. When Mrs. Holbrook did not react strongly or violently, I went back and filled in all the details, watching her carefully. I made it to the end without incident or interruption, but even then, I was apprehensive. I need not have been.

She sat quietly for a moment, then said, "I remember Marie. Ben brought her home once before Carrie."

I felt a surge of relief. "You're not shocked, then," I ventured.

"I am, but not because the baby is Ben's. I'm shocked that Carrie would go to such lengths to conceal it from us." She frowned. "It was a senseless thing to do."

"Well, I'm certainly glad that you can accept it so calmly."

"Accept it?" she repeated. "Mr. Hamilton, when you're in your sixties, you accept many things you might not have accepted fifteen or twenty years earlier. Ben came to us late in our lives. We had given up hopes of ever having children. I was thirty-four years old when he was born. It has always been hard for me to understand young people, and somewhere along the line I saw that the reason I didn't understand them was because I was trying to change them, to make them over in my own image. Perhaps I wouldn't have been so stubborn had Ben come to us earlier in my life. Anyway, I stopped trying to change them and I began to accept them as they are. I don't always understand what motivates them, but I accept them. Young people seem to think we can't look after ourselves. They become overprotective toward us. They try to shield us from unpleasantness and grief and sorrow, not realizing that the years might have made us wiser and our skins thicker, that we are more experienced in heartaches than they. I don't understand why this is so, but it is, and I accept it. I don't know why Carrie should have tried to hide Ben's misdeeds from us. We didn't raise a saint in this house; I've never deluded myself on that score. I deplore what he did, but it's done, and Carrie need not have felt so responsible for it."

"I hadn't thought of it just that way," I said. "I guess I'm still surprised by such a generous reaction."

"You're proving my point. Why should you be surprised? I'm a reasonable person. Or I try to be. I do wish she had told us at the beginning, though. It would have saved so much misunderstanding and grief and unpleasantness.

"I know she's sorry about that."

"She should be," she answered stiffly. "But some things can't be undone. Poor Mr. Holbrook went to his grave thinking the worst of Carrie. That was hardly fair to either of them." She smiled faintly, but it was a smile of regret.

"I guess it seemed right to her at the time."

"No doubt."

I relaxed. The job was done, and it had not been difficult, after all. I had a warm, happy feeling inside, and I did little to hide it. "I know that Carrie will be pleased," I said expansively. "I wish I could offer to see her for you again this week, but I'll be rushed, and I won't be going back that way again until after the Christmas holidays. Anyway, I think it's time for me to get out of your private affairs. I guess you'll be writing to Carrie yourself now."

"What on earth for?" Her words shot out like bullets.

"I just assumed you'd be anxious to get in touch now that—"

"Now that everything is all right?"

"Why—yes, I guess so."

"Your story stopped too soon," she said. "You didn't tell me why, after all these years, Carrie has suddenly decided to send me this information. Why did she wait so long?"

I weighed my answer carefully. "I don't really know," I said, convincing myself that the lie was a white one.

Abruptly, she dropped the subject. "You've been more than generous, Mr. Hamilton. I know you're occupied with your own affairs, and I'm embarrassed that you should have been drawn into ours. At any rate, this is a matter that Carrie and I can settle between us. You've been very kind, and I'm most grateful. I hope you will continue to stop by when you're in town."

"Thank you, but Erskine is not on my regular itinerary, you know. I do appreciate the invitation, though."

"Sometime when you do come back, I wish you'd explain some of Ben's things to me. Actually, they belong to Carrie. The

Army mailed her a box labeled 'Personal Effects,' and she left it here. There are some medals and certificates and odds and ends that must mean *something*, but I just don't understand them."

"If I can remember them myself," I said. "It all seems so long ago. When I'm down this way again, I'll be glad to look at them and see what we can make of them."

But I had no intention of coming back. Indeed, by the time I reached Highway 80 West again, I had pushed the Holbrooks from my mind altogether. I had no time and, to be truthful, no inclination to think of them soon again. The normal pressure of business, and most of all, the delight of Thanksgiving, followed by the excitement of Christmas for two wide-eyed little boys, crowded the Holbrooks from my consciousness as though they had never existed.

✣ 10 ✣

Soon after the first of the year, Mr. Marsh called me into the office to discuss the possibilities of adding Erskine to my territory.

"That's a good account down there, Hamilton," he said, "but our city men just can't look after it properly. Maybe we've been unfair to expect it of them. At any rate, I've been studying the map and your schedule. Erskine is nineteen miles southwest of Fort Worth. You can put it on your itinerary for Monday mornings and get on over to Weatherford afterwards without knocking much of a hole in your present schedule. Or you could add it on the other end—Friday afternoon on your way in. Either way, the adjustments would be rather minor, wouldn't they?" His voice and manner were soft and mild, as though he were asking me for a personal favor.

"Of course, I'm not stupid enough to turn a deaf ear to a new account, Mr. Marsh," I said, "but I've got a pretty full week as it is. It's not always simply a matter of saying hello and good-bye to these people. Sometimes I get stuck for a half day in places where I intended to stay only an hour or thirty minutes."

"I realize that," he said, "and I wouldn't ask you to do this if I didn't think you could handle it without neglecting your other accounts. That Erskine account is old and solid. Think it over and let me know when you come in next week."

Naturally, I accepted the account. What else could I do?

Two weeks later, Erskine became a regular stop on my weekly itinerary. Mr. McCash, the dealer, was delighted. I asked him when he preferred that I come.

"If it's all the same to you, Monday morning will suit me better," he replied.

"Then Monday mornings it will be," I said.

On the third Monday after finishing my work at the Erskine office of American Business Machines, I was getting into my car when Dr. Kriegel's blue station wagon pulled into the parking space adjoining mine. I waited until he got out; then I stepped back onto the sidewalk to speak to him.

"Good morning, Dr. Kriegel," I said. "Remember me? I'm Pete Hamilton from Fort Worth—Ben Holbrook's friend."

"Certainly I remember you," he said cordially. "It's good to see you again." We shook hands. "And what brings you to Erskine this time?"

I explained my new schedule. He looked toward the American Business Machines office. "Oh, yes, I've known Charlie McCash several years," he said. "A fine man. Have you seen Mrs. Holbrook lately?"

"No, I haven't had any extra time since I cranked this new account into my schedule. How is she?"

"She's fine," he said. "She has her ups and downs, but on the whole, I think she is doing nicely. Something's on her mind, though, and I can't figure out what it is. Well—I'll tell her I saw you."

"Please do, and give her my regards."

We chatted for a few minutes, then he was gone.

On the next Monday, Charlie McCash had a message for me. "Mrs. Holbrook called and wants you to call her before you leave town," he said.

"If you have a few moments," Mrs. Holbrook said on the telephone, "I would love for you to drop by and have coffee with me. Alberta made some of her marvelous rolls—I think she makes them with a magic wand. The doctor told me about seeing you, and I was delighted."

"That's very nice of you," I said. "I won't have much time, but I can stop in for a few minutes."

Alberta and Mrs. Holbrook welcomed me warmly. They led me through the musty parlor, through an even mustier dining room crammed with massive furniture and into the breakfast room, an unexpectedly cheerful spot back of the butler's pantry.

The view from the breakfast room was the back side of the hill, the far side from town. The hill sloped gently away from the house and gave way to broad land that rose and fell like heavy waters on the ocean. A highway cut through the fields, bending around one farm and then another, and out of sight over a leisurely rise in the distance. An expanse of pasture, held in by a low wall of native stone, lay just below the house and was joined by the long, straight furrows of a neighboring farm about a half mile away. While I sipped my coffee, my gaze would not stay indoors.

Mrs. Holbrook must have read my mind, for she said wistfully, "It's a wonderful place for a boy. Ben used to have a pony—a shaggy Shetland with a white spot on its nose—that ran loose down there. From up here, it looked like a big overgrown dog. There's an overhang not far down the hill. You can't pick it out from here unless you know where it is." She pointed vaguely and squinted for an instant. "There's not much to it—just a shallow cave in the side of the hill. Actually, it's a bed of rock that refused to follow the contour of the land. It juts out to make a sort of shed. Ben and his friends used to sleep down there on warm summer nights. Once they built a campfire that got out of hand and set the pasture on fire. We had lots of excitement that day. The fire trucks came out from town, but there was nowhere to hook up their hoses, and all they could do was let it burn itself out."

She smiled, remembering. With a sigh, she brought herself back. "It's all going to waste now. I often ask the doctor if I shouldn't get out of this big old house and turn it over to some-body who can use it—it's much too large for only Alberta and me. Gracious! I go for weeks without setting foot in some of the bedrooms upstairs. Sometimes I sit here at the table looking down at all that land and get an urge to go out and roam around, espe-cially when the sun is warm and there's no wind—like we used to do when Mr. Holbrook was alive and we were younger. But climbing back up that hill is more than I can manage nowadays, so I just sit here and remember. It's a shame really, that it doesn't belong to someone who can enjoy it. I can't help but wonder if. . . ."

She was delightful company, and I was glad that I had come.

So glad, in fact, that I returned the following week and the next. As February went by and on into March, my visits became part of my routine in Erskine. Charlie McCash and I usually fin-ished our business by nine o'clock, and I rarely spent more than an hour with Mrs. Holbrook, sometimes not that long. Alberta always had the coffee ready and waiting, sometimes with a pastry hot from the oven, or a plate of light biscuits dripping sweet country butter and spread with her homemade jellies or pre-serves. Sometimes she served us in the sitting room, sometimes in the parlor, and sometimes in the cheery breakfast room. Mrs. Holbrook was always charming, and for the most part rational.

Some days we mentioned Ben or Carrie only in passing. Some days we did not mention them at all. In time, they ceased to be at the core of our association. We became friends on our own terms; our friendship had its own reasons for being. The differ-ence in our ages made no difference. I found her conversation, like her old-fashioned manners, delightful. I had never known anyone like her, and as regularly as I called on Charlie McCash, I called on Mrs. Holbrook in the big house on the hill. But some-how, I never got around to reporting these visits to Amy.

She knew, of course, that I had added Erskine to my territory. She heard me speak of Charlie McCash. I had told her about seeing Dr. Kriegel on the streets and about Mrs. Holbrook's invitation for coffee that first time. But I never told her more, I suppose, because my visits became so routine that they scarcely seemed worth mentioning. I did not think to tell her where I ate lunch on Thursdays or who I drank coffee with on Wednesdays or what movie I saw on Tuesdays, and similarly, I did not tell her of my Monday morning coffee visits with Mrs. Holbrook.

The old Holbrook house itself began to take on a familiar feel. Although I became accustomed to its gloom, I was forever analyzing its unfriendliness. It needed frivolity and a touch of youth. It gasped for air, for light, for happy colors and unchecked laughter, a bit of carelessness and disorder; or maybe it only yearned for people to live in it, upstairs, downstairs, outside and in. Mrs. Holbrook was right: it was too much for only two people.

Her moods varied from week to week, but never from a cordiality that made me feel welcome. Occasionally she had difficulty concentrating on her own words, and her mind would wander briefly into the past; then she spoke of Ben as though he were in the next room or in the town below or playing in the pasture on the side of the hill. Not so with her husband. He was dead, definitely part of her past, and she was reconciled to the remainder of her life without him. The difference, I think, lay in the fact that she had seen one cold and still in death but not the other. Perhaps I brought something of Ben with me each time I came, but that doesn't sound right; it sounds as though I did her favors by spending my time with her when, in truth, I looked forward to those Monday mornings as much as she apparently did herself.

She spoke of her friends, who had thinned out as the years went by, and of her life in Erskine, which was no longer as active and useful as it once had been. She told me of how she went down the hill to the town less and less frequently, to church only occasionally and to visit sick friends every now and then. A scattering of people still called on her irregularly. Her minister came; her lawyer stopped in when there was business to transact;

(85)

someone from the bank brought papers to sign, and that was about the extent of it. Except for Dr. Kriegel. He was a case apart.

He came every day, usually in the afternoons after office hours, sometimes popping in and out and sometimes staying on for dinner and a few hands of gin rummy afterward. She quoted him on an infinite range of topics, never speaking his name but referring to him as "the doctor." She saw local events through his eyes: the state of business, the outlook for the crops, deaths, marriages, divorces, sickness, newcomers, and such gossip as the little town afforded. The doctor was her authority on politics, world affairs, the stock market, the weather. A word from him was gospel. Her daily routine was under his constant scrutiny. She ate, slept, awoke, rested and entertained herself according to his prescriptions. Any modification, no matter how slight, had to carry his sanction, or she would have no part of it.

"He's determined to protect me from loneliness," she said one morning. "I think he's made it his mission in life."

"Maybe he's lonely, too," I suggested.

"Yes, I'm sure of it. His wife was a lovely person. We were the best of friends—like sisters. After she died, he was absolutely lost; he came up here two and three times a day sometimes—he just didn't know what to do with himself. If a day or two went by and we didn't hear from him, we would get worried and run down to see about him, and more often than not bring him back up here with us. He's part of this household and has been for years. He lives alone, too, but he's been more sensible than I have. He sold his house—you must have seen it many times; it's the two-story white brick colonial just across the street from the Methodist Church. A beautiful place. He sold it and moved into an apartment. I often ask him if I should do the same thing, but he won't tell me. He says I'd have to make up my mind without advice from him. That's a business matter, he says."

"Does he look after many of your business affairs for you?"

"Yes and no. He runs errands and does anything that needs doing on the spot, but when it comes to pure business—anything about the estate, for example—he won't open his mouth. He says he's a doctor, not a businessman, and friendship and business don't mix. I'm sure he's right. He says why pay my lawyer—Mr. Tolliver; you may remember hearing me speak of him—he says why pay Mr. Tolliver for advice if I go somewhere else to get it? But he doesn't realize that Mr. Tolliver's interest is professional while his own is personal. It makes quite a difference."

"It sounds like a good arrangement, nevertheless," I said.

"You know, the doctor is getting awfully curious about you. He can't imagine what brings you here each week, and he has quizzed me unmercifully about you. He says nine o'clock on Monday morning is a strange hour for social calls. Of course, it's really not. Gracious! Alberta and I are up rattling around in this house long before then anyway. I explained your work-and-travel schedule and how nicely it fits in. I twitted him about it—I told him he must be jealous, and he admitted it! Isn't that priceless?" She laughed. "Don't be surprised if you find him here some Monday morning. He wants to size you up, I think."

The prospect made me uncomfortable.

"I didn't realize you knew the doctor until he told me about seeing you on the street one day," she went on. "Of course, I was delighted. Anyway, I think you should expect to see him here before long." She looked out the window. "Spring's coming on," she said softly. "Any day now, and it'll be with us. I love spring. On a sunny day in April, with the entire world bursting into bloom, I get caught up in a feeling that's so good it's almost religious . . . it's inconceivable that anything can go wrong."

❧ 11 ❧

When I pulled up in front of the Holbrook house the next
week, Dr. Kriegel's blue station wagon was parked in the driveway. Alberta admitted me, but she was not her usual self. "Mrs.
Holbrook's sick," she announced. "She can't come downstairs."

"What's wrong?"

"I don't know," she said, a worried frown crossing her dark
face. "You'll have to ask the doctor. He's up there now."

"Is it one of her spells?"

"No, sir. It ain't one of her spells." She glanced uneasily up the
stairs. "I took her some coffee jes' like I always do, and she acted
jes' fine. She asked me what dress she ought to wear, and I picked
her one out. The doctor he come in and went up to see her. He
stayed about ten minutes, I reckon, then he come back down and
say Mrs. Holbrook's sick and was goin' to stay in bed."

"Did he say why?"

"No, sir, 'cept she ought to be quiet today and nobody ought
to disturb her. He went back up, and he ain't been back down
since."

She followed me into the parlor.

"Well, surely she must be sick if Dr. Kriegel says—"

"Good morning, Mr. Hamilton."

I wheeled around to face the rugged, towering figure of Dr.

Kriegel. He advanced with a bumbling, shuffling gate and shook my hand. While he was pleasant enough, his greeting was lacking in warmth.

"Mrs. Holbrook is disappointed that she's not up to par today and won't be able to see you," he said, his deep voice filling the room. "She asked me to tell you she's sorry."

He moved toward the sofa. "If you have a moment, suppose we sit down here and talk. Then you can be on your way. I understand you have a long way to drive today."

He dismissed Alberta with a glance. She hesitated, wavering between speaking and leaving. She left the room.

"Don't worry about it," I said cheerfully. "I've got myself into a kind of routine of stopping by here on Mondays, and gradually, I've adjusted my schedule to fit it. Anyway, falling behind schedule is an occupational hazard in my line of work. I've got plenty of time." I smiled at him.

"Yes, you seem to have." The sofa creaked under his weight as he lowered himself onto it. His baggy brown tweed jacket hung open carelessly to reveal a wrinkled blue shirt that needed tucking in more tightly beneath his belt. He humped forward, elbows on his knees, head down, looking at the floor between his feet. I did not move. He looked up at me appraisingly.

"Well, go ahead and sit down," he said with a trace of impatience.

I moved toward a chair, but I did not sit down. "What's wrong with Henrietta?" I asked.

His shaggy eyebrows arched. "It's *Henrietta* now, is it?"

I laughed. "We fell into that more or less. She asked me to call her Henrietta, but I choked on it at first. Eventually, however, it came naturally."

"You might as well sit down," he said, waving a giant paw toward a chair. "You did say you had time, I believe."

I dropped into a chair. "I wasn't being standoffish," I said. "I was just worried about what's wrong with—"

"Mrs. Holbrook?" he interjected swiftly and pointedly. "It's nothing to get excited about. She gets tired and worn out. It

(89)

happens to all of us, and I think it'll be better for her to remain quiet today. She'll feel all the better for it tomorrow."

"I wonder if I could just speak to her a minute—I won't stay long. Since I'm already here? I'll just stick my head in the door and say hello. I brought a snapshot of Ben that she didn't seem to have, and I'd like to give it to her."

He fumbled in a side pocket for a cigarette. Finding one and lighting it, he returned the package to his pocket. "I'm sorry," he said suddenly, retrieving the package. "Would you like a cigarette?"

"No, thanks. I was saying that I'd like to give this snapshot to Henrietta and explain its setting—then I'll be on my way. If it's all right."

He studied the smoke curling up from his cigarette and let me wait. The silence that lay between us was uncomfortable. Finally, he stirred and smiled mysteriously. "I think not," he said slowly.

"But if she's not really sick, why not?"

"Because I think it best for you not to. Anyway, she's probably asleep by now."

"Asleep? But it's only nine o'clock. Did you give her something?"

His manner changed. His expression froze. He fixed his eyes on me with firmness. "Mr. Hamilton, you put me through the third degree once, and I don't intend to subject myself to another. I'm not accustomed to discussing the treatment of my patients with outsiders."

"I'm sorry. I meant no offense, but you caught me by surprise. Henrietta was expecting me. Alberta said she was getting ready when—"

"Alberta says a lot of things. She means well, but she's not the doctor. She's the maid."

I was bewildered by his short, snappish manner. "I apologize," I said. "But surely you can appreciate my concern."

"I can. As a matter of fact, your concern is what I'd like to talk to you about. Did you persuade Mrs. Holbrook to take Carrie back into this household?"

"Persuade her?" I chuckled. "Not quite! I did come by here one day to tell her Carrie's side of the story, but I struck out. Zero. I haven't mentioned the subject since. And I never got back to Foley to tell Carrie how it turned out. In other words, I delivered the message, and that was the end of it."

"Then apparently you didn't know she has written Carrie and asked her to come back."

"She mentioned it once, but Carrie said she didn't get the letter, so I assumed she had imagined it—during one of her sick spells."

"She's written her since, and Carrie got the letter. Henrietta told me that ridiculous story you brought her from Carrie—about Ben and his old girl friend. Surely you didn't believe a trumped-up tale like that!"

"I'll admit that it didn't go down easy, but I finally believed it. Otherwise, I would never have told Henrietta."

"You had your common sense. You must have recognized it as pure invention."

"You would have had to hear it in person to understand my reactions to it. I ended up by giving Carrie the benefit of the doubt, I guess."

"Whether you believed it or not, the harm's done. It created problems. I wish you had checked with me first."

"Oh—maybe I should have, but—well, it just didn't occur to me."

"Surely you can't have forgotten our talk in my office. I told you then that the subject of Carrie upset her. In view of that, it seems that you could have consulted me. I was very frank and detailed with you that day, because I thought you were genuinely concerned—perhaps over-alarmed, but I didn't doubt your sincerity." He paused and ran a hand through his thick white hair. His eyes darkened. "Why did you come here with a story like that?"

"I was only delivering a message from Carrie. If it upset Henrietta, she didn't show it."

From behind the forest of eyebrows, he watched me. "But why did you do it?"

"Carrie asked me to."

"Why didn't she write it in a letter?"

"I'm not certain. Probably because the story was too long and involved. Anyway, you'll have to ask Carrie that one."

"But why you?"

"Carrie asked me to," I repeated flatly. "I did her a favor, that's all."

"A simple act of kindness, eh?" His words carried a sting.

"Well—I hadn't thought of it exactly like that, but if you want to call it that—okay. Is anything wrong with that?"

"Kindness is not always the simple motive it's made out to be."

"I don't follow you."

"Some acts of kindness can have ulterior purposes," he said.

"Then it wouldn't be kindness. It would be a device or ruse or a trick," I said. "I don't understand this conversation, Doctor. I don't know what's bothering you, but whatever it is, I'd appreciate your coming out with it so I can step down from this witness chair."

He stared at me for a moment then said, "Mrs. Holbrook has almost worried herself sick over this entire business. That's what's bothering me. She had adjusted to the way things were."

"She hasn't seemed upset—at least, not to me."

"But you see her only a few minutes each week. I see her the rest of the time. I wonder if you have any conception of what you've done to her."

"I know that she and I have become good friends. That's no big crime. At least, not where I came from."

He ignored me. "You posed a dilemma that even a stable person would have difficulty coping with. Imagine what it does to a person like Mrs. Holbrook, who's not equipped to handle it."

"But if she's been wrong about Carrie—"

"That has yet to be proven," he snapped. "Still, I can't get it out of her mind that she has been wrong."

"Why try?"

"Because it's not good for her to think she's been wrong all these years," he said testily.

"Do you mean you'd let her perpetuate a five-year-old wrong for the sake of her peace of mind?"

"I would." His words carried no emotion. "Your question is academic, anyway," he went on. "The wrong has not yet been proven."

"But surely you're not opposed to righting a wrong?"

"Not in the least. That is, if a wrong has been committed. And I'm not sure that it has. But assume for a moment that it has. Your story has burdened her with a guilt that was new to her—"

"Now come on, Doctor," I broke in. "The first time I ever saw her, she said she often wondered if she had been unfair to Carrie."

"She was speculating—wondering," he countered. "But now she's convinced that she and Mr. Holbrook did the wrong thing. She believes you. Consequently, she's weighed down with a remorse that she can't handle. She's started to brood over what she's done to Carrie these past years."

"Well, I'm sorry about that. I really am. But don't you think you're being a little unfair to me? Remember, it was Carrie who lied. Henrietta was critical of her bad judgment—even hostile. Maybe Carrie should make a few amends to Henrietta."

The doctor was obstinate. "I happen to think that upsetting her the way you've done is not good. You should have consulted me before you told her. If bringing Carrie back here was the thing to do, there would have been ways to prepare Mrs. Holbrook for it. I should have had the opportunity to do it."

"I certainly meant her no harm," I said, "and to be truthful, I'm having a hard time believing it's as bad as you say."

He sprang up and jammed his fists into his pockets. He began to take long strides up and down the room. He stopped in front of the empty fireplace.

"Let's stop all this," he boomed. "Let's get to the point without further ado."

"I wish we would."

(93)

"All right—here it is. You're not good for Henrietta, and I want you to stop coming here."

"Stop coming here? Why?"

"Because you've done enough damage as it is, and I don't want to risk more. As Henrietta's friend, as well as her doctor, I know what's good for her and what's not. You're not good for her."

I sat silent for a while. When I finally spoke, it was with deliberation. "You know, Doctor," I said. "I've been sitting here on the receiving end of an awful lot of insinuations, and I've done my dead-level best to overlook them. Now you've finally come out with it. I don't know who or *what* you think I am, but nobody has ever talked like this to me, and I don't like it. I don't like it at all." I leaned back in my chair. He had not moved from in front of the fireplace. "Now, I'll tell you what I'll do," I went on, hoping that I sounded more confident than I felt. "I'll stop coming here when Henrietta tells me to stop. But not one minute before."

He resumed his pacing and stopped in front of my chair. "You mean you won't stop coming?" he asked.

"That's about the size of it," I said. "I'm not accustomed to this kind of treatment, but if that's the way it's to be, I can be just as direct and tactless as you can."

"You sound pretty sure of yourself."

"I'm not sure of myself at all. But what would *you* do in my shoes? Apologize and thank you for putting me in my place?"

He glared at me for a moment. Then he snorted impatiently. "I can see there's no point in continuing this conversation," he said. He turned and stomped out of the room.

I sat listening to his heavy tread on the stairs.

❧ 12 ❧

Amy's mother in St. Louis had not been well for several weeks, and while she was not seriously ill, Amy thought perhaps she should take the boys and spend a few days with her. We discussed it during the weekend following my unpleasant encounter with Dr. Kriegel.

"We probably wouldn't stay more than a couple of weeks," she said.

"Having you and the kids in the house might be the tonic she needs," I agreed.

"I wish you would go with us," she said.

"I'm afraid not," I said. "This is the wrong time of year for me. I'll see your mother when she comes next time. When do you think you should go?"

"How about the end of the week? Then you could drive us to the airport."

"Okay—I'll make the reservations," I said.

Driving to Erskine Monday, I realized that, despite his unfairness, Dr. Kriegel had made me hesitant about seeing Henrietta again. And yet I wanted to find out how she was.

I found her as excited as a young girl getting ready for her first dance. Carrie and Ben were coming back. Next week. I pretended to be surprised.

"This is the only thing I can remember that the doctor could not talk me out of," she said, triumph in her voice. "He thinks it's the most awful thing in the world. I made it clear to him, though, that Carrie will be a member of this family and that he must treat her accordingly. I just cannot allow a situation to develop between the two of them."

I made no comment.

"It's a tremendous load off my mind," she went on. "It's made a new person of me. Think of it! People in the house once more —and to make it all the more exciting—*Carrie!* Do you know what I'm going to do? I'm going to turn this house over to her and let her do with it as she pleases. It's going to be all hers. She can decorate, redecorate, paint, move furniture, slip-cover and— oh, just whatever she wants to do with it. I've had more than forty years of it, and I'm tired. I'll enjoy looking on and watching what she does with the old place."

She was brimming over with plans. Carrie could take the large bedroom above the entrance hall and Ben the small room overlooking the hill at the rear. She had already telephoned a store about swings, a gym set and a wading pool for the yard. She intended to clear out a storage room in the basement and convert it into a playroom. She must, however, get someone to clean out the old garage and spread new gravel on the driveway.

"I've got to get a man out here to look at that barn, too," she said. "I don't know whether it's still safe. Ben and his friends loved it when they were small. They climbed among the rafters and sometimes stayed in there all day long when it rained. Maybe little Ben will love it, too." Her eyes glowed as she talked. "The only real problem is what Carrie will do with herself," she said. "I don't know the young people in Erskine any more, and she has never been here long enough at one time to make friends of her own. I don't see Ben's friends nowadays, either. I doubt if any of them are still in town. You and Amy must come down and lend a hand."

"Carrie will do all right," I said. "After a couple of weeks, you'll probably wonder why you worried about her at all."

"Then she hasn't changed?" she asked anxiously.

"No—not enough to notice."

As I was leaving, she said, "Now don't forget when you come two weeks from today, Carrie will be here. Why don't you arrange to stay a while longer that day?"

"I'm afraid I can't do that," I said. "I have too much ground to cover on Mondays. Anyway, if she's coming back to stay, I'll have plenty of other chances to see her."

Saturday morning, I drove my family to the Dallas airport.

As we walked toward the loading gate, Amy had last-minute misgivings. "We should have waited until Monday, rather than leave during your weekend at home."

"Then you wouldn't have anybody to take you to the airport," I said. "Besides, you'd miss seeing Aunt Dora." Amy's aunt had been staying with her mother, but was scheduled to go back to Chicago on Sunday.

"Are you sure you'll be all right? We can still wait until Monday, you know—Aunt Dora or no Aunt Dora."

"No, you can't. To change your plans now would be more complicated than going ahead. Don't worry about a thing." I kissed her and the boys good-bye.

"I love you, darling," she said. She handed Kenny to a stewardess and took Skeeter from my arms. The three of them hurried along the ramp.

I stood on the observation deck and watched the plane taxi away from the terminal out of sight then into view again at the end of the runway. I waited until it roared past and swooped itself up into the sky. Then I went back to Jones Hill, washed the breakfast dishes and did some yard work.

I did not see Henrietta Holbrook on my Monday stop in Erskine; I waited a week, so that I could greet Carrie and Ben.

The moment I entered the front door, I felt a change in the house. For one thing, Alberta was not herself. She was sullen and withdrawn.

"Has the other Mrs. Holbrook arrived?" I asked.

"She's here," Alberta said, avoiding my eyes. "She came last week." She turned away with my hat. I wandered into the parlor for a look around.

Yellow jonquils filled the two vases on the mantel; the stiff white antimacassars had disappeared; the chairs had been regrouped and the sofa turned toward the fireplace. A magazine lay open in a chair by the window. A red sweater was crumpled at one end of the sofa, and a toy airplane stood in the middle of the floor, poised and ready for takeoff. The room had come alive.

Alberta reappeared in the doorway. "Miss Carrie said for me to show you into the little—the sitting room," she mumbled unhappily. "Go on in there, Mr. Hamilton. I reckon they'll be down in a minute."

The sitting room had also received a transfusion. More yellow jonquils, these on the long library table, and a huge bower of spring greenery on the hearth had transformed the room so completely that it was as if I had never seen it before. The curtains had been drawn back. The sun splashed through the windows and danced across the floor, up the walls and out into the big hall beyond.

Carrie came downstairs first, and if Henrietta's lovely fairness was at odds with the dull, old-fashioned house, her daughter-in-law's blond brilliance made for an outright clash. She wore a dress with orange and yellow designs that complemented the yellow jonquils and yellow sunlight, but her mood was something else. She greeted me with peculiar restraint, uttering the usual amenities as though I were a casual acquaintance. She made no reference to our long visit in Foley.

During the hour that followed, she remained aloof toward me, but toward her mother-in-law she was on the cosiest terms. Conducting herself engagingly, there was nothing so conspicuous as a word or an overt gesture to mark the difference in her treatment of me. When she turned her green eyes on me, their expression did not coincide with the words on her lips. Clearly, she was holding me at arm's length, and I was at a loss to understand why.

Henrietta was happy and full of chitchat about her new routine, giddy with delight at the confusion, the noise, the laughter, the disorder and disruptions that had shaken the old house out of its doldrums. That she was enchanted by her daughter-in-law was obvious in every glance, and I'll have to say for Carrie that she seemed to return the feeling in full measure. Whatever had happened between them in private, however awkward and difficult their first meeting and subsequent adjustments might have been, their reconciliation was unmistakably a success. Henrietta was particularly happy over Ben's quick adaptation to his new surroundings.

"He made himself at home the first thing!" she said proudly. "You should have seen him exploring this place! He was everywhere at once—upstairs and down, in and out. I had forgotten how quickly little boys can appear and disappear. He pops in and out like a jack-in-the-box. He's already found that overhang down on the slope back of the house." She turned to Carrie. "Perhaps you'd better go and take a look at it soon, dear. I have no idea what's down there—but just go see if it's safe."

Carrie nodded. "I'll see about it, but so far, I haven't had time to think straight."

Henrietta had yielded her customary place behind the coffee table to Carrie, who was the complete hostess and looked after us with charm, although I thought she overdid it.

Alberta was the sole member of the household to appear uncomfortable with the new arrangements. She slipped in and out of the room silently, watching the elder Mrs. Holbrook with anxiety and the younger with resentment.

"I think I got off to a bad start with Alberta," Carrie said at one point.

"Nonsense!" said Henrietta. "She'll get used to you. It's just that she's not accustomed to having anyone around but me."

"It's about the room," Carrie explained to me. "She's always had the room across the hall from Mother Holbrook, but since that's no longer necessary, I moved her down into the basement. There's a nice room down there with a bath and outside entrance. I told her to pick her own colors and wallpaper and we'd redo it—new furniture and all. I don't think she likes being there, though."

Henrietta came to Alberta's defense. "You've got to remember, she's been upstairs with me a long time. She probably feels uprooted—dispossessed."

"I could have moved her into the little room at the end of the hall and moved Ben into hers," Carrie went on. "But I think we might do over her old room for a guest room." A note of arrogance had crept into her voice and manner. I wondered if it was the moving Alberta objected to or the manner in which she had been ordered to do it.

When the conversation turned to Erskine and how Carrie would occupy herself, Henrietta reminded me that she was counting on Amy and me to lend a hand. Carrie frowned.

"You make me sound like a case for a social worker," she said peevishly.

"Oh, no, dear!" Henrietta said quickly. "It's just that with you and Pete being old friends, we should all know Amy too." She turned to me. "Why not come next Saturday?"

Carrie interrupted. "But Mother Holbrook, we haven't fixed the guest room yet."

"Oh—I didn't mean for the weekend, Carrie," she said. She smiled at me. "I just thought you and Amy and the boys might come down for lunch. We can drive out in the country, if you like. Mr. Tolliver tells me I've got some beautiful new Black Angus whose feelings are getting hurt because I haven't been out to look at them yet." She laughed.

"Don't worry about it, Henrietta," I said. "Amy and the boys aren't at home, anyway. They're in St. Louis visiting Amy's mother."

"Then if you're alone, it's all the more reason you should come," Henrietta said. She looked at Carrie as if unsure of her ground. "Don't you think so, dear?"

"Whatever you say." Carrie's voice was cold.

Henrietta was troubled. "Well—I only thought—"

I had no particular desire to return to Erskine on Saturday for lunch or a drive into the country. I had enough to occupy me until Monday morning in my own house, in my own yard, with my own errands and odd jobs. But I resented Carrie's taking advantage of Henrietta's good nature and generosity.

"I'm sure you and Carrie have lots to do before you start entertaining," I said uncomfortably.

Henrietta had withdrawn into herself and appeared not to hear.

Carrie stirred. "Mother Holbrook, if you want Pete for lunch on Saturday, why shouldn't you ask him?" Her voice was silky.

Henrietta's blue eyes lighted up. "Will you come, Pete?"

To refuse would be to give in to Carrie's mood—whatever it was—and for Henrietta's sake, I determined not to do that. "Of course," I said. "I'll be delighted."

Carrie murmured something about how nice that would be.

"I'm *so* glad, Pete," Henrietta exclaimed. "And tell Amy we'll be expecting her as soon as she and the children come home."

In the entrance hall a few minutes later, we watched Henrietta go up the dark stairs to her room. Carrie brought my hat.

"You seem to be well settled," I said, trying to make things pleasant again.

"So do you," she replied with significance.

"How do you mean?"

She smiled mockingly. "I was referring specifically to the cosy Henrietta-Pete relationship you've got going here. How long has it been going on?"

"Whatever you're talking about, you make it sound shady."

"Do I? She told me you came every week, but somehow I didn't get the picture."

"What are you talking about?"

From somewhere in the rear of the house, Ben called, "Mama?"

"Yes, darling?" She turned toward the door at the end of the hall.

"Come look at my store!" he shouted.
"In a minute!" she answered. "I'll be there in just a minute."
She stepped around me and opened the front door.
I left without saying good-bye.

❧ 13 ❧

Driving down the hill, I began to make excuses for Carrie. Coming back surely had been difficult for her in many ways. She had had more than enough to occupy anyone's time and mind, to say nothing of coping with all the old memories that must have swept her up and carried her back to happier days. She needed time to settle into her new life. By Friday, I had convinced myself that her mood had been unintentional and temporary, that when I returned to Erskine the next day I would find the real Carrie Holbrook again—as I had in Foley.

I slept late Saturday morning, and it was almost noon when I arrived in Erskine. It was an April day to enchant Henrietta—the sun was bright, the sky ice-blue and cloudless. The shrubbery and trees, bursting now with lacy green life, stirred in a cool, soft breeze, and there was a freshness on the earth that filled me with vigor and a sense of well-being. All my apprehensions about coming were swept away. I walked into the conservatory for a leisurely look down the side of the Holbrook house toward the old barn and the back of the hill; then I went inside, my spirits soaring.

Carrie had driven downtown on an errand, and Henrietta was upstairs having a map. Alberta told me to make myself at home and returned to the kitchen. The house was quiet, and I moved about the parlor noiselessly for a few minutes before I felt pulled outdoors again, into the sunshine.

I struck out across the driveway down the road in front and tramped around the bottom of the hill toward the back slopes. When I broke out of the trees and into the open, I quickened my pace and followed the rock wall along the property line. The drop in the land was so gentle that, when I looked back at the house, its height astonished me. The cupola rose in the sky like a turret on a castle, commanding the view of the countryside and all approaches. From the rear, the lines of the house were straight and clean, infinitely less dismal than the front, where they were shadowed by trees and zigzag angles. The hill itself, and the pasture that stretched from its lower slope, had been set in motion by a sea of untamed prairie grass shimmying in the wind. A hawk circled overhead. A dog barked at the farmhouse over the fields. Out on the highway, one automobile scooted around another and glided out of sight over a distant hill.

I stopped and perched atop the rock wall to smoke a cigarette and enjoy the crispness of the air, before beginning the climb back up the hill. My eyes and mind roamed. Suddenly, my attention was arrested by a dark splotch on the landscape, about a hundred yards below the house. Then I saw movement. I shaded my eyes and stared until the scene came into focus. The movement was Ben.

Against the backdrop of the hill, he looked no larger than an insect. The dark splotch, I assumed, was the overhang that Henrietta had mentioned several times. Lazily, I eased off the wall, crushed the cigarette under my heel and struck out across the grassy expanse to see for myself. The *swish-swish* of the grass brushing the cuff of my trousers intrigued me with its rhythm, and I alternated my pace, fast, then slow again, listening to the variance in the tempo. The ground sloped down and up again. The sun beat down on me with new strength. I took off my sweater and threw it across my arm. When I reached the overhang, the uphill climb had taken my wind.

The overhang was a freak of nature, a ravine or gully turned on its side. It seemed to be eight or ten feet across, and its ceiling was field stone. I saw immediately why it had attracted little Ben and his father before him. As I approached, the boy was amusing himself by jumping off the edge of the rocks to the ground below, three feet at the most, then climbing back to the top without going around the end. He did not see me until I was almost upon him.

"Hi!" I called out. "Having a good time?"

He jumped down from the rocks once more and stood looking at me. He pointed to his feet. "I jumped this far," he said. "Last time, I jumped *that* far." He pointed to a spot close by.

"Not bad," I said approvingly. "Not bad at all."

"Do you want to see my store?" he asked.

"Sure. Where is it?"

"It's in here," he said, dropping to his knees and crawling beneath the jutting rocks.

I bent down for a better view. He was sitting with his legs crossed, looking out at me expectantly. "Come in and see," he said. He scooted to one side.

I dropped to my knees and crawled in alongside him. The ceiling was too low for me to sit upright, so I hunched forward, sitting one way and then another, trying to find a comfortable position.

"What kind of store is it?" I asked, looking about with interest.

"It's just a store," he said. "Alberta gives me stuff to put in it."

He shifted and showed me a collection of jars, bottles and cans lined up against the back wall. Some were empty, some contained dirt and rocks, others muddy water. I examined the arrangement carefully.

"I didn't know you had a store," I said. "I thought this was your hideout. If this were my place, I'd make a pirate's cave out of it."

"You mean like in *Peter Pan?*"

"I guess so."

"I don't know how to play that."

"It's real easy. All you have to do is pretend that all the wavy grass down there is the ocean, and that farmhouse is your ship. This is your cave where you hide the loot."

"Loot?"

"Treasure. Stuff that pirates steal from ships. They bring it ashore and hide it in their caves—like this one."

"You want to see me jump off the rock?" he asked suddenly.

"Go ahead. I'm getting cramped in here, anyway."

When I crawled out into the sunlight, he was standing on the edge of a jutting rock, poised and waiting. "Watch!"

"I'm watching." I moved a few feet down the slope.

With a whoop, he leaped and hit the ground with both feet. I complimented him and moved back up the hill.

"You want to buy something from the store?" he asked.

"What have you got?"

"Soda pop and cereal."

He scrambled back underneath and emerged with a bottle of dirty water and a cardboard carton full of rocks.

"What's this?"

"Medicine."

"Well—I'm not sick, but I might get sick later. So maybe I'd better buy a bottle."

We completed the imaginary transaction. I left the bottle with him for safekeeping and went on up the hill.

Carrie had returned and greeted me somewhat more warmly than I had anticipated, but she looked worried.

"I saw your car in the driveway," she said. "Alberta told me where you were. Did you see Ben down there?"

"He's all right. He's playing store and jumping off the rocks. Don't worry about him."

"It looks like today won't be exactly what Mother Holbrook had in mind," she said. "She's not feeling well."

"Has the doctor been here?"

"Not yet. I called him to come. She's acting so strangely! She says she feels fine, but she won't get out of bed."

"Alberta didn't mention it when I arrived."

"She was all right when I went downtown. It's happened since. Alberta says it's one of her spells."

We were standing in the breakfast room. Alberta was laying the table for lunch, glancing at us with interest as she padded in and out.

"When I came in," Carrie continued, "she began to talk about Ben and how the Army is holding him prisoner on an island in the Pacific. You can't imagine the weird feeling—she said he was homesick and hungry and no one cares whether he comes home or not—no one but her. I've never seen such a change in a person! I hardly knew her."

Alberta entered the room again and stood surveying the table. "You about ready for lunch, Mr. Hamilton?" she asked cheerfully.

"Whenever you say, Alberta."

Carrie watched her leave the room. "She doesn't seem upset about it," she said wonderingly.

"She's been through it before—many times. She knows what to do."

"Thank God somebody knows. I certainly don't."

"Maybe I ought to clear out and go back home," I suggested. "My being here might upset her more."

"Please don't go!" she said with alarm. "I'm worried about Ben—little Ben. It's an awful thing to say, but I'm afraid she might do something to him."

"He'll be okay. With you and Alberta here, nothing will happen to him."

"But I can't watch him every minute," she said. "He runs in and out of Mother Holbrook's room all the time. She encourages it."

Alberta announced lunch, and Carrie went out to call Ben.

We had no sooner sat down to the table than we heard Dr. Kriegel enter the front door and go directly upstairs. We sat in silence, listening for his movements on the floor above. Presently, his heavy steps descended again, and he appeared in the doorway, filling the space with his bulk. His disheveled clothes and a blankness of expression gave him the appearance of one who had recently been roused from a nap. He stood glaring at us with distaste. Abruptly, he announced that he would send a prescription out from the drugstore.

"Just follow the directions on the label," he said in his deep bass. Then he was gone.

"Friendly, isn't he?" I said dryly.

"That's the way he's been with me ever since I came back," Carrie said. "He hasn't been rude exactly, but he just doesn't have anything to—" She broke off. "Now *what* happened to Ben?"

His chair was empty. Carrie started to get up.

"I'll go," I offered. "Sit down."

"See if he's upstairs," she said, sinking back into her chair. "Don't let him bother Mother Holbrook."

I found Henrietta's room and paused before the door listening for Ben's voice inside. Hearing nothing, I went from door to door calling his name softly. I found him in his room—the small room at the rear of the house—leaning on the window sill and staring out at the back slope.

"Your mother wants you to come back and finish your lunch," I said.

"I'm not hungry," he replied without looking around. "I've got to go back to my cave. I've been playing pirate like you said."

"She wants you to come downstairs, anyway."

He turned away from the window and went out the door. I moved to the window and looked out to see what had fascinated him, but I noticed nothing I had not seen before. I went back downstairs.

"But she won't eat nothin' when she have a spell," Alberta was explaining to Carrie. "I'll take her something later."

"I think I'll go see about her anyway," Carrie said anxiously.

Alberta went back into the kitchen shaking her head and mumbling to herself. Carrie went upstairs, leaving Ben and me to finish our lunch. Moments later, she returned.

"Maybe Alberta's right," she said. "Mother Holbrook's asleep, so I didn't bother her. I just peeped in the door."

She sat down and looked at the table ruefully. "I've lost my appetite," she said. She regarded me with unexpected friendliness. "I'm glad you're here, Pete," she said. "Really I am. I don't know what to do, and I'm just glad to have you around." She paused. "Don't pay any attention to my moods. It's just taking me a while to get used to things. I'm sorry if I haven't been exactly cordial to you. It doesn't mean anything."

"Don't worry about it, but I do think I ought to go home. You and Alberta will get along better without me under foot. She knows what to do, and the doctor is only a phone call away. You can explain to Henrietta when she feels better. Alberta says these spells sometimes last for two and three days."

"Do what you think best, Pete. You may be right."

Ben left the table and sauntered from the room. Carrie sank into a pensive silence.

I sat and sipped my coffee, looking out over the countryside, thinking what a pity it was that Henrietta was in no condition to enjoy such a day—

The silence was ruptured by a scream.

Piercing and blood-curdling, it lifted me out of my chair. The mechanism in my mind and body ground to a halt. Carrie was already on her feet, staring at me, too stunned to move.

"Upstairs," she whispered, her face drained of all color.

We burst into simultaneous action and darted from the breakfast room, through the butler's pantry, the dining room, the parlor, into the front hall and onto the stairs.

Alberta was standing at the top of the stairs, her face contorted with terror. She was wringing her hands and babbling.

"Hurry, Miss Carrie," she wailed. "It's Mrs. Holbrook. Hurry!"

Carrie was halfway up the stairs with me at her heels.

"What is it, Alberta?" she gasped. "What on earth's the matter?"

"I think she's dead," Alberta cried. "I think Mrs. Holbrook's dead."

❧ 14 ❧

Henrietta seemed to be asleep. I had to look closely to find a suggestion of discomfort on her face. But it was there, a thin crease across her forehead and a fine line that drew her mouth down at one corner. Her delicate hands gripped the light blanket that covered her.

Carrie snatched the blanket away and placed an ear against Henrietta's chest, motioning to Alberta and me to silence. I grasped a wrist, searching for a pulsebeat. I found none. Swiftly, I placed my fingertips against Henrietta's temples, then her ankles and again on her wrist. I felt no stirring of life anywhere.

Alberta was standing at the foot of the bed, wringing her hands and sobbing. "As soon as I looked, I knowed something was wrong," she moaned. "I just knowed. I just knowed. I just knowed. Oh, Lord Jesus, I knowed, I knowed, I knowed, I—"

"Alberta!" I said, surprised at my own sharpness.

I could have saved my breath, for the sounds continued to tumble from her mouth. Her body swayed from side to side in rhythm, then forward and backward. "I knowed, I knowed, I knowed, I knowed, I knowed. . . ."

"Alberta! Get hold of yourself!" I said, raising my voice above the commotion. "Go call Dr. Kriegel."

Carrie straightened up and backed away from the bed, her eyes fixed on Henrietta in a glassy stare. "You'll have to call him, Pete," she said in a shaky voice. She did not turn her head or shift her gaze. "She's in no shape to do it."

I ran out into the hall and found the telephone at the head of the stairs.

The operator was aghast. "Oh, no; not Mrs.—"

Slamming down the receiver, I raced back into the bedroom, where I found Alberta on her knees at the foot of the bed, her face buried in the bedclothes. She was crying aloud now, her body heaving with great sobs. Carrie stood by the window looking out.

"Did you find him?" she asked without turning around.

"The operator's trying."

"There's nothing the doctor can do," she said, her voice a dead monotone. "He's too late. All of us are too late."

Alberta raised her head and looked up at me, her eyes wet, her face twisted. I reached out and laid a hand on her shoulder.

"How come she died, Mr. Hamilton?" she asked.

"I don't know, Alberta. Maybe she was sicker than we thought."

She squared her shoulders and pushed herself to her feet. "No, she wasn't," she said with firmness. "She wasn't sick enough to die. I know that much. She wasn't sick enough to die." She took a handkerchief from her pocket and blew her nose loudly. She stood briefly, contemplating the body of her mistress. "I got to fix her before the doctor comes. She don't want the doctor to find her not fixed."

Carrie turned from the window. "You'd better leave her alone, Alberta," she said.

"No. I got to fix her." She moved with determination around to the side of the bed. "She's awful particular about how she look when the doctor comes."

From a drawer in the night table, she took a silver-backed brush. Carrie looked on with increasing horror.

"Alberta, leave her alone," she said evenly. "We can't bother her until the doctor comes. Leave her alone."

"No, ma'am. I know what Mrs. Holbrook want me to do."

She sat on the edge of the bed and began to stroke Henrietta's hair, lightly, tenderly and with obvious love and pride.

"Alberta! I said leave her alone!" Carrie commanded. Her face was pale, her lips set in a hard line.

Alberta went on with her brushing. She took up a kind of chant in cadence with the stroke of the brush:

> "I brush one
> I brush two
> They ain't nobody
> As pretty as you.
> I brush one
> I brush two. . . ."

"Alberta!" Carrie screamed.

"I brush one . . ."

"Pete! Make her stop!"

I said nothing. Alberta continued.

> "I brush one,
> I brush two,
> They ain't nobody
> As pretty as you. . . ."

"Alberta!"

"She's not hurting anything," I said gently. "If she wants to brush her hair, let her. Come on. Let's go downstairs."

"I'm not going anywhere," said Carrie. "Make Alberta stop!"

"I ain't gonna leave Mrs. Holbrook," said Alberta. "Nobody ain't gonna make me leave Mrs. Holbrook. She want me to brush her hair. I brush one. . . ."

Carrie started toward her. I stepped in front of her and held her back.

"Carrie! You're hysterical! Now settle down and go find Ben."

Ben's name was like a dash of cold water. Abruptly, the grim hardness disappeared from her face. "Ben! I'd forgotten about him! Go find him, Pete!"

"Not unless you go with me."

"He's probably out back somewhere."

I took her arm and led her gently toward the door. She glanced back at the bed and covered her face with her hands. A shudder ran through her body.

Ben appeared in the doorway.

"What's the matter, Mama?" he asked, his dark eyes wide with alarm. He turned to Alberta and the still form of Henrietta, then back to his mother.

"Come look, Ben," Alberta called to him. A strand of Henrietta's white hair lay across her palm. She drew the brush through it tenderly. "Come see how pretty she looks. Ain't she pretty? I brush one . . . I brush two . . . ain't she pretty?"

Carrie hurried to the doorway, shielding Ben from the sight. "Come on, darling, and let's go downstairs." She pushed him back through the door. He craned his neck around her skirt.

"What's the matter, Mama?" he repeated. "Why does Alberta want me to look?"

"Ain't she pretty?" Alberta was repeating. "Mrs. Holbrook's the prettiest lady in the whole world. Come see how pretty she looks, Ben. Come look and see. . . ."

But Ben was already out in the hall with his mother. I followed them toward the stairs. Alberta's chant grew fainter and fainter behind me.

> "I brush one . . .
> I brush two. . . ."

15

Dr. Kriegel came down the stairs, his shoulders drooping, his long arms dangling loosely, an air of defeat about him. He looked through and beyond me as though I did not exist. At the bottom of the stairs, where I waited, he brushed past me into the parlor without speaking. I followed him through the door.

"Dr. Kriegel, I—"

"Where's Carrie?"

"She's with Ben—out back somewhere."

Wearily, he lowered himself into a chair and sighed heavily. "Were you in the room with her?" He jerked his head toward the stairs.

"No. Alberta called us—Carrie and me."

Hooking an arm over the back of his chair, he ran his fingers through his shock of white hair and stared at the floor, puzzled and hurt, the deep, rigid lines motionless on his face. His mind seemed to be at work trying to assemble the pieces, to reconstruct a sensible whole from the terrible parts. I stood by anxiously, feeling like an intruder but waiting, nevertheless, for his diagnosis or opinion. He gave no evidence that he intended to provide either.

"Do you know what it was?" I asked at last.

"No. It could have been her heart—but that's only a guess." He rubbed his jaw slowly. Apparently, he intended to say no more.

"Is there anything I can do?" I asked. "If I can help, just say so. There must be some telephone calls to make, people to notify, lots of details to look after, so if you'll tell me. . . ."

He stirred and shifted his gaze toward me.

"You can leave," he said calmly.

"I beg your pardon?"

"Just go back to wherever you came from," he said with tired resignation.

"I don't understand—"

"Just go back where you came from," he repeated. "Wherever that is, just go. People will be coming up the hill before long—people you don't know and who don't know you—friends of Henrietta's." He turned his face away from me. "I don't know how to explain you to them. I can't even explain you to myself. We don't need you, so why don't you just go away and leave us alone?"

I was not certain when the shock wore off. I struggled to say something in my own defense, but against what?

"Doctor, I think I can make my own explanations," I said. "You're not responsible for me or for my presence here."

"I can't argue with you about it," he said. He humped forward, elbows on his knees. "I asked you once not to come here any more, and you wouldn't listen." His voice cracked. "I didn't know it would come to this."

"What are you talking about?"

He covered his face with his hands. For a moment, I thought he was crying. "Just go—please," he said in a muffled voice.

"Do as he says, Pete."

I spun around. Carrie stood in the doorway. She was regarding me with detachment.

"Carrie!"

She nodded toward Dr. Kriegel. "Please do as he says. He knows what's best."

"But—"

She moved into the room. "It'll be easier if you go. Leave me your telephone number, and I'll call you later about the arrangements."

"But *why?*"

"Pete, just go—please."

Dr. Kriegel sat motionless, his hands still covering his face. As far as he was concerned, I had already gone.

"Carrie—"

She watched me without speaking.

Turning suddenly, I hurried through the parlor and out the front door.

I drove back to Jones Hill, humiliated and bewildered. I had been ordered to leave as though I were a thrill-seeking spectator hindering work to be done. And Carrie had not lifted a finger in my defense.

Whistle Smith was working in his yard next door when I turned into my driveway. I pulled into the carport and got out.

"Hi, Pete!" he yelled, starting toward me. When he got closer, he asked, "What do you hear from Amy?"

"Oh—they're getting along fine," I said. "Everybody okay at your house?"

"We're fine, too. Linda wanted me to watch for you and ask you over for dinner. How about it?"

"I'd better take a rain check," I said. My mind improvised rapidly. "I brought a batch of stuff home from the office that I've got to finish before Monday morning, and the sooner I get started the better. Please thank Linda for me, though."

"Too bad. If you change your mind later, come on over for a drink or whatever."

He returned to his yard work, and I went into the house. I had to sort out the swift, terrible events and put them into some kind of perspective, or at least try. I wandered through the house, unable to stay in one place. I lay on the sofa or sat at the kitchen table, trying to think sensibly. Henrietta Holbrook had died, but my natural concern, my desire to be of assistance, my friendship with Henrietta had counted for nothing.

Darkness came on, and I poured myself a double bourbon and

water. While I was drinking it, I heard cars out front, doors slamming and loud voices. I went to the living room without turning on the lights and looked through the window. Across the street, the porch light was burning on the Mansfields' front porch. Several people were going up the sidewalk, laughing and talking. I tried to remember if either of the Mansfields, JoAnne or Jack, had left word for me about a party. I couldn't remember.

I went back to the kitchen and turned on the light over the sink. Amy had stocked the freezer compartment of the refrigerator with good things for me to eat and posted a list on the door with instructions for preparing them. I scanned the list, but I had no appetite. I wandered out into the back yard with a fresh drink in my hand. Later, I refilled my glass again, and probably still another time. At any rate, when I felt soggy through and through, I went to bed and slept. I awoke at three o'clock with a nasty headache and a dirty taste in my mouth and lay awake until daylight, feeling horrible. When I heard the Sunday paper plop against the front door, I went and brought it in.

Henrietta's death was listed on the obituary page under STATE DEATHS. It was accompanied by a short news article that noted she was the widow of a pioneer Texas cattleman and land owner and the mother of one son who had been a casualty of World War II. The cause of death had not been determined, but it appeared to have been from natural causes. She had been discovered in her bed by her maid and daughter-in-law. My presence was not mentioned, either because it had not been reported or because the reporter had not considered it important.

I stayed in the house all day, waiting for a telephone call from Carrie. I tried to pass the time by napping, but I stayed wide awake and alert. I turned on the radio, drank coffee until the pot was empty, smoked countless cigarettes, paced the floor. I made myself a highball and drank it down as though it were plain water.

At four o'clock, the telephone rang. It was the operator with a long distance call from Erskine for a Mr. Peter D. Hamilton.

"This is Mr. Hamilton speaking."

"Your party is on the line."

"Hello, Carrie?" I said eagerly.

A man's voice replied.

"I'm sorry," I said. "I was expecting to hear from someone else. Would you mind repeating your name?"

"Page. Vernon Page. I'm the coroner of Erskine County. I'm calling to inform you about an inquest tomorrow at ten o'clock. Your presence will be required."

"An inquest? What kind of inquest?"

"It's about Mrs. Holbrook's death. I understand you were present at the time."

"I was in the house—yes."

"Then can we count on your presence tomorrow at ten? It'll be in the courthouse here. Just ask anyone where to find the coroner's office."

I tried to make sense of what he was saying. "But why do you want me?" I asked.

"It's required," he said. "I could ask the authorities there in Fort Worth to serve you with a subpoena, but it's a lot of trouble and red tape, especially on Sunday afternoon. If you can assure me you'll be present, we won't need to do that."

I was speechless. He waited.

"Mr. Hamilton? Are you still on the line?"

"I'm here."

"Shall I use the subpoena?"

"No—no, that's not necessary. But I don't understand why you're having an inquest."

"It's required in cases where the cause of death is unexplained. Usually, it's only a formality. For the record."

"But couldn't the doctor determine the cause? He told me it could have been a heart attack."

"The death certificate doesn't say that, though. It says the cause is unknown."

"But surely Dr. Kriegel knows the cause by now."

"I can't discuss the details with you, Mr. Hamilton. Can I count on you tomorrow?"

"Why, I guess so—sure, I'll be there. But can't you tell me—"

"I'll see you then. Good-bye." There was a click as he hung up.

I sat with the telephone in my hands unable to assimilate what I had heard. Then I began to connect coroner's inquests with all the mystery novels I had read and all the movie thrillers I had seen; with suspected evil, with wrongdoing, with criminals, with—

I slammed down the receiver, then picked it up again immediately and dialed the long-distance operator.

"Get me Mrs. Carrie Holbrook, Erskine," I said breathlessly. "And hurry!"

Some confusion on the other end; then a strange voice, a woman's, identified herself to the operator as a family friend. She agreed to ask Mrs. Holbrook if she felt like talking.

"Tell her to talk anyway!" I shouted.

"I'm trying to get your party, sir," the operator said with disapproval.

Impatiently, I pressed the receiver against my ear, trying to interpret the background noises at the other end of the line. An eternity seemed to pass before a voice spoke to me again.

"Hello?"

"Carrie? Is that you, Carrie?"

"Yes—who is this?"

"It's Pete. You were supposed to call me."

"I know. But so much has happened, and the house has been so full of people and—"

"Carrie, what's all this about an inquest? I had a call from the coroner there. He wants me to come to an inquest tomorrow. Why are they holding an inquest?"

"I'm sorry, Pete. I thought you knew."

"How would I know? I've been waiting to hear from you. *Why are they holding an inquest?*"

"Pete, stop shouting. It's awful. Absolutely awful. Dr. Kriegel asked for an autopsy. They found poison."

"What kind of poison?"

"I don't know the name of it. It's technical. Look, Pete. I can't talk any more. The house is full of people, and—well, you'll hear about it tomorrow."

"Carrie, who gave her the poison?" I demanded.

"For heaven's sake, Pete—I don't know."

"*Somebody* must know."

"I don't think they do—that's why they're having the inquest—to see if it was accidental or—or somebody gave it to her."

"Who would do *that?*" I asked.

"Pete, you're shouting again. I don't know. Please—people are listening—I've got to hang up."

"Carrie, don't hang up. When is—"

I heard a click at the other end, and the line went dead.

❦16❧

I drove by the office on Monday morning and told Mr. Marsh I would be in Erskine that day for a funeral. I was too bewildered about the inquest to mention it and have to discuss it. Mrs. Holbrook had been a close friend, I told him, the mother of a wartime friend, and the family would be expecting me. Mr. Marsh was sympathetic. He lent me his secretary to help adjust my appointments and schedule and said to telephone him if I needed more time. I assured him that one day would be enough and that I would be out on the road tomorrow.

The Erskine County Court House, huge, creaky and drafty, was all windows and rock granite, imprisoned on the town square by Erskine's business establishments and topped by the inevitable dome, this one sporting a new coat of white paint. Two or three loiterers on the steps eyed me with no particular interest as I came up the long walk and glanced at the clock high above, stuck into the side of the dome like a monocle. It was ten minutes before ten.

Inside, the corridor was deserted save for a colored janitor who seemed happy for an excuse to stop his lackadaisical sweeping long enough to direct me to Mr. Page's office on the second floor. Upstairs, I met an assortment of people filing out of an office and streaming down the corridor in little knots of twos and threes. A slight, wiry man of perhaps fifty, with thin, sandy hair and rimless spectacles, detached himself from one of the groups and came to meet me.

"Mr. Hamilton? I'm Vernon Page—we talked yesterday. The proceedings will be in the county courtroom. That's where we're going now."

I fell in with the others and followed them through the corridor to the courtroom.

"Just take a seat anywhere," Mr. Page said when we got inside. "We'll call you when you're needed."

A straggle of onlookers dotted the courtroom and watched us make our way down the aisle. Carrie sat alone on the front row, chic, elegant, and dramatic in black. The only touch missing was a black veil, but she had made her point without it. Two youngish women, wide-eyed and curious, sat behind her and to one side, their heads together and tongues wagging, sizing her up with interest.

Dr. Kriegel sat across the aisle, engaged in low conversation with a man in the next seat. Alberta sat on the opposite side of the room wearing what must have been her best dress, a shrieking affair of yellow flowers on a dark blue background, and a straw hat with still more flowers perched atop her gray head. She smiled at me apprehensively, not certain that a full nod or a wave of the hand would be proper. I smiled back at her and waved, and her face broke into a grin.

I took a seat in the row behind Carrie, away from the two young women and a few seats, down where she could see me if she chose to look around. But she did not. She kept her head and eyes to the front. Dr. Kriegel finished his conversation and turned to survey the courtroom. His eyes stopped on me for an instant, but they contained no greeting. Only recognition.

People finally settled down. Mr. Page stepped to the front and explained that a coroner's inquest is traditionally more informal than a trial, and our use of the courtroom should not be interpreted as a desire for formality. He warned us, however, that a coroner's inquest was an instrument of the law, and its findings were binding on the people and the State of Texas. All testimony would be given under oath, and while not subject to the rules of evidence, it was subject to the laws that governed perjury. The purpose of the inquest was to investigate the circumstances surrounding the death of Mrs. Henrietta Holbrook. He took his seat behind a long table and nodded to a clerk who read from a paper in a singsong voice.

The inquest had officially begun.

Despite my own involvement, the proceedings were unbelievably dull, at least until the county medical examiner took the stand and read from his report of the autopsy. But even he read in such a monotone that I had to listen closely to learn that the presence of a chemical called drenathine had been discovered in the stomach of the deceased, a quantity sufficient to be capable of causing death. Death occurred at approximately one-fifteen P.M. on Saturday, April 22, 1950, at the deceased's home in Erskine, County of Erskine, State of Texas.

Drenathine, the medical examiner said, was an ingredient sometimes found in certain old-fashioned household cleaning compounds that he doubted had been sold in Erskine or anywhere else for twenty, perhaps thirty, years. Local druggists and grocers had been requested to examine their stocks of cleaning compounds. None of them had been able to locate a product containing drenathine; nor could any of them recall such a product.

"I must take the assumption, then," said the medical examiner, "that such a cleaning compound is no longer on the market. And in the short time allotted me, I have not been able to ascertain the brand name of such a compound, past or present. The chemical drenathine itself is clear as water, almost odorless and tasteless. That's why it might be dangerous in a household. A small amount of it in a glass of water, for example, would not be noticeable—either in taste or appearance. I found traces of it in a water pitcher, some in a water tumbler that was on Mrs. Holbrook's night table. I presume that the deceased had drunk from that glass."

Having established all facts and circumstances that could be ascertained from official records, the coroner bent his efforts toward determining the identity of the person or persons who might have administered the poison that had caused the death of Mrs. Henrietta Holbrook, and any fact or circumstance that might shed light on whether the death was accidental or willful.

"All deaths," he said, "must necessarily fall into one of four categories: accidental, from natural causes, suicide or homicide."

Carrie, Dr. Kriegel, Alberta and I were called to the stand in turn and asked to describe our actions on Saturday morning prior to Mrs. Holbrook's death. The interrogation of the others followed the same pattern as my own. Did the deceased ever express to me or in my presence a fear for her own safety? Did she ever mention a threat on her life? Did I know of any person who bore her ill will or who might be classified as her enemy? Would her death benefit me or improve my circumstances in any way, morally, spiritually, emotionally or materially? Did I have reason to suspect that the deceased had suicidal tendencies?

Dr. Kriegel's testimony was interlarded with medical opinions and technical phrases; otherwise, his answers to the questions were probably no more illuminating than mine.

Carrie testified that although she was not familiar with the provisions of her mother-in-law's will, she naturally assumed that she would be remembered and provided for, but to what extent, she had no way of knowing. The matter had never been discussed with her or in her presence, and she wanted to make that clear and unmistakable to the coroner.

Alberta testified that she had filled the water pitcher in the hall bathroom earlier in the morning and left it temporarily on the lavatory because she had been distracted by some small chore —the telephone ringing or the doorbell, she didn't remember what. She did not think of it again until Miss Carrie, Mr. Hamilton and Ben were eating lunch. So remembering, she hurried upstairs during lunch and took the pitcher into Mrs. Holbrook's room and poured some water from it into the glass on the night table. Mrs. Holbrook stirred when she heard Alberta.

"Jes' as I was leavin' the room," Alberta testified, "Mrs. Holbrook raised herself up and taken a drink from that glass. I went on back downstairs to the kitchen and stayed there until I went up to Mrs. Holbrook's room again and find her dead." She began to cry. "If I'd of knowed what was in that glass, I'd of drank it myself before I'd of let Mrs. Holbrook drink it," she moaned into her handkerchief. "I'd of jes' drank it all myself."

After she had composed herself, she was questioned about the types of cleaning compounds used in the Holbrook household. She named a few well-known brands. She was not, however, familiar with the ingredients of them.

"We got a whole closetful of bottles in the hall-bathroom closet," she said, "and we got some more in the kitchen pantry, but I don't use all of them. Some of them I ain't never opened up. They been in the house ever since I been working for Mrs. Holbrook. If I could see the bottle you is talking about, I could tell you if I used it or not."

But there was no bottle. At least, the sheriff of Erskine County, a man named Natwick, testified that he had not been able to find it.

"We ransacked all the bathrooms, my deputy and I," he said. "We went through the medicine cabinets, pantries, closets, kitchen cabinets, and a storage room off the screened back porch. We searched the basement and even went through a lot of boxes and cartons stored in the barn down back of the house. We went up into the attic, but you could tell by the thick layer of dust—undisturbed—on the floor, that no one had set foot up there in months. The maid said maybe it had been years."

With all the testimony in and recorded, the coroner's jury retired and returned in less than ten minutes to announce its verdict, in the words I dreaded: homicide at the hands of a person or persons unknown. Actually hearing those words was an anticlimax—and the verdict was wrong. Henrietta's death had been a grotesque accident. It had to be. No one could possibly kill a person as gentle and good as Henrietta Holbrook. No one in the world. No matter what the coroner's jury had decided, it was impossible for me to link an act of violence to her. There had to be another explanation somewhere.

It was noon when Mr. Page adjourned the inquest.

Carrie hurried to the front of the room to talk to Mr. Page. I waited in the aisle for her. Dr. Kriegel brushed past me without speaking. Alberta made her way out by the opposite aisle. Some of the jurors filed past, looking at me indifferently; the stenographer with her hands full of pencils and pads strolled toward the door, examining her notes. Mr. Page shook hands with Carrie and turned to some papers on the table. A half-bald, spectacled, owlish-looking man hurried up to Carrie and shook her hand, bowing slightly and talking rapidly. He fidgeted and pranced, obsequious yet clearly excited. Carrie listened for a few minutes, hardly responding, then disengaged herself and turned to go.

As she came abreast of me, I fell in with her. We left the courtroom along with the others. Neither of us spoke until we approached the main entrance and were free of the people who had walked down the stairs with us.

"Carrie, you don't really think she was murdered, do you?" I asked.

"I don't know what else to think." She kept her eyes straight ahead.

"But if it was murder, they would suspect someone who was present at the time, and apparently they don't. Otherwise, they wouldn't have released all of us."

"They can reach out and grab us any time they choose—any of us." When we reached the door, she looked up at me. "Goodbye," she said abruptly. "Alberta's waiting for me."

I followed her outside. At the foot of the courthouse steps, Alberta was standing alone, crying. The owlish-looking man stood not far from her on the sidewalk, watching her with open interest. He turned his attention to us as we came out onto the steps. I drew Carrie aside on the wide top step, away from the door.

"Carrie, what went wrong between us?" I asked.

"I haven't figured that out yet," she said, rather crisply, I thought, but not unkindly. She looked up into my face; she seemed to be studying me, yet her mind seemed to be on something else. "None of this is what I—" She shook her head quickly and looked away.

"It must be *something*," I went on. "I did everything you asked. I explained everything to Henrietta, and evidently it worked. But for all that, you've held me at arm's length. You even chased me out of the house Saturday. I don't get it. Don't you think you owe me some kind of explanation?"

"There's one thing you've got to remember," she said. "Considering the way I left Erskine several years ago, my coming back was a wee bit awkward. I couldn't simply walk in the house and unpack my bags as though I'd been away on a two-week vacation. Mother Holbrook and I had to feel our way along, adjust—"

"I've figured all that," I broke in. "But I mean something about *me*—not you and Henrietta. I wish you'd tell me."

"Look, Pete," she said in a harder tone, "it's not that I don't appreciate what you've done; but why don't you just forget us? You've done all you can do."

"But your troubles are just beginning, Carrie! Your mother-in-law was murdered—that's the verdict. Somebody will be accused, probably, and you'll find yourself big news all over the State of Texas and maybe beyond. You'll be facing this all alone —surely you can see that!"

"I've been facing things alone for several years," she said. There was little feeling in her voice. "Just go on back to Amy and the boys," she said evenly. "That's where you belong."

"But Carrie, I can't just walk away as though I were a stranger. Henrietta and I were close friends. I'm as grieved over her death as you are, and Alberta and Dr. Kriegel. If nothing else, there was Ben—another close friend. So I feel some kind of responsibility to pitch in and help—"

"What I'm trying to tell you, Pete, is that you're *not* responsible. Don't worry about me—really, I'd rather you didn't try to help me. I'll make out."

I sighed. "Well, I hope you know what you're doing." I started down the steps, then turned back. "Will you call me if you need me?"

"I'll call you," she said flatly. There was no smile or suggestion of warmth on her face.

I left her there and went on down the steps. At the bottom, I paused long enough to offer my sympathy to Alberta. No one else seemed to need it.

❧ 17 ❧

At the edge of Fort Worth, I turned off the highway into a public park. It was deserted. I drove down through the trees on a road that rambled alongside a creek past a playground and clusters of picnic tables and barbecue grills. Just beyond, I pulled off into a parking area overlooking the creek and turned off the engine. Rolling down the window, I listened to the wind gushing through the trees and watched it whip up the dead underbrush. A squirrel scampered up the trunk of a gnarled oak and then down again and across the road out of sight. A piece of newspaper floated by and lodged itself in a bush, flapping helplessly to get free. I sat motionless, intending to think but afraid to. My mind was a jumble of memories, old and new, haphazard and confusing.

Henrietta Holbrook was dead, and I had to think about that, to face the awful knowledge that someone had caused her death. I tried to say the word, but it stuck in my throat.

If there was a crime, someone had to be the criminal. And the most difficult thought of all: the criminal had to be someone I knew, someone who had been in the house Saturday morning. The list of possibilities was short. Aside from young Ben and me, only Dr. Kriegel, Alberta and Carrie had been in the house. I rejected all of them.

Not Dr. Kriegel. No doctor of medicine with murder on his mind would be clumsy enough to poison his victim. He could kill a person, particularly a patient, dozens of ways with little danger of detection. Besides, Dr. Kriegel had refused to certify the cause of death on the death certificate and had, in fact, requested the autopsy, certainly not the actions of a guilty man. His medical opinion on a piece of paper not only would have absolved everyone of suspicion and guilt; it would have concealed the crime itself.

Nor could Alberta have done it. Feeling, rather than logic, convinced me of that. Alberta loved Henrietta with a proprietary love that ran deep and maternal. I remembered the two of them laughing like schoolgirls one day because Henrietta had not paid Alberta her wages.

"You must think back, Alberta, and remember when I gave you money last," Henrietta chided. "This isn't right. Now when was it?"

Alberta chuckled. "I don't know, Mrs. Holbrook. I remember once I gave *you* two dollars to pay the paper boy. But that ain't what you is askin', is it?" She whooped with delight.

Henrietta joined in the laughter. "When was that?" she asked.

"I don't know."

"Did I pay you back?"

"I don't remember that, neither."

Whereupon the two of them broke up in new peals of laughter.

The relationship was not one to breed murder.

That left Carrie.

Not Carrie! Not Carrie Holbrook, wife of Ben Holbrook, deceased. Not Carrie who lived to play, to laugh, to dance. . . .

"Dance with me, Pete," I heard her say.

The music played and we danced. Ben sat at the table and looked on. Old slowpoke, straitlaced Ben Holbrook looked on while Carrie danced. The music was lively. . . .

Not you, Carrie . . . not you . . . Ben, you ought to dance with Carrie more than you do . . . come on and dance with

Carrie . . . not you, Carrie . . . not you . . . you like the lively music. . . .

I dropped off into a confused sleep.

When I awoke, the park was gray with dusk. Across the creek and through the trees, an early street light flickered. I sat up straight, not comprehending, not remembering. Groggy with sleep, I shook myself to get my bearings. I was cold, and my teeth chattered. Tense and rigid, I started the engine, turned on the heater and relaxed gradually as the air wafted warm and comforting around me.

Later when I let myself into my own house, the telephone was ringing. It was Mr. Marsh. He was calling from the office.

"Hamilton? We've been trying to locate you all afternoon. Has anyone from Erskine been able to get hold of you?"

"Not since noon," I said. "I left there around noon, and I've just now walked in the front door. Is anything wrong?"

He hesitated. "No—but maybe yes. There's a lawyer down there trying to get in touch with you. He's called the office several times. I couldn't make too much sense of what he was saying. It's about a will."

"A will?"

"Yes—your friend's will." He sounded puzzled. "It's something about your inheriting her estate."

⚡18⚡

Mr. Marsh was wrong. Or maybe I had misunderstood him. I groped for words.

"Hello? Hamilton?"

"I'm here, Mr. Marsh," I managed to say. "You knocked the wind out of me. Did you say I inherited Mrs. Holbrook's estate?"

"Why, yes—that's what the lawyer told me. Didn't you know about it?"

"No, sir."

"Naturally, I assumed you knew—your being down there today for the funeral."

"They didn't have the funeral today."

"But I thought that's why you went." He changed his tone. "Look here, Hamilton. Did you know your friend was murdered?"

I drew in a deep breath. This entire day had been unreal. Today was a bad dream. Tomorrow I would wake up, take my suitcase, my catalogs, leave town, call on my dealers and not think of today at all. My knees threatened to buckle. I sank into a chair by the telephone table. "Yes, sir," I said meekly, "I know it."

"You didn't mention it this morning."

"I didn't know it then—not exactly."

A troubled stillness lay at the other end of the line. "Hamilton, is there something about all this I should know?"

"I don't know, Mr. Marsh. I—I just don't know."

"I don't like the sound of it. Won't it be in the newspapers?"

Amy!

Mr. Marsh was still talking.

"—inevitably involve the name of the company," Mr. Marsh was saying.

"I'm sorry, Mr. Marsh. I didn't hear—"

"Hamilton, if you're going to be home a while, I'm coming out. The company's got to be let in on what's going on. Will you be there, and is it all right if I come?"

"Sure, it's all right. I'll be here."

"Give me twenty minutes."

"Mr. Marsh? What's the name of the lawyer who's trying to get me?"

"Just a minute." I heard a rustle of papers. "Here it is—Tolliver. J. A. Tolliver. I don't have his number—at least, I can't find it. You shouldn't have any trouble reaching him, though."

"I'll call him while I wait for you."

He rang off.

My fingers trembled so that I could hardly dial the operator. One telephone call would correct Mr. Marsh's misinformation. One question and one answer, and the mistake would be rectified. The operator located Mr. Tolliver readily. He came on the line chattering about how difficult it had been to reach me. He spoke rapidly in a high, thin voice.

"I'm afraid I have the advantage over you," he chirped. "I've seen you around town and knew who you were. Then I was at the inquest this morning. Of course, you don't know me."

But I did. The voice was a perfect match for the owlish, balding, excited man at the inquest.

"I would prefer to talk to you face-to-face about a matter as delicate as this," he said breathlessly.

"Exactly *what* is this matter, Mr. Tolliver?" I asked.

"You mean, you don't know? Word's all over town by now."

"I heard something—but I won't believe it until it's confirmed."

"Oh, dear me! And I assumed that someone had told you," he said. "Mrs. Holbrook has named you principal beneficiary in her will, and I can't imagine why you hadn't heard it from another source. It's big news here in Erskine."

"Then it's true."

"Yes indeed it's true. I need to arrange a personal consultation with you—at your convenience, of course—but you shouldn't delay it any longer than necessary. These things are time-consuming enough as it is. The district attorney served me with a court order requiring the will to be read this afternoon. Otherwise, I would have waited until after the funeral services—it would have been more respectful. But the law is the law, you know, and it cannot be kept waiting for reasons of decorum and appearances. I hope you understand that it was not *my* choice. Normally, I would have notified the beneficiaries by more formal and dignified means, but in a case with criminal potentials, we—"

"Wait a minute!" I was aghast. "You mean that someone is *suspected?*"

"I wouldn't know about *that*, but the sheriff's office is still trying to establish a motive for this horrible thing. It's been *such* a blow to all of us, believe me. You can't imagine the shock! We're all stunned. *Positively* stunned. The will was read this afternoon, just in case it might give a clue."

I clutched the telephone tighter. "Did the—did the will give a clue?" I asked.

"Well, *really*, Mr. Hamilton, the sheriff didn't discuss it with me. It's not my concern, you know." He paused. "I know enough about the law, however, to know that establishing a motive is not enough. There won't be any criminal charges against anyone until they find that bottle of whatever the name of it is. That's the weapon, so to speak, and it must be physically linked to a person, and if they don't find it, they can't link it." He paused again. "Mr. Hamilton, if you don't mind my advising you—quite informally, of course—I think you should retain an attorney before you come down here."

"Why?"

"Why?" he echoed. "Are you serious? If you are, I'll tell you why. One reason, which I happen to think is quite good, is that Mrs. Holbrook—the young Mrs. Holbrook, a *most* lovely person, I must say—has already signified her intention to contest the will. Those were almost the first words to come from her mouth after she heard. She was sitting right here in this very office, not six feet away from where I am now. Dr. Kriegel, whom you may know—very respected in the community. *Very.* He's been a pillar of strength to poor Mrs. Holbrook since Mr. Holbrook passed away. Well, Dr. Kriegel is in an absolute rage about the whole matter. He'll do anything to invalidate the will. He makes no bones about that!"

I began to breathe freely again. "Oh, if that's all you mean—"

"If that's *all?* Good heavens! Isn't that enough?"

"There's been a mistake of some kind," I said. "That much is obvious, and the sooner it's straightened out, the better it will be for everybody, including me. I won't stand in the way of—"

"*You need counsel,*" Mr. Tolliver interjected swiftly. "You should have legal assistance before you commit yourself."

"Do you mean that I should oppose Carrie's—Mrs. Holbrook's —actions?"

"I did not say that!" he screamed. "I did not say that at all! I only said that you should consult with an attorney before you reach a decision of such magnitude. There are implications in these matters that laymen cannot possibly understand or appreciate fully. Mr. Hamilton, I do hope I'm not being presumptuous, but I've found in my profession that many people consult lawyers only after their own bumbling has made for dreadfully wicked complications." He sighed. "I just don't understand it. They go to doctors for physical checkups and take their automobiles to garages for preventive maintenance, but they just won't go to lawyers until they're already in trouble." He stopped short. "Oh, Mr. Hamilton! I can assure you that I meant no offense. But if people would only get legal advice before they do anything at all, they would save themselves untold heartaches and trouble. But there's another reason you should have legal advice." He paused. "The sheriff wants to question you—as I understand it, that is."

"The sheriff wants to see me?" I repeated.

"Oh, good grief!" Mr. Tolliver was horrified. "Do you mean you haven't heard from him yet?"

"I've been out all afternoon."

"I hope you realize, Mr. Hamilton, that I was not informing you officially. I certainly would never presume to speak for the sheriff. Not *him!* He's frightfully jealous of his prerogatives. I just happen to know that he wants to talk to you. Still, if I were in your place, I'd retain an attorney immediately. I only tell you this because you seem to be rather at a loss."

I did not know any lawyers, and I asked Mr. Tolliver if his own services might be available.

"I'm frightfully sorry—really I am," he said. "But I'm representing the estate. I was associated with poor Mrs. Holbrook for a number of years—seventeen to be exact—and loved every minute of it. As a matter of fact, I'm the executor of the will. I'm afraid you can't retain me. Don't you know any attorneys at all?"

"No. I've never needed one."

"But *everybody* knows a lawyer. We're not that scarce."

"I don't, though. Can you recommend one?"

"I might suggest that you contact the local bar association there in Fort Worth. They'll be able to give you some names and basic information about each. They won't actually recommend one over the other, but I'm sure you won't have any trouble. Meanwhile, I need you to sign some papers. Can you come tomorrow? You understand, of course, that the estate can't be distributed yet. We have a restraining order, and we mustn't buck the law, you know. But I still need your signature

(137)

on some papers—formalities, really. I think you should expect this thing to be tied up in litigation for some time to come. Some of these things take *ages*. So don't get impatient."

"I'm not impatient."

"I didn't mean to imply that you *were!* I only want you to know how things stand. Can you come tomorrow?"

"If the sheriff wants me, I don't have much choice, do I?"

"He can come get you. It's not dignified, but it's much more exciting. The sheriff here is no Texas Ranger, but he'll bring you in when he wants you. You aren't thinking of fleeing, are you?"

I laughed. "Not quite. I'm not experienced enough."

"It's just as well," he said. "I doubt that our sheriff here could raise a posse that would do credit to the county, anyway."

"One more thing," I said. "Are you advising me to get an attorney on account of the will, or because of Mrs. Holbrook's death?"

"Both."

"But I don't have anything to hide. I didn't have legal counsel at the inquest."

"That was different. You weren't accused of anything."

"Do you mean that I'm—"

"Mr. Hamilton! You're reading meanings into what I say, and it's not fair! It's not fair at all!"

"Then I don't understand what you mean."

"Do you really want me to tell you?"

"Yes."

"Very well. I mean that somewhere along the line you can be charged with Mrs. Holbrook's death—now don't fly off the handle, *please!* I'm not saying that you *will* be charged. After all, there's the matter of evidence to consider. But *somebody* is going to be accused before this is all over, and you're in a precarious position at the moment."

"Why me?"

Mr. Tolliver let out a scream. "Mr. Hamilton! I refuse to believe that you're so naïve! I absolutely refuse to believe it! *You are inheriting the estate,* that's why! You've got a motive. Surely you can see that much!"

I was silent.

"You do see, don't you?"

"I guess so."

"Then retaining a lawyer is only common sense."

I apologized for my denseness.

"Oh, don't worry about that," he hurried on to say. "In my profession, I'm accustomed to dealing with people under stress. This whole nasty business has us all on edge. The entire town is in a positive dither. Imagine! Our most prominent family. Why, there wasn't a more genteel lady in—"

The doorbell rang.

"You'll have to excuse me, Mr. Tolliver. Someone's at the door. I'll see you tomorrow."

"Yes. Tomorrow. Any time will do. And Mr. Hamilton?"

"Yes?"

"Do try to keep calm. It does no good to get excited, and you must not let yourself get overwrought. Keep cool."

The house was dark by now, and on my way to the front door, I flicked on the lights. Mr. Marsh stood on the front porch. He stepped inside.

"Did you get in touch with the lawyer?" he asked. He held his hat in his hand.

"Yes."

"How big is the estate?"

"What?"

"The estate." He regarded me almost paternally. "Is it a large one? I gathered that it is, or there wouldn't be all this fuss about it."

I stared at Mr. Marsh for a moment. "You know," I said slowly. "I forgot to ask him."

❧ 19 ❧

Mr. Marsh stayed more than an hour while I told of my wartime friendship with Ben and Carrie Holbrook, of Carrie's unexpected appearance that day when I was with Amy and the boys, and of how Carrie and I had resumed our association after a five-year lapse. Of course, I was discreet enough to omit the circumstances of little Ben's birth and the ill feelings in the family because of it. Most importantly, I explained my short friendship with Henrietta Holbrook and why my being named her beneficiary had so completely stunned me.

The more I talked, however, the more fictitious I made the story sound, and I weakened it even further by qualifying and justifying it quite needlessly. As I described my reactions to Henrietta's will, I was neither talented nor resourceful enough to re-create my shock and my unwillingness to believe what I had heard. I protested that money, no matter how much, was not worth the tragedy and grief, and that I wanted no part of it. My attention to both the Mrs. Holbrooks was motivated by friendship and nothing more. The fact that I did not yet know the size of the estate would seem to be significant in that respect. But I went too far. I was overanxious to convince. To my ears, my own words had the ring of a guilty man trying to sound innocent.

"What does your wife think about all this?" he asked when I had finished.

"She doesn't know," I replied, hoping he would let the matter stand at that.

"You mean she doesn't know about Mrs. Holbrook's death?" He seemed puzzled as his eyes swept the room.

"Oh—I'm sorry. I should have told you. She's not here. She's in St. Louis visiting her mother."

"Yes, I think you did mention that earlier. But I assumed that you probably called her—a close family friend like that. . . ."

"Amy never met Mrs. Holbrook."

"Well—naturally, I thought it was more of a family connection. You mentioned visiting Mrs. Holbrook frequently."

"I always stopped in to see her on Monday mornings after I worked our Erskine account, so of course, Amy was never with me. And Mrs. Holbrook never came here."

"I see." He nodded his bald head. "How about the young Mrs. Holbrook?"

"No. Amy has never met her, either."

"Oh."

The one word fell between us with a thud. Mr. Marsh looked down at the floor, then at his hands, unable to hide his discomfort. He took off his spectacles, wiped them with his handkerchief and put them on again. He studied his fingernails and said nothing. With the resources of the entire English language at my disposal, I sat helplessly, unable to find a word or phrase to dispel the suspicion that was obviously forming in his mind.

The silence grew painful. Then he stood up to go.

"I'll notify our dealers not to expect you for the rest of the week," he said gently. "Maybe things will be cleared up by Monday. I hope so. At any rate, I think you should straighten out your affairs in Erskine without delay, Hamilton, and I'll appreciate it if you can keep the company's name out of it." His manner was now more assured. "In the meantime, you must keep me posted. Our board will be interested in this—especially when it

(141)

comes out in the newspapers. The publicity can be damaging. The company can't cope with it if we're kept in the dark."

"I'll do my best," I said.

"We'll help you any way we can," he went on. "That is, if any help is needed." His discomfort returned. "Frankly, I'm not sure of the significance and implications of what you've told me." He moved toward the door. I followed him.

I opened the door. He stepped outside onto the porch, then turned back.

"Hamilton—I know everything will be all right," he said.

Then he hurried off into the darkness.

I wandered into the kitchen and sat down at the table. I leaned back in my chair. The slick, wet fabric of my shirt was cold against my back. I drank three glasses of water to soften the dryness in my throat. I plugged in the coffee pot, then took a hot bath. I stretched out in the tub, ashamed of the crippling self-consciousness that had so colored my appearance before Mr. Marsh. I tried to relax and build up enough confidence to telephone Amy.

Amy was delighted to hear from me, but what was I doing at home on a Monday night? Was I sick? Her mother was feeling better and sent her love, and couldn't I take off a few days and drive up to St. Louis? All of us could have a vacation trip on the way home, and we'd worry about using up our summer vacation time when we got to it.

"No, that's impossible," I said. "I can't come, Amy. I've got to talk to you."

"But you are talking, darling," she said facetiously.

"No—not like you think. Something's happened. Just listen and don't interrupt me, or I'll never finish."

"Pete, what on earth? You sound like the world is coming to an end."

"It may be. Do you remember the Holbrooks?"

"Certainly, I remember them. Have you run into some of them again?"

"Amy, *please!* I'm trying to tell you. Let me talk."

(142)

She murmured an apology along with a reminder that I need not bite her head off.

"Mrs. Holbrook died Saturday, and today I found out that I'm her principal heir."

"Principal heir! What do you mean?"

"She named me in her will to inherit her estate."

I heard a gasp. "You mean she left you her money?"

"Yes."

"Why? I mean, why did she leave it to you?"

"No one knows."

"How much is it?"

"I don't know that, either. A lot, I think. A fortune."

"Is this some kind of a joke?"

"Oh, Lord, no! It's not a joke. I wish it were."

"Pete, let me get this straight before I cut loose and wake the boys and all Mother's neighbors. Are you trying to tell me that Mrs. Holbrook died and left you—Peter D. Hamilton, Jones Hill, Texas—*all* her money?"

"Yes—but—"

She let out a squeal and started to chatter incoherently. I tried to stop her.

"Amy, I haven't got it yet! None of it. I might never get it— you don't understand—"

She did not hear me. She was screaming excitedly to her mother, and in the background, her mother was adding to the confusion and the noise.

"Amy, listen to me! *Listen!* Don't get excited—not yet. I just found out about it today. Don't get your hopes up. There's been a mistake of some kind."

"You mean you might not get it?"

"I'm not finished yet!"

She waited.

"There's something else," I said. "I was there when she died."

"Where, darling? At the hospital?"

"No. She was at home. I was there."

"What was wrong? Had she been ill?"

"She was poisoned."

She did not respond. She had not understood. I gulped and added, "She was murdered."

She began to pelt me with questions, and I must have answered them. I don't know.

". . . and I've been stopping in to see her every week," I found myself saying into the mouthpiece. "I didn't intend to keep it from you, but somehow—"

"Pete—you're not making any sense. You've never mentioned that you saw Mrs. Holbrook every week. Slow down and start over. *Who* poisoned her?"

"Nobody knows. I've got to go down there tomorrow. The sheriff wants to question me. I mean—not just me. He wants to talk to all of us—everyone who was there. Alberta, Carrie and—"

"Carrie? Was she in Erskine?"

"She moved back."

"You didn't tell me that."

"That's what I mean. I didn't tell you lots of things. I can't explain it all on the telephone. But do you remember that night in Foley I told you about—"

"But I thought you went in the daytime on your way to—"

"Amy!" I said impatiently. "Please—it was sort of late when I left, but that's not important. If your mother's feeling better, can you come home? I need you. Mr. Marsh was here tonight, and he's suspicious about everything I told him. I've got to go back to Erskine tomorrow. Carrie is contesting the will, which isn't surprising, considering Henrietta's mental condition. It won't hold up—"

"Henrietta? Who's Henrietta?"

"Mrs. Holbrook."

"Oh. I didn't—"

"Amy! Please— I can't explain it on the telephone. Please come home."

Her voice softened. "Certainly, I'll come home. You don't sound like yourself at all."

"I'm not, but you still don't understand."

"Understand what?"

"I'm the only person who seems to have a motive."

"Motive for what?"

"For poisoning Henrietta."

"Oh—Pete—" A long pause followed. "Do you mean they think *you* did it?"

"Nobody's said that yet. I didn't know about Henrietta's will. I didn't have the faintest idea. I've got to tell that to somebody tomorrow, but I don't think they'll believe me. It sounds too thin. Can you come home?"

"You know I can."

"I don't suppose you know what time you can get here?"

"I'll check on the flights as soon as we hang up. But don't worry, darling. All three of us will get there as soon as we can make it."

"Look—I probably won't be able to meet your plane. I don't know when I'll get back from Erskine. I think there's an airport limousine you can—"

"Don't worry," she cut in. "Don't you think I can find my own way home?"

❧ 20 ❧

". . . and all the rest, residue, and remainder of my estate, real, personal and mixed, wheresoever it is located, I give, devise and bequeath to the good friend of my deceased son, Benjamin, and my own good friend, Peter Dewitt Hamilton, to his absolute use forever. . . ."

J. A. Tolliver read on, glancing smugly at me from time to time to gauge my appreciation of his shamelessly dramatic performance. I watched him, half amused, only partly understanding the legal jargon. Standing squarely at stage center, he had no intention of relinquishing the spotlight until his role had been squeezed dry.

He held the paper with long, slim fingers, while his other hand caressed his thin hair which was parted on the side and plastered tightly into an arch across his skull. His eyes, magnified by the thick lenses of his black-rimmed spectacles, devoured the words greedily. His puffy jaws worked up and down like a chipmunk chewing its food. He illustrated the reading with an extravagant repertoire of limp and fluttery gestures. Watching him, I concluded that he was a middle-aged bachelor, overindulged and pampered, probably by an aging mother or spinster sister, and the owner but not necessarily the master of the household in which they lived.

He finished the reading and sat back.

"Well now—that wasn't so tedious, was it?"

I scarcely knew whether to ask him questions or applaud. He watched me eagerly.

"It gave no indication of the size of the estate," I said.

"Oh, wills never do," he replied. "They must be couched in terms to cover any and all contingencies. Estates fluctuate, you know."

"Can you give me an idea?"

I had scored heavily. It was the question he had been waiting for.

"Why, I might be able to do that," he said. "Yes, I just might." He smiled. "But only an approximation, you understand. An exact accounting would require a financial rendering by the bank. Then that would be good only for today. Tomorrow it might be different."

He took a manila folder from his desk and flipped it open, humming happily and making a production of studying a mass of figures on long sheets of paper.

"A most handsome estate—*most* handsome," he said. "Mr. Holbrook did well in his lifetime, believe me. He didn't just sit back and live on his inherited wealth, although he could have done that. No, indeed! He added to it—and he was *such* a gentleman. Beautiful manners. Beautiful! Anybody in Erskine will tell you that. Of course, there's the matter of taxes, state and federal, attorney's fees, to say nothing of the restraining order that has been clamped on us. Now let me see. . . ."

He resumed his humming as he ran his fingers down the pages. Abruptly, he ceased operations and exclaimed, "Oh, my! What must you think? Here I am humming and singing and poor Mrs. Holbrook's not yet in her grave. The funeral is to be this afternoon, you know. Or maybe you didn't know. It was decided only this morning." He peered into my face. "Did you know?"

I shook my head.

He assumed an expression of piety and returned to his paper. After a suitable interval, he laid the folder aside.

"All in all, I would estimate—and *please*, you must promise not to take these figures literally. They're subject to enormous amounts of revision and change. You must keep that in mind. I would estimate that poor Mrs. Holbrook's estate runs in the neighborhood of a million dollars. Isn't that a nice neighborhood?" He leaned back and lost himself in a peal of high-pitched giggling.

I whistled long and low. "I had no idea. . . ."

"You're in an enviable position, Mr. Hamilton," he said. "You understand, I'm sure, that the estate is not readily convertible into cash. Large estates never are. There's real estate here and in Fort Worth and Dallas, and oodles and oodles of ranchland somewhere out in the boondocks. There are stocks and investments and at least two producing oil wells." He lifted his eyes to the ceiling and rolled them around. "Not heavy producers, but oil is oil, you know." He shivered deliciously.

"I had no idea that Mrs. Holbrook was worth all that much."

"Oh, heavens, yes!" Then, confidentially, "I already knew, of course. Some people, however, will be surprised that it is not more. People always exaggerate wealth—especially small-town people. But make no mistake about it, my boy, you have come into a lovely estate. Lovely, lovely, lovely. And it's all solid as a rock. No flyers in the stock. It's blue-chip and gilt-edged all the way. As trustworthy as her diamonds—they're yours too, you know. I hope you can see now why I advised you to seek legal counsel. There's far too much at stake."

"Not really," I said.

He looked at me blankly. "I don't believe I understand," he said.

"That estate doesn't belong to me. I know it, and if you handled Mrs. Holbrook's affairs, you knew her mental condition, and you must have known it when you drew up this will. You must have known it was a mistake."

"Certainly, I knew her mental condition. Everybody knew about it. And I don't mind telling you that she changed her will frequently. That, too, was common knowledge."

"Then the whole thing belongs to Carrie, not to me."

"It does belong to you," he said firmly. "Nobody but you. Don't ever forget that." He grew thoughtful. "Carrie *is* a problem, I'll admit. The boy is the only living relative, and he's directly in line. The law listens with great respect to such claimants. He'll be your biggest problem." He lowered his voice and leaned forward. "It's common knowledge that poor Mrs. Holbrook refused to accept either the boy or his mother until recently. Let me tell you, when she came back here, this whole town was positively agog. And she's such a beautiful girl. *Perfectly* gorgeous! And poor Mrs. Holbrook was an exquisite creature herself."

"Why didn't Mrs. Holbrook revise her will to provide for Carrie and the boy?"

Mr. Tolliver raised his eyebrows. "Who can say? Perhaps she intended to but just never got around to it. Heavens! How could she have known that she would be murdered in her own bed?" He shuddered.

"But you must have known something of her intentions. Didn't she say anything about providing for Carrie and Ben?"

"Tick-a-lock-tick-a-lock-all-the-way-round, Mr. Hamilton!" he sang, running his fingers around his lips. "That's for me to know and you to find out. Privileged information, you know. A lawyer is bound to respect the confidences of his clients."

"Okay—but suppose she *did* intend to change her will, even though she didn't—wouldn't that put a different face on the matter?"

"No. Absolutely no! A thousand times no! Whatever she might have intended to do doesn't count. It's what she actually did that's important. That's all. It's the law. The significant thing is that she did *not* change her will. It's as legal as the day is long, dear sir—so far, anyway. You've got a fight on your hands, but in the meantime, the estate is yours—the cattle, the land, the oil wells, the stocks, the bonds, even that old pile of bricks on the hill where she lived. It's all yours. I hope you know something about cows. She's got cows strolling all the way from here to Waco—Black Angus, a very expensive breed. You won't find any Flossies and Bessies among Black Angus. They're far too aristocratic for peasant names like that."

"What if I don't want to fight?" I asked.

Mr. Tolliver stiffened. He removed his spectacles to reveal a pair of tiny green eyes. He blinked them rapidly. "Would you mind repeating what you just said?"

"I said, what if I don't want to fight?"

"Surely you can't be serious, Mr. Hamilton," he said in a whisper. "You don't realize what you're saying."

"Why not? The whole thing's a fluke. There's no reason for me to get Mrs. Holbrook's money—not even part of it. I knew her for only a few months. She must have made this will during one of her spells. There's no reason to think it will stick. Furthermore, I don't have the time or the money for a lot of legal battles that I can't win and have no right to win. I've got a job—a good job—and I want to get back to it. This kind of thing doesn't happen to people like me, and I'd be kidding myself to think otherwise. So, tell me this: suppose I just step aside and waive my rights to the estate?"

He slipped his spectacles back on and glared at me. "May the Lord bless us all!" he said. "You're good for a surprise a minute, aren't you? Well, just take off your shoes and sit back and listen to this. The State would hold it and consider all claims against it. And you may be assured that claimants will be coming out of the woodwork. As far as we know, there are no surviving relatives of Mr. and Mrs. Holbrook, but it's possible that a far, far distant cousin whom nobody knows will show up from nowhere and claim it. If he can prove the relationship, he'll get the estate. And let me insert a parenthetical statement to you, while I'm at it: when an estate is up for grabs, fortune seekers come on the scene like a plague of locusts. Oooooh! They'll be around—don't you worry about that! In any event, the State can hold the estate indefinitely. Some estates have been held in a legal limbo for seventy, eighty or a hundred years. Possibly, Alberta can file a claim against it as a longtime friend, protector and body servant, but she has no legal status or rights, as such. Dr. Kriegel can do the same."

"How about Carrie?"

"Her position would be similar to theirs. She's an in-law, and as such, she has no survivor rights. She could file a claim, though, and hope for the best. Keep one thing in mind: the State of Texas wouldn't love you for waiving your rights. For the State, it would be nothing but an endless series of headaches, defending it against one claimant and then the next—and the State is obligated to actually *defend* it against all claimants. So, when all's said and done, it costs the State a lot of money to take over an estate like this. So that, young fellow, is why you'll make no Brownie points with the Lone Star State by waiving your rights."

"All right," I said, "but I wasn't thinking about the State of Texas so much as I was thinking about Carrie. Isn't there some way I can let her win by default?"

"Certainly not! She has to present a case of her own, regardless of what you do or don't do. Your name is on that will, and the only way Carrie or anybody else can get it off is to prove that it got there by some unapproved or frowned-upon methods. Of course, she doesn't know at this stage just how that can be done."

"I'm sure I don't know how my name got there either," I said. "Maybe Carrie will find a way."

"You sound as though you hope she does." He looked disappointed. Then he brightened. "But then, who wouldn't? A gorgeous creature like her! I'd be less than human if I didn't wish her every success in the world."

"It's not that. It's just that—"

"Don't you want a million dollars?"

"Who doesn't? But not this way. Let's be realistic about it, Mr. Tolliver. As Mrs. Holbrook's attorney, you must have *some* kind of moral obligation to speak up about her state of mind when she made this will."

Mr. Tolliver bounced up from his chair and pranced back and forth. "Now listen to what I have to say," he said. "You'll find it very relevant. It was Mrs. Holbrook's privilege to do whatever

(151)

she wished with her money, and that includes giving it to you."
He pointed a lean, white finger at me and wagged it primly.
"There's no legal requirement that anyone has to agree with her
choice in the matter. That's why old women can leave fortunes
to their cats—it's their own affair. The citizens of Erskine can
picket your home, burn you in effigy, sign petitions against you,
and it would not weaken your legal claim to the estate or your
justifiable position in trying to hold onto it. It's *yours*. And I
would deplore—positively *deplore*—your giving it up without so
much as a struggle." He waited for that to sink in. "But aside
from the legalities and technicalities of the law, people just don't
give away a million dollars. They just don't, and I plead with
you not to be so casual about such a possibility. It makes my
skin crawl!"

"Why are you—you personally—so upset by the prospects of
my not getting the money, Mr. Tolliver?"

He stopped his prancing and came to rest in front of me, poised
and balanced, ready to take off again at any moment.

"Mr. Hamilton, first of all, I respect the law, and if the law
says the money belongs to you, I listen with reverence. Second,
I am a man of principle. I don't simply preach about my principles—I live by them. And in principle, I'm unalterably and irre-
vocably opposed to giving away a million dollars. You or anybody else. You can't do it. *I just don't believe in it!* And I can't
let you do it. I just cannot!" His voice rose into a screech. "It's—
it's—" His face turned red, and tiny crystals of saliva spewed
from a corner of his mouth as he sputtered and searched for the
right word. "It's, it's—it's *immoral!*"

I broke into laughter. He looked at me with surprise.

"I certainly don't see anything funny," he said peevishly.
"You aren't compelled to take my advice, you know. You
haven't retained me." His voice took on a wistful tinge, his eyes
a wistful cast. "But I wish you had. Oh, you can't possibly know
how much I would love to represent you in this matter. At this
moment, I'd rather have you for a client than anyone I know.
Wills are extremely difficult to break, and this one has built-in

obstacles that the best attorney in Texas could stub his toe on—not to mention the unpleasant prospect of having me for an adversary. By the way, did you contact an attorney?"

I told him that I had left home too early to attend to it.

"Well, never mind. They'll find you. Just sit still long enough, and they'll be knocking on your door. Have you seen the papers this morning?"

The events in Erskine had moved to the front pages of the Fort Worth newspapers, not in the lead-off position but conspicuous, nevertheless. The details had been scant, but enough to start my telephone ringing before I had opened my eyes. The first two calls had come from crackpots, the third from a reporter who said he had come to my house but was unable to rouse anybody. He asked me for a comment. I told him that I was in no position to comment on the Holbrook will until I had seen it with my own eyes. I received other calls, but I made no attempt to talk to the callers. I reported all that to Mr. Tolliver.

"All the reporters will be after you, never fear. You'll be hearing from lawyers, too. Just don't take the first one that comes along. He'll be an ambulance chaser for sure. Believe me, you'll get more offers of assistance than you can handle. Don't let yourself get taken in. Keep your independence."

He looked at me longingly. Then his owlish face broke into a smile. It was real and it was warm, like a firm and hearty handshake. Against my will, I found something appealing about the absurd, fluttery, excitable J. A. Tolliver. I was not convinced that my personal interests were his prime motivator, but then he had made no such claim, and I could not criticize him for that.

"I assume you'll be attending services for poor Mrs. Holbrook." He looked pious once more. "It will probably be the largest turnout since her husband died. And that was the longest funeral procession ever to drive through the streets of Erskine. The first car drove through the cemetery gates before the last one left the church."

"I don't know if I'll go or not—or whether I should."

"Oh, I think you should, by all means, Mr. Hamilton. You should attend. Your absence would be frightfully conspicuous."

"So would my presence."

He giggled again. "That's quite good. Quite witty—really!"

"There's the matter of the sheriff," I said. "I haven't seen him yet."

"Oh, good grief! I'd forgotten all about him!" Mr. Tolliver's eyes widened with alarm. "He called the first thing this morning and asked me to get in touch with him as soon as you arrived."

He stuck his face into an intercom on his desk and flipped a switch. "Miss Strange, will you please call Mr. Natwick's office and tell him that Mr. Hamilton is here? We should have done that hours ago. Literally *hours!* It's a wonder he hasn't sent out a posse to bring us in. We must keep on the good side of the law."

He straightened up and laughed happily. "As you can see, Mr. Hamilton, everything in a lawyer's office is not necessarily grim. We have our moments of levity, too. Isn't that evident?"

I laughed along with him. It seemed to be the least I could do.

(154)

❦ 21 ❦

A peculiar thing happened midway in the sheriff's interrogation: I could not recall the sequence of Saturday morning's events. Mr. Natwick, the sheriff, was patient, but whether or not he was understanding, I could not determine.

The man had been an enigma from the beginning. At first, I thought perhaps his deadpan expression, the chill in his gray eyes and his seeming indifference to anything I said were tools of his trade, to be taken out and used when needed. Eventually, however, I decided that off duty or on, he would have been the same. He was flat, dull and uncongenial. Probably in his early forties, his was a description to fit hundreds of men who had no physical distinctions to cull them out of a crowd. He was perhaps five feet ten, of from slight to medium build, with short brown hair and ears that seemed to be pinned flat against his head. I cannot recall now how he was dressed except that he was presentable. He did have an annoying habit of flicking constantly at his cigarette even when there were no ashes to flick, and he smoked incessantly.

His manner gave me no overt cause for complaint. On the contrary, he treated me courteously and with respect. It was just that our dealings were marked by a singular lack of rapport; no feeling flowed between us. I had a notion that he could question me for weeks without cease, then meet me in a corridor or on the street and pass me as though he had never seen me before.

I answered his questions as directly as possible, never certain how he was reacting. He listened passively, reaching out every so often to adjust the volume on a tape recorder at his elbow.

"I know this sounds peculiar, Mr. Natwick," I said, "but I just can't remember who went upstairs first—Carrie or me. It was not important at the time, and I didn't pay any attention."

"It might be important now," he said in his flat voice.

"I know—it's embarrassing."

"Start over—back at the point where you came up the hill after seeing the boy."

He lighted a fresh cigarette from the butt of the old one.

I started again, feeling like a child staying after school to recite his lessons until he had committed them to memory. Tense and anxious to please, I was overcautious. Instead of concentrating on what actually happened, my mind kept going back to how I had told it previously, then leaping ahead to test its sound before saying it again. Consequently, when I came to the sequence in question, I did no better the second time than the first.

"This kind of questioning is a new experience for me," I said by way of apology.

"It is for most people," he said. "Let it go for a while."

"But I'd like to straighten it out. It's a simple thing—too simple to get twisted like this. What did Carrie—Mrs. Holbrook—say about it?"

"You don't need to concern yourself about that." He was looking at me through half-closed eyelids. "There's one thing I'm not clear on," he continued. "Ben Holbrook was your best friend, you say. After the war, you settled down in Jones Hill, twenty or so miles from Ben's home. Five years later, you decided to come down here and drop in on Ben's parents to say hello. Five years is a long wait for that kind of visit. According to your own account, seeing Carrie in the doctor's office is what triggered it. Will you give me more details about that?"

"I don't know any more details. I've already told you all there is. Seeing Carrie revived a lot of old memories, that's all. Maybe I had an attack of conscience, too. Ben and Carrie had meant a lot to me. After the war, I meant to come down to see Ben's parents, but I kept putting it off. Then I had to go to Erskine on business one day, so I called on Mrs. Holbrook while I was there. Later on, my company added Erskine to my regular accounts."

Mr. Natwick sat mute and comfortable, flicking imaginary ashes from his cigarette, waiting for me to continue; while I, in turn, waited for him to prompt me. The silence grew heavy. I gave in first.

"Naturally, I was curious about Carrie's not speaking to me that day. That might have had something to do with it."

"Well—did it?"

"Maybe. I'm not sure. I was concerned, naturally. I wondered what was wrong with her, and that started me to thinking about the Holbrooks—all of them. I didn't go see Mrs. Holbrook for the specific purpose of asking about Carrie, though. That wasn't it at all."

"How many times did you go to Foley?"

"Twice."

"A while ago, you mentioned only one trip. When was the second?"

"The trip I mentioned was the second. I had been once before, but I didn't think to mention it."

"Seems like a peculiar oversight."

"Oh. Well, I didn't see Carrie the first time."

"Why did you go then? Do you have customers in Foley?"

"No."

"Any business at all?"

"No. It's a tiny place. Not large enough to support a business machines dealership."

"What took you there then?"

"A detour from the main highway took me there."

"Did you stop?"

"Yes."

"Why?"

"Well, there I was. I had a Coke in the drugstore."

"Did you try to see Carrie?"

"No."

"Did you inquire about Carrie?"

"Yes. From the man who owns the drugstore. He told me about her and her son, Ben, and about her teaching school and how highly she was regarded in Foley."

"Did you try to telephone her?"

"No. School was in session, and I didn't want to bother her."

"Did you leave a message for her—something like 'Give her my regards' or 'Tell her that Mr. Hamilton inquired about her' or anything like that?"

"No. The druggist asked me to leave my name and he'd tell her I had been in. But I didn't do it."

"Why not?"

"Well . . . she wouldn't speak to me that day in Fort Worth, remember, which would have made any messages from me rather awkward."

"But you *were* checking up on her, weren't you?"

"I wasn't checking up on anybody," I said, raising my voice more than I intended to do.

He lifted an eyebrow slightly and his mouth moved as if to smile. It was the nearest he had come to a visible reaction. "Did you know all along that the Holbrooks were rich people?" he asked.

"I guess I did."

"You knew it, or you didn't. Which was it?"

"Ben never came right out and said his parents were rich, if that's what you mean. But of course, I knew enough about him to piece it all together. I knew that the Holbrooks were of above-average means—I knew that Mr. Holbrook owned a lot of land and cattle. Ben used to follow the stock market, and he'd mention some of his father's stock every now and then. And Carrie used to joke about the oil wells that only dripped oil. She said she wished they would blow their tops. Things like that."

"Did you know that Ben was an only child?"

"Yes, I knew that."

"Did you know that he had no blood relatives other than his parents?"

"Yes, I knew that too. He always said he envied people with aunts, uncles and cousins."

"You knew, then, no doubt, that Carrie was logically in line for the Holbrook estate?"

"I don't remember thinking about it one way or the other."

"You seem to have gone to a lot of trouble to find out if she had remarried. Didn't it occur to you that she was the only person left to inherit the Holbrook money?"

"Not that I recall."

"But you did know it?" he persisted.

"Well, yes. When you put it that way, I guess I did."

He shifted in his chair, looked at his watch and stopped the tape recorder. "You can take time out for a trip down the hall, if you like. Or you can get a cup of coffee down on the first floor."

"I'd rather finish," I said without moving.

"Okay. Suit yourself." He started the recorder again. "Why did you agree to see Mrs. Holbrook for Carrie?"

"Carrie asked me to. She wasn't on friendly terms with her mother-in-law, you see. She wrote her letters, but Mrs. Holbrook didn't answer any of them. She wasn't sure that Mrs. Holbrook even *read* them."

"Why weren't they on friendly terms?"

"It was a family matter—strictly personal. I'd rather you ask Carrie that question."

"Okay. But didn't it take a lot of your time to see Mrs. Holbrook?"

"I didn't mind that. Don't forget—I was in Erskine on Mondays, anyway. It didn't take much extra time, and I did it as a favor—for old time's sake, you might say."

"And that's all?"

"Certainly that's all. Why wouldn't it be?"

"I just asked the question. You answered it."

"She didn't promise me anything in return, if that's what you're getting at."

He let my words hang suspended and waited for me to go on.

"That's what you were leading up to, isn't it?" I asked, irked at myself for anticipating him.

"I might not have been leading up to anything," he said in a monotone. "But since you mentioned it, just go ahead with it. It might be interesting."

"That's all there is to it."

"Why did you mention it, then?"

"I went through all this once with Dr. Kriegel. That might be why I'm touchy on the subject. He doubted my motives—like you do."

Mr. Natwick raised his eyebrows again, this time higher and more spontaneously than before. "Me? I didn't say I doubted your motives."

"Well, Dr. Kriegel did. He seemed to think that you can't do a favor for a friend without ulterior motives."

Mr. Natwick leaned back in his chair and clasped his hands behind his head. The inevitable cigarette dangled loosely from his pale, thin lips. "Carrie Holbrook's a good-looking girl," he said with too much significance to sit well with me. "Dr. Kriegel knows that as well as I do. Maybe that's why he doubted your motives. Anyway, she's too good-looking to have been a widow all this time. And when you add a million dollars, she's better-looking than ever."

His voice trailed off, but I determined to wait him out this time. He watched me placidly, squinting his eyes against the cigarette smoke. Again the silence became thick and heavy. After a time, he sat forward, took the cigarette from his lips and flicked ashes into the wastebasket.

"Does she have a boyfriend?" he asked.

"Why ask me?"

"You're good friends—you said. I thought you might know."

"I don't, though. I guess you'll want to know next if *I'm* her boyfriend."

"I ought to thank you, Mr. Hamilton," he said. "You're saving me lots of time. This is twice you've done it now. Go ahead and answer your own question."

"Well, let's get something straight once and for all, Mr. Natwick," I said heatedly. "There's nothing between Carrie Holbrook and me, and there never has been. That's point Number One. I'm a married man—happily married with two children. That's point Number Two."

I stood up and glared down at him. He was watching the revolving reels on the tape recorder.

"I've never had any designs on Carrie Holbrook or whatever money she might inherit," I continued. "That's point Number Three. And the last and main point is that we did not conspire to do away with her mother-in-law and split the money."

I sat down abruptly. Mr. Natwick hadn't moved.

"Now—that should take care of the rest of your questions and suspicions," I said. "I've read a few detective stories, too, Mr. Natwick, and your plot just won't fit the pattern. You'll have to think up another."

He continued to watch the tape recorder. "I didn't think up that one," he said. "You did."

"All right, then," I said. "Let me finish the story for you. I didn't know about Mrs. Holbrook's will. It was a complete surprise to me."

He said nothing.

"Oh—I forgot one thing," I said. "I did not poison Mrs. Holbrook. Now—is there anything else you'd like to ask?"

"Yes," he said. He shifted in his chair and looked at his watch again. "You haven't mentioned your wife in all this. Is she a friend of Carrie's, too?"

"No. They have never met."

"How about the old Mrs. Holbrook?"

"She didn't know her either."

"Then what did she think about your coming down here so often?"

"I come every week. It's my job. I have an account here."

"I know that. But what did she think about your visiting Mrs. Holbrook every Monday morning?"

"She didn't know anything about it."

This time, his surprise seemed genuine. "Not at *all?*"

"Not after the first couple of visits."

"I see," he said quietly.

But I could see that he did not.

"That'll be all, Mr. Hamilton," he said getting to his feet. "Thank you for coming in. You've been very cooperative."

"But you *don't* see," I said in sudden panic.

"Don't see what?"

"About me and my wife—about her not knowing."

"Then go ahead and explain it—if there's anything you think I ought to know." He dropped back into his chair.

"It wasn't exactly a secret," I said miserably. "My not telling her was of no significance. I don't always tell her about where I eat, who I see, what I do, where I stay when I'm out on the road. I wasn't hiding anything from her. She knew that I had seen Carrie in Foley. The thing you've got to remember is that I usually saw Mrs. Holbrook on Monday morning, and I didn't get back home until Friday night. That's almost a week, and I see a lot of people and cover a lot of miles during that time. Besides, after being gone all week, I'm usually busy when I get home. I've got a wife and two children that I like to be with as much as possible, and there's always something to do around the house or in the yard. Sometimes I go into the office on Saturdays. So—Mrs. Holbrook didn't always figure in our conversations on the weekends. That's the way it's been."

Mr. Natwick gazed at me thoughtfully. "Okay," he said, getting to his feet again. "Anything else?"

"You mean you don't have any more questions?"

"Not for now. Maybe later."

"When?"

"I'll get in touch with you."

"You mean I can go now?"

"Yes. Why not?"

(162)

"I don't know. I just thought that—"

He turned away. I got up to go. At the door, I stopped and looked back. Mr. Natwick was taking a reel off the tape recorder.

❦ 22 ❧

In Mr. Natwick's outer office, a young man with a crew cut and an intricate, oversized camera was waiting for me. He stationed himself squarely in my path, clicked a shutter and set off a blinding explosion in my face. Little circles of purple brilliance hung in a field of darkness, dancing and blinking. When they cleared, I could make out three or four strange men, all carrying cameras.

"One more!" said a voice.

Several explosions this time. The circles multiplied and converged. A hot chemical odor filled the room.

"How long have you known Mrs. Holbrook, Mr. Hamilton?" A telephone rang . . . a door slammed shut. . . . "Why is your wife in St. Louis, Mr. Hamilton?" "Is your wife a friend of young Mrs. Holbrook's?" "No comment," I said. "What's the name of your lawyer, Mr. Hamilton? Why isn't he here?" "No comment," I said. Mr. Natwick was standing in the doorway of his office. . . . From behind her typewriter, his secretary watched and listened. . . .

"Did you know Mrs. Holbrook before she married Ben Holbrook?" "Have you figured out what you're gonna do with the money?" "What's the size of the estate?" The strange men were talking to each other . . . one of them was talking to the stenog-

rapher . . . the stenographer was talking into the telephone . . .
"How often have you seen young Mrs. Holbrook since her husband died?" "Did Mrs. Holbrook tell you she was putting you
in her will?" A door opened and more strangers jammed into
the room . . . Mr. Natwick moved to my elbow, speaking in
his flat voice . . . "—and nobody's being held for anything. This
was preliminary questioning." More questions. . . . "No comment. . . ." "No comment. . . ." More flashbulbs . . . more
noises . . . more purple circles. . . .

Suddenly it was all over.

The stenographer returned to her typewriter. Mr. Natwick
disappeared behind his closed door. The strangers with cameras
pushed out into the corridor. Without knowing exactly how I
got there, I found myself outside and alone.

I stood at the top of the courthouse steps, looking across the
lawn past the rows of parking meters that enclosed the square
like pickets on a fence. Erskine was occupied with itself. People
were hurrying along the sidewalk, getting in automobiles and
getting out, disappearing around corners, darting in doorways,
coming out, going in. Two men came out of the marble-faced
bank on the corner, lingered for a moment in conversation and
walked away in opposite directions. Automobiles turned onto the
square then off again. A boy in a white apron, laden with brown
paper bags, came through the door of a grocery store followed
by a lady. He led her to an automobile where she stood by while
he loaded the bags into the back seat. He stood on the curb and
watched her drive away; then reaching under his apron, he
fished out a cigarette, lighted it and sauntered back into the
store. Incredible as it seemed, business in Erskine was proceed-
ing without interruption. Life flowed in and around the square
and around me as though this day were like any other.

I had almost an hour on my hands before Henrietta's funeral.
Crossing the street, I strolled aimlessly along the sidewalk, uneasy about my performance in the sheriff's office. I had had no
reason to be so defensive against Mr. Natwick's questioning. I had nothing to hide.

I peered through the plate glass window of a café where a blonde, overblown waitress looked up and eyed me indifferently. I walked around three sides of the square and turned back when I saw the office of American Business Machines a few doors ahead of me. I had no desire to talk to Charlie McCash. I returned to my car parked in front of the courthouse. A pain in my stomach reminded me that I had not eaten since the day before, and remembering a drive-in restaurant on the Fort Worth highway, I backed away from the curb and headed for it.

By the time I arrived, the lunch hour had ended, and the restaurant was deserted except for the counterman, who was leaning over a newspaper. He took my order and went back to his reading until the jingle of a bell in the kitchen roused him. Placing my lunch before me, he returned to his newspaper. The quiet sleepiness of the empty restaurant was soothing, and I tried to shut out all reflections, but they pressed in and throbbed like a headache.

By any reckoning, a million dollars was ample motive for murder; and from the sheriff's viewpoint, I had had more than an ample opportunity to murder. With no one to observe me, I had been upstairs while Henrietta slept. I could have slipped in and out of her room without Carrie and Alberta knowing. So Mr. Natwick had the motive and the opportunity in his palm. The third essential—the weapon—thus far had eluded him, but no doubt he was trying for it.

As far as I knew, a bottle of cleaning compound like that described by the medical examiner had not been found. Without it, no complete case could be built against me or anybody else. The bottle was like a missing gun; the suspect had to be linked physically to the gun that killed the victim, and Mr. Natwick had to link somebody to the bottle, or else he had no case. And so far, he had no case. Otherwise, I would not be sitting alone on the outskirts of Erskine, trying to whip up an appetite for a plate of soggy food.

If the coroner's hypothesis proved to be correct, the physical existence of the bottle was a fact; and if it was a fact, the bottle most likely was somewhere on the Holbrook premises. How completely had Mr. Natwick and his deputy searched the house? Had they looked in dresser drawers? In bureaus? In desks? Had they searched pockets of clothes that hung in closets? To be thorough, they must have opened trunks, suitcases, storage cartons, but had they? In a house as large and rambling as Holbrooks', there must be dozens—hundreds—of places to hide items as small as a bottle of cleaning compound. The house was a huge assembly of nooks and crannies, shadows and dark corners. But suppose no one was actually trying to *hide* the bottle. Suppose the bottle was empty and merely had to be disposed of? Had Mr. Natwick searched the garbage cans out back—

Out back?

The phrase turned itself over and again in my head.

A door in a dark corner of my mind came ajar to admit a tiny slit of light. If I was right. . . .

I dropped my fork. It hit the counter and bounced onto the floor with a clatter.

"May I have the check, please?" I said to the counterman.

He looked up from his newspaper, surprised. Moving down the counter, he surveyed my lunch, which had scarcely been disturbed.

"Something wrong with your dinner?" he asked.

"What? Oh—no. No, it was fine. I just remembered—how much do I owe you?"

He looked doubtful. "It's seventy cents, but—"

I gave him a bill and waited for my change.

"I don't like to take your money, mister, since you didn't eat. You're not sick, are you?"

"No, I'm all right, thanks."

I walked slowly back to my car and stood for a minute with my hand on the door handle. Then I got in and drove back toward the center of town and the courthouse. Because of an accident up ahead, I had to turn off the highway a block short of the main intersection, and I suddenly found myself approaching the church where Henrietta Holbrook's funeral was to be conducted. It was an ugly red-brick structure with a squat bell tower and gaudy imitation stained-glass windows. A few cars had already parked at the curb. A small group of early arrivals were going inside.

After my discussion with J. A. Tolliver, I had decided to attend Henrietta's funeral service after all. But my experience with the newspaper reporters had changed my mind. My presence among Henrietta's friends might disturb the dignity of the final rites. I parked before I reached the church, in the shade of a giant elm that stretched halfway across the street, too far away to be noticed but near enough for a clear view of the church entrance. I turned off the engine and sat watching the people arrive.

Cars quickly lined the curb in front of the church and along the side, disgorging people to converge on the building. Soon, cars pulled into the parking spaces in front of me, to the rear and across the street. In twos and threes, men, women and children streamed past me on the sidewalk, on their way to Henrietta Holbrook's funeral.

Presently, a motorcycle policeman rounded the far corner and came toward the church. He stopped in the middle of the intersection nearest me and dismounted. Immediately a hearse came into view, followed by a line of cars with their headlights burning. The cars were dark with people. The hearse came to a halt before the church entrance. The other cars pulled up behind, one at a time. The passengers alighted and gathered uncertainly on the sidewalk and on the grass, waiting for the pallbearers to take the bronze casket into the church.

There was a lump in my throat as I watched Carrie, still in black, holding onto Ben's hand. Dr. Kriegel's unruly hair towered above the cluster of mourners like a white banner. Alberta stood alone and to one side. She was crying into her handkerchief. Mr. Tolliver pranced around the edges of the crowd, craning his neck for a better view. Most of the other people appeared to be old and well dressed—white-haired men in dark suits and old ladies wearing perky little hats. These were her friends.

I started my engine and maneuvered away from the curb. The courthouse square was virtually deserted. A funeral wreath hung on the entrance to the bank; many of the stores and offices were dark. The town had paused for a farewell to one of its leading citizens. I wondered how many people felt genuine grief.

I parked in front of the courthouse and went inside. Mr. Natwick had on his hat, preparing to leave.

"I think I know where the bottle is," I said without preface or explanation.

He took off his hat and laid it on his desk. "And where's that?" he asked, regarding me with only mild interest.

"It's down in the overhang back of the house."

"The what?"

"It's a cave—in the pasture that extends a quarter of a mile or more from the house to the farm below," I said. "It's the back side of Holbrooks' hill, actually."

"I know that," he said, "but how do you know the bottle is in a cave down there?"

"I don't. It's an idea that came to me while I was having lunch. It might work out and it might not. If you'll go out there with me, we can see for ourselves. I'll explain my idea on the way."

"Why aren't you at the funeral?" he asked abruptly.

"I decided that it would be best for me to stay away," I said. "Some reporters might be there, not to mention the town's newfound curiosity about me. Very likely no one would have noticed me, but I didn't want to risk it."

He was silent for a moment. "Okay," he said. "Let's go. I was thinking about going out to Holbrooks' myself and looking around again while everybody was gone."

We went in his car.

The Holbrook house glared silently down on us as we drew near. We turned in at the gate and drove up the hill through the trees. The old house looked gloomier than ever. A family had departed; an era had ended. One at a time, the Holbrooks had gone, never to return. First Ben, then his father, and finally and tragically, his mother. All in all, it had been an unhappy story, and the house seemed to bear silent testimony to the heartbreak it had witnessed.

Getting out of Natwick's car, I waited on the graveled driveway while he stepped onto the veranda and rang the doorbell. We both stood listening for the sound of voices or a sign of activity, perhaps a friend or neighbor who had stayed to straighten the place while everyone else attended the funeral. I heard nothing but the whine of the wind sweeping through crazy zigzags of the old mansion. When no one came to the door, Natwick joined me again.

We walked around to the rear. The dry grass and dead leaves that had blown up around the foundation crackled under our feet. We made our way along the brickwork, past the cellar opening and under the breakfast room windows. I led him to the overhang without a swerve in direction, surprised that it was no farther from the house.

"Here it is," I said. "If I'm right, it will be inside among a lot of bottles, jars and boxes." I leaped from the jutting edge and dropped to my knees on the ground below.

"Hold it!" Natwick said, louder and with more force than usual. "I'm going in there with you."

I crawled under the sheltering rocks with him behind me and strained my eyes into the cool darkness.

Ben's "store" was intact, or at least it seemed to be. I ran my fingers over the random collection of bottles, cans and jars. What was I looking for? With a shock, it came to me that I didn't know. The cleaning compound had a name, but no one knew what it was. I had no conception of the bottle's size or shape. Suppose the label had been torn off or mutilated beyond recognition? How would I recognize one glass bottle from another? My eyes fell on a bottle that was larger and cleaner than the others. The label was intact. I uttered a cry and grabbed it. Holding my breath, I passed it to Natwick.

"See if this is it," I said.

"Just a minute." He took a handkerchief from his pocket, laid it across the palm of his hand and took the bottle from me.

We backed out into the sunlight where we could read the label: ADAMS HOUSEHOLD CLEANING COMPOUND.

The label was multicolored and ornate, bordered in scrolls and curlicues and crowded with printed directions. Its most arresting feature was a gaily colored drawing somewhat like those in comic books, of a bungalow, green grass, red and yellow flowers and a round yellow sun. It was easy to understand how the colorful label might have caught the eye of a child not yet old enough to read the words on it. Hurriedly, I searched among the list of ingredients for the crucial one. It was listed last: *Drenathine*, followed by some percentages and decimal numbers.

We went around the edge of the overhang and started up the hill to the house, climbing rapidly.

"Take it easy," Natwick said. "We're not going to a fire, you know."

Exhilaration and impatience, however, would not let me slow my pace. Although the upward climb was more difficult than I remembered, I trudged on ahead of him, while he followed, panting. We stopped on the circular driveway to catch our breath.

"Okay," he said then, "tell me again how you say that bottle got into that cave."

I repeated what I had said in the car. He listened dutifully as if for the first time, never taking his eyes from my face. When I finished, I knew with dead certainty that he did not believe a word I had said.

"Suppose we go back down to the courthouse," he said. "You can tell me all this again. Me and the tape recorder."

23

Earlier in the day, the sheriff's office had been ominously quiet; now it was permeated by the hum of action and an air of excitement. Mr. Natwick had brought in a burly, athletic, dark-haired fellow, younger than himself but older than I, who could have been a wrestler for all I knew and probably was. No one bothered to tell me his name. His sole function, apparently, was to sit in a chair by the door and train his eyes on me, a job which he performed with thoroughness and persistence. If he turned away from me once, I didn't see him do it.

At a table by a window sat a dreary, thin-faced, middle-aged woman, who either fretted with the tape recorder or scribbled intermittently in a stenographer's notebook, but neither with consistency. I never figured out what her true function was, but she looked to be as efficient as the tape recorder, and Mr. Natwick treated her as impersonally.

Mr. Natwick himself had changed. He looked the same, but his voice now was edged with hardness; his manner was crisper, more decisive, and infinitely less patient. His dull passivity had vanished, and whereas he had previously held back his suspicions with professional restraint, now he gave them full rein. Forcing me through my story again and again, he listened each time as though it were the first; then he pounced on it piece by piece, sentence by sentence, with the undisguised intention of tearing it to shreds. Relentlessly and militantly, he probed. By comparison, our session before noon had been as gracious and cozy as a tea party.

Battered and exhausted, I slugged it out with him, while from each word he seemed to gain momentum and fresh breath. As the afternoon wore on and the weakening sun lay across the floor in tired streaks, I got an inkling of how false confessions are made, signed and sworn to. At times I could have been persuaded to trade a confession for a few minutes of privacy and consider my end of it a bargain. I concluded that physical and mental stamina are the crucial factors in an interrogation, not the guilt or innocence of the suspect.

"Please, let's stop for a while," I pleaded. "I can't think any more. I can't add to what I've already told you. We've been over the same thing again and again."

Mr. Natwick looked at the stenographer by the window. He glanced at his watch.

"Okay, Hamilton," he said. "Take a few minutes. The men's room is down the hall." He jerked a thumb toward the big man by the door. "He'll go with you," he added.

I ignored his invitation or suggestion or whatever it was. My only thought, and it was a pleasant one, was that I was to have a recess, an interlude all my own. Everything else was secondary. The big man stepped forward.

"You want to go down the hall?" he asked with a gentleness that surprised me. It was the first time I had heard the sound of his voice.

I shook my head.

"Cup of coffee?"

I nodded.

The thin-faced lady walked across the room and mumbled something through the door. In a moment, a hand reached back through the door with a paper cup of black coffee. I stood by the window drinking it. It was tasteless. My entire being was like a foot gone to sleep.

(173)

The door opened and closed. A chair scraped the floor. I heard voices behind me. The sound of my own name brought me around.

"Okay, Hamilton, let's go," said Mr. Natwick.

I took my seat mechanically. The thin-faced woman was at her table again, pencil poised, ready to write. She turned on the tape recorder and the two reels began their revolutions.

"You know, I've questioned lots of people who didn't mind shoving the blame off onto somebody else," Mr. Natwick began. "That's nothing. Hoodlums and petty crooks do it all the time. But this is the first time I've ever questioned anybody who tried to blame a murder on a five-year-old child. For my money, that's sinking pretty low."

"I didn't say he murdered her," I said. "You keep twisting it around. A five-year-old child doesn't murder anybody. He didn't know what he was doing. He wanted the bottle for his store, so he emptied it into Mrs. Holbrook's water pitcher and took it, that's all. It wasn't murder. It was an accident."

"The coroner said it was homicide."

"That's his version. Mine is that Ben did it, but not willfully nor maliciously."

"Where did he get the bottle?"

"From wherever it was kept in the house. In a closet, I guess."

"Which closet?"

"How should I know which closet? Ask Alberta."

"You have theories on everything else. I thought you might have a theory on this. Did you give it to him?"

"Certainly not!"

"Do you know who did?"

"No—I mean, I don't know that anybody gave it to him."

"How about Alberta?"

"No—she wouldn't give him a bottle that was not empty."

"You're only supposing, Hamilton."

"What else do you expect? I wasn't an eyewitness. How about fingerprints?"

"Yours are on the bottle."

"Certainly my fingerprints are on the bottle! I picked it up and handed it to you."

"I know that. All I said is that your prints are on the bottle."

"You could have prevented my touching that bottle, you know."

"I'm not concerned with fingerprints," he said. "I'm concerned with your intelligence, which I'm beginning to suspect. Now just listen to what you did. Just listen to how brilliant it all sounds."

He had been standing with one elbow resting on a file cabinet. Now he stood up straight and moved a step toward me. "First of all," he said, "you tried the oldest gag in the business: you teamed up with a good-looking widow for her money. The only original angle was that you teamed up with *two* widows—the young one who was in line to inherit the money *plus* the old one who already had it. That's a switch, I'll admit. You had it made, either way, but apparently you figured your best route was through the young one. So you came back here to help patch things up between Carrie and her mother-in-law. Then later, the two of you could take care of the old lady and split the money."

He hoisted a foot onto a chair and leaned an elbow on his knee. "Now doesn't all that sound familiar? I must have seen a .hundred movies with variations on that plot. They grind them out like weenies. It doesn't take a smart man to know that in a homicide case where there's money and a good-looking blonde widow, police will immediately look for a boyfriend, especially the johnny-come-latelies—the ones who show up out of the blue. That's you.

"But things didn't work out exactly as planned. They worked even better. Mrs. Holbrook left *you* her money. I don't know how you engineered it, and for some reason I doubt that you engineered it at all. Don't ask me why. I just doubt it. Anyway, there you are, not with half a fortune but all of it. What more could you want? But suppose that somewhere along the line Mrs. Holbrook changed her mind and took you out of her will and put Carrie in? You wouldn't want that, now would you? Why split a million dollars if you can have it all to yourself? So you had to act fast and get rid of Mrs. Holbrook before she changed her will again."

I listened in wonder and saw that, given another cast of characters, Mr. Natwick's cock-and-bull story even had a ring of probability. He continued:

"So on Saturday, you went upstairs, emptied that bottle into the water pitcher and hid the bottle until you could get rid of it permanently; then you went back to eat lunch. But now, here's where you were dumb again. Why in hell didn't you get rid of that bottle? I can think of a hundred ways you could have done it. Breaking it into little pieces or sticking it in your pocket or in your car and taking it back to Fort Worth are simple ones. I'll say this, though: you hid it well. I went over that place from top to bottom, but I didn't think about that cave. You could have wiped the prints off and put the bottle back in the closet easier than you could have taken it down that hill. But it's like I said, I'm having doubts about your intelligence."

He paused and cocked his head to one side. "So that's how it is—the way I figure it. And there's one thing for sure, Hamilton. You're no professional. Little Ben Holbrook could have figured this one out."

"And little Ben Holbrook would be just as wrong as you are," I said. "You don't even believe that story yourself. If you did, your own intelligence would be suspect."

"How do you figure that?" He was looking at me keenly.

"Because, first of all, I had no way of knowing that Mrs. Holbrook owned a bottle of Adams Cleaning Compound. And even if I did, I would not have known where she kept it. Until I went looking for Ben, I had never been upstairs in that house. What's more, I did not stay upstairs long enough to search for and find the bottle and pour it into Mrs. Holbrook's water pitcher. This can be put to the test. Work it out for yourself and see how long it takes. Check with Carrie and Alberta and see how long I stayed upstairs. Then see if I had enough time. In the second place, taking that bottle to the overhang would be the surest way in the world to get caught. It's out in the wide open. Everybody in the house could have seen me if I had run down that hill in broad daylight. None of this is to mention the insane possibility that I might know of an obscure chemical in an obscure cleaning compound that not even the local merchants know about. So you see, Mr. Natwick? You can't possibly believe your own story—you've got more intelligence than that."

"How do I know that you didn't put that bottle in the overhang yourself?" he asked. "You say you didn't, but how do I know that? I went along with you to *find* it certainly, but how do I know that you didn't set up the whole thing so you could say, 'The sheriff of Erskine County was present when I found it'? Don't be juvenile, Hamilton. None of that overhang business has been proven by a long shot. Not yet."

"You're stuck with it, though," I said. "You've got to believe and promote the overhang story or else admit that the bottle was somewhere else on the premises. You swore that you searched the house from top to bottom. You can't afford to admit that you simply overlooked it. No, Mr. Natwick, you're stuck with the overhang story."

"No, I'm not," he said. "For all I know you could have had it in your glove compartment while we were searching the house. The important thing is that you were the only person who knew where it was. That's all I need for what I've got to do. You led me straight to it without a hitch." He took his foot down from the chair and sat up straight. "Why didn't you tell your wife about all your visits with Mrs. Holbrook?" he asked suddenly.

I covered my face with my hands and groaned. "Not again! We've been through that a dozen times. I have an account in Erskine and—"

"Okay—you didn't want her to know what was going on between you and Carrie Holbrook. Isn't that it?"

"No, no, no- -that is not it. Nothing was going on!"

"You said Carrie sent you to see Mrs. Holbrook. What kind of deal did she make with you?"

"She didn't make a deal with me."

"Oh, yes—I forgot. You did it out of the goodness of your heart. Are you still hanging onto that one? That's cornier than the plot itself."

"I don't see what's so hard to believe about it," I said. "What's so strange about doing a favor for somebody?"

He took a long, tired breath and let it out slowly. "Just this," he said. "When a favor involves a million dollars and ends up in homicide, it's hard to believe that it was purely a friendly favor and nothing else."

"According to your reasoning, then, you judge the motives of an act by how the act itself turns out."

"Look, Hamilton. This might surprise you, but I've been to school. College. Surprised? I've been around, and I know a thing or two. I'm not one of your small-town hick constables, fresh in off the farm with straw in his hair. And I don't intend to be sheriff of Erskine County for the rest of my life. But I got elected to this job to deal in law enforcement, not philosophy. But if you want to put all this on a moral plane, I happen to believe that a person must be responsible for the consequences of his actions, and the fact that his motives might be as pure as the driven snow doesn't lessen that responsibility in the least. That's why people can be held liable for accidents. So when you did this big favor for Carrie and started this whole ball to rolling, you must—whether you like it or not—bear some responsibility for what happened later. That's the moral angle to the generous favor you did for Carrie."

He walked to a window and leaned against the sill. "But I don't work on that level," he said. "I work on the legal level. In my business, I start figuring from the opposite end. I start with the act and work my way *backwards* to the motive. That's exactly what I've done in your case. I've got an act of homicide on my hands. I've got a motive that fits like a glove. I've connected you physically with the lethal weapon; and you had ample opportunity to commit the act. That's one-two-three. Just like that. It's all I need. Do you think you can convince your wife of this claptrap you've been giving me?"

"Amy? Of course I can," I said. "And that reminds me: she should be back home tonight or maybe she's already there. I need to call and tell her where I am."

"We'll get in touch with her and tell her."

"You mean I can't make a phone call?"

"You can call a lawyer if you like."

"A lawyer? I don't know any lawyers."

"It might behoove you to find one," he said indifferently.

"What's going on here?" I exclaimed, half rising from my chair. "Are you arresting me?"

He nodded grimly.

"On this pulp-fiction evidence you've got?" I asked.

"It's enough."

"You're reaching, Mr. Natwick," I said. "Why, my own two children could punch holes in your fairy tale."

"Then maybe you'd better get your own two children to come in and start punching," he said, "because I'm holding you on a charge of homicide."

"You must be out of your head!" I said, getting to my feet. "You can't get an indictment against me, and you know that as well as I do."

He shrugged. "If not, you'll be turned loose," he said. "It's that simple. Meanwhile, you're under arrest. I'll leave the indictment to the grand jury."

"Where do you intend to hold me?"

"In the county jail."

I sank back into my chair and stared at him.

"Do you want a lawyer?" he repeated. "I'll get you the telephone if you do."

"I don't want but one thing from you," I said, "and that's for you to leave me alone."

Mr. Natwick stretched lazily and looked at the recording machine. The tape had almost run out. "Okay," he said. He yawned and looked at me curiously. "What I can't figure out, though, is how you can hold out for so long without a trip down the hall."

He moved about the room, speaking to the thin-faced lady by the window and the big man by the door. I was conscious of their voices but not what they said.

I sat in silence. The big man opened the door and motioned to me, and at last, I stirred. The stenographer outside had covered her typewriter and was tidying her desk before leaving. As we passed through the office, she looked at me curiously. The big man and I went to the men's room and back again without saying a word.

❧24❧

The Erskine County jail sat to itself, isolated from everything that looked decent, on a leftover, forgotten street on the seedy fringes of the business district. In a scraggly area dotted by warehouses, storage tanks, a loading dock and a cotton gin, the narrow, two-story building sat back from the street alongside the railroad tracks and a heap of oil drums. Squarely across the street, an old auction shed, long since abandoned to the weeds and the rats, leaned at a perilous angle contemplating its own collapse.

The big man from Mr. Natwick's office got out of the car. He seemed ashamed. "This is it," he said softly. "You'll be treated okay." Apparently, it was as close to an apology as he dared get.

The jail was faded by the weather and worn slick by age, the kind of building that endures stubbornly year after year, resistant to change, still too serviceable and sturdy to tear down. The dirty grilled windows leered at me obscenely.

Inside, in an ill-lighted cracker box of a room, the big man signed some papers and turned me over to a toothless old man with hacking cough and a bald head, who stared at me in wonder, as though I were an exhibit in a sideshow. He tore himself away long enough to gather up a towel, a bar of unwrapped soap and a dingy white mattress cover.

"He's staring at your clothes," the big man explained. "They're too good. He's not used to anyone who looks like he can afford a square meal."

The old man dumped the articles on the counter, and I picked them up. He took a key from the desk behind him and motioned me through a door. The big man watched me go.

"Somebody will be around to see you about a lawyer," he said.

"Will you call my wife?"

"We'll keep trying," he answered. He smiled faintly.

Upstairs, the cells, perhaps six in all, adjoined one another in a single row. They opened out onto a narrow aisle that ran the length of the building and looked out over the vacant lot and the backsides of Erskine's business district. The old jailer locked me into a cell alone; those on either side were empty. At least, I would have a measure of privacy. He went down the stairs, coughing and wheezing, and a door closed behind him. Then all was quiet.

Somewhere along the aisle, a man began humming fragments of a tune. He stopped abruptly. "Who are you?" he called out.

I did not answer.

"Which cell? Number Two or Number One?"

I said nothing.

"What're you in for?" the man asked. His voice was husky, and it was not unkind. He waited. The quiet was oppressive. I did not disturb it. I did not trust my own voice.

"You and me are the only ones up here," he said helpfully. "Another guy was in Number One, but he got out yesterday. I been up here by myself ever since. . . . You'll be talking by tomorrow," the voice went on. "This place will make you talk soon enough. They ain't nothing to do but look out the window, and they ain't nothing to see when you do. Take a good look outside before it gets dark and see for yourself."

He went back to his humming.

I stood in the middle of the floor, unable to move. The mattress rolled up on the bunk and the two faded brown blankets stacked on top, the discolored lavatory and the open zinc toilet in the corner, the stone walls lined with obscene drawings, dirty words and filthy verses, all were temporary. They had nothing to do with me. I wouldn't let them. The naked light bulb suspended from the ceiling by a single cord was not burning, and I resolved that when night came I would not let it burn. To cover the place with darkness might help.

"You eat supper before you come?" asked the voice.

I opened my mouth and formed the word "no," but no sound came out.

"They already fed me," the voice went on. "You didn't miss nothin'. Nothin' at all."

I thought about the clean modern lines of our house in Jones Hill, the snug comfort of our bedroom, of Kenny or Skeeter crying out in the night, of Amy leaping from the bed, of the soft words and soft crooning, of darkness again. Familiar darkness. . . .

Voices downstairs, a general commotion and the opening and closing of doors brought me back with a start. Someone was coming up the stairs. I turned my back to the door. Swift, choppy steps came on up the stairs, into the aisle and stopped before my cell. I didn't move.

"Oh, *there* you are, Mr. Hamilton!"

I spun around to see Mr. Tolliver, peering at me anxiously from behind his thick-lensed spectacles, his eyes large and wide. His face was a comic mixture of alarm, sympathy and curiosity.

"I was never so glad to see—" I began.

"I brought you two sandwiches," he said, sticking a brown paper bag through the bars. "One's ham and the other's chicken salad. I don't guarantee either of them. As a matter of fact, I should warn you against them. They came from Erskine's leading café, where the food is atrocious! It's probably no better than the hobo rations you get here."

I took the bag gratefully and tried to thank him, but he went on chattering and paid no attention.

"I don't know why you didn't listen to me about the lawyer," he admonished. "You might not be in this sinkhole if you had

(183)

listened. *Really*, Mr. Hamilton! You've got to take somebody's advice on these matters. You're *so* inexperienced."

"Things happened too fast," I said. "There wasn't time. From the minute I got out of bed this morning until this very moment, it's as though I've been in the middle of a whirlwind."

"Don't you worry about that. I'll get you out. I'm going to call Fort Worth and find you a good attorney. The selection in Erskine is limited. I'm the best in town, but unfortunately I'm not available." He raised his hands, palms forward. "Now don't get too upset. I know how tragic that is, but perhaps I can represent you some other time when you get yourself into another jam. You need an intelligent attorney—one who's frightfully expensive. In the meantime, I want you to promise me that you won't talk to anyone about your case. Did you sign a confession? I hope they didn't use a rubber hose on you."

"No—nothing like that."

"Thank heavens!" he exclaimed. "Lawyers are always getting saddled with clients after they've signed some foolish confession that complicates things wickedly. Don't sign your name to anything—not even a letter to your wife. Put your X on it. It may be tomorrow before I can get anyone down here to see you. Don't talk to any reporters, either. Why haven't you had your supper?"

"Nobody offered me any. Anyway, I'm not hungry."

"Eat those sandwiches and you'll feel better. On the other hand, you might feel worse. I just don't understand why somebody doesn't open a decent restaurant here. Going out for dinner in Erskine is a depressing experience—vastly less cheerful than funerals. If I weren't a lawyer, I'd be a restaurateur myself. I'm a good cook—when I have time. Don't forget what I told you about the reporters, now."

"I talked to some reporters this morning in Mr. Natwick's office, and one tried to talk to me on the telephone in Jones Hill before I left home."

"Oh, that didn't count." He dismissed it with a fluttery wave of the hand. "That was before your arrest. You're big news now.

They'll be around again, screaming and carrying on something awful. Just don't you say one word to them. Not even hello and good-bye."

"Can't the jailer keep them out?"

"*That* old fool?" Mr. Tolliver screwed up his face in disgust. "There's a rule against visitors up here in the cells, but he doesn't know it. I could have walked up those stairs with a toolkit full of hacksaws without bothering to conceal a thing. His only qualification for the job is that he went on relief during the Depression and stayed on it for three years after the Relief Act was terminated. If the reporters come up here, just turn your back and pretend not to see them. Like you did me."

I agreed.

"They've already been out to poor Mrs. Holbrook's house taking pictures and driving Alberta and Carrie out of their minds. It was on the radio—six o'clock news from Dallas. Oh, it'll be tomorrow's headlines, all right. You can count on that. Why, when I went after those sandwiches, everybody was talking about you. That impossible waitress—she has warts on her hands as big as quarters—when she discovered that the sandwiches were for you, she almost wet her pants! She bellowed it to everybody in the café, and they all stopped eating. You can't blame them for that. They needed something to take their minds off that food. I'm telling you, this whole town is agog. *Positively agog!* Nothing like this has ever happened in Erskine before. We haven't been on the front page of the Dallas newspapers since a tornado blew the roof off the depot back in 'thirty-seven."

"This is bad enough without publicity," I said. "I do appreciate your interest in me, though. You must have lots of your own affairs that need looking after."

"I'll look after them later. For a man with a million dollars, you don't have as many friends as you should," he said. He leaned back from the bars and lost himself in a fit of high-pitched giggling. "Don't mind my witticisms, Mr. Hamilton. I'm just trying to cheer you up. I'm irrepressible. Frankly, I don't see how you stand this dreadful place." He shuddered. "I went to a council meeting once and brought up the subject of a new jail—or a bucket of paint for this one. No one listened to me. Jails always have the lowest priority on a county budget. One of the councilmen said, 'If people don't like our jail, they ought to stay out of trouble and not get locked up in it.' I couldn't believe my ears when I heard that Natwick had arrested you. He's a cold number, that one, but I never *dreamed* that he'd lock you up. You're not the type. You look too respectable, and let's face it, this just isn't a coat-and-tie jail. But why did he turn you loose this morning, then arrest you this afternoon? So he could chase you through the streets and capture you in front of the voters? It's common knowledge that he's got his eye on a job with the law-enforcement division of the Attorney General's office in Austin, but he doesn't need to be *this* theatrical to get it. Gracious!"

"He's dreamed up a case that not even a third-grader would swallow. I'm positive that he doesn't believe it himself. But it's the only case he's got, so I guess he's playing the grandstand with it."

"Well, you know what they say: half a case is better than none. You know, I just made that up on the spot. Wasn't it dreadful? Tell me all about your case so I can ration my sympathy in proper proportions. I don't promise to advise you, though."

I explained about the overhang and the cleaning compound and Mr. Natwick's three-hour grilling. Mr. Tolliver clutched the bars with both hands, peering through them eagerly. Before I had finished, he was sputtering.

"Mr. Hamilton! Leaving you alone even a minute is perilous!" he wailed. "You had no business leading Natwick to that evidence, sonny boy. I think you're trying to convict yourself. You just might succeed, too."

"What should I have done—kept my mouth shut?"

"Yes *indeedy!*" he screamed. He put his hand to his forehead and closed his eyes as if nauseated. "Yes, yes, indeedy, yes! Listen. Natwick gets paid for finding household cleaning compounds in caves. He got himself elected to public office to get to the bottom of crimes—not to lead lambs to slaughter. You *gave* him his case. It was an outright donation. He lacked only one thing—your connection with that bottle, and you gave him that. No rubber hose. No bloodhounds. No truth serums. No lie detectors. You *forced* it on him. Why didn't you gift-wrap it while you were at it?"

"But I had a theory on where the bottle was, and why," I said. "It worked out right, too. Are you trying to tell me that I have no moral obligations to help set the facts straight?"

He snorted. "The law is a moral instrument, you know," he said. "It's not exactly insensitive to the plight of individuals under suspicion or otherwise in trouble. It has little provisions scattered around here and there to keep people like you from convicting themselves unwittingly. One of the better known is the Fifth Amendment to the Constitution of the United States. It's a neat little paragraph. You ought to sit around and read it for pastime instead of going around getting your neck measured for nooses. I'll bring a newspaper in the morning so you can see how they get everything twisted. They will. They always do."

The man in the other cell coughed. Mr. Tolliver cocked an ear in that direction. "Who's that? Billy the Kid?" he whispered.

I shook my head.

"I should have lowered my voice," he said. "My advice is too expensive and sought-after to let him have it free of charge."

He studied my face for a moment then shook his head in disbelief.

"You know, a photographer was outside the church snapping pictures of poor Mrs. Holbrook's casket when we came out. It was such a lovely funeral, and the music was sad, sad, sad. I could hear 'Rock of Ages' at a horse race and start weeping. I have never seen so many flowers in my life. I wouldn't be surprised if the local florist doesn't buy himself a yacht and take a Caribbean cruise after that one. But wasn't that an outrageous thing to do? If anybody takes pictures of my casket, I'll rise up and haunt them on the spot. Carrie didn't take it nearly as hard as everybody expected. Just between us, she didn't seem to be grieved at all." He sighed dreamily. "But how can you tell? Grief probably doesn't show on a gorgeous face like hers. Poor Alberta was the most distraught of all. She was inconsolable. You should have been there; you'd have been better off at the funeral than out playing Dick Tracy. I told you this morning that your absence would be conspicuous, but I never *dreamed* it would land you in jail. When you get your own attorney, I hope you don't ignore his advice the way you've ignored mine—free counsel, I might add."

He looked at his wristwatch. The ugly light had come on while he was chattering. Later I would reach up and unscrew the bulb. "I'm going out to find you a lawyer now—unless you think American Business Machines will do it for you. Do you want me to contact them and see?"

"I hadn't thought about it. I wouldn't like to burden them, and this isn't their problem. But do what you think best."

"All righty. Give me your home phone number so I can charge all the calls to you. Is there anything else I can do for you?"

"Mr. Natwick said he'd get in touch with Amy, but I hate for her to get this news from a sheriff."

Mr. Tolliver looked past me at the cell, distaste all over his face. "I can't blame you for that," he said. "I'll try to get in touch with her before Natwick does."

He took a pen and an envelope from his pocket. "Oh, good grief!" he cried, studying the envelope. "I haven't answered this letter yet. It's from my aunt in Beaumont. She's ninety-three and not at all well."

He scratched down the telephone number I gave him.

"What happens next?" I asked. "Exactly what am I waiting for?"

"The grand jury. There's no indictment yet, you know. Bail has to be set. You'll probably be expensive."

"I'd like to talk to Carrie, if it can be arranged," I said. "This is a terrible thing I accused little Ben of doing, and I'd like to tell her about it myself. She might get too many versions from other people."

"Oh, good grief! I forgot to tell you! Natwick's questioning her now. As I came out of the café, I saw her going into the courthouse with Natwick and that big gorilla who works for him. They tell me he can do more than fifty push-ups with one hand. I understand he's studying to be a stevedore. Anyway, Carrie was walking between him and Natwick—just like Marie Antoinette en route to the guillotine. Maybe she'll corroborate your story."

"A fat chance!" I said. "Why should she? If Natwick doesn't believe me, why should Carrie?"

"To corroborate doesn't necessarily mean that she has to tell the *same* story. You ought to read a law book, Mr. Hamilton. If you're going to stay mixed up with the law, you should at least learn a smattering of the words and terms. It would make conversation easier."

He looked beyond me again and studied the details of my sorry surroundings once more.

"Aren't you going to fix your bed? You might as well make yourself comfortable. Perhaps I should have brought you a can of bedbug killer." He snickered then hastened to add, "Don't mind me! I'm apt to say anything—but you do need cheering up. I can tell. Do you have anything to read—aside from that literature scrawled on your walls?"

"I couldn't concentrate on it if I did."

"I'll bring you some magazines tomorrow," he said, still studying the walls. "In the meantime, see if you can find time to wash away your murals." He pointed to a crudely printed inscription. "That one's wrong. The authentic version is above the first stool in the City Hall. I've got to go. I promised that old fool downstairs that I'd stay only a few minutes, although I doubt that he remembers me at all by now. Too bad you're not a bona fide criminal—a desperado. Escape would be *so* easy." He turned to go. "Now don't forget what I told you about the reporters.

They'll probably overpower the jailer and tie him up. The next time he comes up here—if he can remember the way—why don't you just ask him for the key? Well—I must be off. Ta-ta, Mr. Hamilton. Don't take any wooden nickels."

He dashed out of sight before I had a chance to thank him for coming. I heard his footsteps on the stairs, then his high-pitched voice raised in excitement. I assumed that he was berating the jailer.

𝕸 25 𝕸

Amy came the next morning. She waited for me in a bare room with a dusty concrete floor and an uncovered grimy window. A battered, scarred table and three rickety chairs made up the furnishings. The toothless jailer turned me into the room and locked the door behind me.

I stopped just inside the door. Amy was standing by the window. Her eyes were red.

"You haven't shaved," she said timidly. Her voice was small and frightened—not hers at all.

"I couldn't—not in this place—and I didn't have my things."

"I brought them—"

Suddenly we were in each other's arms, talking and not talking, but it didn't matter. Amy was the only reality in the room, and even the touch, the smell, the feel of her was so incongruous with the dirty room that she might have been an apparition. She cried softly for a bit, then pushed herself away from me and dabbed at her eyes with her bare hand.

"I don't know what to say," she stammered.

A lump in my throat threatened to choke me. "How are the boys?" I asked.

"They're fine." She was trying to look at me, but her eyes would not stay on my face. "Skeeter fussed for half the flight home because I wouldn't let him run up and down the aisle."

"Neither of them got airsick?"

"No, they did fine. I left them at a twenty-four hour nursery close to the Jones Hill shopping center." She took a step toward the table and sat down. I sat down and held her hand.

"Last night we rode the airport limousine from Dallas to Fort Worth then took a taxi home," she went on. "You weren't there, of course, and I didn't know how to get in touch with you. When we got in the house, the telephone was ringing, and it's hardly stopped since. Lawyers, reporters, crackpots—I didn't know what they were talking about. A Mr. Tolliver called and told me you were—you were down here. As we were leaving this morning, JoAnne Mansfield came out to the car and asked if she could do anything for us. She offered to keep Skeeter and Kenny. She tactfully avoided mentioning—this. It might have been easier for both of us if she had just come out with it." She shook her head and tried to smile, but she was not entirely successful.

"I guess the whole neighborhood is upset," I said.

"I'm sure they are. A picture of you and the sheriff was on the front page of the paper this morning."

"On the *front* page! Now that's just dandy, isn't it? Amy, you've been having an awful time of it, and I'm sorry. You don't know how sorry I am."

"Well, here I am with all my faculties intact, so apparently it hasn't killed me. Anyway, as I was saying, Linda Smith came over while I was dressing the boys. She took over while I straightened the house. She was too sweet to mention all this, too."

"What about your mother?" I asked. "Won't she see the papers?"

"If the story gets in the St. Louis papers, of course, she will. Anyway, I called her last night and told her what I could. Mr. Marsh telephoned. He was upset by all the publicity. He asked if you needed help finding a lawyer, but I told him I'd talk to him later if you did. A man from one of the newspapers came to the house, but I wouldn't talk to him."

She stopped. This time, something broke inside her. She buried her face in her hands and wept. Quickly, I moved to her and took her in my arms again until she had finished crying.

"Looks like I've loused us up, doesn't it?"

She backed away from me. "Nobody's proven that to me yet!" she said.

"How did you get down here?" I asked suddenly.

"Oh—I almost forgot. A lawyer named Burnsides brought me. This Mr. Tolliver had arranged for him to look into all this. He picked me up this morning and drove us by the nursery. He went on to the courthouse and said he'd come back after we've had a chance to talk. He's very nice. I think you'll like him. All the way down here, he asked me questions about you."

"I hope you gave him a good report," I said, smiling.

"What else? But when we got off onto the Holbrooks, I struck out. Pete? What's been going on? Why don't I know more about all this than I do?"

"I don't know if it will make any sense to you or not," I said, "but if you'll sit down here at the table, I'll try to put it all together—just like it happened. I've been over it again and again in my mind, trying to figure out the best way to make you understand."

"Just tell me, and let me worry about the understanding," she said.

We sat at the table while I went over the events since that night in Foley. By now it had become a recitation, neat, mechanical and nonstop, made smooth and glib by practice. Yet, had she cried out for a halt anywhere along the line, I would have been grateful. But she listened without speaking, her expression changing every now and then to reflect shades of feeling too subtle for me to interpret, which was as well, for I dared not try. At last, I finished and waited for her to speak.

"It's as though you've been talking about somebody else," she said gravely.

"I know. It seems that way to me, too. Do you believe me?"

A shadow crossed her face. "Don't I always?"

It was not what I had hoped to hear. Something tightened in me.

"I'm not talking about the facts," I said. "What I mean is— do you understand?"

She studied her hands which lay folded on the table. "Darling —I'd give anything in this world if I could say yes," she said. "I mean that with all my heart. But I don't," she said in a small voice. "I don't understand why you kept me in the dark about all this." She turned to look out the window at the old auction shed across the way, but she was not seeing it. "There's a reason somewhere, an explanation of some kind. That's what I want to hear, so I can try to understand that."

"I'd give ten years of my life if I could explain it," I said miserably.

"Well, *try!*" she said earnestly. "Just try, and maybe it'll come through for both of us. Just try to describe how you got so completely involved in the lives of people I don't even know. See if you can figure out how you came to know so much about them, all the ins and outs of their affairs, business and personal, public and private, and how it went on for months without my knowing about it. I've *got* to understand that—and I can't do it alone."

"But Amy, it wasn't as if you didn't know who the Holbrooks were," I protested feebly. "The Holbrooks weren't a deep, dark secret that I kept from you. You know how it all started."

"Certainly I did, but you stopped mentioning them, so I assumed, when I thought of them at all, that they had dropped out of your life. Now I find out that you were seeing them *regularly*. I can't imagine why, in the normal course of events, you didn't say, 'I had coffee with Mrs. Holbrook again Monday morning,' or, 'Carrie Holbrook has patched it up with her mother-in-law and is moving back to Erskine,' or something like that. You tell me dozens of little things that happen to you in Brownwood or San Angelo or Big Spring or wherever you go. I'm familiar with the names of lots of the people you deal with—you mention them as a natural thing. But not this."

"You've got to remember the time lapse between my visits to Mrs. Holbrook and when I saw you next. From Monday to Friday each time. Other things happened in between."

"I can understand that up to a point, but we're not talking about one or two occasions. We're talking about a routine that apparently became almost a phase of your life. So it couldn't possibly have slipped your mind for months on end just because it wasn't worth mentioning. Did you not want to tell me because I objected to your repeating Carrie's tale to Mrs. Holbrook?"

"Maybe," I said reluctantly. "You didn't believe Carrie's story, and I did. That probably was somewhere in the back of my head. I can't say for sure. It was Thanksgiving week when I told Mrs. Holbrook the story, and I didn't see her again until after the first of the year when Mr. Marsh added Erskine to my territory. With Christmas in between, I honestly didn't think much about the Holbrooks. That's as near as I can figure it out."

She sighed. "If you ever figure it out, will you tell me? No matter how painful or embarrassing or senseless, will you tell me?"

"Certainly, I'll tell you."

She smiled. "I'll wait for that," she said.

"Amy, I love you," I said. "I love you so much it hurts."

"You know, I'd like for you to keep saying that all day long, but we've got business to discuss. And I don't know where to start. The lawyer will want a lot of money. I know he will, and we don't have it."

"We'll get it—borrow it somewhere."

"Where?"

"I don't know—the bank or—lots of places. We've got my insurance and the house and our savings. People always get lawyers when they need them—people in worse shape than we're in. We'll find a way. We'll just have to see what the lawyer says."

She glanced nervously at the door. "He should be back soon."

"Amy—there's one more thing," I said. "Whatever you hear, and however guilty you may come to think me, I love—"

"*Guilty?*" She got up from her chair and came around the

table. "Darling, I don't think that! It hadn't even crossed my mind. That's the one thing in this whole mess that I don't question in the least." She laid a hand on my cheek. "Don't you think I know you couldn't have done an awful thing like this?"

I grasped her hand and kissed it. She withdrew it gently.

"We've still got lots of figuring to do—"

She was interrupted by a knock on the door and a key turning in the lock.

"That must be Mr. Burnsides," she said.

It was.

❦ 26 ❧

Arthur Burnsides, of the firm of Burnsides, Whittier & Palmer, greeted me with a businesslike cordiality that put me at ease immediately and gave me a glimmer of hope that at last here was a man who just might introduce a note of sanity into my insane situation. His hair was gray at the temples, his eyes were clear and friendly, and his manner pleasant. His dark suit, obviously the work of an expensive tailor, was perfectly complemented by a snowy-white shirt, a blue figured necktie and plain platinum cuff links. There was about him an easy perfection that seemed natural and unstudied.

His questions were surprisingly few and uncomplex, not the long-drawn-out prying I had learned to expect. He proceeded with an efficiency that would allow for no delays or interferences. He would devote as much time as necessary to me, but no more; his talent lay in gauging just how much that should be. Here was a man, I thought, who would treat me personally and with warmth, but as attorney-to-client and never as man-to-man. I liked that, too. He drew a delicate, barely perceptible line between us, and its very presence was a tribute to his skill and a measure of his professionalism.

"Is that all you need to know?" I asked when he seemed to have finished.

"Far from it," he answered. "But enough to make up my mind. I'd like to take your case, Mr. Hamilton."

A weight fell from my shoulders. He recognized what was happening and jumped in to caution me against too much optimism.

"I'm no miracle worker," he said. "You'll do me a disservice if you think I am. But for what it may be worth to your personal hopes and feelings, I believe I can do justice to your case. Otherwise, I would refuse it."

Amy leaned forward eagerly. "Do you mean you can get him acquitted?"

He laughed. "You're too fast, Mrs. Hamilton. He hasn't been indicted for anything yet. The case interests me—it has merit. That's all I meant."

"Oh—of course," she murmured, sitting back in her chair.

"Now let's be practical and talk about fees," he said. "I believe in complete understanding and agreement about money matters at the outset. My fee will be five thousand dollars with a thousand-dollar retainer to begin with."

Amy gasped and turned to me. I was speechless.

"I didn't realize it would be so much," she said.

"We don't have that kind of money, Mr. Burnsides," I managed to say.

He offered no apology or justification; he merely awaited my decision. The next move was mine.

"We're not trying to bargain with you," I said. "It's just that we are not used to dealing in such figures. We're flabbergasted."

"It's your decision," he said kindly. "I can't help you with it. I'm sorry. I do believe, though, that you should make some inquiries about me before you decide. In other words, I don't require an answer on the spot."

"That part of it is okay," I said. "If Mr. Tolliver asked you to come—that's fine with me. But we'll need some time to raise that much money."

"I expected that. Most people would. I made some inquiries about you in Fort Worth. I talked to Mr. Marsh at your company. The company holds you in high esteem. High enough, in fact, to stand behind the fee. Mr. Marsh said, in effect, that American Business Machines would guarantee payment. I didn't check further, because if a company like American Business Machines will say that, I'd have a hard time finding a better recommendation."

I was incredulous. "I hadn't expected that kind of treatment from the company," I said.

"Mr. Marsh described some of your accomplishments and said they're as anxious as you are to get all this straightened out."

Amy smiled at me.

"I don't know how long it will take to raise the money, Mr. Burnsides, but—"

He raised his hand to interrupt me. "There's one condition I haven't mentioned yet. I'll want your assurance that I'll have first option on your case when the young Mrs. Holbrook contests the will."

The incredible events of the past two days had crowded the will from my mind. Now that Mr. Burnsides was forcing me to consider it, I saw that I had no opinions on it one way or the other.

"Well, certainly—but that's in the future, isn't it?" I said. "Anyway, by the time all this is cleared up, I don't know if I'll be able to afford an attorney or not."

"Just your word is all I want for the present," he said. "We'll work out a fair percentage, and that will be the fee. All I'm requesting is the option. It's not binding on you. You can turn me down. By the same token, I might turn *you* down. But I do want the right to see the case first."

"But what does the will have to do with this charge against Pete?" Amy asked.

"Money," said Mr. Burnsides. He smiled broadly. "Attorneys don't make their money in criminal law. They make reputations, perhaps, but not money. When Mrs. Holbrook contests the will, half the lawyers in the State of Texas will be after you."

"How can you be certain she'll contest it at all?"

"Because the *other* half will be after her to make sure that she does."

There was a pause. I looked at Amy. She nodded her comment.

"It's agreed, Mr. Burnsides," I said. "I don't know how we'll raise the money, but if you're willing to take the case on the chance that we can, it's agreed."

"That's an acceptable risk," he said smiling. "Now let me tell you my own ground rules before we make the agreement final. I'll be in complete charge of the case. You may not always like what I do or how I do it, but I insist on autonomy—complete. If at any time you become dissatisfied, you can dismiss me. That's your prerogative, and you'll always have it. I'll keep you informed about what I do and my rationale for doing it. I'll ask you many personal and intimate questions about matters that might seem remote and irrelevant, but before we're through, I intend to know as much about you as you know yourself, and maybe more. It is imperative that I do. If my probing offends you, try to understand that it will be for a purpose. Anything you tell me will be privileged. That means that I cannot be required by law, moral or legal, to divulge it. You must turn yourself over to me with no reservations. Otherwise, you tie my hands. I'll have to do your thinking for you, and I can't do it if I don't know all."

He stopped and let that sink in for a moment.

"Do you object to anything I've said thus far?" he asked. He looked from me to Amy. Both of us shook our heads.

"There's more," he said. "You're not to discuss this case with anyone without my permission and unless I'm present. This includes the district attorney, the sheriff, and above all, news reporters. Is that understood?"

"I've already talked to Mr. Tolliver about it—quite a bit."

"Including Mr. Tolliver." He was firm.

"I agree."

He turned to Amy. "And you, Mrs. Hamilton—I want you to go back to Jones Hill and not come back here without my full knowledge and consent. Here in Erskine, you'd be in the spotlight. Some of the local people would be kind to you, and you'd be tempted to yield to their kindness. But kindness can cause lots of damage. Sometimes I think that kind people are the most dangerous of all. Everything I've said to your husband about discussing the case must apply to you, too."

She agreed. He resumed. "I'll try to get us on the grand jury docket as soon as possible and work out the bail. It shouldn't be difficult. The district attorney is confident that he can get an indictment against you, and you might as well know that. After that, we'll work in Fort Worth, which will be easier on all of us." He stood up. "Now, have I laid down any rules that you feel you cannot abide by? If so, tell me now."

I was so grateful to have someone else take over my problems, I said quickly, "Not as far as I'm concerned." I looked at Amy. She shook her head. Neither of us knew enough about what lay ahead to ask questions.

"I think we'll get along fine—all of us," he said pleasantly. "I don't require myself to be personally fond of my clients. I've defended people I despised, but it had no effect on my representation of them. And I've defended people who despised me, too, which I'll confess complicated my work, but not enough to make it impossible. You should feel under no strain or obligation to like me personally. But I do want your confidence. You must trust me implicitly. You may come to regard me as a tyrant. I hope not, but if you should, be assured that you won't be the first."

He picked up his hat and moved toward the door. "I know this is easier said than done," he said, "but let me do the thinking and worrying—try to, anyway." He rapped sharply on the door for the jailer to let him out. "I'm probably a better worrier than you. At least, I know what to worry about, and you don't."

The jailer unlocked the door. Mr. Burnsides smiled at us and departed.

For the first time since Saturday afternoon, I felt like a member of the human race. I reached across the table and took Amy's hand again.

"What do you think?" I asked.

She withdrew it gently. "Nothing," she said. "He told us to let him do the thinking."

We used the rest of our time together devising ways and means to raise five thousand dollars.

❦27❧

During the days that followed, Amy stayed at home according to Arthur Burnsides' instructions, and I did not see her. She sent me clothes and things to eat and wrote me notes. She tried to make her words cheerful, but the effort showed. The boys were fine. The neighbors were considerate. The Smiths, the Mansfields, the Thompsons continued to offer their assistance. Jack Mansfield came over after work one day to see if he could do any odd jobs around the yard; Clay Thompson stopped by and asked if the car needed looking after; Whistle Smith offered to run errands for her.

Amy's mother had telephoned and volunteered to come down and look after Skeeter and Kenny, but Amy persuaded her not to. She asked where we got the money for the lawyer, and how much was it? Amy explained that we had used our savings for the retainer and arranged terms with Mr. Burnsides for the balance. She did not tell her, however, that I had borrowed money on my insurance. Mr. Marsh had telephoned to repeat the company's willingness to stand behind Mr. Burnsides' fee. He sent word to me not to worry about my territory "until this is all cleared up."

Arthur Burnsides came every day to the jail and more than confirmed my first impressions. He took command of my affairs, methodically, firmly and with assurance. He asked me questions, made notes, delved into my background, my family, my friends, and pulled from me everything I knew about the organization, workings and personnel of American Business Machines Company.

By the following Monday when the grand jury met, I felt that a lifetime rather than a mere week had gone by since the day of the inquest. Sometimes, after our day's session had ended and Mr. Burnsides had returned to Fort Worth, I would stand in the center of my cell or sit on my bunk with my eyes closed and review the entire sequence of events, from the day I had seen Carrie in the doctor's office to the night the toothless old jailer had shut me in my cage; but long before I could reach the end, the principal character had ceased to be Pete Hamilton and become a stranger. I could not begin to calculate the effects of these crazy happenings on me, because I could not keep myself in the center of them. I was an onlooker, an interested observer.

On Monday, the assistant district attorney presented an indictment of first-degree murder to the grand jury, and the foreman returned it with "A True Bill" written across its face. Mr. Burnsides had asked for a lesser charge, but to no avail. "You might as well prepare yourself for the worst," he had warned me. "If he has any case against you at all, it will be first-degree." I had been optimistic, nevertheless, and the impact of the findings staggered me.

The hearing was like a one-sided trial in which I was judged guilty with no opportunity to offer one word in my own defense. The assistant district attorney built his case expertly, without once raising his voice. The grand jury listened and was convinced. That's all there was to it.

For once, I was glad to get back to my cell where no one could see me. Arthur Burnsides had tried to warn me, but I had been totally unprepared to hear myself described as a greedy, calculating, cold-blooded killer of a defenseless old woman. When the wheezing old jailer clanged the door shut behind me, I wanted to crawl under my bunk and stay there.

I was arraigned the following afternoon and bond was set at $50,000. Mr. Burnsides had a bondsman standing by to make the arrangements. I signed my name to a contract and was free. J. A. Tolliver was flitting around the corridor waiting for me. He rushed forward and extended a limp hand.

"I just wanted to say—oh, good grief! Here come those awful reporters! They came to see me this morning, and I thought I'd *never* get rid of them—they're like flypaper." Quickly, he stepped between me and several men, some with cameras.

"Mr. Hamilton, I'm from the Fort Worth *Globe*, and I'd—"

"Go way, go way, go way!" Mr. Tolliver screamed. "You, too!" he added, turning on the others and shooing them off as though they were chickens.

They ignored him and moved in closer. I looked around for Mr. Burnsides. He had fallen behind and was talking to one of the court officials.

"Is your wife here today, Mr. Hamilton?" asked the first reporter.

"Yoo-hoo, *Arthur!*" Mr. Tolliver was waving frantically. "Over here! Hurry!"

Mr. Burnsides looked up, nodded and joined us promptly. He extended a hand to one of the reporters. "I'm Arthur Burnsides," he said pleasantly. "Mr. Hamilton's attorney." Then before the man could reply, he turned to another and smiled. "I know you'll understand, but we're in a rush. Can you call me at my office? Maybe we can arrange something there, but at the moment—oh, hello, J.A.! It's good to see you again. Ready, Pete?"

Then we were outside in the sunshine with Mr. Tolliver at our heels.

"I just don't see how you do it, Arthur," he said. "Really I don't. And you're so polite while you're giving them the bum's rush! It's a blessing that I'm not a celebrity. My press relations would be disastrous. I was ready to take the flyswatter to those dreadful—where are you going now?"

"I'm going to take Pete home," Mr. Burnsides said.

We went down the steps and out onto the sidewalk. A cluster

of loiterers parted and let us pass. "Thanks, J.A.," said Mr. Burnsides over his shoulder. "I hope you'll excuse us for running, but we've got lots of things to do, and Pete is anxious to see his family."

Mr. Tolliver looked back at the courthouse and went into action again. "You'd better hurry, then," he said. "Here they come again. Go on! I'll stay behind and titillate them with the story of my life. It's never been published, you know. Ta-ta, Arthur. You, too, Mr. Hamilton." He turned back and flew at the approaching reporters.

At Jones Hill, Mr. Burnsides let me out in front of my house and drove off down the street. During the drive from Erskine, I had been conscious of a strangeness and a tightening inside me, but it was not until Mr. Burnsides had left me standing alone on my own sidewalk that I could define it. The strangeness was the odd sensation of freedom, which when I had thought of it at all, I had always taken for granted. The tightening was apprehension. I didn't realize it until I started up the sidewalk and noticed a lag in my steps. After all, how does a person leave a jail cell under $50,000 bond, with a charge of first-degree murder against him, and walk through his own front door to greet his wife and two children? What's expected of him? What can he, in fairness, expect of them? An automobile turned onto the street at the corner, and I hurried into the house.

Amy met me with Kenny in her arms and Skeeter at her feet. I grabbed the three of them and tried to kiss them all at once. We chattered incoherently and made a terrible racket. Skeeter was squealing, Kenny was gurgling, and Amy was crying. I think I cried, too.

"Pete—you're crushing Kenny!" Amy exclaimed, trying to free herself.

"He'll survive," I said.

I kissed all of them again. Then I sat down on the floor and swept Skeeter up in my arms.

"Here—I'll give you another one," Amy said, depositing Kenny in my lap.

"I'll take you, too," I said, tugging at the hem of her dress. She dropped down beside us, and the four of us sat on the floor in the open doorway, babbling, laughing and squealing.

"At least we can close the door!" Amy said after a time. "What will the neighbors think if they see us piled down on the floor like this?"

"Who cares?" I said.

She got to her feet anyway and closed the door.

I stood up, holding Skeeter and Kenny close to me. "The first thing I want to do is take a shower and scrub that—that place off myself," I said. "It'll take at least two bars of soap."

"Go ahead," Amy said. "Use *three* bars if you like."

"No," I said suddenly. "I've changed my mind. I'm going to sit down here and stare at all of you. That's all—just stare."

Skeeter wandered off into the kitchen. Amy took Kenny into his room for his nap. I remained seated and wallowed in the simple luxury of being in my own home, in my own living room, with my family. I had no desire to move. I wanted nothing but to sit and wait for any or all of them to appear in the doorway again. Amy was gone a long time.

"What were you doing?" I asked when she returned with a magazine in her hand.

She lined it up with some others on a table. "Just straightening up," she said. She did not look at me. She started back toward the kitchen. "I didn't take anything out of the freezer this morning," she explained. "Now I've got to figure out what will thaw the fastest—or something else."

"Amy—can't it wait?"

She hesitated in the doorway, then went on out of the room. I followed her.

"You don't know how good this place looks," I said, coming up behind her. She was leaning into the refrigerator.

"It looks even better with you in it," she said, trying to sound bright, but her cheerfulness was strained. It had a false ring. "I thought I had a package of pork chops, but I guess I don't." She turned away from the refrigerator and moved past me to the cabinet.

"Amy—"

"Pete, go see about Skeeter, will you?" she said. "He's too quiet."

"He's all right. Can't we—"

"He'll get into the dresser drawers again," she said. "He opened one this morning and poured face powder all over the carpet."

She hurried away. I walked out into the back yard, but when I saw Linda Smith puttering in the flower bed next door, I went back inside before she could see me. I was not ready to explain my new status. Maybe later. I took a shower, put on fresh clothes, looked through an accumulation of mail and returned to the kitchen. Amy stood at the cabinet with her back to me. She was mixing something in a bowl. She did not look around.

"I don't suppose you feel up to making a trip to the grocery store for me, do you?" she asked.

"Not unless it's a dire emergency," I said. "What do you need?"

"Oh—well, it doesn't matter. I just needed a package of—but it's okay." She opened a cabinet door and searched the shelves. She took out a bottle of seasoning. "I'll just use this," she said. "Is Kenny awake?"

"You'll hear him when he is."

"I thought I heard him—"

"No, you didn't, Amy," I said. "You don't think you heard him at all. Something's happened to you. What is it?"

She bent her head low and continued her mixing. "Maybe after I get dinner on the way and things settle down—"

"Things are as settled as they're going to be," I said. "I've been home two hours now, and you've been working yourself into a frazzle so you wouldn't have to talk to me. What's the matter?"

She turned to face me. Her eyes were red. "I wish I knew," she said. "I hate myself for it, but ever since you walked into the house, I've been—I've been—I'm not sure what it is, but I think I'm *embarrassed*, of all things! I can't think of anything to say."

"Then how about sitting down here at the table, and let's think of something—just anything."

She grabbed a tissue and wiped her eyes. She moved to the kitchen table and dropped into a chair, but she sat on it sideways as though prepared to get up any minute. She looked out the window and waited for me to speak.

"Now tell me what it is," I said as calmly as I could.

She turned from the window. Her eyes were dry now. "Pete —I can't—I just can't!" She turned to the window again.

"Look—there's nothing outside that window that you haven't seen a thousand times, so why don't you turn around here and let's get to the bottom of things. Is it this thing about Carrie and me? I've been reading the papers, too, you know."

"I've done my dead-level best to ignore it," she said miserably. "You don't know how I've worked on *not* thinking about it, but it won't go away. The newspapers call you a longtime friend of Carrie's. They keep linking your name to hers in the most insidious ways: the beautiful war widow and the business-machine salesman, or the traveling salesman and the would-be heiress, or the young Mrs. Holbrook and her dead husband's best friend— nothing actually wrong, but they always manage to make them *sound* wrong. They make you sound indecent and cheap, and I know that you're not. It's always you and Carrie—Carrie and you —never one or the other. I've begun to feel like the apex of a triangle. I can't help it. Mother has danced all the way around this very question without actually asking it. Mr. Marsh has been bending over backwards to avoid mentioning her name— and that's worse than his coming out and saying it. The Smiths and the Mansfields have not referred to Carrie *or* you. They intend to be discreet, I suppose, but by sidestepping so completely, every one of them shines a big white spotlight on it, and I guess it's just got next to me."

She stood up and went back to her mixing bowl.

"So all week long, I've thought of nothing else," she continued. "I haven't even worried about you in that jail cell. I knew you could cope with that. It was awful for you, but I knew it wouldn't get you down. I haven't worried about the trial. It will come out all right—it must. I haven't worried about any of the things a wife should worry about when her husband is in the terrible trouble you're in. It's this—this other. It won't go away. You can't drive it away, either. I've got to do that for myself."

She bent her head low. She was crying again.

"Pete, I'm so ashamed—"

"Would it be easier for you if I didn't stay here?" The question was out of my mouth before I realized that I didn't have the courage to ask it.

"Go somewhere else?" she repeated. "Why would you do that? And where would you go? Anyway, you can't."

"If you want me to, I can."

"Pete! Stop and think a minute! If you went somewhere else, you'd only give weight to what people already think. You have to stay here. It's part of your defense."

"But I don't want you to be bothered."

"Bothered?" She turned to face me. "Oh, Pete, how can you use a word like *bother*, of all things?" she exclaimed. "We went in hock up to our necks to retain a lawyer, and I don't know how much the bail money is costing us. Your job's all washed up. You can count on that. Mr. Marsh made it clear that the company can't stand the notoriety. Our neighbors are nice to us— but what else can they be? They're nice people, and they've got us in their midst. Two days ago, I drove three miles to the other side of Jones Hill until I found a supermarket where nobody knew me. Mother called two nights ago and begged me to come home until this all blows over. The St. Louis papers picked up the story because of me. They asked her for photographs, but so far she's fought them off. She doesn't know how to deal with all this. And beyond it all, you've got a terrible criminal charge hanging over your head. And you don't want me to be *bothered!* I'm in trouble, too, Pete! Your going or staying won't change that. I'm in deep, deep trouble, too."

(210)

"I'm sorry. I wish I could convince you of that much, at least."
"You don't need to convince me," she said. "I know you're sorry, but it doesn't alter our situation. We're in trouble—both of us. We've got to figure how to make the best of it."

"Okay—but first, let's get one thing settled," I said. "There is nothing between Carrie and me. There never has been. I had not said that to you before because I didn't have any idea it was necessary. All I can do is tell you. I don't know how to prove it."

"I don't ask you for proof," she said. "You're not on trial. The rules of evidence don't apply in your own kitchen."

I struggled for the right words. "Amy, I want to say this," I said awkwardly. "I love you just as much as I ever did. I've never been a great one for saying it over and over again. You've never needed to hear it over and over to know it and feel it. I love you. I hope you believe that. It's the only thing in this whole world that hasn't changed. The only thing."

"And I love you, too," she said quietly. "That's what this is all about."

Later, I lay awake staring into the darkness. Alongside me, Amy scarcely moved. I knew that she lay awake, too.

✲ 28 ✲

Beginning the next morning and for the next couple of weeks, I spent my days seventeen stories above downtown Fort Worth in the offices of Burnsides, Whittier & Palmer, closeted with the senior member of the firm. In a small but elegant consultation room, rich with mahogany, fine leather and deep carpeting, we shut ourselves away from all everyday activities. Occasionally, a secretary slipped in and out to bring us coffee, to empty ashtrays or to hand Mr. Burnsides a note. Otherwise we could have been in a tree house or hidden in the deepest reaches of a cave. Sometimes he ordered sandwiches sent in for lunch, or he might dismiss me to go out and find my own.

At home, the chasm widened between Amy and me. We took care of essential matters with the minimum of words. At breakfast, we turned on the radio and listened to the news with exaggerated interest. Sometimes Amy had toast and coffee by herself then woke me for a plateful of bacon and eggs alone. Or she might busy herself with the boys or a machineful of laundry or a basket of ironing that somehow could not wait until I left the house. In the evenings I found chores to do in the garage or yard while she spent endless time preparing dinner and cleaning up afterwards. I gave the boys their baths and let them splash longer than they should. I played two and three games with them instead of one, keeping them awake longer than I should. Amy reorganized cabinet drawers, wrote letters, checked bank statements, read the newspaper from front to back, top to bottom. Then when our ingenuity ran out and we came face to face with nowhere else to go or nothing else to do, we sat and uttered words to fill holes, to get us through the evening, to keep up some semblance of being a happily married couple.

My days, however, were fuller and more active than I would have thought possible. While Mr. Burnsides listened, I talked about myself, sometimes for thirty and forty minutes at a stretch, wandering backward and forward through the years, stumbling onto little-remembered episodes, magnifying the importance of some and down-playing others. Sometimes he forced me to answer questions that I tried to sidestep, taking me into domains that I considered none of his business. Bit by bit, I transferred my life over to him, the past, the present and, most significantly of all, the future.

At first, it was difficult; my inhibitions were many, and some all but crippling. But as I talked, talking became easier. Breaking through one restraint made the next less rigid. I soon learned to talk without evaluating my words; evaluation was his responsibility, not mine, and I realized I had no clues to his judgment of what was important and what was not.

"What went on between you and Carrie that night in Foley?" he asked suddenly one day. I had been describing a trivial incident in college.

"I've been through all that," I said. "Do you want to hear it again?"

"No—let it go," he said with a grin.

"Did you think you'd catch me changing my story?"

"It never hurts to try," he said, still grinning.

"How much longer does this soul-searching go on?"

"Are you getting tired of it?"

"I can't shake off the feeling that time will slip up on us. We haven't got to the heart of the matter yet—Henrietta Holbrook's death."

"We've discussed most of it," he said. "You told me your hypothesis about little Ben Holbrook and the cleaning compound just as you told it to Natwick. He looked into it and got nowhere. There were no witnesses, and Ben doesn't remember anything about it. Why should he? He was playing, and he plays every day. In his memory, that day was no different from any other. As interesting as your hypothesis is—and plausible in a strange way—it is probably the toughest one you could possibly come up with. We are entirely dependent on the memory and words of a little boy, and legally, that's not worth a tinker's damn one way or the other. A five-year-old child cannot be held legally responsible for what he does or what he says—if anything —on a witness stand. We need an eyewitness, which of course we don't have. I think Natwick discarded that one from the first. In his shoes, I might have done the same. Carrie was not at all cooperative, but in *her* shoes, I probably would have done no differently. So, you see? We don't have much to discuss."

"Doesn't finding that bottle at the overhang mean anything at all?"

"Pete, even if you could convince a jury that you found that bottle on a hunch, you'd still have to prove how and when the compound got from the bottle into Mrs. Holbrook's glass. Now you've *really* got nothing to go on there but another hypothesis. That's all—a supposition. I would never base your main line of defense on it. And there are other things to consider. Both of us know that you couldn't have known about that bottle of cleaning compound upstairs, but can we convince a jury of that? After all, you were in that house every Monday week after week. Alberta might testify that to the best of her knowledge you had never been upstairs. But what good would that do? You were not under her constant surveillance. You could have gone upstairs many times without her knowledge. It's a case of proving a negative, a tough thing to do. So again, it would depend on your gift of persuasion. It's a shaky proposition at best. I don't mean that we can't introduce these things into your defense—or

(214)

at least, try—but I don't see it as your main line. If that's all we have, the district attorney will chop us into little bits. We'll have to do something else."

"There's something wrong with all this," I argued. "I don't want to win this case on a technicality or by a legal maneuver or trick. I want to win it on the basis of my innocence—that's all. The only tangible proof I've got is that empty bottle in Ben Holbrook's store, and you're down-playing that one. The only way I can prove beyond all doubt that I'm innocent is to prove that somebody else is guilty. It's that cut and dried with me. I don't get your approach. I don't get it at all."

Mr. Burnsides' manner softened. "Pete, listen to me," he said gently. "Nobody is going to throw you to the wolves. The only way we can get that story into the record is for you to get on the stand and tell it yourself. That's the only way. And there's nothing to corroborate it. Natwick was with you when you found it, certainly. But he believes you planted it, or he could never have arrested you. And that's exactly what the jury will be asked to believe. The grand jury has already considered it probable, or else you would not have been indicted. Right or wrong has nothing to do with my position on this. It's all a matter of what we can make stick and what we can't. There's no trick, no legal maneuver up my sleeve. Just stay with me on this, Pete, and we'll make it."

He switched back to my college experiences as abruptly as he had turned away from them. "You were talking about how many of your classmates were going into the Army and Navy. . . ."

That's the way it went. On the whole, the experience was cleansing, a sort of catharsis.

"I'm getting a bigger kick out of this than I should," I remarked toward the end of our long sessions. "I've never told the story of my life before."

"Is there any reason you shouldn't get a kick out of it?"

"Well—I would have imagined that spilling my insides this way would be upsetting."

"Only if you had uncovered anything worth getting upset about," he said. "Let's face it, Pete, you've led a rather humdrum life up to now."

"Humdrum? I've never thought of it as such."

"All right—call it unexciting," he said. He stood up and poured himself a glass of water. "I could match your story all over the United States. There's scarcely anything in it that's interesting. *Really* interesting, I mean."

"Well, that's a flattering sum-up," I said.

He carried the glass of water to the window and looked out as he drank it. "A written report on you would make dull reading," he said when he had finished and returned the glass to the table. "You had a normal, happy childhood, fine parents, comfortable home, were educated all the way through college with no great strain financially or mentally. Your military service was undistinguished. I mean no offense, but thousands of boys can match your war record. You lost both parents, but that happens to a lot of people. You met Amy, fell in love, got married, bought a home on the GI Bill, had two babies—all without a bobble. You haven't had a struggle with money, and your job's gone as smoothly as everything else. Security, security, security all the way. You've done well, make no mistake about it. Everything's almost too much all right with you. You've had no stumbling blocks, no setbacks, no blighted hopes, no hard knocks. You don't bear any scars from anything. You don't have any strong likes or dislikes. You don't have any extreme or violent opinions, and if you have any hidebound prejudices, I haven't spotted them. You're getting along just fine. You always have, so why shouldn't everyone else get along just as well?" He paused. "And I think that's the clue to your proclivity to meddle," he added.

"Meddle?"

"Why, yes," he said, looking surprised. "A man needs to have a release of some sort. In your case, though, there doesn't seem to be anything that needs releasing. I can't find anything that's pent up. But maybe that's a clue, too. Meddling is essentially an idle occupation. Busy people don't have time."

"I don't follow you," I said. "Where did you get the idea that I meddle?"

"By your own account, that's exactly what you've been doing. It's what got you into your present predicament. You can substitute another word, if you like, but it was meddling, nevertheless."

"I explained how I got involved," I said.

"You did. Suppose you listen while I tell it back to you. Listen to how it sounds from where I sit."

He perched himself on the edge of the table and stuck a forefinger in the air. Wrapping a fist around it, he began to talk.

"First, you went to Foley and inquired about Carrie Holbrook. You made no attempt to see her. You wouldn't even leave your name with the druggist. If you had been genuinely interested in Carrie, you would have called her up, knocked on her door, seen for yourself how she was getting along. But you didn't. You were activated by curiosity, not interest. That's a clear-cut instance of meddling."

"But that's not the way it—"

"I've got the floor now," he reminded me. He released his forefinger and grasped the one next to it.

"Second. You went to the Holbrooks' to see what you could see. That's all in God's world you went for. Let's be honest: whatever deep and abiding interest you once had in the Holbrook family, it had withered away with the years. You don't need to be ashamed of that. It was natural. You've got to have a very special feeling for somebody to keep an interest alive for five years with no contact whatsoever. Your feeling was not that special. Oh, you've convinced yourself since that it was, but it wasn't. Your curiosity about Carrie had not been satisfied, so you focused it on Ben's parents. You went to see Mrs. Holbrook as a sightseer. That's the second instance of meddling.

I lighted a cigarette, and he stared at it keenly as if it were important to what he was saying.

"Third. At Mrs. Holbrook's, you discovered a situation more dramatic than you had bargained for. Aha! Your meddling suddenly turned up something intriguing. So when you got that letter from Mrs. Holbrook, you went back. And what did you do that time? You called on the family physician, who was closer to Mrs. Holbrook than a blood relative, and you told him about his patient and his friend. Then you asked him what he was doing for her, how he was treating her, what he intended to do in light of your revelations. That was rather presumptuous, if you ask me. You didn't tell him one blessed thing that he did not already know. You might have been the best friend Ben Holbrook ever had, but you were a stranger to his mother and her friends. That is the third instance of your meddling."

I was beginning to squirm. "You're putting the wrong face on all this," I said. "You're making it sound worse than it was."

"Am I?" He raised an eyebrow and shifted his weight to the edge of the table. "That's too bad," he said, "because I'm not finished."

He took hold of the end of his little finger. "Fourth. Even after Dr. Kriegel attempted to pacify your fears and make you see that he and Alberta were capable of looking after Mrs. Holbrook without your help, you would not stay out of her affairs. You went back to Foley, this time to warn Carrie not to come to Erskine because her mother-in-law had threatened to kill her. Carrie did not take the threat seriously. She's the second person you tried to upset. You weren't having much luck, were you? You couldn't find anybody who needed your help. You were the only person to be upset by Mrs. Holbrook's state of mind. This all seems to indicate that they knew her much better than you did, and why not?"

He went back to his forefinger. "Fifth. Carrie persuaded you to plead her case with Mrs. Holbrook. You had a struggle with your conscience now. Somewhat tardily, I'd say, but you struggled, nevertheless—and ended up by doing what Carrie wanted. From all the evidence, you pleaded her case well. Apparently it never occurred to you that for a matter so personal, an emissary would be an intruder—"

"I told Carrie that this was a matter for the family! Not an outsider's business at all!" I broke in.

"Okay. You told her. But you went anyway. Had you refused her, you would have had no excuse to go back to see Mrs. Holbrook."

He dropped his hand and stopped talking. I waited for him to continue, wondering what else he might add to so much flimflammery.

"Do you get the picture?" he said after a time. "You stuck your nose into everybody's business, into every situation, none of which concerned you—"

"Now just a minute, Mr. Burnsides! You're getting a bit carried away with all this picking and analyzing, aren't you?" I started to my feet. He motioned me back into my chair.

"You're supposed to listen to me," he said. "Remember? I listened to you. Now, you listen to me."

I sat back as though he had shoved me. He stood down from the table, pulled out a chair and sat in it. He leaned forward, both elbows on the table.

"You're *too* helpful, Pete," he said. "That's the whole thing in a nutshell. You're a do-gooder."

"A *what?*"

"A do-gooder. Do you know what a do-gooder is? He's a meddler. He's a person who goes around improving things for somebody else, whether they want him to or not—whether they need improving or not. He decides what's good and what's bad, what's moral and what's immoral, what fits and what doesn't fit. He makes his own diagnosis of who's happy and who's unhappy. In other words, he uses his own values as yardsticks for his improvements. Now get that: his *own* values. But, of course, that's what makes him tick—his own diagnosis based on his own values. It bothers him just a little to run across somebody he can do nothing for—somebody who doesn't need or, worse, doesn't *want* his help. He resents them, which is why you resent Dr. Kriegel."

"But I don't resent Dr. Kriegel," I said. "I don't know what gave you that idea. It's the other way around—he resented me. He told me to stop seeing Henrietta, and on the day she died, he even chased me out of the house. You can't expect me to have a warm feeling of affection for him after that. But I don't resent him—not as you're making it sound."

"You know, I got this story from you," he replied.

"Then you got it wrong. I thought I was a better communicator than that."

He got up from his chair and walked to the door and back again. He circled the table then leaned against the wall with his arms folded and one foot thrown across the other. He was a fine figure, and even though I disliked what he was saying, it was impossible not to be fascinated by the manner in which he said it. He seemed to have finished talking now, but there was no letdown in his manner.

"In summary," he continued, as though he had never stopped talking, "It didn't suit you to believe that Mrs. Holbrook could work out her own affairs without your help. She was aging and alone, which gave you an edge and plenty of room in which to demonstrate a superiority."

"Now *you* listen, Mr. Burnsides!" I sprang to my feet. "I'm not paying you five thous—"

"Sit down!"

His sudden fierceness shocked me into submission. I dropped into my seat while he continued as though there had been no interruption.

"The tragedy of your good works is that they led to the death of a woman who—"

I was out of my chair again. "You're not going to make me be quiet this time!" I shouted. "How in God's name could you listen to me day after day, hours on end, and come up with this kind of cock-and-bull story? Haven't you listened to anything I've said? Didn't you understand a single word? I was trying to help a friend—two friends, as it turned out—and you make me sound guilty of some major felony. Even Natwick's version is better than yours. At least, he made his sound obvious."

"Sit down, Pete," he said quietly. "I didn't say you were guilty. You're innocent, all right. Do-gooders usually are—"

"Stop calling me a do-gooder!"

He ignored me. "You're not guilty of murder or any other crime on the statute books," he said. "Don't you think I know that? You're not guilty of malicious intent toward anyone. I know that, too. You never had the remotest idea of getting material benefits from Henrietta Holbrook's money or anything else. I also know that. The only thing you're guilty of is something that no court in the land can ever convict you of: meddling in other people's affairs."

This time, there was a letup in his manner, and I knew that he was willing for me to take the floor. I took it.

"Okay—now I'd like to give you a little diagnosis of my own," I said. "Yours and Natwick's have one thing in common: neither of you believe your own story. His is too obvious and pat, but he's stuck with it because it's the only one he's got. As for yours, you cannot point to one instance in my entire life—and you've heard it all—where the do-gooder analysis is substantiated. You can't make it stand up with examples from my past. I don't have a history of it. But like Natwick, you've got to explain me. Do you know what I think? I think you've been bugged all your life by somebody's helpfulness. I don't know who, but that's your business, not mine. So you've found yourself a substitute to work on, and you're having a grand time doing it. And you know, the odd thing about both your and Natwick's versions is that they are both reasonable. They make sense. They're believable. Except for one thing: you've both got the wrong person in the leading role."

Mr. Burnsides' features had been immobile as he listened to me. Now he raised his eyebrows slightly. His arms remained folded. One foot still lay across the other. He was holding a pose as rigidly as an artist's model sitting for a portrait.

"Congratulations!" he said. "You've been holding out on me.

I didn't suspect that you were a psychologist and an analyst along with it." Strangely, his tone was devoid of ridicule.

He straightened up and moved to the conference table. "All right, Pete," he said after a long pause. "Natwick and I both seem to be wrong—according to you. But we're both right about one thing, and you can't deny it. You set off a hell of a big chain of events when you called on Henrietta Holbrook in Carrie's behalf. Who's responsible for that? The man in the moon?"

I said, "Well, I won't deny that my visit to Henrietta Holbrook set off a chain of events that landed me in the mess I'm in now. But who's to say that many of those events would not have happened without me? Who can say that Carrie would not have worked her way back into Henrietta's favor and moved back to Erskine without my intercession? Who's to say that Henrietta would not have died from that cleaning compound without me? Things happen, Mr. Burnsides. And you won't always find a specific person or a specific set of circumstances to pin the responsibility on. I don't know why—I'm not God. Just because the world has come tumbling down around my ears doesn't necessarily mean that I, Peter D. Hamilton, made all these things happen, by word, motive or deed, unwitting or otherwise."

Mr. Burnsides smiled. "That was a good speech, Pete," he said. "Is there anything else?"

"Yes. You're just a little too quick to pin labels on people," I said. "You've got all your facts straight. I did all the things you said I did. But does that make me what you say I *am?*"

"How do you take the measure of a man if not by what he does?"

"Would you say that every man convicted of a crime is a criminal?"

"Technically, yes."

"But only technically," I said. "An innocent man wrongly convicted of a crime is technically a criminal but not morally. By your system of reasoning, everybody who sings a song is a musician; everybody who tells a white lie is a liar; everybody who helps himself to a paper clip from the next desk is a thief."

(222)

"Then you're convinced that I've figured you out wrong."

"Yes, I am. You attributed the wrong reasons to everything I did. You *want* to believe I'm a meddler. I'll go further. You've *got* to believe it."

"Everything points to it," he said.

"Because you pointed it, that's why. What do you do? Carry a little template in your pocket searching for somebody to fit it?"

"Well, Pete, I'm merely trying to get you to see what I see. I think I know whom I'm defending. I want you to know that, too."

I got up from my chair. "I only hope, Mr. Burnsides, that you've got the skill to free whoever it is you've been talking about."

❦ 29 ❦

Mr. Burnsides was scheduled for an appointment with the district attorney in Erskine the next day, so I could not see him.

"I think I'll try to talk to Carrie while I'm down there," he told me. "Perhaps I can get something out of her—or little Ben, if she'll let me see him—about that cleaning compound and the overhang. But aside from that, I'd like a chance to size her up at close range. I've come to regard her as the villain in this piece."

"Carrie's not the villain," I said. "I don't think this piece has a villain."

He regarded me thoughtfully for a moment. "And when I finish with Carrie," he said with no change in voice or manner, "I want to see if I can figure out why you're so quick to defend her each time her name is mentioned."

I welcomed a recess from him. His accusations still smarted, but Mr. Burnsides himself bothered me even more. His polished manner, his all-knowing pronouncements, his air of invincibility were grating on me. I had cooperated all the way, turning myself over to him in little slices and large chunks, confident that he knew best. Now I was not so certain. Doubts were beginning to seep through. He was wrong about me, yet I did not want to pull against him. I needed time, therefore, to back away and decide how to cope with him best.

I had made no attempt to detail each day's session to Amy. For the most part, it would have meant recitations of chapters of my life with which she was already familiar, and I saw no point in that, although I knew she would be interested in an accounting. She had to be.

She was clearing off the breakfast table. I was leaning against the end of the cabinet drinking the last cup of coffee from the pot so she could wash it. We had been making small talk, and not much of that.

"Amy, am I a do-gooder?" I asked suddenly.

She stacked some dishes by the sink. "Certainly not," she said, her attention still on the dishes. "Who said you were?"

"Mr. Burnsides. Yesterday. He told me I was a do-gooder, and that's what got me into all this trouble. He went into the damnedest spiel you ever heard in your life to prove it."

I went on to reconstruct the essentials of our discussion.

". . . and so that's his version," I said in conclusion. "He seemed to be more upset about it than I was. Do you agree that I'm a do-gooder?"

She had finished clearing the table by now and was drawing water into the sink. "I don't know where he got all that," she said. "But suppose you were? What would that prove that's important to your defense?"

"Beats me. I haven't figured it out yet. I assume he knows what he's doing."

"For five thousand dollars, I hope so."

She turned on the water again and watched it run. We were silent until she turned it off and put a stack of plates into it.

"If you're not seeing Mr. Burnsides today, maybe you should see Mr. Marsh," she suggested. "For the company's sake as well as our own."

I had not talked to Mr. Marsh since the night he came to our house—the night he told me about Henrietta's will.

"I thought maybe he would get in touch with me," I said.

"Maybe he's waiting for you."

I would rather have let the status remain undisturbed, but I went.

An expectant, breathless hush accompanied me through the main offices of the American Business Machines Company. Looking straight ahead, I made my way to Mr. Marsh's office. From the front door, past the receptionist's desk, the cashier's cage, past the long row of desks and open cubicles, everything came to a halt as I went by—typewriters, adding machines, calculators and conversations. Mr. Marsh closed the door behind me, and the buzz of voices started up again.

Mr. Marsh was pleasant but embarrassed. He adjusted his spectacles more often than they needed it, and he fussed with his necktie, which was perfectly knotted and in place. He glanced at the closed door frequently as though expecting someone to come through it. We made small talk until it ran out. I took the initiative.

"I don't know exactly what to say, Mr. Marsh, but I've left you holding the bag about my work. I know that. You've been good about not pushing me, but it seems we should discuss it."

"Yes, you're right," he said. "I appreciate your coming. I considered calling and asking you to come, but I knew how busy you were."

"I don't know what you can expect from me," I said. "I can't see far enough ahead to predict."

"We want to do the right thing, Hamilton," he said, his nervousness increasing, "and frankly, we've had trouble knowing exactly what the right thing is. You must appreciate the fact that this situation is unprecedented for us, too. We've been tremendously pleased with your work, most assuredly. You've been good for us in the West Texas territory, and we don't want to appear insensible to that. You've known for some time that we've had our eye on you for other things—bigger and better things." He gave me an uneasy smile, and I returned an uneasy one of my own. "Naturally, all of us have been upset about events of the past few weeks. I can't tell you how upset we've been." He took a paper clip from his desk and turned it idly in his fingers. "We've tried to assess your potential value to us in face of all—all the recent events, and I think you must see that it poses a problem."

I felt a sudden compassion for this kindly man who was trying to perform an unpleasant task in a pleasant manner. "I'm aware of where this is leading, Mr. Marsh," I said. "Would you like my resignation?"

My directness flustered him. His face turned red. He frowned and ran a hand across his bald head. "You make it sound so cold-blooded!" he protested. "It's not that way at all. We don't intend to simply turn you out and wash our hands of you. Even though we must view this thing impersonally, it doesn't mean that we don't feel a personal interest in you."

"Thank you for that. But you do want my resignation, don't you?"

He studied the paper clip, then dropped it and locked his fingers together. He took a deep breath and looked straight at me. "Yes, Hamilton," he said. "I'm afraid we do."

He breathed more easily. "It was not an easy decision to reach," he added. "It's too much like kicking a man when he's down, and none of us like that. The publicity on this thing has been tremendous, and the company is squarely in the middle of it. Newspaper people are always telephoning and coming in here for new angles on their stories—your business colleagues, the dealers you call on, the towns you go to—things like that. We've got to protect our own people, of course, and we can't let our dealers get caught up in unpleasant publicity. If you don't mind my speaking very frankly, we can't visualize your going back out into your territory even after this is all over. You'll be too much of a curiosity—if you'll pardon my saying it—to the people in those smaller towns. We've considered making a place for you here in the office, but there's nothing opening up just yet that you'd be interested in. Anyway, we don't know what the time-table is—we don't have a schedule we can plan on. In other words, we can't predict your availability. So this seems like the only way for us, and in the long run, for you, too. It would make for a less sticky situation if you—"

I jumped in to ease the situation for him.

"Of course you'll have my resignation, Mr. Marsh, if that's the way it's to be," I said. "I see your side of it. I wish I didn't, but I do. This has been a pleasant job with a good future. I hate to give it up. I've developed a kind of proprietary interest in American Business Machines. It's a personal thing with me."

"And that's the way it should be," he said. "It accounts for the good showing you've made." He brightened and switched moods. "Now, there are a couple of things we can do, and I want you to consider them carefully. Our board has discussed your—ah—your circumstances, and we're prepared to give what assistance we can afford. We can take care of your attorney's fees, or we can give you six months' salary, but we can't do both. Either one should help, and we want the choice to be yours."

I was stunned. I had hoped at the very most to salvage my job, but I would have felt fortunate to receive one month's salary in lieu of a standard termination notice. In other words, I fully expected to walk away with nothing.

"This is almost too generous," I said. "The alternatives are uneven, though. Five thousand dollars—the attorney's fee—is more than I would make in six months without commissions."

"True, but we're not offering you the five thousand dollars in cash. We would pay that directly to your attorney," he said. "I called Mr. Burnsides and persuaded him to tell me his fee. We had to know before we could determine the size of our offer. You did open up the West Texas territory for us, don't forget, and you've done a bang-up job out there. We want to do something for you, and we thought this might help."

"It certainly will," I said, still overwhelmed. "Mr. Burnsides told me that you were ready to guarantee his fee, and I had no idea there would be anything else. I thought that alone was a generous thing for you to do."

"Well, don't be too impressed with us for that guarantee," he said, smiling. "We offered that as a kind of backstop—sort of like cosigning a note, you might say. We've never feared that we'd be *forced* to pay it."

"We're almost ruined financially," I said. "I don't know when we'll see daylight again. We made arrangements with Mr. Burnsides, of course, so we don't need any cash for him at the moment. We do need money to live on, though, and we're just about ready to scrape the bottom of the barrel. I'm forced to take the six months' salary. I'll confess that it's embarrassing. It's like charity, almost."

"No, no! Not in the least! You've earned every cent of it, and I think you made a sensible choice." He got to his feet and came around the edge of his desk, pleased that we had reached agreement so quickly and amicably. "You understand, this is your basic salary—minus commissions and bonuses—but it should help. Shall I have a check drawn up for the entire amount, or do you need some of it now—in cash?"

I did not fancy waiting for a check to be processed. Neither did I relish the idea of Mr. Marsh or anybody else counting money into my hands as though it were a payoff.

"Can you mail the check?" I asked.

He understood at once. "No trouble at all. It'll be in the mail before closing time today. I'm sorry about all this. I wish it could be some other way, but this was not a hurried decision, nor was it mine alone. We can't leave your territory uncovered indefinitely. I went out myself two weeks ago, but it was a stop-gap measure, and that has its limitations. We hope to start breaking in someone next week, but we don't know exactly who yet. We have one or two people in mind."

"I have a few books and catalogs at home that I should bring back. Your new man will need them."

"Whenever it's convenient for you."

I looked around the office and felt a great sadness. I got up to go. "I guess that's about it, isn't it?" I said. "I don't know how to terminate a conversation of this kind. It's my first experience."

"We'll give you references."

"I'll need them."

"I hope things turn out well for you. I mean that. When all this blows over, come back to see us. Maybe we can work out something."

"Thank you. That may be a long time from now."

"Do you want to get the things from your desk?"

I shook my head. "If you don't mind, just ask one of the girls to clean it out. If she thinks there's something I might want, maybe she can drop it in the mail."

"Be glad to do it. Glad to do it."

An awkward silence followed.

"Hamilton, don't think too hard of us," he said softly. "This is a business we're running, and I'm sure you appreciate that." He extended his hand. "Would you like to say good-bye to anyone? Some of the others might—"

"No, I believe not."

"As you wish." He opened the door. "I'll walk to the front door with you, if it's all right?"

I was not certain that I could get there, otherwise.

At the front entrance, with all the company employees craning their necks and straining their eyes and ears behind us, Mr. Marsh gulped noisily and said, "I'm infernally curious about one thing, Hamilton. I don't mean to pry, but can't you draw any money against that estate you inherited?"

"I haven't tried."

"Haven't tried?" He was incredulous. "Why, I thought you'd—"

"My plans, such as they are, don't include any money from the Holbrook estate."

"I see," he said, but I knew that he did not.

"Well, good-bye, Hamilton." He seemed wistful. "I'm sorry—really sorry. Mail me your letter of resignation as soon as you have time. It will look better in your file than a company explanation."

He turned back. The typewriters and business machines started up their clacking again.

I found myself outside in the sunshine, unemployed. The six months' pay and Mr. Marsh's sympathy and last gesture should have softened the blow, but they represented the wrong thing. A tie had been broken; a link had been severed. I had one less root to hold me down. I had never felt more insecure.

I walked past the company's parking lot and around the corner onto Fort Worth's main thoroughfare, wandering aimlessly along the sidewalk, mechanically dodging the other pedestrians. I was in no hurry. I had nowhere to go and nothing to do. I had no job; I was an awkward presence in my own home; I was an embarrassment to my neighbors; I was free only at the price of a $50,000 bail bond; an indictment for first degree murder hung over my head; my name was headline news; I was scheduled to inherit one million dollars; and I had nowhere to go and nothing to do. I smiled at the irony of my situation. Had it not been so serious, and had it not been happening to me, Peter D. Hamilton, I would have laughed aloud.

With my head down and my eyes trained on the sidewalk, I circled the block and strolled aimlessly back to the American Business Machines parking lot and the privacy of my own automobile.

At home, Amy met me at the door, distraught. Carrie Holbrook had just telephoned from Fort Worth. She was on her way out to Jones Hill, to our house.

❦ 30 ❧

Amy could not take her eyes off Carrie. I think she had planned to dislike everything about her, but once we were settled in the living room where she could examine her at leisure and at close range, she became so absorbed in what she saw that her critical faculties seemed to fail her. She gave herself over to outright admiration of Carrie's smile, her green eyes, her blonde hair, her creamy complexion, her green cardigan, gray skirt, the orange bauble that hung from her neck and should have been garish but was not, her well-turned ankles and the plain black pumps that encased her perfectly shaped feet. I watched Amy take it all in, and I knew that she found Carrie faultless.

Meanwhile, Carrie had been sizing up Amy with equal interest and the same open admiration. She overlooked no detail. She seemed delighted by Amy's well-scrubbed, wholesome charm. As for myself, I had never seen Amy look quite so alive, so genuine and so completely the American ideal of an attractive young matron, mother and homemaker.

"You're just right for Pete!" Carrie exclaimed. "Without actually having a mental picture of you, you're exactly what I knew you'd be."

Amy was flattered and scarcely bothered to conceal it. I sat with my mouth open as she and Carrie bypassed the normal stiffness of a first meeting and, with every circumstance working against them, established a rapport without apparent effort. I was the only one who felt ill at ease.

While they talked and I listened, I was filled with a fresh appreciation of Amy. She had none of Carrie's glamour, but she did not suffer by comparison. Actually, her face had more depth of expression, her features were somehow more interesting, and in all probability her charm would be more enduring. Carrie glittered, Amy was winsome. By any standard, Amy was pretty, and I had never seen her look prettier than she did while sitting on the sofa talking to our visitor. She was gracious, too; and while she was enchanted by Carrie Holbrook, she kept both feet on the ground, every inch the hostess, never once betraying an avid curiosity that surely must have consumed her.

Carrie asked to see the boys, who were having their naps. I waited while Amy led her into their bedroom.

"Pete, they're *adorable!*" Carrie said when they returned. "I'd love to see them awake. I know they're precious!"

Then as naturally as she breathed, she turned the conversation to me and the purpose of her visit.

"Your lawyer came to see me today with that fantastic tale about Ben and the cleaning compound," she said. "The sheriff had already told me, but since he seemed to pooh-pooh the whole idea, I did too. Now your lawyer's trying to open it up again. He says he wants to get it into the record at the trial. I'm horrified. You can't do that to Ben, and I want you to stop trying."

"But I think he put the liquid into Henrietta's pitcher," I said. "He didn't know what he was doing—I'm quite aware of that, but I still believe he did it."

"But he's just a baby! You have no idea what you're blaming him for!"

"*No idea!* How can you say that? Do you think I'm enjoying this? It's the worst thing I've ever done in my life! You can't possibly think I would dream up a thing like this to get myself off the hook. But it isn't a question of blame, Carrie. *There was no murder.* It was an accident, that's all."

She shook her head obstinately. "I don't know what put such a wild idea in your head."

"There was nothing wild about it," I said. "As far as I could figure, the overhang was the only place the sheriff and his deputy hadn't looked. So we went to the overhang, Natwick and I, and there was the bottle. And it had to be Ben who put it there."

"It did not," she said quickly. "You could have put it there yourself."

I felt a compassion for her. Not for Carrie Holbrook, the beautiful widow, but for Carrie Holbrook, mother, protecting her little boy from hurt.

"Carrie, did you ever see Ben's store?" I asked.

"No."

"When you get home, go down to the overhang and take a look. You'll see what I'm talking about. He pretended to sell me a bottle of medicine, and we went through the transaction from beginning to end. When we went into the house for lunch, he still had the store on his mind. He found a bottle in the closet that caught his eye—a pretty bottle—and he wanted it for his store. He took it. Alberta wouldn't give him a bottle unless it was empty, so he emptied it. He emptied it into Henrietta's water pitcher because it was handy. *He was playing*, Carrie! He didn't commit a crime."

Carrie would have none of it. Her green eyes flashed. "That is not true," she exclaimed violently. "*That is just not true!* You've got no right to tell that to me or anybody else."

"Don't you think I realize the seriousness of what I'm saying? I've got two children of my own, don't forget. And you must know me well enough to realize that I would not involve a child in a thing like this without some solid reason. That empty bottle was in Ben's store because he took it there. There isn't any other explanation." She started to answer, but I went right on. "Did Mr. Burnsides talk to Ben today?"

"Yes, but Ben didn't confirm anything you've said."

"He didn't deny—"

"*Pete!* Ben didn't confirm or deny anything! He's too young.

Mr. Burnsides couldn't get Ben's mind on the overhang at all. He talked, all right, but not about that. Ben talks in circles. All children do."

I waited to hear more. Little Ben Holbrook was my entire case. Regardless of how Arthur Burnsides intended to handle my defense, without Ben Holbrook to back me up, I was doomed. A last chance was passing by, and I groped for a way to hang onto it. I turned to Amy, who was still staring at Carrie. She turned her head slowly and looked into my eyes. Something passed between us, and she sat up straight and turned to Carrie.

"But surely that's not the end of it," she said. "Mr. Burnsides must plan on talking to Ben again."

"Not if I can help it," said Carrie with fierce determination. "What good would it do? He's a harmless, innocent little child, and I have no intention of allowing a lot of adults to gang up on him."

"You don't seem to understand the spot I'm in," I broke in. "I'm the one who's been indicted. I'm the one with the motive. I'm the one who profits by Henrietta's death. I'm the outsider no one can explain. I'm the Number One suspect. I'm the *only* suspect. And do you know what my defense is? My defense is my own words that I didn't do it. That'll sound pretty weak in a court of law. Now, what would you have me do? Sit back and rest until my turn comes, then get up on the stand and tell the jury that I'm innocent and they've got to believe me? Do you think I'm a good enough orator to put that one over? 'Truth is mighty and will prevail'—is that the idea? Maybe so, but I just happen to believe that truth won't come out unassisted."

"Now, Pete, you know you'll never get convicted on the case Natwick has built up," Carrie said.

"Maybe not by a jury," I said, "but unless the whole truth is laid out for everybody to see, plenty of people will always convict me in their minds. Look, Carrie, if I wanted to invent a story —tell lies to get myself off the hook—don't you think I could have been more ingenious than this?"

Carrie had not taken her eyes off me while I talked. Her face was a mask. I could not determine how she was receiving my words. Her reply, however, left no doubt. It was cold, deadly and calculating.

"I think it is the most ingenious story I ever heard," she said evenly.

Amy gasped. My mouth fell open. "You can't believe that!" I whispered.

"I most certainly do."

"Do you mean to sit there and tell me you believe I fabricated this story out of thin air?"

"I do. And you're not going to get away with it, Pete," she said. "I'll do anything in the world to stop you."

"What can you do?"

"I'll send Ben away where no one can find him. There's no law that can keep him here. The district attorney can keep me here, maybe, but he can't keep Ben."

"You wouldn't do that."

"Try me," she said threateningly. "Just try me. If you think I'm going to have something like this hanging over Ben's head for the rest of his life, you've got another think coming. I'll send him as far away as I can and for as long as I have to."

"Even if it means I get convicted?"

Carrie looked at Amy. The two of them gazed at one another in charged silence. Carrie turned back to me.

"Yes," she said. "Even if it means you get convicted."

Amy drew back as though Carrie had struck her. Her eyes filled with horror and disbelief. She shaped her lips around a word and held it for a moment. "You believe Pete!" she said at last. "I can tell. You *know* that Ben did it."

"I know no such thing!"

"*You know Ben did it,* but you'd let Pete take the blame! You believe Pete! You be—"

"Stop saying that!" Carrie stormed. "If I believed Pete, I wouldn't be here."

"No—that's the reason you *are* here," Amy said, in measured tones. "You're afraid to let Mr. Burnsides talk to Ben again. If

you thought Pete invented that story, you wouldn't be afraid—
and you *are* afraid."

"You're damned right I'm afraid," Carrie said. "I'm afraid
plenty, because I know that a five-year-old child can't match
wits with an experienced attorney. As soon as Ben saw Mr. Burnsides, he liked him. He doesn't take to strangers easily, but he
took to Mr. Burnsides; and I know that, given enough time, Mr.
Burnsides could twist Ben around his little finger and make him
say anything he wants to hear."

"But he wouldn't do that," Amy said. "Don't you believe he
has any principles? Don't you trust *anybody* to do the right
thing?"

"I don't intend to give him the chance." She turned back to
me. "So stay away, Pete. Leave Ben alone."

"You know, Carrie, you don't trust anybody. You're too much
on your own. I thought I knew you, but maybe you've changed.
Or maybe I never did know you—maybe I've been counting on
something that was never there in the first place."

"I don't know what you've been counting on," she said, her
chin tilted upward, "but I can tell you one thing. During the
years, I've had to look after Carrie Holbrook because there was
no one else to do it. And I've learned that nobody hands you
anything on a silver platter. If you want something, you have to
figure a way to get it, then get it. If you want something not to
happen, you have to figure a way to stop it, then stop it. And this
thing you've cooked up against Ben is not going to happen. I'll
stop you any way I can."

There was nothing left to say. Carrie had said what she came
to say, and for us to try again would have been useless. Her
visit was finished, and by all that was sensible, I should have been
finished with Carrie. I tried to convince myself of that, but I
couldn't. Her aloneness touched me. She was ruthless, but people
don't become ruthless without provocation. At least, that's the
way I saw it. Or perhaps I only imagined I saw it that way. Even
now, I'm not certain.

(237)

Carrie stood up to go. Amy did not move from the sofa. Carrie looked down at her.

"I'm sorry, Amy," she said. "Really I am. I wish it could have been some other way between us—all of us." Her words rang true.

"Did you make the trip from Erskine just for this?" Amy asked.

"Yes. Why?" Carrie seemed puzzled.

Amy got to her feet and went to the front door before she replied. With her hand on the knob, she turned back to face Carrie. "It seems like a lot of trouble and bother just to run down a story that you believe to be pure invention."

Carrie chose not to reply. Instead, she stood in the doorway and appraised Amy, not without kindness.

"Amy?"

"Yes?"

"I wish we had. . . ."

Amy said quickly, "But we didn't. . . ."

Carrie lingered for a moment. "No," she said wistfully. "We didn't, and it's a pity." Then she crossed the porch and stepped down the sidewalk.

Amy closed the door and stood listening until she heard Carrie shift gears and pull away from the curb. She came back into the living room.

"What do you think?" I asked.

"I think that Carrie Holbrook is one of the most beautiful women I've ever seen," she said.

Then she went into the bedroom and closed the door.

❦ 31 ❦

I telephoned Arthur Burnsides at his home that evening to report on Carrie's threat to send Ben away.

"There's nothing to prevent her doing it," he said. "As a matter of fact, Carrie herself is free to leave any time she chooses—until she is actually served with a subpoena."

"I'd like to talk to Ben myself," I said. "At any rate, I'd like to try. Do you think you can arrange it?"

"Perhaps," he said, "if the district attorney will give his consent again. Carrie's his witness, and a question of ethics is involved."

"Do you think he'll consent?"

"He might. He's got a personal interest in this case. He and Ben Holbrook grew up together. I don't suppose we can lose anything by asking."

Douglas Fenton, the district attorney, agreed readily enough, but with the stipulation that he be present when I talked to Ben.

Mr. Burnsides was pleased. "It will be to our advantage to have him along," he said the following morning during our drive to Erskine. "If Carrie is not cooperative—and she just might resist us—the authority of his office could smooth out the entire operation. Besides, if Ben tells us anything, Fenton will be our witness for what might turn out to be one-time testimony. Even if Ben talks, he might not talk the second time and for the record. Fenton will be good insurance."

He turned to look at me appraisingly. "Douglas Fenton is about your age, I'd say. This is his first term in office, but he doesn't have blood in his eye like so many new prosecutors. Maybe that's because he's a home town boy. I doubt if he'll measure up to your image of a district attorney."

He didn't. Douglas Fenton was not the adversary I expected. Well-mannered and soft-voiced, he was interested in my friendship with Ben Holbrook and offered a few recollections of his own.

"Ben and I went down to Galveston one summer to work at the beach," he said. "We decided to enjoy ourselves for a day or so before we looked for a job. The day or so stretched into a week, and we ran out of money. Then we couldn't find a job. We telephoned home—collect—and our folks told us to get home the best way we could, or else find a job like we went down there to do. We thumbed our way back to Erskine without one red cent between us. Home never looked so good before or since."

He smiled at the memory; then, turning to the business at hand, he said he felt obliged to warn us that our visit to little Ben Holbrook could work to the State's advantage.

"Suppose your hypothesis doesn't pan out," he said, "and I come away from the Holbrooks' with a new and unflattering opinion of the defendant here?" He nodded toward me. "Do you get what I'm saying?"

"Precisely," said Mr. Burnsides, "and we're willing to take the risk."

"Very well. Just so you know."

His eyes kept straying to me. I was the object of a wonderment that was personal, not official. Had we met at a college reunion, we would have understood one another more readily than as adversaries ordained by law.

"Why didn't we do this before the grand jury met?" he asked.

"There just wasn't time," said Mr. Burnsides. "We were busy

getting acquainted, and there was a lot of emotional upheaval. Anyway, at that stage, I could not have decided whether or not it was a good idea. Besides, Pete was in custody, which would have made it awkward and complicated. My one attempt to talk to the boy later got me nowhere. Pete hopes to do better."

Fenton smiled and got up from his desk. "You know, it's going to take me a long time to build a reputation this way. My job is to go to court—not stay out of it."

He excused himself to settle some routine office business and to telephone Carrie that we were coming.

"That could have been a tactical error," he said, hanging up the telephone and reaching for his hat. "We might have done better by walking in unannounced. Come on. Let's go."

Alberta's face lighted up at the sight of me.

"Have you been all right, Alberta?" I asked, giving her my hat.

"It ain't been good around here, Mr. Hamilton," she said with sadness. "It ain't good at all. I guess I'll jes' go on missin' Mrs. Holbrook until I die, too. It ain't like it was when you was comin' all the time and you and Mrs. Holbrook was havin' such a good time and enjoyin' yourself. Miss Carrie will be right down. How you been feelin'?"

"Fine. Just fine." We filed into the parlor.

The draperies had been pulled back to admit the sun in full, but the old room was depressing, nevertheless. The flower vases were empty. Nothing was out of place. Alberta followed me, mumbling.

"I don't like to hear all them things they said you done," she said. "I know you didn't do none of them—not none. Would you gentlemen like to sit down?"

We didn't have to wait long before Ben bounced into the room followed by his mother. The three of us stood up. Ben hardly looked at me, but when he saw Mr. Burnsides he went toward him.

"Hello, Ben," Mr. Burnsides greeted him cheerily. "You didn't expect to see me again so soon, did you?"

"See where I cut my finger?" He held out his hand.

(241)

Mr. Burnsides took the small hand in his and examined it. "I'll bet that didn't hurt much, did it?"

"Not much," Ben said.

Carrie regarded the three of us with hostility, but she did motion us to sit down.

"I don't like this," she said. "I don't like it at all. It's a terrible thing you're doing—all of you." She took me in with a dark frown. "It took the district attorney to get me to do it." She lifted her eyebrows and appraised Fenton with new interest. "And I'm surprised to see you here," she said. "After all, you are the prosecutor, aren't you? You sound like one of them." She nodded toward Mr. Burnsides and me.

"I'm interested in justice—whatever that turns out to be," he said. "That's part of my job, too. Actually it *is* my job."

"Do you believe their story?"

"I neither believe nor disbelieve. They have an interesting theory, and I'm obligated to examine it. If it will be any consolation to you, I wish I had never heard of this case. I was a friend of Ben's, too, you see."

"You're doing this over my protest," she said stubbornly.

"I understand that. May we talk to Ben now?"

Ben was standing by the window absorbed in something outside.

"Ben?" Carrie called to him halfheartedly. "These men want to talk to you."

"There's a squirrel in the tree!" he cried. "Come look at the squirrel, Mama!"

"I'll see it later, darling. Mr. Hamilton wants to talk to you."

He did not move.

"Ben—"

I got up, stepped to the window and stooped down beside Ben.

"Where's a squirrel?" I asked.

Ben pressed the end of his finger against the windowpane. "There—see? Up at the top. See him?"

I inched closer to the window. "Hey! That's a big one! There's a squirrel that comes into my back yard sometimes."

"Do you feed him?"

"No, I'm afraid not," I said. "He never stays long enough. How about you? Do you ever feed that one?"

"No. Mama said that squirrels find their own food."

My eyes took in the wooded hillside. "That looks like a good yard to play in," I said. "What do you play when you go outside?"

"Different things," he replied. "When Scottie and Jimmie come up here, we climb trees. One day we walked the stone wall and Scottie fell off and hurt his foot."

"When I was here once before, you were playing store, down at the overhang," I reminded him. "Do you still have your store?"

"No. One day when Jimmie was here, we threw rocks at the bottles and broke them."

"I guess that was fun, too, wasn't it?" I said. "Do you remember the day I came to your store and you sold me a bottle of medicine?"

He stared at me for a moment. I could not determine whether or not I had rekindled a memory. For fear that I had not, I added, "You were showing me how far you could jump off the top of the overhang. I ate lunch with you in this house that day. Do you remember all that?"

"Did you know that my grandmother died?" he asked abruptly.

I saw that his mind had made a significant connection, and I seized on it. "I was here the day she died. Remember?" I said. "She was sick in bed that day. She couldn't eat lunch with us."

I glanced back at the others. They were sitting like rocks, their attention fastened on the scene at the window. Of the three, only Carrie's face portrayed any emotion. She was leaning forward, straining to remain silent. Her green eyes were dark with anxiety. I turned back to Ben.

"Ben, did you take any new bottles to your store that day?"

His interest had shifted back to the wooded hillside. "The squirrel's gone!" he said.

"Ben, you're not listening to what I'm saying. *Listen* to me!"

"Stop it, Pete!" Carrie commanded, standing up. "This has gone far enough. Can't you see that? You're getting nowhere with him. Leave him alone!"

"Please, Mrs. Holbrook," Fenton interceded. "Let him try."

"Ben—look at me," I pleaded. "Please, listen to me. Please."

He looked at me obediently.

I drew a deep breath and tried again. "Now listen to what I'm asking you," I said. "Did you take a new bottle to your store when your grandmother was sick in bed?"

"Alberta gave me a bucket," he said.

"I don't care what Alberta gave you!" I said, exasperated. "Did *you* take a bottle from the—"

"Pete!"

Ben looked around at his mother expectantly.

"Ben! Listen to me!" I said. "Did you—"

"Pete! I'm warning you!"

Ben was alarmed now. He looked from his mother to me then back again. "Mama?" He started toward her.

"Ben, come back here!" I knew that I should not have shouted at him so harshly, but I couldn't help it.

"Stop it, Pete!" Carrie screamed. She held out her arms. Ben ran to her.

"Ben! I'm talking to you!" I said.

Carrie sat down again and drew Ben close.

"Mama, are you mad at me?" he asked, frightened.

"No, darling, I'm not mad at you," she said. She stroked his dark, tousled hair. "You've been real nice," she said softly. She bent down and kissed the top of his head. She raised her eyes and looked at Fenton imploringly.

"But he didn't answer any of my questions!" I protested. "Ben, let's talk about your store. . . ."

Carrie clapped a hand over his ear. "Don't listen, darling!" she cried. "Don't listen!" Her face was pale. Ben pulled away from her and looked into her face, his eyes wide with fright.

"Come on, tell me," I went on, trying to control my voice. "Tell me about getting the bottle out of. . . ."

"Stop it! Stop it! Stop it!" Carrie screamed. She wrapped her arms around him tightly, holding his face against her breast. "Don't listen, Ben."

"Mrs. Holbrook, you're not making things any better," Fenton said, standing up.

"Am I supposed to?" Carrie cried. "This was your idea, not mine!" She still held Ben to her.

"I was hoping you'd be more cooperative."

"You want me to tell him what to say? I'm his mother—remember?"

Fenton sighed. "I think we'd better go," he said quietly.

"But he didn't answer my questions!" I said again. "We can't go until—"

Fenton patted Ben's head. "You're a fine boy, Ben." He turned to Mr. Burnsides. "Maybe we can try again later."

"No, you can't! I won't let you. You asked if you could see him this once, and I agreed—but that's all. If you try to see him again, you'll have to use every legal maneuver in the book to get inside the front door. I won't let you talk to him. I won't let you! Look what you've already done to him!"

Mr. Burnsides spoke up. "Mrs. Holbrook, I can understand your feelings. I don't blame you in the least for wanting to protect him. This is a terrible thing we have to do here, but it must be done. We're here looking for the truth, and none of us is getting one iota of pleasure from the task. But we've done nothing to Ben, and I think you realize that. We have not upset him in the least. That's the crux of the problem—we have not communicated with him at all."

He nodded slightly and left the room to wait for us in the hall.

"I grew up with your husband," Fenton said to Carrie. "We went through school together." His eyes took in the room. "I've been in this house—this room—more times than I can remember. I'm sorry we had to come here today like this. I'd rather remember the good times. I'm sorry."

Carrie stared at him mutely and watched him join Mr. Burnsides. I moved past her. "I'll be back," I said. "I'm not through."

We let Fenton out at the courthouse. "I don't know if I wish it had turned out differently or not," he said, sticking his head back inside. "I don't know my own mind about this case. All I know is that I wish this whole miserable mess could be erased from the records. Getting a straight story from a small child is the toughest thing in the world, if he's not interested. Mr. Burnsides will tell you that—and you've just tried it for yourself."

"I'll tell *you* something, Fenton," Mr. Burnsides said. "Carrie believes Pete's story. She gave herself away at every scream."

Fenton said nothing, but he smiled. He stood on the curb watching us drive away.

We drove back to Fort Worth, trying to pick the flaws in our approach.

"There must be something else we can do," I said, as the Fort Worth skyline formed itself on the horizon.

"We could get a psychiatrist—a child specialist," Mr. Burnsides said, thinking aloud. "But that would take a lot of time and a lot of money. Anybody would have a tough job now. Carrie will see to that. She'll fix it so that Ben remembers nothing about that day. She'll make certain."

"How?"

"Many ways. She can substitute a whole series of events for that day. Little by little she can lead him away from the memory of the overhang, his grandmother's illness and everything connected to that day; then she can drill other events into his head until they're real to him. It wouldn't be difficult—he seems to be very much under her influence."

"But Carrie wouldn't do a thing like that!"

"Put yourself in her shoes, Pete. Can you think of anything you wouldn't do to protect one of your own boys from the knowledge that he had poisoned his own grandmother?"

"Not if it meant convicting an innocent person."

We reached the edge of Fort Worth and slipped into the stream of inbound traffic.

"You're not convicted yet," he said. "I told you before that I didn't intend to base your defense on this story. It was just that we needed to make the attempt—and we made it. You might feel that you're walking the plank, but you're nowhere near the end of it—not yet."

"Pirates," I said.

"How's that?"

"Pirates." I repeated it slowly.

Mr. Burnsides glanced at me. "What do you mean?" he asked.

"I forgot about the pirates."

"What are you talking about?"

"Turn around and go back," I said.

"Go back where?"

"Back to Erskine."

"Pete, you're not making any sense."

"I told Ben how to play pirates and hide his loot in the cave. He wasn't playing store at all—he was playing pirates." My excitement was mounting. "He took the bottle out of the house and hid it because he was a pirate, not a storekeeper. You see? I was trying to make him remember the store, but *I* had started *him* on the pirate thing. Turn around."

"Why did you tell him how to play pirates?"

"I'd played it when I was a kid. I told him how to pretend that the overhang was a pirate's cave and the grass was the ocean. I told him how the farmhouse below could be a ship. He didn't know anything about pirates, and I had to explain to him the meaning of the word 'loot'."

"Why should you have told him what to play?"

"There wasn't any reason. I just saw all that pasture and space, and the idea came to me. It's probably what I would have played."

"Perhaps he didn't follow your suggestion. You went back up

to the house and left him there. You can't be positive that he played pirates at all."

"But he did. When I went upstairs to call him back to lunch, he was looking out a window toward the overhang. He told me then that he was a pirate. Then he left the table before Alberta found Henrietta. He had gone outside again."

Without speaking, he maneuvered the car over to the curb and turned off the ignition. He leaned back in his seat and turned to face me. He seemed pleased. "Congratulations," he said. "You finally did it."

"Did what?"

"You finally managed to connect yourself directly to Henrietta Holbrook's death." He sounded almost triumphant.

I was baffled. "I connected—?"

"Yes—you finally did it. It took a while, but you made it. I suppose I should add this as Number Six to your list of do-gooder activities."

"What are you talking about?"

"You planted the idea, that's what. You told me so yourself a moment ago."

"I only meant the idea of playing pirate."

"But that's what did it," he said with complete confidence. "Surely you can see that."

"Well, how about explaining it to me just in case I can't?"

"It's quite simple. Or at least, it's quite apparent," he said. "If Ben was playing pirate, he had to take something that did not belong to him and hide it. So he went into the house and took a bottle that he knew Alberta would never give him. You taught him the rules of the game. It was another of your do-good—"

"Now don't get strung out on *that* line again!" I broke in, irritated. "Do-gooding may be your favorite subject, but it's not mine. Why not concentrate on the problem at hand instead of trying to prove all your little private theories?"

He was watching me intently. Then with a half smile, he looked at his watch.

"No more speeches, eh?" he said, looking up. The half smile broadened.

"Not unless you can think of a new one."

"You know, you're wounding my ego," he said. "I've always been considered a good speechmaker."

"You are," I agreed, "and that's the problem. You're so good that you almost convince me—not by what you say, but by how you say it."

He laughed outright. "Well, that restores part of my vanity, so you're forgiven."

"Thanks," I said, my mood softening. "Now. How about it? Can we go back to Erskine and take another crack at Ben?"

He studied his watch again. "All right," he said decisively. "But this time, we'll do something we should have done the first time. We'll take the cleaning compound bottle with us. That is, if Fenton will permit it. If your theory is right, you won't need that pirate story. The bottle itself should do it."

❧ 32 ❧

Douglas Fenton was reluctant to go with us a second time. "Your timing is psychologically wrong," he said. "It's been less than two hours since we left Mrs. Holbrook in a mood to slit our throats. She might not let us back in the house without a court order."

"Her very mood might make our timing psychologically *right*," Mr. Burnsides argued.

"If that's true, then we'd be taking advantage of her, and I don't like that," said Fenton.

"Normally I would agree," said Mr. Burnsides. "But if the truth is buried there somewhere, and if we find it, even by taking advantage of Carrie, I'll have to advocate that we do it. We're dealing with a man's whole life and the life of his wife and children and everybody connected with them. I would not like to put all that in jeopardy for the sake of Carrie Holbrook's personal feelings. She'll get her feelings back into good running order soon enough. But reinstating a man with his family, his employers, his neighbors and friends and with society at large—that's another matter."

"You believe Hamilton's story, don't you?" Fenton asked.

Mr. Burnsides stared at the floor for a moment. "Yes, I guess

I do," he said. "Something's got to make sense, and to be truthful, Fenton, this is the only thing I've heard that does."

"We can't invade the place, you know," said Fenton. "But aside from that, she's my witness. I do have an obligation to keep her good will."

Mr. Burnsides was persuasive. "You told us that you have no enthusiasm for this case, Fenton, and if we can wrap it up here and now, so much the better. I believe if we handle it right, the cleaning-compound bottle will bring it all back to Ben, and we can settle that matter once and for all. We can hardly afford not to try."

"I'll agree that we should have taken the bottle with us before," Fenton admitted. "And once while Hamilton was talking to Ben by the window, the thought crossed my mind. But everybody got so emotional that I didn't think of it again." He gazed at his desk, littered with paper and books. "I have other things that need my attention," he said with a sigh.

"If we're right, you'll have fewer," said Mr. Burnsides.

Fenton pushed back his chair and stood up. "All right. But if we're wrong," he went on, "I'll have the devil of a time wooing Carrie Holbrook back into my camp."

Alberta was so surprised to see us that she forgot to take our hats. Carrie appeared at the top of the stairs.

"No!" she screamed.

"We have to see him again, Mrs. Holbrook," Fenton called out.

She stood tall and unyielding. "No! You can't! I won't let you see him." She made no move to come down the stairs.

Alberta stood by the parlor door, her dark face troubled, unable to decide whether to go or stay. Her training won out, and she disappeared through the parlor.

We moved deeper into the hall, the district attorney first; he stepped to the foot of the stairs. Mr. Burnsides and I stopped at the parlor door.

"You can't talk to him," Carrie repeated, her voice shaking. "Go away—all of you."

"I wish we could," said Fenton. "There's nothing I'd rather do. But you must realize that if Mr. Hamilton is correct, the facts will come out one way or the other, and possibly in a way that will be more painful than this. If he's wrong, maybe we can establish that here and now, and your worries will be over." He stood with his hat in his hand, his head tilted back, his eyes on Carrie at the top of the stairs. "Please, Mrs. Holbrook," he said gently. "Please, don't force me to get a court order."

"If you want to see Ben, you'll have to get it," she said with fire. "But until you do, just go away—all of you."

Suddenly her bravado crumbled.

"Please . . . go away. . . ." she pleaded. "Leave him alone. . . ."

"We can't do that, Mrs. Holbrook—not yet," said Fenton.

Her fear was out in the open now. She abandoned any attempt to hide it. "Please, don't. I beg you. He doesn't know what you're trying to do," she said. "It's not fair—three of you against a baby—he doesn't know what he's doing. It's not fair . . . it's not fair. I'm begging you to leave him alone."

The door at the rear of the hall opened and Ben wandered through it. Carrie leaned over the banister to follow our gaze. Her eyes widened. "Go back!" she shrieked. "Ben, go back!"

Ben looked up at her, his dark eyes big with curiosity. His mother had come halfway down the stairs, leaning over the banister and motioning to him. "Go back, Ben! Go back—go back!"

Ben stood as if fastened to the floor. She reached the bottom of the stairs and swooped down upon him.

"What's the matter, Mama?" His voice was small and frightened.

Throwing herself in front of him, she spun him around and shoved him toward the door through which he had entered. "Go outside and play—go, darling—go!" she babbled. "Don't come in here—see if you can find Scottie and Jimmie—don't stay here."

"Mrs. Holbrook, this isn't doing any good," Fenton said, trying to make himself heard, but Carrie was pushing Ben past the foot of the stairs, past the sitting-room door, past the hall closet. They reached the end of the hall. Her hand reached out for the knob.

In a second, I saw one chance.

"Ben!" I called, stepping forward. "Look what I found in your pirate's cave!" I held out the empty bottle.

He peered around his mother's skirt, his face suddenly eager. He disengaged himself and came out into full view. Carrie clutched at him, but he was too quick for her.

"*Ben, come back!* Don't talk. . . ."

I moved closer. "Where did you get this, Ben?" I spoke as quietly as I could, offering him the bottle.

Carrie flew at him from behind and grabbed him by the shoulders. He broke loose. She turned on me.

"I'll get you for this, Pete Hamilton!" she screamed. "If it's the last thing I ever—"

"You're making it all worse, Mrs. Holbrook," I heard Fenton say.

Somehow, all of us were back at the front of the hall again. Carrie had fallen into a crumpled heap at the bottom of the stairs, quiet, her face buried in her arms.

Ben was holding the compound bottle and examining it with pleased recognition.

"Do you remember taking that out to your cave?" I asked.

His face broke into a smile. "This was some of my loot," he said. "I put it in my pirate's cave one day."

The hall was still. From the corner of my eye, I thought I saw Carrie raise her head, but I dared not take my eyes off Ben.

"Where did you get it?" I asked.

"In the bathroom," he said casually, still fondling the bottle.

"Which bathroom?"

"The one upstairs."

"Will you show me where?" I said.

"If you promise not to tell Alberta."

"I promise."

"Okay!"

He hopped nimbly around his mother and took the steps as fast as his short legs would allow.

"Ben, don't go! Don't!" Carrie cried out, but he was already at the top of the stairs. "Ben—baby! Come back, darling!"

I followed him, the other men behind me. Ben led me to the hall bathroom and darted inside. Flinging open a closet door, he pointed.

"I got it in there," he said proudly.

The closet was a jumble of bottles, jars, tubes and cans. Ben dropped to his knees and crawled on the floor under the shelves.

"Was it empty?" I asked, keeping my voice calm.

He laughed. "No. That's why I don't want Alberta to know. She told me not to take any bottles that have anything in them."

"What did you do with it?" I asked.

"I hid it in the cave."

I was not there yet. The crucial question was yet unasked. The sweat stood on my forehead. "I mean *before* you hid it in the cave."

"I poured it out over there," he said, pointing to the lavatory.

"Did you pour it down the drain?"

He thought about that for a moment. I stopped breathing.

Fenton spoke up. "Did you pour it into a pitcher on the lavatory, Ben?" he asked gently.

Ben nodded. "I think so," he said. "I took it out the front door so Alberta wouldn't see me with it. I went up to my room to get it."

"Where was Alberta?" he asked.

"She was in the kitchen," he said.

I tried to speak, but the words were not there.

There was more—from Fenton and Mr. Burnsides—but I didn't listen. Later—I don't know how much later—I followed the others downstairs. I felt nothing at all, not even relief.

Carrie's face, pale and drawn, was turned up toward us. Fenton stopped and looked down at her.

"I'm not at all certain that we had the legal right to do this,

Mrs. Holbrook," he said softly. "Especially the manner in which we did it. You might be justified in seeking legal recourse against me. But we had a moral obligation to do it. I'm convinced of that." He moved past her toward the front door.

Carrie buried her face in her arms again. A faraway sensation told me I should feel sorry for her, but I had no energy to fix on it. Not then. My eyes were trained on the rectangle of light framed by the front door. As I stepped across the threshold, I was dimly aware of Alberta's dark figure somewhere in the background.

Outside, I crossed the circular driveway and dropped to the ground. There I sat, huddled in silence, staring through the trees to the bottom of the hill.

After a time, I stirred and looked around for the others. Mr. Burnsides was coming down the steps while Fenton stood in the doorway talking to Alberta. Carrie was nowhere in sight. I got to my feet and to the car. Mr. Burnsides came up from the other side. He settled himself behind the steering wheel and fumbled for his keys. I crawled into the back seat. Then it came, a nauseating revulsion at this thing I had done. Two dark, eager eyes looked up at me; an innocent little face swam before me. I saw a small finger pointing. . . .

I bolted from the car and onto the grass, where I retched until I felt hollow inside.

☙ 33 ❧

Quashing the indictment was not the automatic transaction I had assumed it would be. For Fenton and Mr. Burnsides, it was a cut-and-dried legal-administrative procedure involving a brief of the new evidence, a few affidavits and depositions, all bound together and filed with the office of the district attorney. But for me, it was an agonizing, long-drawn-out action of red tape and bureaucratic delays, during which I was sustained by an optimism that was not absolute, no matter how well founded, and a patience that quickly wore as thin as tissue paper. Friday and the weekend and two more days dragged by, while Mr. Burnsides had the documents and the motion for dismissal itself prepared and Fenton arranged a hearing at which he could present them. I wandered around the house, half listening when Amy spoke, half thinking when I responded.

If she shared my optimism while we waited, she said little to let me know it. She was withdrawn and closemouthed, but I knew that it was anxiety and a fear of expecting too much too soon that made her seem remote. I did not assess her mood beyond that. She cared. Quite aside from a natural concern for our future as a family, she cared for my sake. I was confident of that.

On Wednesday, when the waiting came to an end, I entered the house without much feeling.

"It's over," I said.

Amy came in from the kitchen to listen while I described the formalities that had set me free from all restraint and suspicion. "I'm glad, Pete," she said warmly when I had finished. "But I guess that goes without saying. I'm so glad—and relieved—I could cry."

"Go ahead," I said. "Go ahead and cry. Maybe I'll join you."

She dropped into a chair at the dining-room table. I stood in the middle of the living room. Her eyes were wet, but not wet enough to camouflage the emotions struggling to break through the restraints that had held them in check.

"I think I'll just turn loose and do that," she said, her voice trembling. "I just might."

And she did. She laid her head on the table in the crook of her arm and wept. I still stood in the living room, unable to move.

At last, she looked up and dried her eyes.

"Most of all, I'm glad for you," she said.

"For me? You mean for *us?*" I moved toward her and leaned against the doorway.

"All right. For us. But this has been yours from the beginning. I've really had little to do with it."

Her words had a chilly ring.

"Amy, how can you say that?"

"I'm not being ugly about it, darling," she said. "I'm not being vindictive. At least, I don't intend to be. But I've never felt as involved as I should have been in a thing of this magnitude. I don't mean I haven't cared. I've cared with everything in me. But it's been a kind of helpless anxiety—a sort of stand-by-and-wait proposition—rather than total immersion. I even feel guilty about it."

"But Amy, you told me yourself that when I'm in trouble, you're in trouble, too!"

"That's true," she said. "But it's the kind of trouble I was in when Kenny had the flu. That's not a good analogy. Kenny's flu had nothing to do with how he lived, his habits, his way of life. Your trouble did, and—I hate to keep harping on this, Pete

(257)

—but I was frozen out of a rather large portion of your life, and I don't know how to deal with it. I don't think I'm being selfish. I realize we have to lead our own lives—up to a point. We do it in many ways. All married people do. They have to, or else they'd drive one another crazy. But you took on a new segment of existence, which I knew nothing about. If it had been business-connected, I wouldn't question it for a minute. But it had nothing to do with business. It was another set of interests, a separate orientation, and I've been asked to understand it after the fact. I could have shared those interests with you—and the minimum would have been for me to at least know the interests existed. So all I can get from it is that you didn't *want* me to share it. I don't know how to deal with that."

"Are you leading up to something?" I asked.

"Yes," she said quietly. "I've got to get away from here. I can't think any more. I'm so mixed up and confused that I don't know what's what and who's who."

I moved back to the sofa and sank onto it, afraid to listen to more, but I prompted her, nevertheless. "And so?" I said.

"I've decided to go back to Mother's and see if I can get things straightened out."

"For how long?"

"I don't know. Until I straighten them out, I guess."

"What if you can't straighten them out?"

Her eyes filled with tears again. "Pete, that's not fair!" she cried. She turned her head away. "How can I know? I've just got to get away from here—from Jones Hill, from the neighbors, from the newspapers, from—from—*you!*"

Quickly, she turned back to me. "Oh! I didn't mean that like it sounds!" she said. "I didn't mean that, darling! I didn't mean it at all!" She got up from the table and rushed across the living room to me. I pulled her down into my lap.

"I know you didn't," I said. "I don't know what you *do* mean, but I know you didn't mean *that*."

She buried her face in my shoulder. "I've just got to get

away," she sobbed. "I've just got to go. Please—please, let me go!"

"Amy, Amy, Amy!" I murmured, holding her tighter. "It's not a matter of my letting you go. If you want to go, why, you'll go. That's all there is to it. It'll work out. You'll see. I just wish you were going for another reason."

"I wish I *had* another reason," she said.

I held her a while longer then she lifted her head from my shoulder and sat up straight.

"Give me your handkerchief," she said.

"Then get up, or I can't reach in my hip pocket for it."

She stood on her feet, and I gave her my handkerchief. She blew her nose rather noisily.

"I've got to ask you something," I said.

She returned my handkerchief and waited.

"Are we separating?"

"I only said I've got to get away. Do we have to formalize it with a title?"

"Okay—but I've got to ask you something else," I said. "Does your leaving me have anything to do with this talk about Carrie and me?"

She sat down on the sofa, this time on the end opposite me. "I wish I could deny it," she said in almost a whisper. She took a deep breath and looked at me imploringly. "Pete, why are you so interested in her?"

My heart went out to her. "Amy, there's nothing between Carrie and me. There never was. What I tried to do for her, I would have done for any close friend—Whistle Smith, Clay Thompson or Jack Mansfield. Well—things didn't pan out, but who in a thousand years would have predicted they would have come to a pass like this?"

"And that poor little boy—"

"I'll see him and hear him until the day I die," I said, "but it had to happen. A happy ending was impossible."

"I've stayed awake nights trying to find the answer," she said.

"Carrie has a hold on you that doesn't make sense. I couldn't believe my ears when I learned that you told Mrs. Holbrook that tale about the baby. Let's face it, Pete, you believed that story because you *wanted* to believe it. You've got no common sense about Carrie. Your reason has gone haywire. You're so concerned about her personally that you've got no rational view of the things she does. You rule out any possibility of the tiniest wrongdoing on her part. I don't get it—unless you're in love with her—"

"But I love you," I broke in.

"—unless you're so infatuated with her that you don't know what you're doing," she went on. "I don't really know what to think. That's why I've got to get away from here and straighten things out in my own mind."

"Amy, you don't believe that I'm in love with Carrie. Whether you hear me say it or not, you don't believe that. If you do, then I've got to wonder if you still love me."

"Whatever gave you that idea?"

"Well? Do you still love me or not?"

"Darling, if I loved you any more than I do right this minute, I'd explode all over this living room. But I don't understand your feelings about Carrie. Call me the jealous wife, if you like, or the third apex on that triangle, but at least, I've got some justification for it."

"Nothing that makes sense."

"Don't be too sure. What time did you leave Foley that night?"

"Oh—so that's it!" I said. "I see what's gnawing at you now. Well, I don't remember the time. Midnight maybe."

"Could it have been morning?"

"Suppose it had been broad open daylight the next day? Do you think I'd be stupid enough to sit here and admit it to you?"

A knowing expression appeared in her eyes.

"And you can get that smug look off your face, too," I went on. "Nothing illegal, illicit or immoral happened between Carrie and me."

"How can I be sure of that?"

"Because I'm telling you, that's how!"

"And that's supposed to be enough?"

"If it's not, then maybe you *ought* to leave!" I exclaimed.

"If you'll recall—that's what I intend to do," she said, standing up and starting from the room.

My anger quickly changed to panic, then remorse.

"Amy—come back," I said. "Please come back and sit down. Why don't we calm down and talk like adults? This is a serious thing you're doing."

"I'm aware of that." She stopped in the doorway and waited.

"Are you being fair to the boys?" I asked.

"No. Things like this are never fair to children."

"What about the money—the will?"

Her eyes narrowed. "What about it?" she asked suspiciously.

"It hasn't been settled yet."

"You won't need me for that."

"But it's yours, too. If it's mine, it's yours."

A quick flash of indignation crossed her face. "You're not going to get that money," she said with decision. "You have no right to it. Whatever I think of Carrie Holbrook's story of the baby, that money is hers. She ought to get every cent of it. Think of what she's got to live with for the rest of her life. How would you like to wrestle with her problem? Should she tell Ben before he hears it elsewhere? Or should she try to hide it from him altogether? How would you like for that to be hanging over Kenny's or Skeeter's head? Whatever I said to her that day in this house, I was in sympathy with what drove her. I couldn't help myself. Maybe she should take Ben away where no one knows them. But that takes money, and she hasn't got any. I don't think you'll enjoy the money, even if you get it. I certainly wouldn't."

"Do you think I should just step aside?"

"You'll have to decide that for yourself."

"I can't. When I make a decision, everybody says it's wrong, or it's prompted by the wrong motives. So what difference does it make what I do? I guess your going to St. Louis is calculated to bring me to my senses, isn't it? It's probably my punishment."

"I'm not trying to punish anybody." She turned and started through the door again.

"This isn't right, Amy," I told her, following her down the hall toward our bedroom. "It's not right at all."

She reached for a suitcase in the top of the closet, but her arms were not long enough. I got it for her.

"You might as well get the other two while you're at it," she said. "And my makeup kit, too."

"What if I refused?"

"I'd stand on a chair and get them for myself," she said, placing the suitcase on the bed. She fumbled with the catches.

I brought the other luggage from the closet.

"Take the big one into the boys' room," she said. "I'll come in there and pack their things later."

The boys were having their naps, and I went in and out of their room on tiptoe.

"Look, Amy," I said. "If you want to go visit your mother again, go ahead. But don't go off as the long-suffering wife whose husband has been stepping out on her. You don't realize what you're doing."

"I admit that. I don't know what I'm doing, but I'm going to try and find out."

"Once a break like this is made, it's awkward to patch it up later," I persisted. "You'd better think about that."

"I've already thought about it," she said flatly.

So it went. I might have stood over her arguing and pleading until she finished packing if it had not been for the boys. First Skeeter woke up crying, then Kenny. I picked them up, dressed them and took them out to the back yard.

In the evening, I drove my family to the airport in Dallas. Skeeter stood between Amy and me, babbling and bouncing around on the car seat. Amy held Kenny.

"Amy, where did we make the wrong turn this afternoon?" I asked. "We were doing fine. I didn't want you to go, but I agreed to it because you felt it was the thing to do. Then this

Carrie business came up, and we've been—well, out of touch ever since."

"Maybe we should have started out with Carrie and saved all the other," she said primly.

"Now just knock it off, Amy!" I protested. "You're just trying to give yourself a recognizable reason for leaving. I'm telling you for the last time that there's nothing between Carrie and me. You'd better get that straight with this telling, too, because I don't intend to repeat it every time her name is mentioned."

We drove to the airport without another direct word between us. When we entered the terminal, the St. Louis flight was being announced. We hurried through the baggage check and to the loading gate with no time for last minute considerations. I hugged and kissed the boys. Amy and I stood and looked at each other for as long as we dared. The airline agent at the gate spoke up.

"This is the last call, miss," he said.

He broke up our mood.

Amy laughed merrily. "Did you hear him call me *miss?*" she said. "And I'm standing here with two children in tow!"

"I love you, Amy," I said.

"I love you, too, darling."

She turned to go. A stewardess took Kenny from her arms.

"Hurry back!" I called after her.

"We'll see," she called over her shoulder.

They disappeared into the night.

Back home again, I telephoned Arthur Burnsides at his home.

"Should I come see you tomorrow?" I asked. "We haven't talked about the will yet."

"Well, of course, we've had our hands full of other matters," he said pleasantly. "I won't need to see you for a few days yet—not until I can get an agreement drawn up for you to mull over."

"How much time do we have?"

"I don't really know," he said. "I haven't been in touch with anybody in Erskine about the schedule for the probate hearings. In other words, I just haven't had time to zero my attention in on the will at all. That's another reason I'm not quite ready to talk about it. But don't worry, we won't come up short on the time. I'll make sure of that."

"I'm probably overanxious about it," I said. "Amy and I had a big hassle about it, and she took the boys and went back to St. Louis."

"Oh, that's too bad," he said. "I'm sorry to hear it. I hate to do this, Pete, but I'll have to hang up. We have dinner guests."

"I'm sorry—I shouldn't have called you at home."

"Don't worry about it. It's all right," he said. "Good night."

I hung up, went into the kitchen and poured myself a stiff drink of bourbon. I scarcely felt its effects, so I poured myself another. I could think of nothing else to do.

≱ 34 ≰

Our newspaper carried the story the next morning. It was at the bottom of the front page and was headlined, "ERSKINE DEATH RULED ACCIDENTAL." Although the account reported that the indictment against Peter D. Hamilton, Fort Worth salesman, had been dismissed and why, the emphasis was on a child's game that led to a fatal accident. My innocence was only incidental, it seemed. Later in the day, I drove to the shopping center for the Dallas newspapers. They, too, had given little more than a casual nod in my direction.

The telephone rang several times, and I ignored it. The doorbell sounded often enough to convince me that the neighbors wanted to tell me they knew and were glad, but I didn't answer. Perhaps I behaved badly, but the idea of facing people and trying to act natural was too much for me. Whistle Smith staked me out, though, and eventually caught me.

"Look, Pete, we all know how you feel," he said. He had been puttering under the hood of his automobile when I pulled into our carport. He had hurried across the driveway before I could get out of my car and into the house. "The whole world has sort of tumbled down around your ears—all that business in Erskine and Amy taking the kids to St. Louis—but don't take it out on us."

"I know, Whistle," I said, "and I appreciate what you're saying. But you don't know how hard it is to face people and try to carry on an ordinary conversation and act like nothing has happened."

"Well, you can't stay hidden forever," he said. "You might as well face that. So, here's my remedy. Come over in about five minutes and have a drink with Linda and me. If you'll stay for supper, we'll be tickled to death. If you don't, we won't push you. And we promise not to ask you any questions."

I laughed bitterly. "You'll be the first, if you don't."

I went, and although Whistle and Linda were determined to stick to their promise, I released them from it and told them about my friendship with Ben and Carrie Holbrook and later, with Henrietta. When I returned to my own house, I was relaxed and in better spirits than I had been in weeks.

After that, it was easy. Jack and JoAnne Mansfield invited me over for steaks in their back yard. Clay and Polly Thompson dropped in on a Sunday afternoon with a bottle of wine and some cooked cheese that Polly's mother in Lubbock had taught her to make. While we ate the cheese and drank the wine, I even made a joke or two about being a potential millionaire with no money in the bank. If Amy, Skeeter and Kenny had been at home, I might have considered rejoining the human race.

If I had any doubts that Henrietta's will must be dealt with soon, a letter from J. A. Tolliver several days later removed them. The will was being entered on the calendar for probate, which meant that I would have to act immediately. "The procedure will be brief," he wrote. "Carrie has announced her intentions to contest the action, as you know, but before she can file her petition, she must wait until the probate proceedings have been instituted formally. Therefore, the proceedings themselves will be little more than a formality. I have advised Arthur Burnsides accordingly." He concluded by saying that he planned to be in Fort Worth soon and would call me for lunch.

A week or so later, he made his word good, naming a restaurant that was small, quiet, excellent and expensive. I looked forward to his chatter and gossip. He did not disappoint me.

"You know, I should move to a city," he said, taking in the restaurant with an approving sweep of his saucerlike eyes and commenting on the appearances of at least a half dozen fellow diners. We had disposed of the menus and as much preliminary talk as was possible with J. A. Tolliver. "A city would give me more scope," he said. "But not this one! Heavens! I might as well live in Erskine as this overgrown village." He shuddered. "Dallas perhaps. Maybe New York or Boston. I've always thought I'd make a good Bostonian. I'm snobbish enough. I wanted to call you after that dreadful indictment was dismissed, but I was afraid I'd say the wrong thing. There was that poor, lovely Carrie Holbrook with that *frightful* situation on her hands, and I couldn't very well congratulate you in the face of that, could I? Think how it would have sounded! Wasn't that a tragic thing? I just don't know how she can ever cope with it."

He shook his head sorrowfully. "The people in Erskine don't know how to treat her. She's not well known there personally. Can you imagine not knowing someone who looks like *that!* But as I was saying, people simply don't know what to say to her. I suppose that in their own untutored way, they do their best, but they're standoffish. How can you rake up common, ordinary pity for one so *un*common and so *extra*ordinary? She's too chic and too elegant. That's her pitfall. You know yourself that it's easier to feel sorry for an ugly woman in a print housedress than a pretty one dressed liked a movie star. She just doesn't *look* sad and pathetic enough to suit them. She needs more of an underprivileged air about her—remind me to inquire about your family the minute I finish telling you this.

"Well, she stays up on that hill with that poor, poor unfortunate child, and when she does come down, looking like Miss America, everybody gawks at her as if she had two heads. They wouldn't stare so brutally if she had stringy hair and fat legs. She doesn't waste much time downtown, though. She gets back

(267)

up on that hill as fast as those shapely legs can carry her. She was in Carter's Drugstore the other day, and Miss Strange, my secretary, saw her and actually spoke to her before she realized that she had never met her personally. Carrie bought some shampoo, but Miss Strange was too far away to see the brand. It was in a tube, though."

The waiter brought our lunch, and while he served it, Mr. Tolliver bewildered him with a spirited monologue on recipes and exotic seasonings. He watched the waiter until he was out of sight. "He didn't understand a word," he said, shaking his head. "Not the first word. He's probably the parking lot attendant on his day off. Alberta left, you know."

"No, I didn't know."

"She and Carrie didn't get along," he explained. "*Surely* you must have known that—it's common knowledge. Everybody's wondering how long Carrie can hold out in that old warehouse without any domestic help. It's like housekeeping in the Methodist Church. Imagine!"

"Where did Alberta go?"

"She probably went back to the slave quarters singing 'Swing Low, Sweet Chariot,' or maybe to the cotton fields. A red kerchief around her head would fit her personality. The talk is that Carrie fired her, but I happen to know that Alberta chugged out of the house under her own steam. Just between us, Carrie didn't have the money to pay her wages. She's living on credit herself, and I cannot alter her plight. Everyone thinks I'm an old Scrooge, but I can't release a penny of poor Mrs. Holbrook's money to her. Not one red cent. The law, you know. I don't know what will become of her. I just don't know. She'd make a beautiful, tragic mistress for somebody. I'd approach her myself, but the scandal might not be good for my law practice."

We concentrated on our lunch for a while. At least, I did. Mr. Tolliver had an amazing ability to eat while talking incessantly.

"Dr. Kriegel doesn't help matters at all," he continued. "He still won't have anything to do with her. I don't know if you're aware of it, but he was *violently* opposed to her returning to

Erskine. At the funeral, he cut her dead. I saw it with my own eyes. He came out to the house afterwards and talked to everyone but Carrie. I think poor Mrs. Holbrook's death has been hard on him. He hasn't looked at all well recently. He's kept to himself, brooding and looking dramatically moody. He's a Heathcliff type, you know. He needs a couple of hounds at his heels and a moor to stand on and look out over. When he was younger, so many of his women patients were in love with him that it was fashionable. The few who were not, were considered to be queer. You know, he and poor Mrs. Holbrook were the *closest* of friends." He savored the words juicily.

"Some people think he's upset because he got cut out of the will," he said, "but that's only gossip. Small-town people are frightful gossips—they'll say *anything*, and you can't depend on a word of it. I happen to know that he's grieving for her; that's his trouble. Pure grief. For a while, I had the idea they might get married; they weren't too old—*she* certainly wasn't. Speaking of old, we had a couple in Erskine who got married last spring. He was eighty-two and she was eighty-one. He had lumbago, and she had asthma. Before they left on their honeymoon, the boy in Carter's Drugstore sold him a bottle of rubbing liniment and a package of Cubeb cigarettes. Don't you know they had a good time, wheezing and rubbing? How did you get along with Arthur Burnsides?"

"All right, I guess."

"You *guess?* Can't you make up your mind?"

"Well—okay. We got along all right."

"You sound so tentative. He's a good man to have on your side."

"What about you?" I asked suddenly. "Whose side are you on?"

He bent over his plate, then looked up. "Everybody's," he said. "Everybody who doesn't forbid it, that is. And most people don't. I don't have enemies. They're too much trouble and bother. I'm on your side, but of course, you're a special case."

"I never look a gift horse in the mouth, but why should you be on my side, and why am I a special case?"

"I'm no gift horse, and you're a special case because you are potentially so wealthy!" He snickered. "I've been representing the Holbrook estate for seventeen years and loving every minute of it. It gives me a status of sorts—don't forget the Holbrooks were the absolute top strata of Erskine business and society. Maybe that doesn't mean much to an outsider, but it's sort of a big-frog-in-a-little-pond proposition, and I enjoy that. I just do—make what you will of it. But that's not all. I love money, you see. I love to handle it and talk about it and deal with it and spend it. When poor Mrs. Holbrook passed away and left her money to you, I saw no reason not to go on handling it, even though it might change hands. But you wouldn't retain me if you didn't know me and admire my fine qualities—I have many, many more that you haven't discovered yet. So I waged an aggressive campaign to get acquainted with you."

I laughed. "But why don't you bend your efforts to keeping the money in the family—in Carrie's hands? As the family retainer, wouldn't that be more proper?"

"Oh, I'm not ignoring Carrie," he said happily. "Do you think I'm crazy? She might get all the money and leave you out in the cold without a cent, so I advise her too—more than I do you, actually, because she's infinitely prettier. I'm collecting some papers for her now, getting them ready for her attorneys. She retained a firm in Dallas—Teague and Folmer, an *excellent* firm. I could name you some of their bigger cases, but you'd have to be a lawyer to understand, and if there is anything that you're not, dear Pete, it's a lawyer. You proved that to me long ago. Anyway, Teague and Folmer will give you and Arthur Burnsides a stiff battle. Carrie came to see me not long ago for a briefing on the estate. She *is* a member of the Holbrook family, after all, and she needs to know what she is fighting for. I encouraged her to go ahead with her suit, by all means. You see, the way I've mapped it out is that if she wins, I'll stay on with the estate. It's very clever of me really."

"But what if she loses and I win?"

"It's perfectly all right," he said. "I've thought of that. My strategy embraces either eventuality. I wasn't born yesterday. If you win, you'll be indebted to me and retain me out of gratitude —then as we go along you'll be overcome with admiration for my skills. I've been laying the groundwork."

I laughed again. "Did it ever occur to you that I might not *want* to retain you?"

"Oh yes! Yes, yes, indeedy yes! This doodad hanging from my pocket is not a watch fob, you know. It's a Phi Beta Kappa key. If you decide to keep Arthur Burnsides to represent the estate afterwards—or anyone else, for that matter—I'll poison your mind against him. I can be vicious. At the moment, however, until I see reason to bare my fangs, I'm using the positive approach. That's why I called you for lunch—I'm trying to impress you. If you don't cooperate, I can always switch."

"You certainly aren't lacking in confidence," I said.

"I looked you over carefully at the very beginning and made up my mind quickly. I'm not a dawdler. I decided that you *deserved* me. How much did Arthur Burnsides charge you?" He held up his hand. "That's an unethical question, I know, but how else can I know? I certainly can't ask Arthur!"

"I don't mind, Mr. Tolliver—"

"You can call me J.A.," he broke in. "Now that you're no longer a criminal suspect, you don't need to be stiff and formal with me. I meant to tell you earlier to call me J.A., so you'd be more relaxed."

"The fee was five thousand dollars."

"You got him cheap." He nodded approvingly. "*Very* cheap. He can command much higher fees, you know. He's handled some really big cases in Texas, and I suspect that he cut his rates for you. Where did you get the money?"

"Savings, insurance, that sort of thing, and the company gave me six months' salary."

He looked at me keenly. "Are you in bad shape?" he asked.

"Well, it's not good. I'm not working, you know."

"Can you hold out until the will is settled?"

"How long?"

"It could take a year, maybe longer. Some of these cases stay in litigation for five, ten, twenty years, and some of them stay forever. I know of one case that was in litigation for so long that when the judgment was rendered the entire estate had been eaten up by attorney and court costs. It had been an empty exercise for all parties concerned."

"I can't hold out for even a few months. I've got to find something to do, but I was hoping to settle the will first. I don't want to start a new job with this thing hanging fire. It wouldn't be fair to my new employer—if I can find one, that is. Anyway, I haven't counted on winning it. The money's not mine, really—morally, that is."

He dropped his fork with a clatter. "Now don't start *that* again!" he exclaimed. "I won't listen. I'll stop up my ears. We went through all this once in my office. The money is *legally* yours. The law is on your side this time. The law gives it to you, and the law will fight anyone who tries to take it away from you. This isn't the *State of Texas* versus *Peter D. Hamilton* this time. You've got the State of Texas in your corner, and it's quite a large state, even if I do say so myself. Have you made up your mind about Arthur Burnsides? I mean is he going to represent you in the suit? That's really what I've been leading up to all this time."

"I gave him first option, but he might not be interested."

"Are you out of your mind? Of course, he'll be interested! And you couldn't have done better."

I shook my head in wonderment. "You really are on everybody's side, aren't you?"

"Actually, I'm in the middle. I've already told you that. My job is to distribute the estate as the court prescribes. If Carrie wins, I'll give it to her. If you win, I'll give it to you. Makes me feel like Santa Claus. I think it's exciting, don't you? In the meantime, I have to retain the affections of you both."

We finished our lunch, and Mr. Tolliver asked for the check.

"When we came in, I planned to let you wrestle me for the check," he said. "It makes a better impression on the waiter. But since you're so poor, I'll take care of it this time. When you come into your estate, you can buy me a lunch. I know a place that's vastly more expensive than this. It's in Dallas."

"You mean, *if* I come into the estate," I corrected.

"If—when—those are only words," he said, getting to his feet. "You have to maintain your optimism. By the way, you were supposed to remind me to inquire about your family, and you didn't. How are they?"

I delayed my reply until we were outside on the sidewalk. "They left me," I said. "They went back to St. Louis."

He made a clucking noise with his tongue. "And you sat all through lunch without saying a word about it! You should have got it off your chest. You mustn't get too pent up. It's not good for you. Do you need a ride somewhere? I hold the all-time record for traffic tickets in Erskine but I can get you to where you want to go. If nothing else, I can put you in a taxi cab."

"Thanks, but I've got my car."

"Is your wife going to divorce you?"

"I hope not. We haven't discussed it."

"Don't mention it to her," he said, extending his hand. "Let it be her idea. The plaintiff is always at a disadvantage—burden of proof and that sort of thing. Maintain your advantage, Pete. Keep your edge."

"I don't want any advantage or edge over Amy. It's not that kind of situation. I just want her to bring the boys and come home."

"Oh." He peered into my face, apparently trying to judge whether or not I was sincere. "Maybe she will," he said. "I wish you had told me, though. I could have been cheering you up all this time."

❧ 35 ❧

Carlton Sheffield III, tall, thin, blond and bookish-looking, was as stuffy as his name sounded. His handshake was as anemic as his appearance, cold and limp. He could have been no more than four years out of college, and I could not imagine why Arthur Burnsides had assigned an associate so young to a case involving a million dollars. What's more, I did not approve.

Disapproving of an Arthur Burnsides action felt good. My life was no longer teetering on the brink of a precipice. I was not now on the defensive in a life-or-death struggle. The law was on my side. J. A. Tolliver had taught me that, and he had taught me well. I had bargaining power—lots of it—and I had no intention of being intimidated by an arrogant, overbearing upstart named Carlton Sheffield III.

He sat in my living room, stiff and formal, his eyes roaming the room, taking it in with obvious distaste. I had to bow to his judgment there; the place was a shambles. A thin coat of dust covered the tables; the ashtrays brimmed with cigarette butts; several days' newspapers were strewn over the sofa and the floor, but I refused to explain that I was my own housekeeper. He must have known it, anyway.

Placing a brown leather attaché case on his knees, he fumbled with the catches. The lid flew open. The case was as new and unscarred as its owner. I waited while he took out a sheaf of papers, snapped the lid shut and looked about the room inquiringly.

"A desk would help," he said.

"We can use the dining table." I led the way. Spreading the papers on the table, he sat down before them. I sat down opposite.

"First, there's the agreement," he said, shoving a long, blue-bound document across the table. I ran my eyes down the first page, dismayed that my recently acquired facility with legal jargon was of little help to me now. He recognized my bewilderment and seemed to take satisfaction from it.

"You may follow me with that copy while I explain it to you," he said smugly. "The essence of the agreement, or contract if you will, is that for representing your interests in any and all legal actions against your claim to the Holbrook estate, you will pay to the firm of Burnsides, Whittier and Palmer fifteen percent of the value of the estate. That is, provided the judgment is in your favor."

I whistled long and loud. "Fifteen percent! I didn't realize it would be so much."

Sheffield was prim and unyielding. "That is our figure," he said.

I was shaken. "But that can turn out to be a hundred and fifty thousand dollars! That's a fortune in itself."

"Quite possibly. I have a statement of the assets here. We can go over them in a moment, if you like." He picked up a manila folder. "But our fee will be fifteen percent of the value of the estate at the time judgment is rendered. It can fluctuate up or down in the meantime."

"What's the current value?"

"My figures may be off slightly," he said, "but as of one week ago, it was a trifle under a million dollars. Very little of that is in real moneys, you understand. You'd probably want to convert enough into cash to pay the fee."

My head reeled. What did I know about converting assets into

$150,000? For that matter, what did I know about $150,000 in any shape, form or fashion? I was accustomed to dealing with monthly paychecks, commissions and price lists. Money, to me, meant columns of neatly printed figures, bound and indexed in thick catalogs or listed on invoices. Money was a fixed commodity that came in and went out in regular, fixed amounts. It was predictable and steady and presented no problems other than how to stretch it as far as it would go.

"I wouldn't have the foggiest idea of how to convert the money," I heard myself saying.

"Naturally, we would expect to guide you there," Sheffield said, apparently pleased by my discomfort. "That's in the agreement, too. Our firm has attorneys and analysts who are quite capable in these matters, and it would be to our interest as well as yours to see that you get the best returns possible."

"How soon would you want the money?"

"Within five years of the date of judgment. That is to allow you the maximum accommodation of market prices and values and stock quotations. And during the five-year period, our firm will expect to represent your estate in any and all actions. In other words, we would occupy the same position in relation to the estate that one Mr. J. A. Tolliver, Erskine attorney, occupied during Mrs. Holbrook's lifetime. During that same period, we would arrange for the spaced transfer of our fee. But perhaps I should explain more fully."

He launched into a long, laborious recitation of figures, percentages, grosses and nets, much of which passed over my head. In essence, however, he said that raising $150,000, and doing it properly, demanded considerable expertise. "Knowing when to sell can be as crucial as knowing what to sell," he said. He stopped and watched my face.

"We will not want you to transfer the moneys to us in a lump sum," he went on. "To insure that you have the moneys on the dates transfer is due, will require extremely careful management of conversion procedures." He glanced at the document. "I hope I haven't gone too fast."

"No—I just hadn't realized we'd be dealing in such figures."

"It's a substantial estate, Mr. Hamilton. Of course, we have represented larger ones, but even one this size is not uncomplex."

"What else is in the agreement? You might as well deliver the knockout punch while you're at it. How about the inheritance taxes?"

"We will take care of your dealings with the Department of Internal Revenue, certainly, for the duration of our agreement," he said. "We will arrange a tax schedule that will be mutually satisfactory to all parties concerned. Of course, the inheritance tax will not be inconsiderable. There's the state and federal taxes, you see. And that means, too, additional conversion of your assets. Quite a bit, in fact."

"How much?" I held my breath.

"Approximately one-third of the total value."

"*Three hundred and thirty thousand dollars?* You've got to be kidding!"

"Inherited wealth is expensive, Mr. Hamilton."

I could not assimilate it. It had nothing to do with me. The whole thing was becoming more ludicrous each time Sheffield opened his mouth. I picked up the blue-backed document and shoved it across the table. He eyed the paper with suspicion and watched me nervously.

"Now let me see if I've got this straight," I said. "I will pay Burnsides, Whittier and Palmer approximately one hundred and fifty thousand dollars, and I will pay to the State of Texas and the Government of the United States approximately three hundred and thirty thousand—a grand total of four hundred and eighty thousand dollars, give or take a few thousand."

He nodded and waited, but far from serenely. He was becoming agitated. I scarcely knew what to say next. He sat rigid and quiet.

"Now let's take the really drastic view of all this," I said. "Suppose I lose out on the estate and get nothing whatsoever. What is your fee for backing a loser?"

Sheffield's mood brightened. He flipped some pages of his copy of the document. "Mr. Burnsides is taking your case on a contingency basis," he said. "It's in here." He held out a paragraph to me which I ignored, waiting. "In other words, the firm is prepared to take the risk that you will lose. We are prepared to gamble along with you. If you lose, we lose too."

"That doesn't seem like sound business practice," I said.

"It's not unheard of, and it's not as speculative as it may sound in your case. Mr. Burnsides represented you in your criminal charge for five thousand dollars. The indictment was dismissed before the case came to court. Aside from Mr. Burnsides' personal time spent on the case, the expenses for the firm were negligible. None of the staff was ever brought into service, except a typist on a few occasions. If the judgment is not in your favor, Mr. Burnsides feels that the firm will not have worked for nothing."

He paused for a moment, then added, "If I may venture my own opinion, Mr. Burnsides' proposal in this respect is most generous."

"Yes, I guess it is." I picked up the paper and flipped open the blue cover. "Do you realize that to sign this piece of paper means that I will be signing away nearly a half million dollars?" I asked.

"I'm quite aware of that, Mr. Hamilton, but you should remember that approximately three hundred and thirty thousand of that money will go for taxes whether you sign this agreement or not."

"I assume you're not authorized to negotiate?"

He shook his head.

"Did Arthur Burnsides think I would sign this—this contract as casually as I would sign a travel voucher?"

"Mr. Hamilton, I cannot speak with authority on what Mr. Burnsides thinks," he said coldly. "All I can say is that I have explained the agreement in good faith. You are at liberty to ask for a senior member of the firm to go over it with you. Or to negotiate, if you prefer. If that is your desire, I shall relay your request to Mr. Burnsides."

"I might just do that," I said sourly.

"As you wish. I have no fear that you will find my briefing to have been inaccurate in any respect."

"I wasn't worried about that. Look, Sheffield, can you tell me why Mr. Burnsides sent you here?"

He stiffened. "I had hoped that was obvious, but if it is not, may I suggest that you ask Mr. Burnsides?"

"No. You don't understand. Is it a routine policy of your firm to send a new and junior associate to arrange matters of this size? The senior member of Burnsides, Whittier and Palmer personally undertook my defense in a criminal charge. The fee was five thousand dollars. Now here's an action where your firm stands to make thirty times that amount, and he sends a new and young associate. I don't understand why."

Sheffield's manner remained icy. I had offended him. "Mr. Hamilton, I have not been authorized to discuss the firm's rationale in this particular respect."

"Okay. But I'd feel better discussing my case with someone a little more seasoned. You must be younger than I am."

"I'm twenty-seven."

"See? Two years. Tell me. Do you really feel qualified by experience to sit here and conclude a deal of this size and scope?"

"You're overlooking a vital point," he said. "I had nothing to do with drawing up this agreement. Nothing whatsoever. That's where the seasoning is crucial. My function is to explain it to you and to answer your questions. I have the qualifications for that." He paused and swallowed hard. His manner thawed somewhat. "To be truthful, I worked long and hard to prepare myself for this briefing, and I was prepared to answer any question you might ask—except the one you actually did ask." He smiled wistfully. "I suppose I was too pleased with the assignment to question the firm's rationale for giving it to me."

"Maybe it wasn't a fair question," I said. "Still, I'm disturbed by it."

"Am I to conclude then that you find the terms unacceptable?" He could not keep the disappointment from his voice.

"Not necessarily," I said. "I just don't know, that's all. I need to think it over. Wouldn't you need time to think about something like this?"

"In all probability, and of course, that's your prerogative. But may I point out that you don't have unlimited time to decide? Mrs. Holbrook's attorneys will be ready to act as soon as the probate hearings are under way. That will be soon."

"Maybe I can decide by tomorrow, then, if I sleep on it tonight. Can you leave this copy with me?"

"Most assuredly. That's why I brought it."

Glumly, he collected his papers and returned them to the brown attaché case. He had lost his spirit now. At the door he hesitated, then stopped.

"Mr. Hamilton? I hope you'll forgive me for saying this, and I urge you to take it in the spirit in which it is intended—"

"Yes?"

"—but be careful—please."

He was struggling to say something else.

"How do you mean?" I asked.

"I mean no offense, believe me," he said, "but *you're* unseasoned too. I don't like to think that someone will take advantage of you. And they might. That's why I say be careful."

My antagonism abated. "Thank you," I said. "Thank you very much. You've put your finger on my problem. I am unseasoned. That's my whole problem in a nutshell."

He held out his hand. His handshake was still limp and cold, but in his own way, I think it was sincere. He managed a weak smile as he went out the door.

36

As I listened to Carlton Sheffield drive away from the house, I came face to face with the realization that my indecision had nothing to do with the terms of the agreement. The thing that really held me back was so simple that it was complex: I could not make the decision alone.

I needed Amy. I was crippled without her. I had begun at least a dozen letters to her and finished none of them. I could not strike the right tone. They were too self-pitying and melodramatic, filled with pleading and breast beating. She would have been appalled by any of them. Several times I sat with her mother's telephone number in front of me, but I never placed the call. The trouble was that I had been trying to articulate a feeling that was so immense and complete that to be understood, it had to be returned. It was beyond language. The reasons I wanted her to come home, when listed separately, seemed puny and unconvincing. Even when added together, they fell short of the total, for the whole was greater than the sum of its parts. I discovered that love has no component parts.

Signing or not signing the agreement, then, the Holbrook estate notwithstanding, was a matter of no real consequence. Whatever decision I made would be the right decision only if Amy helped me to make it.

The irony of my plight was that, at that very minute, the estate was mine whether I wanted it or not. The law insisted on it. Unless and until someone successfully countered that law, the estate would pass into my hands, decision or no decision. Afterwards, I could do with it as I pleased, but in the meantime I could not change the terms of Henrietta's will. Like it or dislike it, I was the titular head of a million-dollar estate.

I telephoned her that evening. She greeted me calmly and pleasantly, with no show of surprise.

"I've got to make up my mind about the estate," I said after an explanation of Sheffield's terms.

"Pete, I can't get excited about that money," she said. "I've told you that again and again, but you won't believe me."

"But Amy, you can't shut it out of your mind just like that. Please talk to me about it."

"What good will it do? The money's not yours, and the sooner you face that, the easier it will be for both of us."

"But it *is* mine. No matter what you think, the money's mine. The law decreed it."

"Then maybe you don't have to do anything at all."

"It's not that simple. If Carrie contests the will—with no counteraction from me—there's no guarantee that she will win. I might get the estate anyway. I've got to have legal counsel. I don't know what to do."

"Try doing nothing."

"I don't even know how to do nothing."

"Do you think fifteen percent is too much?" she asked.

"How should I know? It's probably a standard percentage."

"Then if that's not the problem—what is?"

"The whole thing, that's what. This whole thing is driving me up the walls. I can't think in terms of a hundred and fifty thousand dollars."

"Is the fifteen percent really what's bothering you?"

"Well—I—yes it is! Try signing your name to an I.O.U. for a hundred and fifty thousand dollars and see if it doesn't bother you."

"What's really bothering you is getting the estate itself—not the fee it costs to get it. Otherwise, you'd be elated at the prospect. Isn't that true?"

"Amy—please come home," I said, suddenly sick all over. "I'm begging you. That's really why I called. Just come home, and we'll figure something out."

"Pete, I can't come yet—not until you work out the money thing."

"Does that mean you will come if—"

"No, no—that's not what I said. All I mean is that you have to decide for yourself. That's one thing I've definitely straightened out in my mind since I've been here."

"But you don't understand. I can't decide without you. This can mean over a half million dollars to us after taxes and lawyers fees. We can be rich—and you ask me to decide that by myself! I can't do it."

"I liked things the way they were," she said.

"So did I, but they're not that way any more."

"They can be," she said softly.

"I hoped you would be more helpful."

"Well, I'm sorry," she said. "Don't think you've got all the problems. I've got a few of my own."

"Amy, answer one question for me, please. Do you *want* to come home?"

She did not answer.

"Do you?"

"That's not fair."

"If you want to come home and don't come—"

"This isn't getting us anywhere, Pete." I detected a tremor in her voice. "And this call is costing money." I heard her take a deep breath. "How have you been?" she asked.

"Terrible. And you?"

"Terrible, too," she said. "All this is so abnormal. Everything is so temporary and confused. We can't stay with Mother forever, and she won't listen to our going anywhere else—unless it's back home. I don't know what to do."

"That's because you don't belong there. You belong here. I love you, darling. I love you, and I miss you and the boys."

"Pete, don't—I hear Kenny. I've got to go."

"Amy, don't hang up. How are the boys?"

"They're fine. Mother's spoiling them. She gives them anything they want when they want it. That's another reason I've got to find somewhere to go."

"You know where that is," I said. "I'm waiting for you."

"Good-bye, Pete."

I heard a click, and the line went dead.

I sat with my hand on the telephone. Amy had no intention of staying away. She was confused; she needed time to think, but she would come back. I had to believe that. And believing it lifted my spirits.

Meanwhile, I knew only one person to whom I could turn now. That was J. A. Tolliver. To him, my position was legally sound. If it had a moral complexion at all, it was the morality of taking what was legally mine versus the immorality of turning it loose without a fight. I called the Erskine operator and asked her to locate Tolliver for me.

He screamed so loudly that I held the receiver away from my ear.

"Sign it!" he squealed. "Sign it, and don't call me again with silly questions. At this very minute, I'm sitting here with green tears of envy streaming down both cheeks. One eye is crying over you, the other over Arthur Burnsides. I don't know whom I envy the most. I take turns."

"You think it's a fair price, then?"

He screamed again. "Fair? Now hear this—these may be the last words you'll ever hear me speak. Somewhere in this tired old world, you might find a firm for ten percent or even five, but any firm that's idiotic enough to let you off that cheap will be fly-by-night—a discount house. Avoid them, boy. Don't touch them with a ten-foot pole. They would fritter away more money than their cut rates could possibly save you. I'm surprised that Arthur Burnsides didn't ask for more. I would. Oh, you can bet your simple little soul, I would. Sign it, and let me hear no more about it."

"But I don't understand the ins and outs of the transaction. It's so full of technicalities that I don't—"

He interrupted with a shriek. "Listen, dear boy. *You* aren't required to understand anything. That's why you hire lawyers—lawyers you can trust. As a matter of fact, this case can go along quite nicely without you. You can stay in bed. This won't be like a murder trial. It will be grossly technical and grossly dull. The thrill-seeking spectators will have to go back to their comic books. Take my word for it, this won't be a show for the unaware, which includes you above all people."

He chattered on until I stopped him.

"But why do I need to be represented at all?" I asked. "You told me yourself that the State of Texas will defend my claim to the estate. So why do I need attorneys of my own for the same purpose?"

"And we send missionaries to Africa!" He groaned. "The State of Texas *will* defend your claim for you, but they won't look after *you* personally. Once you've won—if you do—the State of Texas will have fulfilled its obligation to you. You'll be on your own. Then you'll have to pay inheritance taxes, which means you'll have to sell off some of your assets to get the money. You could squander the entire estate just trying to get enough cash for the taxes. It's been done before. But that's not all. Do you have the foggiest notion of what's involved in simply managing a million-dollar estate? There's never a day goes by that I'm not involved in transactions of some kind on the Holbrook estate—correspondence, telephone calls, visits, decisions. Sometime let me show you how much of my file space is filled with Holbrook business. I deal with stockbrokers, realtors, farmers, oil companies, cattlemen, banks, corporations, other attorneys—it goes on and on. You can't do it alone—you can*not*."

"All right then," I said. "If you say it's fair, I'll sign it. I just wish I knew what I was doing, though. I talked to Amy on the telephone, and she gave me no help."

"Why should she? You're separated."

"I guess Teague and Folmer have already dug in," I said.

"Indeed they have," he said happily. "I coached Carrie for the last time this week and turned her over to her attorneys with my blessings. You'd better get yourself represented, boy, and fast. If I have to advise you one more time, I'll slap my own fee on you, and it will be more expensive than you ever dreamed. I'm really high-priced when I find a client with money. Now run along."

"How's Carrie, by the way? Does she seem to be making out all right?"

"She's not herself at all," he replied. "How could she be? All alone on that hill in that spooky old house with that unfortunate child. She doesn't know what's going on any more than you do. She brought me a *photostat* of Ben's birth certificate to examine before she turned it over to her attorneys. You could hardly make out the doctor's name, and you could argue until dooms-day about whether it read Port Arthur or Port *Aransas*. I said, 'Carrie, darling, you'll need the original, honey—the certified original.' And do you know what she said? She said she's *saving* it! What in heaven's name she's saving it for, I can't imagine. Had she been slatternly, I would have thrown her bodily out onto the street."

I tuned him out. Something did not add up, and I needed a moment to check for the error. It was an obvious one; that I could feel, but with J. A. Tolliver chattering like a canary, I could not pin it down. My mind flashed back to Erskine then to Foley then to Port Arthur. Or was it San Antonio?

"Mr. Tolliver?"

"Don't you remember? I gave you permission to call me J.A."

"Are you sure it was a birth certificate?"

"Well, it certainly wasn't a sales slip. Don't you think I know a birth certificate when I see one? It's labeled across the top. 'Certificate of—' "

"Was it Ben's birth certificate? *Little* Ben Holbrook's?"

"Whose did you think it was—mine?"

"Where did you say it was issued?"

"You can't make it out on the photostat. You'd need infrared eyes. Of course, it was Port Arthur. Carrie told me that, and once you know it, you can make it out as easy as pie."

"Was Carrie's name on the certificate?"

He exploded. "Certainly her name was on it!" he exclaimed. "Where do you think she got Ben? From a head of cabbage?" He stopped abruptly. "Pete, is there something you're not telling me?"

"Do you have that photostat?"

"That's for me to know and you to find out. What if I do?"

"Will you check at the office and see?"

"I'm at the office now. I don't have time to go home. One of those dreary farmers has been bothering me about a fence that he claims is on his property while his neighbor claims it's on his. You've never heard so much carrying on in your life. You would think they were arguing about the Great Wall of China."

"Look and see."

"Look and see what? The photostat? Carrie's got it. I told her to take it back home and get the original. Why do you want to know?"

"Can you get it back from Carrie?"

"Why should I?"

"Will you?"

"Maybe I will and maybe I won't," he said obstinately. "As a matter of fact, I refuse to say another word until you tell me why you want it. *Not one more word.*"

"Please do this for me—J.A."

He changed his tone. "Pete, do you have reason to think something is wrong with that birth certificate?"

"I'm not sure. Something's not adding up, and I don't know what it is."

"Tell me, and let me add it."

"No. You get the certificate first. I may be all wet, but then maybe not. Call me when you get it, and I'll drive down to look at it. Can you get it?"

"Certainly I can get it. I'm resourceful. But there is a question of ethics, you know. I can hardly say, 'Carrie do you mind if your opponent takes a look at your documentary evidence?' After all, you *are* her opponent—remember? You do know what an opponent is, don't you? He's the person on the other side."

"Don't bother about the ethics," I said.

"You can say that—but what about me? If you'd only tell me why you want to see the certificate, perhaps it will persuade me to fudge."

"Not until I see it with my own eyes. Anyway, it would be too complicated to explain on the telephone. If I'm right, that is."

He considered that for a moment then gave in with a sigh. "Oh, all right," he said. "But let me tell you this, Pete Hamilton, and I want you to listen with both ears. Your reason had better be a good one, or else I'll repudiate all the expert advice I've given you, and then where would you be?"

I laughed and told him I would take the risk.

❦ 37 ❧

J. A. Tolliver called at eleven o'clock the following morning. I knocked over a chair getting to the telephone. "What took you so long?" I asked.

"Long? Listen, Pete Hamilton. To get this thing, I had to drink three cups of coffee with Carrie, and I'm not a coffee drinker. It makes my stomach churn. I blush to recall what I did. I feel like I've violated her."

"Never mind that. Did you get it?"

"Certainly I got it. I'm reliable. But be assured that my methods were unethical. Deception usually is. I hope you have bad dreams about it."

"Are you at your office now?"

"Where else? I don't have a million-dollar estate like some people I know. I'm *always* in my office. I've got one of those dismal actions on my hands where the wife is suing her husband for nonsupport. I'm representing the wife, but I'm on the husband's side. She's got a case of halitosis that would fell a moose. Are you coming down?"

"I'm on my way. Stay where you are and wait for me."

"I'll be here. Miss Strange doesn't unlock my leg irons until twelve-thirty."

I got there shortly after noon. J. A. Tolliver sat waiting for me behind a desk that was clear of any indication of work done or to be done. He had been umpiring a battle between his conscience and his curiosity, and now that his conscience was smarting from defeat, he was licking his wounds.

"You certainly took your sweet time getting here," he complained.

"It takes a full hour to get from Jones Hill, across Fort Worth and all the way to Erskine."

"You might have told me," he said. "I've been glued—positively *glued*—to this chair waiting for you. There's no calculating how much jurisprudence I could have been handling in the meantime. What's this all about? I can't stand much more. This isn't a class B movie, you know."

"Let me see the certificate," I said, pulling a chair up to his desk.

He opened a drawer and took out a thick sheet of photographic paper.

"When I think of how I got this little piece of paper, I break out in splotches."

Reaching across his desk, I took the paper from his hand and scanned it avidly. His impatience could not be contained.

"Well? Is it what you want? And if so, *what* is it?"

"Carrie is Ben's mother," I said without looking up.

"Who did you think she was—his landlady?"

"How many months is it from July eighteenth to June twenty-third?"

He began to count on his fingers, then stopped. "Why do you want to know?" he asked.

I made my own count. "It's eleven months and five days. Right?"

He looked at me blankly. "I'll take your count," he said, "although I can assure you that I don't see what it proves."

"It proves this. We left the Port of Debarkation in San Francisco on July eighteenth, 1944—Ben Holbrook and I," I said, oblivious to J. A. Tolliver's stares. "He never saw Carrie again. If Carrie gave birth to a baby in June, 1945—eleven months later

—Ben could not have been the baby's father. So there goes her case right out the window. Little Ben Holbrook is not a Holbrook."

Tolliver took off his spectacles then put them on again. "You'd better read that piece of paper again," he said. "In black and white, it says, 'Father: Benjamin Holbrook.'"

"That's only Carrie's story. She had to list a father's name."

"Obviously."

"But Ben was *not* the father."

"That's a legal document, son," he said. "The law is partial to legal documents. I saw the original with my own eyes. How can you contradict that?"

"I'm contradicting it here and now. If Carrie is the mother, Ben was not the father, legal documents or not. No woman was ever pregnant eleven months and five days."

"It *would* be freakish," he said, adjusting his thick spectacles and assuming the pose of the professional attorney. "My own mother gave up after nine months, I believe it was. But you'll have to back up and explain all this to me. Why would Carrie pretend the baby is—I mean, if the birth certificate—oh, good grief, Pete! Don't be so obtuse!"

"Carrie would have got away with it except for me," I said.

"Got away with *what?* Look, Pete, if you don't explain yourself, I'll throw up here and now—and I can do it, too, after all that coffee."

"Here's how I figure it," I said.

Tolliver leaned over his desk, his eyes bulging.

"I have no idea who Carrie took up with," I began, "but it's evident that she took up with *somebody*—at least once. So there she was, a pregnant widow, which was nothing novel except that she was pregnant by the wrong man. How could she explain it? Of course, she didn't have to explain it to Ben, for he was missing in action, and she was fairly certain that he was dead. Explaining it to her in-laws, however, was the big problem. She figured that if she stayed out of sight, away where no one knew her, she could pass the baby off as Ben's, because as time went by, a couple of months' discrepancy would become blurred and eventually fade altogether. It was a good gamble. Sympathy is usually on the widow's side, especially a war widow with a baby. If she could get away with it, she would have a lifelong claim to the Holbrook estate, even if she remarried some day.

"But she didn't get away with it. The elder Holbrooks were onto her. They threw her out. She hadn't planned on that. But she was not defeated. All she had to do was bide her time until the Holbrooks died, then stake her claim. She had the birth certificate to back it up. Now here's where I entered the picture. And do you know, if she had only spoken to me that day in the doctor's office, I doubt that any of this would have taken place—"

Tolliver broke in. He had not heard about that chance encounter with Carrie, and I reviewed it for him.

When I had finished, he shook his head in wonderment. "Imagine!" he breathed. "She walked through a room one day, nothing was said, then all this. . . ."

I nodded and went on. "She could have told me anything, and I would have believed her—anything at all. She could have said that the boy was a neighbor's child or a relative or that she had remarried, and I would not have questioned it. If she had only treated me as an old friend, I might never have seen her again. But when she pretended not to know me—well, naturally, I was mystified. Wouldn't you have been?"

Tolliver sat so transfixed that he passed up an opportunity to speak.

"But that's what started it," I said. "I couldn't get her off my mind. I couldn't toss off the incident as though it were nothing. So I looked her up in Foley, and she gave me that story about Ben's old girl friend—"

"What girl friend?" Tolliver asked.

"Do you know, J.A., for a man who sees all and knows all, you're surprisingly uninformed about the details of this case."

"Oh, I heard rumors about Carrie and the baby, but I didn't know which one to believe, so I decided not to believe any of them."

"You see?" I said. "Despite the rumors, even you didn't question little Ben's origins. If a doubt existed, you're the one person whose job it was to examine the evidence, but you didn't take the rumors seriously enough to bother. So, Carrie's scheme was working—and it would have been successful, except for me—"

"What about Ben's girl friend? You're supposed to tell me about Ben's old girl friend and Carrie's doing something or the other."

I detoured and told him the story of Marie Scott's affair with Ben Holbrook and Carrie's taking the baby from her. J.A.'s eyes almost left their sockets.

"You *believed* that story?" he exclaimed.

"She convinced me. I know that in the retelling, it comes out a little bit unreal; but remember I was hearing it from Carrie Holbrook's lips, and she did a masterful job of putting it over."

He shook his head ruefully and made a clucking noise with his tongue. "Why you poor, poor gullible boy! That's the corniest tale I ever heard in my life."

"Carrie said that herself. She called it corny—pure *Stella Dallas*, she said. Amy didn't feel that it was on the up-and-up. Dr. Kriegel said it was an outrageous story. Henrietta and I were the only ones who accepted it. There was a good excuse for Henrietta's believing it, I guess, considering her state of mind and her guilty conscience over her treatment of Carrie, but— you're probably right. I was gullible. Well, anyway—sizing up the situation, she saw that I could not go back to Erskine with a story that conflicted with the version she had already given her in-laws, so she made a shrewd move: she *sent* me back with the Marie Scott story. She *begged* me to tell it to her mother-in-law! Wasn't that clever? It made a martyr of poor, misunderstood, mistreated Carrie! For years she had let her reputation be sullied rather than dirty the name of her dear dead husband. It was shrewd enough to convince me, and Henrietta was downright contrite about it. She would have done anything in the world to make amends to Carrie. Both of us were taken in, make no mistake about it.

"Naturally, Carrie never intended to take that Marie Scott story into a court of law. She knew better than that. She had no adoption papers, no birth certificate to back it up and prove such a trumped-up tale. Anyway, she wouldn't need to try it—not if things worked out as she originally planned. No one would question Ben's origins, but if they did, she always had his real birth certificate to prove that he was hers and a Holbrook, too."

I stopped to light a cigarette. Tolliver fidgeted. "I hope you know that this is balderdash," he said. "Every word of it. And you might do me the courtesy of not telling it quite so well so I can disbelieve it more wholeheartedly."

"The thing that went wrong, though, was me," I went on. "I was the fly in her ointment. She hadn't planned on my staying around, but when she saw that I was part of the scenery, she was afraid I'd smell a rat. So she cooled off toward me and tried her best to make me feel unwelcome in Henrietta's house. That didn't work. Given enough time, however, she probably would have got rid of me eventually. But Henrietta died unexpectedly and upset her timetable. Now she had to get me off the scene. On the day Henrietta died, she chased me out of the house. But there was the indictment and the will, and I *couldn't* disappear from her life. Our affairs were mixed together now more than ever. So I ruined her plans completely. I'm the last person on earth she wants to battle for that money. But she has to go through with it now. What else can she do? She can't turn back now, and there's always the chance of a slip. The odds are against her, but for a million dollars, you'd expect the odds to be heavy."

I finished and sat back. Tolliver had calmed down and was watching me in studious silence. We sat for a few moments, neither of us speaking. Then an idea took shape.

"Without my story to contradict hers," I said at last, "wouldn't Carrie have a strong claim on that money?"

"Indeed, she would," Tolliver said. "You've never had this case sewed up all the way. Survivors—whether blood or by marriage—are always in a good position, particularly against a rank outsider like yourself."

"It might be the way out for me," I said softly. "It just might be the answer to my problems. If I keep my mouth shut and don't sign Arthur Burnsides' agreement and let nature take its course, she might get the money as she planned all along. It might be worth a try."

"Do you mean, if you don't counter her action?"

"Something like that."

"And just *give* her a million dollars?"

"I want out of this, J.A.," I said. "I never should have been in it. I don't belong—I never have. This whole thing is a fluke—a freak accident. I want Amy, Skeeter and Kenny to come home. None of this is for me, and that includes inheriting a million dollars."

J. A. Tolliver wheeled around in his chair and looked out the window for a moment, then turned back to face me. A new seriousness had come over him.

"And in the meantime," he said, "what do you intend to do with this story you've just told me?"

"Nothing. I'll just forget it."

"You can't."

"Why not?"

"Because I won't let you. Do you think that it will simply go away? Look here, Pete. You can't have it both ways. You opened this box—I didn't. Everything that spilled out is your clutter—not mine. You've got to clean it up—I won't. You're not going to saddle me with a tale like this, then walk away free, unfettered and unencumbered. You started this, and it's yours to finish."

"But I'm sincere," I protested. "I'm not interested in the Holbrook estate. Carrie can have it."

"I don't care whether you're interested in the Holbrook estate or not," he said, a surprising hardness coming into his voice. "Do you think I'll sit here and help you conceal your little secret about those dates? It's your worry, and you'll not unload it on me. You'll not make me your accomplice. And I won't let you leave me with the untidy task of proving this without you— which I can do. You can't possibly be the only person in the world who can disprove Ben's right of survivorship. There are military records that can be subpoenaed, and there were other men overseas with you who can testify that it was impossible for Ben to have seen Carrie after he left the States. No, my dear sir, no indeed. You started something, and you can just finish it."

Tolliver's face was grave, and he spoke with resolution. For once, he had no quick, fluttery quip, and he kept his voice low.

"And just so you realize what you've started," he said, "let me tell you the rest of it. When this case comes into court and you tell this tale officially—this eleven months and five days, or whatever it is—you'll be accusing Carrie of fraud. That's extremely serious, and she can be prosecuted."

"But I don't want to get Carrie in trouble."

"Well, why didn't you keep your mouth shut, then?" he came back at me angrily. "Why didn't you think of the consequences before you raced down here bursting at the seams to blabber this story about Carrie's indiscretions with another man? What did you have in mind when you told it? You know, you don't make much sense. You can hardly wait to tear down her claim; then after you've done it and made a scarlet woman of her in the bargain, you decide it's not what you wanted after all, so let's all forget it, pick up our marbles and go home. You've stirred up a bushel of trouble for Carrie Holbrook, and you can just see it through to the end."

He quieted down and studied my face. Then he shook his head. "I just don't get you," he said. "I don't get you at all. You would walk away from that million-dollar estate just for her— just to keep her out of trouble." His voice was filled with disbelief. "I've never met anybody quite like you, and even now, I'm not sure you're real. What kind of hold does she have on you?"

I ignored him. I had had my fill of explaining, of justifying, and I had no intention of starting up again. J. A. Tolliver could think whatever he pleased about my relationship with Carrie Holbrook.

"I just don't want Carrie to get in trouble," I repeated.

"She will . . ." His statement had an unfinished ring to it.

"Unless?" I prodded.

"Unless you persuade her to drop her suit."

"Do you think I should?"

"Well, *somebody* should!" he said, some of the old fire returning. "If she isn't stopped, she's headed for trouble, and you've just this minute said you don't want her to get in trouble."

"But why me?"

"Because you dug up the skeleton, that's why! So if you want it buried again, you can do the burying yourself."

"Nothing's simple, is it?" I laughed. It was a short and mirthless laugh. "You take care of one thing only to find that it brings on another."

"I don't know what kind of ivory tower you've been living in all these years, Pete, but even in an ivory tower you must have known that nothing happens in a vacuum. Every action has a consequence, no matter how slight. The consequences are part of your responsibilities, too. That's part of the price you pay. Everything has some kind of price tag attached to it, high or low. Nothing in this world is absolutely free—not even the truth."

"I've heard all that before," I said, "and from the sheriff of Erskine County, of all people."

"Well, it certainly shouldn't have come as a revelation to you," he said.

We sat quietly for a time, neither of us stirring or speaking. A curious depression moved in and settled over me like a fog. I had known all along that my victory would be Carrie's defeat, but I had viewed victory, if at all, through unfocused lenses. The lines had been fuzzy and crooked. Now that they were clear and distinct, I felt no elation nor sense of triumph. I felt only a great and crushing sadness.

"You never know what people will do," Tolliver said softly, breaking the silence.

"How's that?"

"I thought Ben and Carrie were happily married."

My mind had been a thousand miles and five years away.

"They were," I said, "but Carrie liked the lively tunes."

"I don't understand."

"It was nothing. I was only thinking." I got to my feet. "How long are you supposed to hold onto a memory?"

"As long as you can, I suppose," he said. "The good ones, that is. Why?"

"And forget the bad ones?"

"Maybe," he said, apparently understanding my mood if not my question. "While you're juggling your memories, you'd better go tell all this to Arthur Burnsides."

"Why?"

"Because he's likely to be peeved if you don't." He threw up his hands. "Don't be so dense! Arthur Burnsides is your attorney, young fellow. That's a first-class reason. This is a tidbit that just might come in handy as he prepares your case. Now depart in peace."

I started for the door.

"If you run into anyone on your way out—male or female—who is tattered, bedraggled and obviously penniless," he called after me, "it will be one of my clients, no doubt. Tell him or her, as the case may be, to go away—I'm having an attack of the vapors."

❧ 38 ❧

Arthur Burnsides was in court when I tried to see him. I left word for him to call me as soon as he returned. His secretary did not expect him back in the office for two or three days. Perhaps Mr. Whittier could help me. I refused. I had no heart for what I had to do, and to postpone it was a relief.

Two days later, Mr. Burnsides greeted me cordially and apologized for not having been more accessible. "It was an appeal action that's had me tied in knots for over a week," he explained, pushing an arm chair toward his desk and motioning me into it. "I couldn't find any place to turn loose."

He settled himself behind his desk. I took a cigarette from my pocket and lighted it. He shoved an ashtray toward me. "How have you been?" he asked.

"All right, I guess. Of course, things aren't good with Amy and the boys gone, but I'm making out."

"I was sorry to hear about that, and I was sorry not to have talked longer on the telephone, but that night we were having a dinner party and had just sat down to the table."

It seemed unimportant now. "I hope I didn't upset Sheffield too much," I said. "I guess he told you what happened."

"He did, and we've been expecting to hear from you before now about the agreement. We're running out of time."

"Something happened," I said. "Something happened that I hadn't counted on—and I'm afraid it just about wraps up the case for us."

His eyebrows went up. "Afraid?" he said, tilting his head to one side. "You don't sound too cheerful about it."

"I'm not. I saw little Ben Holbrook's birth certificate."

"How did you do that?" he asked.

Tolliver's name was on my tongue, but I caught myself. "Does it matter?" I asked glumly.

"Certainly it matters. Did Tolliver show it to you?"

"Tolliver? Why him?"

"It would have to be either Tolliver or Carrie," he said. "It hardly seems likely that Carrie would show you anything to destroy her own case. There's no need to beat around the bush, Pete. It was Tolliver, wasn't it?"

"He didn't want to do it. He said it was unethical."

"He shouldn't have done it. But at least, I'm glad he knew he was out of line."

"Don't be too hard on him," I said. "Tolliver is too close to all this mess. He thinks he is all business and no feeling, but that's not true. He's sweating out the outcome of all this the same as I am—or Carrie."

"All right. What about the birth certificate?"

"I don't like what Carrie Holbrook did, and that's what the birth certificate is about. I wish I had never seen it." I stopped. Mr. Burnsides sat behind his desk, his face a mask, waiting for me to continue. I took a deep breath. Carefully, methodically, I unfolded my story of the dates and their discrepancies while Mr. Burnsides listened intently and without interrupting me. When I had finished, he asked a series of questions to determine if my story could be documented, which of course, it could, with military travel orders that moved our squadron from North Carolina to Indiana to San Francisco to New Guinea. Would I sign an affidavit to testify that Ben had not seen Carrie after we departed Indiana?

"Do I have to?" I asked miserably.

"Of course! This story and all those military travel orders aren't worth a damn unless you do."

"But that would be like swearing out a formal accusation against Carrie."

"That may be, but it's part of what you started out to do when you looked at that birth certificate, isn't it? Now did you, or did you not, see Ben Holbrook every day for the rest of his life after he left Indiana?"

"Yes. We were together at least part of every day."

"Did he, or did he not, see Carrie again after he left Indiana?"

"No. It would have been impossible."

"Will you, or will you not, sign an affidavit to that effect?"

I stared at him, holding back, searching desperately for a way out, for one reasonable and acceptable excuse for not taking that one last step that would forever ruin Carrie's hoped-for and carefully planned future. He stared back at me, waiting.

"Well?"

"But I hadn't counted on—you don't understand. This makes me her accuser! I don't want it to be this way!"

"What else did you expect?" he asked in exasperation. "Why did you tell me this in the first place? Just to get it off your chest? Your concern comes a wee bit late, I'd say."

"You're not making things any easier."

"What do you expect me to do? Sign those affidavits for you? Tell you to close your eyes and maybe it will go away? You're a big boy now, Pete, and it's time you began to act like one. You can't start something like this and then walk away just because the going gets unpleasant and things get tougher than you anticipated. This was all your idea and nobody else's. You've got to sign the affidavits, or I can't do anything for you. It's either that, or you'll have to go somewhere else."

This was his ultimatum, and I had no doubt that he meant exactly what he said. I knew that if I turned and walked out the door, he would wash his hands of me. I recognized something else, too. I recognized not only the futility of further resistance, but I also recognized a wrongness in it. I had burdened two attorneys-at-law with the story of Carrie Holbrook's fraudulent plan, and I had no right to force them into a position that would require them to take action if I didn't. And either or both of them would do just that. As respected members of the bar, they could do no less. I saw with unrelenting certainty what I had to do.

Mr. Burnsides was watching me closely. In his eyes, I saw a faint, but definite, suggestion of suspense. His concern was personal, not professional.

I moved in my chair. "Looks like I've painted myself into a corner, doesn't it?"

He relaxed. He smiled. A real smile. "Pete, if you can sit there and admit that, you'll make it from here on," he said.

I tried to smile back, but I was not successful. I said, "Tell me what to do. But hurry—before I change my mind."

"You won't change your mind," he said with conviction. "I'm going to turn you over to some of my people. Give them the story as you gave it to me. Monday, bring in the travel orders and anything else that will document your movements—letters, diaries, photographs—from the time you left Indiana, and we'll have the affidavits made up from all that. Then, I'll contact Teague and Folmer and see what they want to do. If this turns out as solid as it now appears, I imagine they'll step out of the case."

I got up to go, feeling that some kind of final explanation was in order but unable to think of one. "I didn't want to do this, Mr. Burnsides," I said.

"Then why did you?"

"Tolliver said I had to do it. Concealing it would make me an accomplice to Carrie's fraud."

"Tolliver was exactly right—about that, anyway." He pressed a button on his desk, and a buzzer sounded in the outer office. His secretary appeared almost immediately.

"Get that Hamilton agreement," he instructed her. "I think Mr. Hamilton is ready to sign now."

"Tolliver told me what happens if I waive my rights," I said. "I didn't realize how it would be."

"Is that what you want to do?"

The secretary hesitated and looked at me quizzically. Mr. Burnsides motioned her out of the office.

"I want out from under somehow," I said after she had gone. "I don't want that estate. I never have wanted it, and I particularly don't want it if I have to walk over Carrie's body to get it."

"You should think long and hard before you sign away a million dollars. You've got a wife and two boys. When you waive your rights, you'll be waiving theirs too. Is that a wise thing to do? You can secure their future with trust funds and that sort of thing. You can educate them, give them a start on their careers—many, many things that parents want to do for their children but can't. So think of them. Then think of this. Even if you don't want the money for yourself, you can turn it over to other people—foundations, charities, schools, churches—and do a tremendous amount of good with it. If the States of Texas takes it, however, it will serve no such useful purpose. The State doesn't need it, and what's more, the State doesn't want it. Think it over carefully before you do anything rash."

"Isn't this a hell of a note?" I said. "I don't know what I think any more. But I do know I'd like to be free of any and all connections with the Holbrook affairs, including the million dollars that seems to be mine, whether I want it or not."

Mr. Burnsides studied my face for a moment then said, "The world is full of people who would laugh out loud if they heard you or anybody else lamenting over the possession of a million dollars."

"I wish I could laugh out loud," I said. "I can't think of anything I'd rather do this minute than laugh out loud."

Then I turned and went out the door.

✤ 39 ✤

As Mr. Burnsides predicted, Teague & Folmer disassociated themselves from Carrie Holbrook's interests. What's more, they advised her to drop her suit.

"That doesn't mean we're home free," Mr. Burnsides cautioned me on the telephone. "Carrie's free to go ahead with her action if she can get someone to represent her. She probably won't find anyone, though. Not now, and I hope she doesn't. The minute she steps inside a courtroom with that claim, she lays herself wide open to a charge of fraud."

"I wouldn't want that to happen."

"Then maybe you can influence her to forget the entire matter."

"I guess that's my job, too, then?"

"That's up to you. I only mentioned it because I know how you feel about her."

"What's that supposed to mean?"

"Not a thing!" he snapped. "What you think of Carrie Holbrook is your own business. Do what you like."

A long stillness lay between us. I thought he had hung up.

"Mr. Burnsides?"

"Yes?"

"Are you sure I should talk to her?"

"Would it stop you if I weren't?"

Less than two hours later, I stood in J. A. Tolliver's office. He was seated at his desk looking out the window, his back to the door. Something was wrong. I sensed it even before Miss Strange had closed the door behind me. The quietness was too heavy. The tumult and ferment that usually swarmed around Tolliver like flies were missing. Slowly, he swiveled around, gripping the armrests. His face was grave.

"You told Arthur Burnsides that *I* showed you the birth certificate." His voice quavered, and he spoke with more regret than reproach. I took out a cigarette and lighted it. He watched silently, waiting for an explanation.

"It was pointless to deny it. It had to be you or Carrie, and he's smart enough to take it from there. I didn't foresee that I'd have to tell him."

The corners of Tolliver's mouth twitched. His jaw muscles moved up and down. He breathed heavily and unevenly. "That doesn't help in the least," he said. "I told you it was unethical for me to get that birth certificate for you. I should never have done it, but it didn't occur to me to swear you to secrecy. I assumed you knew better."

"I did. Believe me, I did, and I'm sorry if it's been embarrassing for you."

"Yes indeed, it's been embarrassing, all right. This little episode has cost me the respect of a very influential member of the Texas Bar Association. I don't think you know what that means." He smiled sadly and gave me no chance to reply. "No—I can see that you don't. This is one of those little things that in and of itself is of no great consequence. But in Arthur Burnsides' eyes, I'm suspect in any future dealings. Oh, this won't get me disbarred or anything so drastic, but it has cost me an association that I prized. If you don't maintain the respect of your own profession, you're in trouble, and I am. He'll never take another case on my recommendation, and he'll never send one to me, either."

He relaxed somewhat. The explanation had obviously been therapeutic. He dropped his eyes.

"Maybe you're overalarmed about it," I suggested.

"I'm not overalarmed," he responded. "I just know what I'm talking about. Arthur Burnsides called me on the telephone and gave me one of the most genteel upbraidings you can imagine. He said that I was under no obligation, moral or legal, and that I had no right, moral or legal, to assist his client in any way, and that he looked on my actions as interference. What could I say? He was right. Dead right. I knew that all along. He didn't have to tell me. Then he said a strange thing. He said, 'Too much helpfulness was at the root of all this difficulty, anyway.' I didn't understand what he meant, and with the situation like it was, I couldn't find a graceful way to ask him."

"I think I know."

"Then tell me." He looked up at me, puzzled rather than curious.

"Arthur Burnsides thinks everybody should look after his own business and let other people look after theirs. He's death on the subject. He contends that I should have stayed out of Carrie's affairs, and so does Amy. That's one of the reasons she left me. I'm about ready to agree with both of them."

He twisted his chair a half turn then back again. "Don't be too hard on yourself," he said. "You know what Carrie was up to."

"I didn't know it then," I said. "But suppose things had worked out for her? Would anyone be in any worse shape? What's the most that could have happened? One day she would have inherited the estate and no one would have been any wiser or unhappier. She and Ben could have lived comfortably for the rest of their lives. The world would keep on turning; the sun would rise tomorrow morning and set tomorrow evening; everybody would go on with their own affairs; business as usual everywhere. No one would be any the worse off, and Carrie would have been better."

"That's a peculiar attitude toward someone who took you for

a sucker." He pointed a slim white finger at me. "And don't delude yourself: she'll take you again, anywhere, any time it suits her purposes. What she planned to do was crooked. You know that, or else you're an idiot. She was wrong."

"Has anything been right in lieu thereof?"

"She was *not* entitled to the money," he said obstinately.

"Do I deserve a pat on the back for stopping her?"

"You would have seen that birth certificate eventually, anyway," he said. "In court you would have had the chance to examine it, and you would have done the same thing—only later. But I don't pat people on the back. Not as a routine thing, that is. Compliments and praise don't come easy from my lips. Still, I don't see why you should be reluctant to take *some* credit for what you did."

"Because I didn't set out to stop her. That just happened."

"Well, just don't beat yourself over the head about it," he said.

"Have you seen Carrie since all this came out?"

"Me?" He looked shocked. "Heavens no! What could I say to her?"

"I thought you might have some unfinished business to wind up, or some final words."

"I don't have any final words for Carrie—nor unfinished business. Carrie and I are finished—through—kaput!"

I surveyed Tolliver with new appreciation. "Well, at least you're honest about it."

"That's the way I am," he said. "I don't claim that as a virtue necessarily, but perhaps I should. What are you going to do now?"

"I'm going home and start building up the courage to talk to Carrie Holbrook. Mr. Burnsides thinks somebody should head her off before she tries to push that claim again. He says she'll get herself in trouble if she tries it."

"I told you that—or at least, I intended to. But I'm no longer sure you should talk to her. You can do nothing for her."

"Maybe I can. I owe her something."

Tolliver shook his head. "You certainly enjoy punishing yourself. You don't owe Carrie Holbrook one solitary thing. Not a thing! She had a long-range plan for getting her hands on that money. It was carefully mapped out, and it was as crooked as a corkscrew. All you did was knock the plan in the head. You prevented her from committing a crime against the State of Texas and its people. What's so terrible about that? And pray tell me, if you can, how that obligates you to her?"

"Don't you have any personal feelings for *anybody?*" I asked, standing up.

"Not when I can avoid it," he replied. "It makes relationships too messy. As a matter of fact, I don't understand the first thing you've been talking about."

"Think about it," I said. "Maybe the light will come on. It takes a while."

"No, I won't do that," he said. "I've got other fish to fry. I told you before that I'm not sure you're real, and this clinches it. But who knows? After all, your attitude toward Carrie may be the right one. I can't say. But if it makes you happy to turn the other cheek, then go right ahead and turn it." He sighed elaborately and smoothed the thin strand of hair across his skull. "It's just not my way of doing things, though. Christian virtues have always embarrassed me just a little, especially when they are practiced so illogically. But maybe that's what makes them Christian."

"I'm not being Christian."

"Oh, for heaven's sake, Pete! You might at least pretend that you are. Otherwise, you look like a fool!"

I laughed and turned to the door. "I guess I'll just have to relax and enjoy it, then," I said.

"Well, ta-ta and good luck," he said with a wave of his hand. "When you get tired of wearing that hair shirt, take it off and come back. I've made up my mind definitely that even though you've got a loose screw somewhere in your head, I shall some day permit you to retain me." He grinned.

Despite his protests to the contrary, I left the office with no doubt that he understood perfectly what I intended to do. Perhaps he was not in sympathy, but he understood.

❧ 40 ❧

The Holbrook house stood gaunt and still against the deepening sky, melancholy and moody in the gathering grayness. A wind—cool for June—blew out of the east, heavy with the threat of rain. It swept around the veranda, leaving an eerie wail in its path. With each gust, a loose shutter banged against the side of the house. A drop of rain touched my cheek as I hurried from my car across the circular driveway and into the shelter of the veranda. The stained-glass panes around the front door were almost black. I rang the bell and suppressed a cold shiver.

A light came on inside. Footsteps approached from the rear of the house. The door swung inward.

Carrie Holbrook stood in the door, a trim silhouette framed in the amber light behind her. I could not make out her face, but I saw her body stiffen, and I heard her breath as she drew it in sharply.

"You!" she gasped.

I moved as if to enter. "Carrie, I want to talk to you."

"Go away!" she said hoarsely. She stepped back to close the door. The light fell on her face. She held her chin high. She was pale; in her eyes I saw a mixture of hostility and arrogance.

"Don't close the door," I said. "Let me come in, please."

"How can you have the nerve?"

"Please, Carrie—it won't take long." I put one foot across the threshold and held out my hand to stop the door.

"Why can't you leave me alone?" Her eyes were blazing. "Haven't you stirred up enough trouble?"

"I won't bother you again—just let me talk to you for a few minutes."

With sudden resignation, she dropped her hand from the door and moved aside. I stepped in and closed the door quietly behind me.

"I had no idea things would turn out this way," I said.

"And just what *did* you have in mind?"

"Nothing. Nothing at all. That's the weird part of it. I had no purpose in mind. No one believes that, but it's the truth. I didn't want things to end this way."

"You're the only person who could have prevented it. But you didn't."

"I know that. I got caught up in a chain of events, and I couldn't get out."

"Is that what you came to tell me?"

"Partly. But primarily, I came because I don't want you to get in trouble."

"You're a bit late worrying about that, aren't you?"

"Not too late. Mr. Burnsides says that if you drop your claim now, nothing can happen to you. But if you persist in it, you'll be liable to a charge of fraud. Somebody should make you understand that, and there didn't seem to be anybody but me to do it."

She smiled bitterly and shook her head. "You know this is crazy—really crazy. You appear in Foley and turn my life upside down. You cut my reputation to shreds. Then you come worrying about me. Why don't you moralize instead? Isn't that what a best friend does when he catches his best friend's wife being unfaithful? Shouldn't you remind me that all this is my comeuppance?"

"Carrie, I didn't come here to talk about that. I won't even try to justify what I did. I just don't want you to ruin your life and Ben's life."

(310)

"You don't need to worry about that," she said, her manner softening. "My attorneys convinced me that I should give up."

"You mean you're through?"

"What else? I know when I've had it. I lost. That's all there is to it." Her mood hardened again. "Is there anything else worrying you?" she asked flippantly.

"You," I said flatly. "Just you. Do you remember how we used to dance, and you'd laugh at Ben because he couldn't keep up with the fast tunes? 'Come dance with me, Pete,' you used to say. 'This one's too fast for old slowpoke Ben.' That's the Carrie Holbrook I'm worried about."

Her expression softened again and grew wistful. "We did have fun, didn't we? Sometimes I think back to those days and wonder if Ben was real or if he was a fantasy. That was another life, and I was another person. We all lived in another world."

"Sometimes I wish we could go back to it. Don't change, Carrie. That's what I really came up here to say. Don't change. All these years, I've been holding onto a Carrie Holbrook who's alive and happy. I can't help believing that she still exists."

She sat down on the stairs and began to cry. She covered her face with her hands. I stood back and waited until she stopped.

"I've made a mess of things, haven't I?" she said without looking up.

"So have I. I should have let you alone after that day in the doctor's office. I hope you'll forgive me."

She dropped her hands from her face. Her eyes were wet and glistening. She said nothing.

I looked through the parlor and out the windows. The rain was coming down now in gusty torrents; the trees were bending under its heavy lash. The loose shutter banged noisily against the house.

"If all this were not so insane, I'd hate you," she said. "But I don't, and I never have. Isn't that strange? I lied to you. I tricked you. I insulted you. I ran you out of the house. I did my damnedest to get rid of you. But I never hated you. Ever since I came back to Erskine you've been the enemy; you've stood in the way of everything I wanted. You made it all possible; then you stopped me from getting it. I should hate you with a passion, but I don't. Somehow, you're the only one left, Pete. There's nobody else to talk to. It doesn't make any sense."

"Where's Ben?" I asked.

"Upstairs. He's taking a nap."

"I don't guess he knows."

"How could he know? I hope he never knows. If I can get away from here—far, far away among strangers—maybe he'll never know. But that's probably a pipe dream like all the others."

"What will you do?"

"Go back to teaching, I suppose. I shouldn't have stopped."

"I know you'll need money, and as soon as the will is settled and we've got our feet on the ground again, I'd like to—"

"Pete?" Bewilderment clouded her eyes, but it turned quickly to disbelief. "Pete—do you mean you don't know?"

"Don't know what?"

She clapped her hand over her mouth, then dropped it limply. "My God! What have we been talking about?"

"What do you mean?"

"Have you been standing here thinking that the estate is ready to be settled on you?"

"Well—naturally, I thought—"

"Pete—when's the last time you talked to Mr. Burnsides?"

"On the telephone several days ago. Why?"

"When did you see J. A. Tolliver?"

"The same day—about three days ago, I guess."

"Then maybe they didn't know—not then."

"What are you talking about, Carrie?"

"Dr. Kriegel," she said. "He filed an affidavit with the probate court along with a complete medical report on Mother Holbrook. A man from the courthouse brought me a copy this morning—and by now, there must be one in your mailbox at Jones Hill. The report was virtually a diary of Mother Holbrook's mental and physical condition for the past two years.

Dr. Kriegel gave his diagnosis a technical name, but it boils down to the fact that, for legal purposes, she has been non compos mentis for the past two years with only rare and short intervals of clearness."

"But we all knew that," I said.

"I know we did, but this report throws doubts on her soundness of mind at the time she changed her will in your favor—and that's its real significance. Several psychiatrists examined it—one was from Austin, I remember. The report was full of incident after incident—dozens of them. Once, for example, she tried to make a will giving all her money to a teller in the bank, and she didn't even know his name! Another time, she tried to claim Alberta as a blood relative and asked Tolliver to make out a power of attorney to her. Tolliver refused. Then she would go for weeks at a time thinking that Dr. Kriegel was Daddy Holbrook. She wrote checks for fantastic sums of money and tried to give them to people. Tolliver made arrangements with the bank to telephone him when one of the checks showed up so he could stop payment on them. She gave Dr. Kriegel a check for five thousand dollars for a bottle of nose drops. He tore it up. It goes on and on like that for pages, citing chapter and verse, names, dates, places. Of course, most people were aware of many of these incidents, but when added together—as Dr. Kriegel added them—they form a pattern that made the overall diagnosis possible. The man from the courthouse says the consensus is that it knocks the will into a cocked hat."

I listened in total fascination. My reaction was strange. A heaviness began to fall away. In huge chunks it dropped to the right and to the left, leaving me light and unfettered, almost giddy. I knew that it was all over now. Beyond question, the entire improbable melodrama was approaching the final curtain. No matter what legal maneuvers Arthur Burnsides might devise, I knew that they would be futile. And I was glad.

"And you didn't know," said Carrie in wonderment. "I thought that's why you came—one loser to commiserate with the other."

"Tolliver didn't know about it, or else he would have told me," I said.

She dismissed him with a wave of the hand. "To hell with Tolliver," she said. "As soon as he saw which way the wind was blowing, he dropped me like a hot rock. He's out for what he can get."

"But he makes no bones about it," I said. "You don't have to worry about him." I smiled. "You can take him or leave him, but at least you know what's in the package."

"You can have him," she said, not unpleasantly.

"He was good to you."

"So were you, Pete. You stopped me from doing something I would have regretted forever."

"Let's not talk about it any more. It's all over."

"But let's not fool ourselves," she said. "We can't take up where we left off years ago, as if nothing had happened between then and now. There's no real reason to try, is there?"

"No. This whole thing has been like the detour that brought me through Foley the first time. The best thing we can do, I guess, is to forget the bad and remember the good."

"Pete, were you ever in love with me?" she asked abruptly. "Even a little?"

"Just the idea of you—I was head over heels in love with that. You might say I've been in love with an abstraction—an image. And the image always glittered. It always gleamed and sparkled. I never told that to Amy. She wouldn't understand."

"I'm sorry to have disillusioned you. You deserve better. I suppose if I were to do the right thing, I'd try to convince you that the idea you've been in love with never existed—that you've been chasing rainbows. That way, I'd let you off the hook." She smiled. "But I seem to have a record of doing the wrong thing—and I want you to keep on chasing that rainbow."

"It's been a beautiful one," I said.

"Well, this is it," she said without rising. "Except for one thing I want to explain."

"You don't owe me any explanations."

"I want to explain anyway, so listen. There was just that one time. I'm not trying to minimize it or justify it, but it was a lark —nothing more. I can hardly remember how he looked."

"Carrie, please—"

She got to her feet and followed me to the door. "I want you to retain as much of that glittering image as you can."

She raised herself on tiptoe and kissed me on the cheek.

"Tell Amy that she's the luckiest woman in the world," she said.

"Amy's gone."

"She'll be back," she said.

The door clicked shut behind me. The rain had stopped. The clouds were breaking and chasing one another across the ice-blue sky. The air was fresh and invigorating, and I gloried in its feel against my face as I drove down the hill. As I turned out of the gate onto the road, the sun was working its way through a cluster of white, puffy clouds.

I did not look back.

❦ 41 ❧

Three days later, Mr. Burnsides laid his hand on a thick, manila-bound document and patted it fondly. "Dr. Kriegel did his homework well," he said. "He's boxed us in on all sides. I submitted this report to one of the best psychiatrists in the State of Texas, and he couldn't punch a hole in it anywhere. He has nothing but praise for the opinions of the two psychiatrists who examined it before him.

"The thing that makes this report unique is Dr. Kriegel's first-hand, everyday, intimate knowledge of his patient. He knew much more about her than doctors normally know about their patients. Usually in cases of this type, a team of experts moves in and makes a study. Their time is necessarily limited, and they have to work from records and the testimony of friends, acquaintances and casual observers. They have no firsthand, on-the-scene knowledge of their own. In this instance, however, Dr. Kriegel not only gives medical evidence of his own, but he gets it certified by two unimpeachable psychiatrists whose testimony would be revered in any court in the United States. Then he backs it up with the intimate, day-to-day knowledge of the patient, with the knowledge of a close friend as well. He's the medical expert, the friend, the physician, the acquaintance, the casual observer all rolled into one package. It's an unbeatable combination. He's the witness all attorneys dream about but never find."

He picked up the report and turned it over in his hands, looking at it with admiration, almost affection. "It's an amazing document," he said. "Our only chance would be to bring in witnesses who knew Mrs. Holbrook as well as he did, and of course, they don't exist."

"How about Alberta?"

"He's boxed us in there, too. He quotes her again and again and cites one incident after another where she substantiates his own observations. She's his—not ours. You see, the law requires only one thing in this regard: the person must be of sound mind *at the time the will is signed.* Mrs. Holbrook could have been off in a fog two minutes before she signed the will and two minutes afterwards, but it doesn't matter so long as she was of sound mind during the actual execution of the instrument. I talked to the people who witnessed her signature—Tolliver's secretary and a friend of hers who works across the hall—and incidentally, anyone who is twenty-one years old and literate is a competent witness to the signing of a will. They both said, 'She seemed all right to me,' or words to that effect. Tolliver said the same. Now, that's rather weak, and it's not very convincing testimony in the face of two years' evidence to the contrary. Five minutes out of two years is what the State is asked to presume, but that has been thrown into serious doubt. It's that five minutes that we will be forced to prove, and we can't do it. We've got nothing to prove it with."

"You seem convinced—and impressed."

"Convinced? Impressed? Make no mistake about it—I am. I admire a good solid victory, even when I'm the loser, if the victor wins with intelligence, skill and thoroughness, and that's what the doctor has done. Oh, we'll go through our paces like obedient children. Actually we won't be required to do anything at first, for the State presumes the will to have been properly executed unless and until proven otherwise. Dr. Kriegel will challenge the State's presumption and move in for the kill. Then we'll counter him by attempting to establish the will as having been properly executed. We've got to make the gesture, but that's all it will be. It will be over before you know it, and in truth, it will be quite painless."

"What happens to the estate afterwards?"

"We'll have to wait until the will is officially and legally invalidated; then we'll see. Probably the estate will be distributed according to the terms of the last will Mrs. Holbrook executed while she was still of sound mind—if such a will exists."

"Why would the doctor go to so much trouble and expense?" I asked. "He had nothing to gain from it—unless he had ambitions of claiming the estate for himself somehow."

"That's highly unlikely. The doctor is in comfortable circumstances. Besides, he's over seventy years old. Any suit he filed would probably be in litigation for a long time, maybe years. I doubt that a man of his age and circumstances would be willing to let himself in for all that."

"Then why?"

Mr. Burnsides walked to the window and stood looking out at the steel and concrete towers of the Fort Worth skyline. "He's a remarkable man," he said. "I asked him that same question, and his answer was unassailable. 'Because it's right,' he said. That's all. He didn't enlarge on it. He didn't justify it or qualify it. He only said, 'Because it's right.' "

He turned back to face me. "Do you believe that?" he asked searchingly.

"Believe that it's right or that he *thinks* it's right?"

"Both—or either."

"I guess so. At least, I know something was wrong with things as they were."

"Then you don't have any regrets or ill feelings? Some day you might look back at what might have been and feel regrets."

"Right now, I'm so relieved to be done with it that I don't care how I may feel later on. Still, I can't get over the pointlessness of it all. Everybody loses. Nobody wins. It's been an exercise in futility."

(318)

"Maybe not," he said. "Who's wise enough to see the point or reasoning or the meaning in everything that happens on this earth?"

"You certainly tried," I replied. "You did your dead level best to explain all my actions, and you struck out. The trouble was that you explained me according to your own personal philosophies—not mine. I'll regret this entire Holbrook affair until the day I die. I'll always wish I had not gone to Erskine that first time, but I went, and let's face it, nothing was wrong with my going. You can trace each of my actions step by step, and you won't find one thing I did that was actually wrong. Not one thing."

"But look how it turned out, Pete!"

"It turned out tragically—everything. But that doesn't prove that my actions per se were wrong. If I had had the faintest inkling, do you believe for an instant that I would have set foot inside the Holbrook house the first time? You know better than that. A family down the street from us started to Colorado last summer for their vacation. A few miles this side of Quanah, their car turned over and killed their two children. Does that mean they should never have planned their vacation and started for Colorado?"

"The trouble with you," he said, "is that you hide behind your own motives. You take refuge in them and excuse your every action on the grounds that since your motives are as pure as the driven snow, nothing could possibly be your fault. Well, that's rather sanctimonious, if you ask me. It's self-righteous, and if that's your attitude, then I'll agree that the exercise has been futile—for you. You expect me to admire your unshakable sense of right and wrong, and I probably would were it not so overdeveloped, and if you weren't so sensitive about it. You don't have a corner on it, you know. You're a good man, Pete Hamilton, and you'd be even a better one if you'd let me make that judgment, not you."

"I'll have to think that over," I said, getting up to go. He followed me to the door. I laughed. "I guess you've put me in my place enough for one day," I said. "So much so that I can't think of a good comeback at the moment."

Now it was his turn to laugh. "That's the best comeback you could have made." He put his hand on the doorknob, but he did not open the door. "Before you go," he said, "I'd like to ask you one more question, if you don't mind."

"Go ahead."

"Could you have *voluntarily* waived your rights to that estate?"

"That's the one question I will not ask myself," I replied.

"Why not?"

"Because I don't know the answer," I said. "Now let me ask you one."

"All right."

"Could *you?*"

He studied the doorknob. Then he looked up at me. "I don't know the answer, either," he said, shaking his head slowly. Then he added, "Who would?"

He opened the door and held it for a moment. "Do you have any idea what you will do now?"

"Right now, I'm going home and call Amy and tell her that we're flat broke with a pile of debts and not a penny in sight," I said.

He grinned and extended his hand. "That's a good start. I hope she comes back soon."

"She will," I said. "This is what she's been waiting to hear."

I walked out of the building into the brilliant Texas sunshine. At the corner, I stood on the curb waiting for the traffic light to change. An elderly gentleman standing at the bus stop eyed me with interest. Halfway across the street, I looked back at him, wondering what it was that had attracted his attention. He smiled at me. Then I knew, and I smiled back. I had been whistling a happy tune.

It had been a long time since I had whistled a happy tune.